Echoes
of the
Mystic
Chords

Echoes of the Mystic Chords

J. Wes Ulm

BOOK 1
THE LEIBNIZ DEMON
TRILOGY

www.echomystic.com | *@echomystic* | *@wesulm*

Original Artwork by Will Chen
Edited by Jon Rauch
Book Design and Typesetting by David DePerro

Opera-Lyrics-Smooth font created by Dennis Báthory-Kitsz. Info at http://malted-media.com/people/bathory/index.html. Used with permission.

Chapter 9 photo illustration adapted from 'Komori Nursemaid', Item # 70330-0001, from Kjeld Duits Collection at MeijiShowa.com. Used with permission.

Tim Shoemaker's harrowing journey will continue in Book 2 of the Leibniz Demon Trilogy.

Contents

A Glimpse of the Nightmare to Come 1

1. The Beckoning 5

2. The Sacred Sight 35

3. Epicenter 63

4. A Sinister Inspiration 95

5. Legacy of Puzzles 125

6. Thunderings of an Immortal Echo 165

7. The Siren Call of the Mystic Chords 189

8. Shards of Memories Lost 209

9. Heralds of a Strange Apocalypse 241

10. Seeds of an Ancient Provenance 267

11. The Soul on the Screen 303

12. The Grand Liaison 329

Epilogue: The Dark Devours 361

Acknowledgments 365

About the Author 367

Previews: Book 2 369

The Echoes Team 379

To my family

and

To Gloria

Let's create our own
grand mystery together.

我愛你，羅世娟

The mystic chords of memory, stretching from every battle-field, and patriot grave, to every living heart and hearthstone, all over this broad land, will yet swell the chorus of the Union, when again touched, as surely they will be, by the better angels of our nature.

Abraham Lincoln

The manner in which by means of a sort of snapshot we take cognizance of this moving universe whirled along by Time, has the contrary effect of immobilizing it.

Marcel Proust

Aufgeschreckt von einem Alptraum,
der mit Angst und Bang gefüllt,
Bebend, schwitzend: es wird dauern,
bis das Morgenlicht enthüllt.
Ist dort etwas, auf uns lauernd,
das versteckt sich in der Nacht?
Wohin gehen, wohin fliehen,
wenn die Finsternis erwacht?

A Glimpse of the Nightmare to Come

SIX YEARS AFTER FISHER'S RECKONING
FRIDAY, MAY 23, 2025, 6:05 P.M.
EAST SHAFT 7A
CARNOCK COAL MINE COMPLEX, LEWISTOWN, KENTUCKY

The six miners wiped their brows and adjusted the lamps on their helmets. The foreman's whistle had just signaled the close of a long week—and a long day to end it. They trudged through the dusty, subterranean wasteland of the work tunnel, savoring every tiny gust of cooler air that caressed their cheeks as they approached the shaft. It was a shortish hike. They arrived at the elevator, coughing and leaning heavily against its rusted walls as they awaited three more of their crew still making their way up from the worksite.

"So, Joss," began one of them, synchronizing his words with his breathing, "heard you and the lady of the household have some enviable plans for the weekend."

This was Kyle.

A second man laughed hoarsely. "If you're so envious of our shed-caulking and gutter-cleaning, you're more than welcome to join us."

"So going on the road with the band's off."

At that moment their three coworkers boarded and stepped behind Joss and Kyle, and Joss launched the elevator with a backhanded smack of his work glove against the UP square on the panel.

"The Lords of Leannain will be back in business soon enough, but it's not gonna be tomorrow or the days to follow. Vocal cords and bitumen dust"—Joss shook his head—"shitty combination."

Kyle grunted in agreement, and the two men slacked against the wall, embracing the respite as the elevator's clacking gears echoed about them in the barebones metal car. The lift inched its way up past a seeming infinitude of caverns and carvings, of aborted paths and half-cleared promontories that were forever imparting new character to the otherwise featureless underworld landscape. A mine on the moon could not have looked much different. The miners, having risen past the half-kilometer mark, patiently awaited the remainder of their journey and breathed a little easier.

"Whoa! What in the—" Kyle grabbed for a bowed handrail on the wall to keep himself from falling. The other men did the same as the elevator jolted to a standstill.

Gone was the loud clacking of gears.

There'd been no signs of an obstruction before the sudden stop. Nor had there been any apparent malfunction; no lights on the panel had lit, the buzzer hadn't sounded. They seemed to have simply lost power. The control panel was without so much as a flicker, and none of the switches was able to do anything to raise or lower the elevator. An older miner attempted a call on an emergency line, but it was a no-go. The old man shook his head.

The group spent the better part of an hour trapped in their positions, passing time with small talk and gallows humor as they waited for attention from above.

A chill wind began harassing the men as it curled throughout the shaft and caverns and about the car, working its way into the small space in substantial drafts, filling the silence with the sterile buzz of ebbing wall lamps and the creaking motion of the car and frozen pulleys above and beneath them. Another hour passed, then another. A sense of restlessness filled the car. The frustration of the younger miners in particular began to bubble toward the surface.

"Bastards!" Kyle exclaimed, ramming his callused fist into a thinly-padded girder. "Six months they've had to fix the bugs and bring this piece of shit to code. Now we can't even call out. Damn regulators, bought off as usual."

"The owners...We don't know that," Joss said.

"We don't? Seriously? We're meat to them, Joss. Numbers on a balance sheet. Triantarchs, Ruling Clans, whatever we're supposed to call these vultures lording it over the country and all us peasants down below—they'll have plenty more desperate warm bodies to replace us with."

"They aren't all the same. I've been riding up and down these shafts for the past decade. The Augustus Clan wasn't like the rest of 'em; they looked after us."

"Maybe so. But they're not the ones in charge anymore, are they? Pyrrhus Clan's been running this racket since my first descent, and that's just about two years ago. Was right after my old man died in one of their death traps. Not Augustus. Pyrrhus."

"Tone it down, Kyle."

"Fifteen-hour days, seven days a week in that pit in West Nebraska, and he died in debt to the evil fucks who owned the shafts. That firedamp blast that brought the mine roof down on him and the other colliers—sometimes I think it was an act of mercy."

"Dammit, you shouldn't say things like that!"

"How would you know, Joss? You really expect some Triantarch rescue-squad to come rushing down here for us?"

"Kyle, the Pyrrhus cousins don't rule the mine country in West Nebraska. That's Vedius territory. The Pyrrhus Clan's Triantarchy, yeah, but are they sadistic creeps like the Crassus Brothers, let alone Clan Longinus or Vedius? No. Don't assume evil and malice when stupidity and laziness are more than enough. You'll drive yourself crazy."

"Like we aren't half-there."

"They're not gonna abandon us here. The Pyrrhus cousins are probably up there sweating bullets, calling their Daddy to extricate them from this mess. They already look like fools. They're not leaving us down here."

"I don't know, Joss."

"One way or another, we'll be out of this mine, and you're gonna see your wife and little girl tonight. Don't tell yourself otherwise, not for one goddamned minute; don't even think it. That sort of thinking's poison, worse than any firedamp seeping out from the rocks around here."

The men withdrew into sudden silence. Something was emerging from above.

ONE WEEK EARLIER . . .

Aufmarschiern die Herrn der Schöpfung,

zepterschwingend mit Gewalt,

Ihre Macht wächst unaufhörlich,

mit der finsteren Gestalt.

Doch was lohnt sich große Macht,

wenn nur Trümmer draus auftauchen?

Wär' die größte Macht dazu,

um große Macht nie zu missbrauchen?

Chapter One

The Beckoning

Symbol of the Guild

THURSDAY, MAY 15, 2025, 5:45 P.M.
DEPARTMENT OF BIOMEDICAL ENGINEERING
DALTON UNIVERSITY, DURHAM, NORTH CAROLINA

"I know you'll cringe to hear this, Zach, but it can wait no longer. There comes a time in a young engineer's career when he's gotta take it straight—the unvarnished truth."

Holding up a heavily marked-up folder, the professor summoned Zach to his table. The table, wooden with sharp borders, was cluttered from edge to edge with papers, journals, and technological bric-a-brac. Beads of sweat stood out on Zach's forehead as he approached the stern-faced older man. He took too deep a breath and ran a hand through his thick black hair. Dark rings stood out under his bloodshot eyes.

Yet the professor of engineering pretended not to notice his student's anxiety. "As your willing advisor and mentor for what I know has been an arduous five years, and as one obligated by my station to level with you as to the good, the bad, and the ugly…Well, Zach, I suppose you knew this was coming."

Zach struggled to meet his teacher's inscrutable stare. The older man was legendary for his poker face, and for the barbs with which he laced his humor. They were no doubt sharp, those verbal barbs of his, but not malicious; he deployed them to seize and focus the drifting attention of those around him, and here they were serving their purpose.

The professor's voice dipped as he set down the folder. "Zach, allow me to say this to you unequivocally: You really must learn how to drain your glass in *one* take. I simply *cannot* bestow a PhD upon a young man so wanting in the art of gentlemanly drinking."

Zach looked up. His mentor grinned and held out a shot glass with the image of a downhill skier stenciled on the side, along with a salt shaker and a wedge of lime. Yet another of the renowned professor's peculiarities: everyone just *had* to love tequila, and show it. Zach licked the webbing between his left forefinger and thumb and salted his hand liberally.

"Cheers!" the professor said.

"Cheers!" "Way to go, Zach!" "Congrats, *Doctor* Zach!" The small crowd of faculty and students seconded the professor's toast, their voices echoing throughout the small amphitheater.

Zach sucked down the liquor and bit into the wedge of lime. He grinned despite the vile taste. He preferred beer. "Please! My esteemed colleagues, please no 'Dr. Zach'!" The burn in his throat gave his voice a temporary rasp. The crowd gathering around him laughed. "Nor, God forbid, 'Dr. Choi'—abominations, both! Especially coming from my not-always-distinguished colleague, the budding Dr. Matt Hansen himself. That is, not unless one of you here has granted my request, and secured for me an afternoon talk show slot to translate our obscure endeavors to the masses—in which case I'll be calling in rich to work in short order."

The professor and the others threw back their own glasses and bit their limes.

"If anyone could pull it off..." the professor growled, affecting disapproval. "You're the only soul from here to Appalachia who could get away with defending a thesis in a spray-painted T-shirt under your suit and tie."

"Well," Zach said, "coming from a man infamous for leading conferences in tattered ski gear, I'm not sure what to make of such commentary. And speaking of ties, what were *you* thinking? A Peter Pan theme? Really?"

"Cut the old prankster a break, will you? That tie is an indispensable *accoutrement* for working one's own silliness into official business."

Well over six feet tall, with close-cropped reddish-brown hair and eyebrows more reddish than brown bushing over his gray-blue eyes, Tim Shoemaker spoke and carried himself in general with the hard-nosed resolve of a military veteran. The past ten years had been a pageant of setbacks and sorrows for him, the toll of which showed on his scarred face.

Yet it was not his nature to hang his head; despite the onslaught of disappointments, Tim took care to maintain an aura of unflappable professionalism. His studied cool served him well. Though in his late forties, more often than not he exhibited a boyish enthusiasm and mischievous humor that endeared him to his colleagues. It was with genuine affection that his young charges had dubbed Tim's laboratory "The Doghouse."

"Aha!" Zach said, waving a finger. "Now I remember where I saw that tie before. I seem to recall the local bigshots called on you, O esteemed keeper of The Doghouse, to give a few pep talks on math and science at the public schools, no? To boost spirits amidst the budget cuts—maybe sucker in a few bright-eyed-and-bushy-tailed youngsters to follow in our misbegotten footsteps."

Zach's comment was answered with more laughter. The new PhD beamed with pride. And yet, his own laughter was tainted by clashing sentiments. Lately he'd been plagued by unwelcome bouts of introspection, following which his chosen profession indeed seemed misbegotten.

For the better part of five years, he had toiled away on a doctoral thesis to gain entry to this exclusive club of elite biomedical engineers. The result was a dissertation on the arcane arts of implantable, color-responsive mimics of the retina in the human eye—a small but vital step in enabling the blind to see. And his efforts had been rewarded—he had been successful in defending his work.

Yet, he could not shake the corrosive suspicion that his achievements would soon be greeted with indifference. At long last, he was embarking on his career, but he could not celebrate his success in a vacuum. The world had undergone a grotesque metamorphosis since he'd begun his studies.

Still, he was here with his colleagues... and *she* was still with him. If for no one else, he must put aside his troubling thoughts for her sake.

Zach called to a young woman in the back of the room.

"Renee! I've been waiting a near eternity to gaze into those pretty brown eyes again."

"Well, not quite an eternity, Zach," the young woman answered as she approached him. "But if we ever endure another four months like that, you'll be waiting *more* than an eternity to gaze into these eyes again!"

"Your eyes are my solace, Renee," Zach said. "I've told you that before, but I'll say it again, and again—a million times. Can you feel that in me?" Zach asked and lifted her from the floor, kissing her as he returned her to her feet. His solace, her eyes...Though sometimes it was her hair. He shifted back and forth between the two.

"There were times when you made me wonder if I'd ever see this day," she said.

"Just thought I'd make things interesting, love." He hugged her close and shut his eyes.

For a moment, they might have been alone; but an authoritative voice behind him cut his thoughts away from Renee. "A bravura performance, Zach. I know I was a late addition to your thesis committee, but I'm honored to have played even a small part in your professional blossoming here. So what's on the horizon for you now?"

Zach pulled away from Renee and turned around, a forced smile on his face.

"Still working on that part, Dr. Malcolm."

Dr. Malcolm snaked an arm around Zach's shoulder and with his other hand slipped a dog-eared business card into Zach's shirt pocket. His grizzled, unshaven face was almost touching Zach's.

"So I've heard. Listen...My brother-in-law's biotech firm...They've wrangled a contract for device development in the neuro-optical arena. They're one of the few such enterprises still afloat, and I'm sure my brother-in-law would be delighted for you to crash one of their brainstorming sessions. Soon."

Zach nodded, on autopilot. Unsatisfied by this reaction, Dr. Malcolm drew him in closer about the shoulders, the professor dialing down his voice another notch.

"Of course, I can't guarantee anything, Zach. It's a gauntlet for all of us out there. But if you talk to him, I'll sing your praises until there's a dotted line awaiting your signature."

"Thanks, Dr. Malcolm. I'll definitely follow up on this."

"Glad to hear it." The professor let him go and, giving Zach a knowing pat on the shoulder, left him to join one of the conversations taking place among the others in the amphitheater. He was sincere in his offer, and equally aware that it would likely amount to nothing, as was Zach himself.

"Excuse me, hon," Zach said feebly to Renee. Before she could say anything, he strode across the room to a work table where lab assistants were setting out trays of hors d'oeuvres. Renee had not followed, but he could feel her eyes on him as he approached the food, could almost hear her thoughts.

Zach sidled up next to Tim, seething—his supposed mentor, and the man was blithely uncorking a bottle of champagne as if he'd done nothing of consequence.

"You just couldn't help yourself, could you?" Zach said under his breath, pretending to inspect a cavernous dish of antipastos and crudités. At just that moment Tim popped the cork. A tuft of foam bubbled up from the bottle of champagne, dribbling wine onto Tim's shoes. A couple of lab assistants holding plastic tumblers of bourbon applauded.

"Help myself?" Tim was pouring out the bottle into a line of disposable champagne glasses. "What's the matter, Zach?"

The younger man leaned over the table and laid the business card against the stem of Tim's glass.

Tim sighed and squeezed his eyes shut, bracing for an unwelcome exchange. He slipped the card under a folded napkin and handed it back to Zach. "Benny Malcolm may lack the gift of good timing, sure—but his heart's in the right place."

"It's not Professor Malcolm who blew the timing, Tim. It's the guy who tipped him off in the first place."

Tim grimaced.

"It was just one of those unforeseen fords in the stream, Zach. We were simply briefing Benny on all the mandatories and usuals at the thesis committee meeting last week and... what can I say, the conversation wandered onto a promising sidetrack."

"That's an excuse, not an explanation."

"Zach, please, listen to me. The committee members got to talking about real hiring prospects we hadn't even conceived of before. Phil Stern made an offhand reference to a five-year-old firm in Maryland, quietly recruiting fresh PhDs with your sort of knowhow. Benny and Sue Markov started enthusing about the local biotech start-ups, how they'd embarked on a rare talent-hunt throughout the Research Triangle, blah blah blah. Word is some new sources of venture capital are trickling right up your alley of expertise. New and unexpected."

"You know as well as I do, that won't make a scintilla of difference in this whole fetid swamp that I've been stuck in."

Tim shook his head.

"Not this time," he said. "They had local contacts, names that not even they themselves suspected were held in common. The kinds of people who won't be swayed by prying eyes from above."

"Then why didn't you duly arrange for us all to convene after the defense, Tim? Slap on some semi-official label about, I don't know, career advising or group mentoring?"

"Because you have to strike when the iron's hot. They were bouncing hard prospects off each other. We're talking the real deal, local names, newly created positions for young up-and-comers. That happens to be you, Zach. It was a critical moment. I had to tell them the whole truth, if for no other reason than to get them pulling strings on your behalf. Give 'em a sense of urgency. We both know the deck's been stacked against you. *I'm* thinking of ways to overcome that. You should do the same."

"You still don't get it." Zach looked hard at Tim, his voice controlled but barely. "I told you why we had to keep this strictly in confidence. My exact words: 'No matter what—'"

"It was for your benefit, dammit. Why can't you see that?"

"You *knew* Renee would be here. You know how she senses things. She could tell something was off, even before Benny Malcolm did his little song and dance. You knew this would happen if you broke the news to the committee, yet you did it anyway."

A champagne bottle popped behind them.

"Whoa, boy!" someone said amidst laughter.

Tim leaned in closer to Zach.

"Yes, I did it anyway. I'm your mentor. It's my job to see the big picture—the picture you can't conceive of at this stage of your career. Especially in the wake of Fisher's Reckoning."

"No, Tim," Zach said. "That isn't your job; it's a manifestation of your *obsession*. You did it for yourself as much as for me."

"Lower your voice. This is supposed to be a party."

Zach glanced over his shoulder. If anyone were eavesdropping on their conversation, their faces didn't show it. Another professor in a tweed suit, holding court at a cluttered table, met Zach's eye and, smiling, raised his shot-glass. Zach smiled back and gave the professor a little wave before turning back to Tim.

"You know what I'm talking about," Zach said.

"Really? Why don't you enlighten me, because I guess I'm a little slow on the uptake today."

"So now I have to ram this through your wall of denial, too? Is that it?"

"You want to make me feel guilty, Zach? Go ahead. Tell me: I'm nuts, right? I have a pathological need to play the rescuer since I couldn't save—"

"No." Zach cut Tim off. "Stop, please."

"Why? Isn't this what you wanted? Was it not you who started this conversation?"

Zach glanced at the table behind them. The champagne glasses Tim had poured were all gone, and a good dent had been made in the trays of hors d'oeuvres.

"I'm sorry, Tim," he said. "Please, I didn't mean to—"

He watched as Tim, with shaking hands, poured himself another glass of champagne and tossed it back in one shot. Tim turned away from Zach and, pushing past the two lab assistants who had earlier applauded his opening of the champagne bottle, sank heavily into a chair at a table covered with file boxes. He'd taken the champagne with him.

Now the tweed-suited professor and a few of the others were looking at them—at Tim and at Zach. Again the professor met Zach's eye, not with a smile but a look of concern.

Without thinking about what he was going to do, Zach turned away from the professor and his mentor, left the amphitheater and strode down the hall toward a steel door under a red EXIT sign.

"Zach! What happened? Is everything okay?"

His hand was on the horizontal bar; a quick shove and he'd be outside. But he couldn't pretend he hadn't heard her—he could lie to her if he had to, but he couldn't walk out on her as though she wasn't there.

He turned around to face Renee.

"It's—" he began, then hesitated; lying wasn't so easy, after all. He sighed. "I wish I could say everything's okay, but it isn't. There's a lot that isn't. Some things that are going horribly wrong in fact—" He ground his teeth together to choke off that last sentiment; it was honest, but he hadn't meant for it to slip out. Not yet at least.

For the millionth time, he waited for Renee—this bright, sweet, beautiful woman who for some reason had chosen him—to roll her eyes, to say something along the lines of "It never ends!" and walk out on him. Maybe tonight would be the night when it finally happened, he thought, as she came down the hall to meet him where he stood.

"Honey," he said as she approached him, "the reservations I made for us at the Gondolier, they're good for 24 hours and... I think we should go tomorrow. I don't feel up to it this evening."

"But we've been planning this for weeks! This was supposed to be *our* night. You're not the only one who's been suffering through this ordeal."

"I know that. And that hasn't changed. We've endured this for months; we'll just have to push it back one more day. That's all, I promise."

"Are you simply going home to sulk? Today?"

"No, not home. Matt and the rest of the Doghouse are planning to do a little bar-hopping in Old Chapel Hill. I'm not much for carousing tonight, but... How to put this... There are some dirty linens that need a good airing, the kinds of things that only your fellow grunts in the trenches can understand. I've been putting it off for too long."

"It's always something, isn't it, Zach?" She was fighting back tears.

Gently, he slipped his right hand beneath her left ear, cradling her neck and drawing her to him. Her hair felt like silk on his fingers.

"I know it seems that way," he said. "But this time really is different from all those other times, and I can't simply set it aside. It's only this night, Renee. I promise you that."

He backed away from her slowly, until he felt the door's exit bar press against his body. He tried to focus on her, to not vanish into his thoughts, as he knew how his eyes looked when that happened—hard and cold—but his thoughts took over. He barely saw her as he turned and shoved the exit bar, disappearing behind the door as it swung shut.

5:59 P.M.

A familiar melody jerked Tim from his unwelcome reverie—his cell phone was ringing. He looked with puzzlement at the digits on the display: The call was from an unfamiliar area code, apparently in Tennessee. He swallowed the stew of emotions still bubbling in his throat, and assumed his typical mien of cool normalcy.

"Hello, this is Tim Shoemaker," he said.

"Tim! Hi—I'm so sorry, I heard about the thesis defense today. Are you free to talk?"

It took a second, but the voice on the other end conjured up a familiar face from a fog of memories.

"Ra— Rachel Bloom? Is that you?"

"Oh, I'm sorry again, Tim. I got ahead of myself."

"Not a problem," he said, hastily burying his astonishment and adopting a congenial tone. He left the table where he'd been sitting for a quiet corner of the lab. He took the champagne bottle with him. "I prefer a bit of awkwardness in reunions; makes them more authentic. Besides, two years isn't exactly an eternity."

"It might as well have been for me."

The edge and angst in her voice rattled Tim. Rachel was not one to sound like this, ever, he thought. She was the crème-de-la-crème in all the glossy announcements about the brightest young prospects in the field—and one who had yet to bolt for less troubled shores overseas.

Tim had assisted her for years in a grand endeavor: tracing the physiology of human sight to designated nerve bundles in the brain's vision processing center. In short order, she won a national fellowship for a breakthrough that he would never savor alongside her. By then his life had become engulfed by a nightmare, outside of which he could see nothing, not even Rachel Bloom.

"From your number," he said, "I take it you're not in Research Triangle Park anymore."

"I wound up at Oak Ridge—the new National Labs out there, Prosthetics and Bioengineering Division."

"Out in the sticks, huh? Good ol' Tennessee."

Rachel laughed, but her reaction didn't sound at all genuine to Tim.

"Even after winning the Steinmetz Fellowship, it was hell securing grant support for my work."

Rachel's tone was earnest, yet laced with a soldier's black humor. There was a subtext to what she was saying and Tim was not keen to it, so for the moment, he kept his assumptions confined to the tried and true.

"Yet another gift of the Reckoning," he said gruffly. "If it's any comfort, you weren't alone."

"That's part of what brought me out here to the National Labs. The funding stream is guaranteed through military research—manna from heaven. Or so I thought."

She sighed audibly. The sound reverberated amid scattered crackles of background static.

"Tim, look, I should cut to the chase. I'm calling you for a major favor. We'll have ample opportunity for small talk if you can make the trip."

"Trip? You mean to Tennessee? When? And what favor?"

"Something's overwhelmed my team recently. It's the vision restoration trials we're conducting—perhaps you've gotten wind of them?"

"Clinical trials?" asked Tim, fretting over a reference that should have been familiar.

"For the veterans from the wars in Iraq and Afghanistan, as well as a few from the recent police action in South Midawan. All of our patients sustained combat wounds that left them blind; most haven't seen for a decade or more. Our efforts showed so much promise at first, but then the horrors took hold."

"The horrors?"

"We don't know what hit us; not the slightest inkling. And lately it's gone from bad to horrendous."

"I'm sorry to hear that," said Tim. He shut his eyes and pressed on his forehead with bent knuckles. One protégé's travails were sufficiently dispiriting for an evening; he dreaded to hear the woes of another.

"And I'm sorry to come to you begging for help. But we've exhausted every other recourse—I have no one else to turn to. I know your sabbatical is on the horizon. All the same, if you could pay us a visit, even for just a weekend... you'd be a ray of hope for us, and it's been months since we've glimpsed one of those."

Tim rubbed his eyes, snared between an impulse to help and a resigned sense of futility. He decided to split the difference.

"I'm always willing to lend a hand, Rachel; I promised you that before. But I don't see how I can be of any use to you now—I know next to nothing about the vision restoration trials. At best I'd be an educated observer, if not a fifth wheel."

"Quite the contrary; you were present at their inception."

"I was?"

Again Rachel sighed, the sound of her breath mixing with static on the line.

"That clinical trial review panel at Cold Spring Harbor, Tim. Around three years ago... remember? It was right before you left for South America."

"Yeah, I remember," he said. "For the retinal implant... Sure. I had to cut that commitment short, for obvious reasons."

He bit his lip. More nasty memories unearthed.

"Anyhow," he said, "I recommended that the trial be deferred. The AP-278 implant showed potential, but it was far too premature for testing in patient cohorts. Its designers made sweeping claims about their growth factor cocktail—supposedly capable of sprouting new axonal bundles straight to the optic nerve itself. But their prior data had too many snags. Nothing to be ashamed of; many of us in the field have been seeking the grail with similar results."

"The panel took your advice, Tim. They voted to postpone the trial."

"Glad to hear it—they voted responsibly. But I'm not following here. If the trial was stopped, why bring it up?"

"Because it didn't stop. The AP-278 became the nucleus of the retinal prosthesis that we eventually used in our efforts here."

"But it wasn't ready for implantation—you just said the panel agreed with me. Even if it had managed a successful link-up with the optic nerve, it wasn't ready."

"Not the version you saw in Cold Spring Harbor," Rachel said, "but outside forces made sure it got an upgrade."

"Come again?"

For a moment Rachel was silent.

"Rachel?"

"Ever since the Ruling Families commandeered half the agencies in the DoD and Department of Energy, the purse strings have been largely controlled by Metacelsus."

"Who?"

"We don't know much about him, other than that he's well-connected in the Triantarchy's upper echelons, apparently within Clan Argentus."

"Argentus," Tim said. The name tasted like battery acid. For the first time since picking up the phone, he took a swig from the bottle of champagne.

"For once, our dear leaders' nepotism has led to a more salutary outcome than the usual corruption of everything they touch. Metacelsus is as drunk on power as the rest of the Triantarchs, but he styles himself a visionary—hence the pretentious sobriquet, apparently some faux-Latin riff on Paracelsus, the Renaissance doctor and scientist. Paracelsus ushered in a revolution in medical thought and practice, and Metacelsus claims he's destined to do the same. In his case, he's preoccupied with neural prosthetics."

"Along with all its lucrative by-products, no doubt."

"That goes without saying—still, he's lavishly funded our research."

"With his cut of the stolen loot. How generous. He sounds more like a fool than a visionary," Tim said. "He had no business Guinea-pigging those devices in human subjects!"

Tim glanced over his shoulder at the party still underway, and reminded himself to keep his voice down.

"We all shared those doubts, believe me. But he did have the implants modified before the testing, supposedly by the tech team of a local contractor."

Tim shook his head.

"I'm sorry, but that story doesn't pass the smell test. Even before the Reckoning, domestic firms with that kind of expertise were shipping all their projects overseas; you could count the holdouts here on one hand."

Rachel said nothing.

"Did you ever get a name?" Tim asked.

"No. Not sure on that count, either," she said. "No one who actually does the work is privy to that kind of information; only those in the privileged castes are kept in the loop. Could be a foreign outfit with a shell office in the States, for all we know. The winning firm was awarded a no-bid contract to alter the implant, so they must have had VIP access, whoever they are."

"No surprise there, eh? Last I heard, bidding on merit's been dead for years now."

"Then we must have had the luck of the angels on our side, because that team wrought a miracle."

Tim sat up, his slack posture gone rigid. He gripped the phone.

"Those soldiers can see again?" he whispered.

"For more than three months now."

Tim shook his head, incredulous, now gnarling his forehead with his knuckles. Still, his excitement lasted only a moment before the question came to mind.

"What about the re-training for the visual cortex? Even the most finely-tuned implant would merely restore the conduit for sight information to the brain. The patients would still need months of hand-holding to interpret all the shapes and colors streaming back in."

"We've seen to that."

"Through what means?"

Tim noticed that Rachel's breathing had become irregular as she fielded his questions; she hesitated, as if fearing his response to the answers she gave. So unlike the Rachel he had known, to be so unsure of her footing from moment to moment.

"Rachel?"

"It's...why we need you, Tim."

Tim pinched the bridge of his nose. Her evasiveness told him the answer.

"The Simitalis?" he asked, incapable of quashing the feebleness in his tone. It was infuriating, what helplessness did to a man; even if he knew he should push back, it took him over, subjugated him like a force of nature. "Is that how you did it?"

"I've spent nearly a week wondering how to tell you." Rachel's voice cracked. Tim closed his eyes and could see her, lovely, brilliant, helpless herself, unable to hold back the tears.

"Tim, please believe me when I tell you, I had nothing to do with the expropriation of your system. I'd heard about the burglary in your lab two years ago, but I never dreamt that— "

Rachel began to cry.

"It's OK, Rachel. I believe you," Tim said, though he wasn't sure he did—not entirely. "Just tell me what happened."

Rachel cleared her throat.

"Excuse me. Nine months before the operations took place, when our surgeons were still ironing out how to place the implants into the patients' eyes, we got a briefing from the higher-ups regarding a confidential technology already in place for the next step. They said it was a specialized computing device, run by a microprocessor capable of learning and adapting so as to guide the patients in regaining their sight. It was a neural network with a wireless link to the eye implants, featuring a recursive learning algorithm to fine-tune the image processing in the occipital cortex."

"Go on," Tim urged her gently after a mutually uncomfortable pause.

"The description was disconcertingly familiar, but I told myself that it couldn't be—they wouldn't have robbed you so brazenly. I was . . . naïve. I realized how naïve once the implants were in and it came time to flip the switch to activate the visual re-learning process."

Tim grunted. His mind was racing. His sense of helplessness was beginning to be eclipsed by anger. This was good, he thought; was not anger a necessary precursor to action? Yes, it was . . . or to more anger and still more anger. Then exhaustion . . . He'd trod this path before.

"They hit you with a gag order, didn't they?" he asked.

"It's one of the reasons they lured me out here in the first place," she said.

If she had betrayed him, he thought, could she feign despair so convincingly? Maybe. Rachel was brilliant—who's to say she could not be a brilliant actress if need be? Tim shook the ugly thoughts away and forced himself to focus on what Rachel was telling him.

"After all, I'd gained first-hand experience with the prototypes that became the Simitalis years later," she added, "under the tutelage of its creator. Metacelsus must have known that, because his minions all but incarcerated us in the facility before showing us the system. Then we had to sign strict non-disclosure agreements, or we'd be . . . there would have been consequences."

"Bastards!" Tim exploded, incandescent with rage, his fear of being overheard gone. "The burglars made off with everything—they took the damn hardware wholesale. But the police barely lifted a finger; they wouldn't touch the case. The whole thing stunk. At first it seemed inexplicable, such complete disinterest. Then we realized, this wasn't a theft of computer equipment, but of what was on it—not just the specs but the entire design process. It became obvious, this had to stretch all the way to the Ruling Clans themselves. We eventually hired a private investigator and she concluded Argentus was behind it, but we never found out where—"

Tim got up from the table, leaving the champagne bottle. He walked to the door his protégé had left by mere minutes earlier and gazed down the empty corridor. Above the door the EXIT sign glowed red under the pale fluorescent lights. He shook his head and chuckled.

"So they steal my life's work," he said, "and now they come groveling to me for help when things don't work out as planned. They wanted you out there because of your relationship to me, now they put you up to the task of recruiting me because *they don't know what they're doing*."

Again Tim chuckled in amused contempt.

"So that's the story, huh?" he added.

"They figured that maybe I could get through to you. They felt they'd get nowhere if they contacted you directly."

"Indeed. They're as craven as they are corrupt," he said. "And if you failed, well, at least they'd know they managed to turn two more of their victims against each other."

"There's been plenty of that around here, too."

Tim sighed. He checked the date on his watch.

"Monday... Monday's a holiday from my remaining duties pre-sabbatical."

"So you'll come?"

Tim shrugged.

"There's a family visit I've been putting off," he said, thinking aloud. "If I go to Tennessee for work, I won't have to guilt-trip myself into a separate outing later on down the line."

He pinched the bridge of his nose. He felt a headache coming on from the champagne. Or maybe it was from the vague feeling that bad winds were stirring, and he was taking the most foolhardy tack imaginable, sailing out instead of staying safe at home in port.

"I'll do it, Rachel, for you—you and any other hapless foot-soldiers embroiled in this mess. And who knows? They're calling me because they need me. If I help them, maybe I can name some conditions of my own—not least among which that they spring you loose from that bottomless pit."

"I wouldn't get my hopes up on that count. They all but have us on lockdown here until the crisis is resolved; I'm surprised they haven't issued us orange jumpsuits yet."

Tim pondered that image.

"I have to say, Rachel, it's not like the Triantarchs to ever own up to anything, no matter how royally they screw up. They just blame someone else and move on. Yet here they are, desperate to fix the mess they made—they actually want to fix something, so bad that they're pleading on hands and knees to the very guy they ripped off in the first place. Must be one serious mess out there in the sticks."

"If only it were just a mess," she said. "My old childhood nightmares seem like pictures of tranquility, compared to the damnation I wake up to every morning."

"That's quite a statement."

Rachel seemed to hesitate for a moment.

"How soon can you get out here, Tim?"

From personal to professional in the blink of an eye, he thought.

"How soon do you need me there, Rachel? A-S-A-P, I take it?"

"More or less, yes. One of my assistants can brief you on the details first thing tomorrow. Don't worry about security clearances. We'll make all the arrangements, and get you quartered in whatever passes for a five-star hotel since the Reckoning. I'll be in before dawn on Saturday, if you can manage it on such short notice."

"What a hideous way to kick off the weekend," Tim said with a chuckle, though he didn't even feel ironic amusement anymore at the situation. Nevertheless, he followed up his hollow joke with another. "I think that qualifies as damnation in itself."

"Well, that's how it's been lately," she said. "At least it'll be relatively low-key. I can give you the guided tour without much fanfare. You know, I don't mean to come off so heavy. The circumstances... Really, I can't thank you enough, Tim. You're literally saving our lives here."

"Let's wait until I arrive before declaring any miracles."

"Considering what they took from you, it's already a miracle that you're coming."

"The Triantarchs have taken far too much from all of us, and that goes doubly for you, Rachel. I won't let your promise melt away on account of their greed and recklessness. I won't let you drown in that quicksand."

"If you can help us chart a path out of this web of strange riddles we've gotten trapped in—that alone will be enough to fulfill my wish list for the next three years. As for getting out of this place or recovering any peace of mind... I'd need my naïveté back to believe in such pretty fantasies. Whatever happens, I'll never regain what I've lost."

Even if she'd felt like elaborating, Tim would have told her to hold off till he saw her in Tennessee. He'd barely slept the night before, and the champagne and the day's events had already left him exhausted. Though dusk had yet to set in, he looked forward to shutting his eyes on the world and drifting off into dreamless sleep.

Tim busied himself with clean-up and office trivialities as the alcohol dissipated into his bloodstream, then set off for home. He was in bed minutes after arriving, barely even mustering the initiative to switch off the bedside table lamp. Yet, as he lay there in the dark, thoughts and images kept his brain stubbornly, sluggishly awake—sleep just wouldn't come.

Like a dog straining to scratch off a stubborn tick, he tried to drive away the thoughts, counting down from three-hundred by threes, then from six-hundred, then from nine-hundred. Without meaning to, he began thinking of Rachel's crying over his stolen work, and he found himself grinding his teeth in impotent rage at what had been done to him. At the same time, he scolded himself for not fully trusting her, for feeling anger toward her for being a participant in events she'd had no control over.

As he thought about it, he realized the true source of the anger he felt toward this rare, talented, and wonderful woman, whom he had come to cherish so much amid the rottenness into which his world had descended. What we despise in others, he thought, almost always mirrors what we hate—or fear—about ourselves. No, it was not her imagined role in the theft that rankled him. It was the morbid helplessness in her voice; she sounded nothing like the Rachel Bloom he had known. It was the terrible defeatism, coming from someone who had been so strong-willed and unflappable before. It was her choice of words...

"I'll never regain what I've lost."

THURSDAY, MAY 15, 8:47 P.M.
CANTINA DE LOS CORAZONES ROTOS
CITY OF OLD CHAPEL HILL, NORTH CAROLINA

Zach looked to his left with a blank expression, out the arched window of the cramped but cozy bar. The plastic coatings of its variegated panes were peeling in places, leaving islands of smudged glass that offered views of the bustling promenade outside. Revelers in varying states of intoxication milled before the window like a lurching pageant, their faces betraying a dissonant mixture of merriment and misery.

Street vendors and performers plied their trades before an audience of tourists, students, and young children who had nowhere else to be. Lonely coffeeshops shared the broken-down block with impromptu nightclubs, squatting amidst a nest of generators in abandoned lots long forgotten by municipal authorities. Lights from the occasional posh restaurant or swanky hotel glittered in the distance, anachronisms in a bleak landscape that had been stripped of such luxuries long enough ago so that people described them in words suggestive of mythology, not history.

"So they say there's a new tent city springing up to the north," called out a familiar voice. The speaker took the unoccupied barstool immediately to Zach's right. "On the grounds of the old Astor Park."

"How charming." Zach tipped back his beer mug and guzzled half of its contents, then made a quarter turn on his stool, halting well short of a face-to-face with his junior colleague Matt Hansen. "So it's only one street down from the Imperial Plaza, the newest little gated city on the hill."

"Oh, no reason to sweat the issue. I'm sure the goon squads from the local lords and manors will raze the place soon enough."

"Pity that. The park's location is unbeatable. Now I'll have to find somewhere else to pitch my tent."

"There you go again, Zach. You pass your thesis defense with a flair and a flourish, and still you couldn't wait a single evening to toss the wet blanket onto your own party."

"A whole *evening*?" Zach took another swig from his mug before angling to address his friend more pointedly. "Please, Matt—you give me far too much credit. I was on it barely an *hour* after the defense."

"Yes, I noticed. You and Tim did a bang-up job muzzling that little tempest you kicked up, but it was obvious that you weren't critiquing the dip. After all he's done for you, Zach... What's gotten into you? You weren't like this two years ago. Sometimes I wonder if the same guy is inhabiting that body you traipse around in."

"Two years ago," Zach said with a nod and an indignant grin. "You just answered your own question."

Matt sighed and put his back against the hard counter, taking a moment to craft his reply.

"What happened to you was terrible," he said. "But you're not the only one who suffered because of the break-in."

"Never said I was, Matt—nor am I pleading for a pity party."

"Then why can't you do like the rest of us, simply count your blessings and move on?"

"Because I lost much more than the fruits of my labor. I *can't* move on because they're determined to hem me in."

"They?"

Zach looked through his colleague, swirling the dregs of his beer.

"We've been in this foxhole for three years now," Matt said. "You, me, Shelley, everyone in the Doghouse; we've been dodging these bullets together. Or not dodging them, as it may be. Whatever's eating you, we of all people can relate."

"Tim never wanted the gaudy horror of it all to hit the big screen. I guess I followed his lead." Zach swiveled his stool to face his colleague, then, as if thinking better of it, began to turn away. Matt grabbed the backrest of the stool, however. Zack looked at Matt's hand and Matt let go of the backrest. Still, Zach didn't turn away from the younger man.

Matt broke the silence.

"I always thought there was more to this story."

"You've barely browsed its cover page. It was ostensibly a routine break-in, yet the police and the university bigwigs wouldn't go near it—an odd coupling of events, with that sweetly putrescent aroma of an official cover-up."

"A cover-up? By whom? Why would the university—"

"Tim hired a private eye—used his own money. She was good. She spent three months digging up all the musty skeletons in the case. Did great work. If you ever need a crack P.I.—"

"Stop. You just said she did great work. And?"

"And? And she didn't dare take a step further. Smart lady."

Matt's ruddy cheeks blanched. "It was one of the Ruling Families, wasn't it?"

Zach studied the bottom of his mug.

"The patriarch of Clan Argentus is one of the worst; even the other Triantarchs fear him. A coldblooded, greedy old bastard. One of his close associates—never learned his name to curse and spit on—set his sights on our work. And not only on the Simitalis." Zach looked up from his mug. "You remember, what became my thesis project was originally a humble side gig, not the pièce de résistance. That was supposed to have been, you may remember—"

"Damn right I remember. We all used to whisper that you had your own pet cyborg stashed away in the locker room, the insane hours you were putting in."

"For all we knew, Old Man Argentus may have had that in mind; there was a rash of intellectual property theft around the same time as our break-in, and it's not even clear that we were the main target. The bottom line is that after the Clan members had drawn first blood, they knew I was too dangerous to be left standing; I knew too much. So they had to pummel me while I was down, to guarantee that no one in the field would ever exhume the truth from the shallow grave where those dreamsnatchers had buried it alive..."

He was about to bring his fist down on the countertop, but he stopped himself. What good was anger if he couldn't channel it to yield results?

"So the Blacklist is real."

"Real?" Zach chuckled.

"I didn't mean anything by—"

"Don't worry about it, Matt. It's just...sort of morbidly amusing to hear someone surprised to learn that what ruined my life actually exists."

Zach signaled the bartender for another beer.

"I never met anyone who was put on it," Matt said. "I figured it was propaganda, to help the Triantarchs keep the masses in their place."

"No one gives you an official notice—though actually, that would be nice. Hell, a phone call would've been nice. They just leave it for you to figure out. One by one, in the months after the burglary, all my prospective work offers were rescinded. I couldn't get a summer internship—couldn't even get work as an office gopher."

"You can't work anywhere? Still?" Matt asked.

Zach shook his head.

"Can't work, can't escape. Imagine if you had to tell Melissa before your wedding day—"

Zach knotted his tongue and locked his lips shut, silently berating himself for turning onto a strictly forbidden avenue of conversation.

"You know," he continued, subtly changing the subject, "the Clans even added a touch of Dantean theatricality to the name—the Blacklist, I mean, is not just 'The Blacklist.' Its official title supposedly is, 'The

Blacklist of the Damned Souls.' The names of the Damned are radioactive; everyone up to your old grade-school buddies from the backyard treehouse will balk at bringing you on staff."

"But you never lifted a finger against the Triantarchs—you were just doing your work!"

The bartender set down a froth-topped mug in front of Zach and took the empty one away. Zach took a sip of foam.

"You know, I actually like beer-foam. The good professor thinks you're nuts if you don't like tequila, but that stuff tastes terrible. The head on a beer, on the other hand... it's like a little preview of the goodness to come. Why does the foam get such a bad rap, Matt?"

"You were just doing your work," Matt said.

"Yes, I was. But they didn't like it. Or rather, they liked it so much they stole it, but they didn't want me doing any more of it for anyone else. Anywhere." Zach took a long drink of beer. "Doesn't matter what I did, Matt. Doesn't matter if it's right or fair or... or what have you. My career has been stubbed out like a cigarette, and that's that. There's no power left in this shell of a continent that can stop them."

"Powerful as they may be, not even they can ruin you on a whim or a whisper. Take Tim—he's managed to keep standing."

"Tim, bless his heart, has enough stature to fend them off for a while. The bloodthirsty knights in our Camelot of Crooks reserve their worst predations for the weak and wounded, and unfortunately for me, I happened to catch the Triantarchs' collective eye *before* I'd gained such stature for myself. You only get that with a career, which, as we've covered, is already off the table for me."

"But Zach, that doesn't mean that—"

"Which is useful to them in another way—I'm too busy surviving each wretched new day to even contemplate fighting back. And that is a concern—survival, I mean. The Ruling Clans often like to attach a fig leaf of legitimacy to Blacklisting, usually some trumped-up accusations of debt or financial profligacy."

"You?" Matt laughed. "In that mass of rust and scrap you call a car? You're about as far from profligate as can be imagined."

Zach leaned in close to Matt.

"The Triantarchs can always find a liability to your name or fabricate one out of whole cloth, so all of us born into the cattle classes are candidates for the Blacklist—or worse. As for those misguided souls who dare to engage someone on the Blacklist…They're next to wind up in the crosshairs. Go home and stay safe, Matt. You don't need to know about this nightmare. Thank your lucky stars you don't."

"I'm no stranger to the Clans' machinations, Zach. Nor is Melissa…" Matt abruptly stayed his tongue. He moved on quickly. "In any event, it still shouldn't be like this. How can they undo so many centuries of hard-won gains—"

"Is that a serious question? They play up every festering rankle or grievance that's rent this country since 1776. They keep us at each other's throats. Thirty families with a chokehold on 300 million people—the numbers may be bigger than ever, but the strategy that got them there is as old as the Bible—older, even."

Matt took a prolonged gulp from his own beer. He set down the mug on its edge and it wobbled on the counter

"I still don't see where the puzzle pieces fit," he said, shaking his head. "Why you, a lowly young gearhead minding his own business?"

"'Lowly' young gearhead? Now there's a spirit-perker for you."

"Zach, come on. You know what I meant."

"Even if I did, am I really supposed to care?"

"I think you should. It'd do you a lot more good than slinking away into this little temple of dark and dismal thoughts you've set up for yourself."

"Which, I take it, is Matt-speak for, 'Zach, stop acting like a first-class jerk about all this.'"

"Actually, Zach, you are acting like a first-class jerk right now, and the thing is, it doesn't bother me a bit, because I know why you're doing it. It's your armor, your antidote to the whispers in your own head, the ones that occasionally gain a voice to sing and chirp about hope. You've been burned bad, I get that. And now you're afraid of the fleeting rays of light that might dare to seep in past your defenses, so damn afraid to hope for any hint of a solution that might crumble into yet another disappointment."

"Hope? That would imply there's something to hope for."

"At the very least, you could get to the bottom of what really happened to you. It wasn't merely about shutting you up. Think about it—why would the Clans even care if you *did* speak up about the burglary? You could shout the truth from the rooftops, and what difference would it make? So the Ruling Families are criminal monsters bleeding our country dry—that's common knowledge, especially to anyone naïve enough to have ever engaged in productive pursuits before having all their efforts stolen away. Why would the Clans care what you said?"

"You really think I have an answer for that?" asked Zach with a disdainful sidelong glance.

"No, but I do think you should be asking more questions. It's been six years since the Triantarchs seized the honeypot of power in this country, and they're more entrenched than ever. So why would they go to such lengths to destroy you?"

"Why do you even presume there *is* a rational explanation for what happened to me, at least that any of us outside their inner circle could comprehend? It must get awfully humdrum within the Triantarchy from time to time; maybe ruining the lives of helpless plebs qualifies as rousing entertainment for bored kleptocrats."

"Zach, dammit, this cynicism of yours will get you nowhere. All I'm saying is that there's far more to the story than some ham-fisted attempt to muzzle you about the burglary. There has to be a deeper reason."

"Oh, Jesus, Matt! A deeper reason?"

Zach's outburst drew tentative gazes from elsewhere in the bar. He lowered his voice.

"The bigwigs in Clan Longinus," he continued, "flattened two towns and butchered 15,000 people back in 2021, all to seal off the region and build a den of debauchery for the murderous hedonists within their orbit. It was three years before the Underground groups could dig up the truth, before all those official lies about a revolt and seizure of the local armory were at last dispelled. That was the 'deeper reason' that 15,000 innocents breathed their last that day—a goddamned pleasure complex!"

"The Mayfly Massacre—I wish you hadn't reminded me. I'm not sure what's more dispiriting, the mass slaughter itself or the apathy that greeted the eventual truth."

"No, Matt, it wasn't mere indifference that greeted the revelations—it was fear, and not only of the Triantarchs themselves. Fifteen thousand perished in the Mayfly Massacre, but fifteen million died on account of the civil war in Tokhariana the year before, including many of our own troops sent in for God knows what reason."

"To say nothing of the other wars in all those countries-for-a-week that sprouted up after the Reckoning."

"Then you know where this is leading. Up to now, most of the Triantarchs have preferred to keep their brutality a bit less overt than the horrors of Mayfly, but not because they have to. They've wiped out virtually anything that would qualify as organized opposition, so whatever hell the Ruling Clans have visited upon this land, what's left of America is too afraid of what would follow in the wake of their ouster. The Clans know this, and it's why they don't need *reasons* for what they've done to me or any of their other victims, only their own unchallengeable whims."

"Maybe so, but I'd be willing to wager that some sort of inter-Clan insider jockeying is at the bottom of all this, a power struggle with you somehow caught in the middle. You're probably not the real target, and you may have more room to maneuver than you think. Heck, maybe we'll all get lucky if they start bumping each other off again. Used to be, what, 150 Clans? Then 90? 80? Maybe they'll solve your problem for you."

"I wouldn't count on such a grim salvation, Matt."

"I think you're being too pessimistic."

"And I wish I could soak up a drop of your dogged optimism, but what you or I think, let alone hope, doesn't matter one iota. For me to survive this, I have to lie low and tend my own garden, and that means fending off any unguarded thoughts about how I came into this plight. I've boiled my own blood too many times while stewing in that pot of speculation and... no, it's not in the blood. It's in the pit of my stomach, that's where I feel it."

"Where you feel what?"

"That vampire despair, the kind that lifers in a Supermax lockdown or the debtors' prisons must wake up to every morning. It drains your spirit pale every day with the knowledge you have nowhere to go, that everywhere you turn there's another wall waiting to close in and crush the life clean out of you. This sick feeling... I can overcome it only because I've learned not to feed it with unanswerable questions whenever my mind strays too close."

"All right, Zach, I can see why you're not pressing this, but that doesn't mean you're limited to helplessly waiting and moping. Why can't you just pick up stakes, like so many of the other promising young talents who don't even have a sword dangling over their heads?"

"The Blacklist upends the exit visa process, too, and regardless, where would I go? My family couldn't come within 100 miles of Korea without setting off all those old vendettas again. We're pariahs anywhere near the old family home."

"Have you thought about crossing the other ocean? At least a few places are somewhat less screwed-up across the Atlantic. You're a trained professional, spent a year in Switzerland, you speak French, Spanish, and German at least passably enough to— "

"Matt, even if I could scheme my way past customs, everybody and his tenth-cousin-once-removed is conniving to get one of those exit visas, and they don't come cheap. I don't have the remotest connection to Europe other than that stint goofing around as a ski instructor."

"Then elsewhere in Asia? What about Renee?"

"What about her?" Zach asked, awkwardly averting his gaze.

"Her family's from Taiwan, right? Used to work in Hong Kong? And in Xiamen on the Chinese Mainland? Plenty of options. I was at the same table with all of you at that Engineering Awards Banquet last year. Her father was gushing about all his new investments in the family tool-and-die shop in south Taiwan."

"I speak enough Mandarin to sweet-talk Renee now and then, Matt. Can't draw much of a paycheck from that."

"Then call it a first step and give it a chance. The Triantarchs can't reach you there."

"I told you it's a non-starter."

"What do you have to lose, for Chrissakes? Renee's parents would corral earth and moon to help you. I'll never forget her father's words when he learned I was your best friend; he made me deaf burbling on about how much he looked forward to introducing Dr. Zach Choi as his son-in-law— "

Zach had seized an unfortunate salad fork in a death grip, gouging its tines into the already pocked and scarred wood of the bar counter. He then arched forward with a pale, blank stare before tilting his forehead meekly downward, overwhelmed by a corrosive mixture of shame and self-devouring rage.

His friend looked on in sympathy and a measure of alarm, the icy waters of realization washing over him.

"That's why you and Tim were locking horns," Matt concluded soberly. "That's what's behind all of this. You still haven't told Renee, have you?"

Zach dug a crumpled wad of dollar bills from his back pocket and dumped them on the counter.

"I think I'll call it a night," he said brusquely, rising from the stool and lumbering toward the exit.

"Zach, wait! I only wanted to—"

Zach paused momentarily at the door, making a half-turn back around; but his shoulder was soon pressing through the threshold. Whatever he dared not disclose in words, he feared his eyes would betray just the same.

Aus der Höhle, der vertrauten,
flattert eine Fledermaus,
Grüßt ganz still das Unbekannte,
wagt sich in die Welt hinaus.
Doch sie kann sie nicht verstehen,
ruft und horcht und fliegt herum—
Was liegt jenseits unsrer Sinnen,
bleibt uns ein Mysterium?

Chapter Two

The Sacred Sight

Chakana

FRIDAY, MAY 16, 4:33 P.M.
PINE GULCH FILLING STATION
GATLINBURG, GREAT SMOKY MOUNTAINS, TENNESSEE

"So yes, rain, rain, and more rain for the weekend, and no *relief in sight; that just about sums up what's on tap for all you determined Great Smoky picnickers and hikers out there. This is Carl Roland with the WBRG Weathertracker. Over to you, Vivian."*

"Thank you, Carl. We will have more on the weekend weather forecast, including live updates and road conditions, later in the broadcast. But first, an update on the worrying events first disclosed early last week, when a computer virus of unknown origin was reported to have infiltrated and hijacked a number of critical regional networks. Among the victims thus far, as confirmed by WBRG field investigators, are local branches of the Humboldt Memorial Hospital and the now-defunct Khemia Corporation, based in the town of Farragut."

Tim yawned as he queued up before the gas station's checkout counter, clutching a bag of salted trail mix to tack onto his tab. He directed his attention sporadically toward an old TV perched precariously behind the counter, its tilted screen beaming out grainy pictures from the local news program. The weather along the drive had been oppressively dank and dreary, his winding course through the mountain passes suffocated by a dense canopy of fog and drizzle that carpeted the road. The journey felt interminable. It had been a struggle for him to keep from nodding off behind the wheel.

Thus it was to his surprise that he found his attention piqued by a curious, violet-hued image materializing on the crackling television screen behind the counter. The image vaguely resembled a nut twirled around a bolt, yet with notched grooves around its perimeter and a multitude of exotic etchings inscribed within. Tim leaned in over the counter to get a better look at the strange iconography as the news reporter continued her narration.

"Experts have recently dubbed this electronic intruder the Chakana Virus, a name originally suggested by retired local anthropologist Haley Rasmussen, who spoke briefly with WBRG reporters this morning at her home in Gatlinburg.

"'Years ago, my team was stationed in Ecuador to train with the region's anthropologists, where we became well-acquainted with a symbol in the Inca mythology called the Chakana. It symbolizes the links between the everyday world we experience and the unseen realms of the gods—their underworld and heaven above, as it were. It's unforgettable to anyone who's seen it, and there it was of all places on the computer monitors at Humboldt Memorial, the ones invaded by that virus that's been kicking up such a fuss. Couldn't guess why or how the symbol wound up at that hospital.'"

"Pretty weird, eh?" mumbled the young clerk behind the counter, his attention briefly diverted as Tim advanced to the front of the line.

"In my line of work, precious little surprises anymore," said Tim, forcing a grin. "I'm at pump number six, by the way, forty bucks, premium unleaded."

"Sure thing," replied the clerk. He rubbed his slightly stubbled chin as he rang up the tab. Tim's eyes went back to the TV.

"Authorities sought to reassure anxious local residents that personal records and hospital test results have not been compromised or made public. Yet these assurances have been met with growing skepticism as days continue to pass with little explanation for the recurring intrusions. An unnamed hospital staff member at Humboldt Memorial, on

condition of anonymity, disclosed to WBRG investigative reporters that the Neurological Imaging Center had been especially hard-hit.

"Meanwhile, a Khemia company representative reported the biotech firm had suffered persistent attacks on its own brain-scan databases. The targeted files had been central to Khemia's clinical trials for stroke rehabilitation drugs. However, they had been shifted to low-security mainframes as part of recent negotiations for the beleaguered enterprise, struggling to emerge from a bankruptcy restructuring under Chapter 11."

"Brain scans?" Tim muttered, incredulous.

"That'll be $43.57 altogether," the clerk said. Tim could scarcely take his eyes off the TV screen as he reached for his wallet.

"So, what in God's green earth brings a professor from Carolina to our mountain hideout on such a dismal Friday afternoon?"

"I..." Tim began. "How'd you know?"

"Your badge, Dr. Shoemaker," laughed the clerk as he took Tim's cash off the counter.

"My badge—oh, forgot I still had it on," Tim said sheepishly, unclasping the insignia and slipping it into a side pocket in his travel knapsack. "Those roads, all the fog closing in on you like a flood tide... I'm telling you, it's surreal. I felt zombified half the time behind the wheel; guess I've yet to fully return to the world of the living. And I suppose you're Ted, at least if your own badge has anything to say about it."

"Theodoric, actually, if you can believe it," said the clerk with a bemused grin, as though incredulous of his own name. "My Dad owns this place, but he's an amateur classicist when he's not busy running the show. He and my mother picked out a slate of names from ancient Rome for me and my little sibs. Always made for awkward introductions, so I've just stayed with Ted ever since high school."

"Well, then, I'll stick with Ted, too."

"Much obliged, Doc. You're right about that fog—it can get pretty bad sometimes, but it's never been quite like this. It's like... sticky. And they say 'thicker than pea soup'? Heck, might as well be our homemade Tennessee corn chowder," Ted quipped as he handed over the change.

"Tennessee corn chowder, huh?" chuckled Tim, slipping the bills into his wallet and checking over his shoulder. The shop was otherwise empty, freeing him to extend the conversation and the sorely needed breather it availed. "Guess I'll have to sample a bowl. As for your question, I came out to help an old friend. She works around here."

"So it's all business for you, eh?"

"Sure don't see much pleasure upcoming on this trip," Tim answered ponderously, "though I'm not sure I'd call it all business, either. More like catching up with familiar names and faces under... awkward circumstances. Since I was roaming around out here anyway, I figured I'd see my cousin in Kingston. He's been bugging me to visit for years. Oh well, I guess I could use a little home cookin' before heading out to Oak Ridge tomorrow."

"Oak Ridge? You've got guts."

"Why do you say that, Ted?"

"Folks mentioning that place around here, seems they're always on the way out and glad of it. None ever said why. But, I don't know—"

"What?"

"It's like they're trying to rinse off some bad mojo bubbling into the premises nowadays, and given the long haul they have ahead, I've never pressed for details. Oh, beg your pardon, Doc; sometimes I lose myself in conversation. This is probably the last thing you want to hear right about now."

"Nah, don't worry about it," Tim said, his roiled mood belying his words. "My bad mojo meter was already maxed out the day I took this crazy assignment. Besides, I've been looking for an excuse to take the scenic route through all these mountain passes. Now, if only I could *see* any of the scenery through this damn corn chowder fog."

"I'm with you on that," Ted replied with a shrug. "It's been a real puzzler. We don't get fog and cloudbursts up here like this, especially not in this season. Heck, most years in May my Dad has me out chopping wood for the stove and planting trees, but lately the whole forest is soaked over like a wet dishrag."

"As are the roads."

Ted nodded.

"You know, living in the mountains, you can just feel things in the air sometimes, like electric jolts tearing through the sky. You might think I'm nuts, but there's something wicked brewing out there, like a storm straight outta Hell itself."

Tim narrowed his eyes, equally curious and apprehensive about the clerk's foreboding words.

"You mean, out there on the mountain passes?"

"Yeah. And I'm betting it's not gonna stay confined to these parts, either. Can't quite put my finger on it, but you know how the weather forecasters on the radio get all in a huff about biblical storms from time to time? Going on about the elements pelting the hills, warning you out-of-towners about what's ahead?"

"On this drive alone, more than I care to admit."

"Well, this is gonna be the real thing. Not sure I could snag a weatherman job making predictions on that basis. All the same, you get pretty good at sensing the currents around here. This thing's comin', and soon. Don't mean to scare you, but—just look at it out there already. Drive safe, Doc."

"You too, Ted, and uh—hey, thanks for the heads-up."

As Tim drove cautiously along the foggy Appalachian thoroughfares, his tank now full and his tired eyes refreshed, anxious thoughts flitted through his mind. The words of the gas station clerk gnawed at him. The certainty with which the young man had uttered his predictions was unnerving, Tim thought. The kid had a keen mind humming beneath that folksy bonhomie; he knew of what he spoke.

The effect of the clerk's malign augurings was compounded by the disorienting weather conditions. The twisting mountain roads, invisible ten feet ahead and behind the car, bewitched Tim's senses like a siren call, a warning from a mystical land into which he had unwisely trespassed.

Now and then the slow crawl along mist-covered roads gave way to dimly-lit hillside tunnels. The fog traveled with him underground, so thick in places that Tim barely noticed the headlights of oncoming cars, as though they were simply materializing beside him. As he neared yet another tunnel, his eyes darted to the inscription on its entryway arch.

It was nothing more than the prosaic monogram of the local Highway Authority, yet it menaced the road below, bathed as it was in the harsh glow of a red safety lamp that strained to illuminate the fog- and rain-swept entrance. The light occasionally pierced the snaking mist, like flaming arrows aimed at oncoming drivers. As the gray-hued daylight gradually subsided within the mouth of the tunnel, Tim could hear the unsettling echo of the clerk's cryptic warning, redounding mercilessly amid the crisp landscape of his recent imaginings: "There's something wicked brewing out there, like a storm straight outta Hell itself."

FRIDAY, MAY 16, 7:22 P.M.
HOME OF ERNEST AND CONNIE SHOEMAKER
KINGSTON, TENNESSEE

"I knew you wore many hats, Ernie, but a chef's? I'd have never guessed." Tim marveled at the colorful platters laid before him. "Quiche on a chafing dish? Caviar? Tomato fondue, *and* a fine merlot to wash it all down? I'm impressed."

Tim's cousin beamed. Ernie's voice was deep and gruff, and his dark, bushy eyebrows framed a broad, heavy-set face topped by a mop of graying dark-brown hair—he looked like a sketch of an old-time seaman. One would never figure him for a gourmand. Ernie was still holding Tim's wet overcoat. He gestured at the food.

"Please, dig in," he said, returning to the foyer to hang up the coat. Tim laced his fingers overhead and stretched his aching back. After so many hours on the road in such miserable weather, he was in a dull state of shock at being inside such a cozy space. It had still been drizzling when he'd pulled into Ernie's driveway ten minutes ago.

"Just because the Reckoning forced me into semi-retirement, I'm not going to sit around twiddling my thumbs," Ernie called from the foyer. "I've tried to make the best of it, indulging all my long-deferred hobbies for better or worse." Returning to the living room, Ernie poured them each a glass of the merlot. The two men sat down, Tim on the sofa and his cousin in a burgundy leather armchair. "In truth, I can't take all the credit here; Connie lent a hand before going to her potluck tonight. She sends her warm regards, by the way."

"Sorry I missed her, Ernie. I came out on such short notice; didn't have time to plan. Cheers, to procrastinating cousins."

"Cheers, to long-awaited reunions that are never a day too late." They clinked glasses. Tim drank down half his glass, prompting his host to raise an eyebrow.

"Speaking of short notice," Ernie said, "What exactly brought you out here? I was spacing out in the backyard yesterday when you called—something about that eye implant trial you were involved in some years back?"

Tim briefed his cousin on his conversation with Rachel Bloom, emptying the rest of his glass as he finished. Ernie poured him a refill.

"I realize you've never been the *bon vivant* type," observed Ernie as he poured, "but most aspiring connoisseurs prefer to, uh, sip the merlot."

"Most merlot sippers haven't been on a two-state odyssey to reach the bar."

"Fair enough. But I'm not sure I'm following here—you said the retinal implants initially delivered on their promises, so what happened? Side effects from the procedure? Unforeseen complications?"

"Unforeseen complications..." Tim's laugh grated with a rasp that bordered on incredulous derision, baffling his host. "I'm sorry, Ernie; if you only knew the understatement in that description."

"So, enlighten me."

"Rachel's team was attempting to restore sight to Marine veterans who'd sustained traumatic eye injuries in the line of duty. After the first flush of success, the vets began exhibiting... how to put this... mental status changes that grew progressively worse—dysphoric episodes, delusions, auditory hallucinations, and all manner of other psychiatric woes."

"Doesn't surprise me, sad to say. Back in '09, they dumped my Army Reserve team straight into eastern Afghanistan, Helmand Province. 'Hell's playground,' we called it. About half the squad had full-blown PTSD by the end of our tour. Even minor checkups with the docs would flare it right back up again."

Tim leaned forward and set his wine glass on the coffee table. Ernie poured him another refill.

"I don't mean to make light of your experiences in that meat-grinder, Ernie, but this is something else. The Oak Ridge phenomenon is a far different animal from post-traumatic stress. It's as if the insanity were... *coordinated* somehow. The affliction appears to be shared in kind among the veterans."

"Come again?"

"Imagine a schizophrenic passing his delusions along to others as readily as a cold from a sneeze."

"Like a ... what's that French term for a delusion shared between two people?"

"A *folie à deux*," Tim said with a nervous twitch of the nose. "It is that, but also dreadfully more."

"In what way?"

"Rachel's assistant treated me to a nonstop horror show on the various dimensions of the syndrome. I've yet to hear the lowdown on all the fine points, but she said it's all-consuming—a full-blown psychosis that's contagious not only in the delusions themselves but also in the patients' behavior, speech patterns, even their movement. The functional decline is insidious, moving as if in waves from one soldier to another, always manifesting first in a certain Marine among the group before overwhelming the rest. Nothing of the sort has ever been documented before."

"You sure about that?" Ernie asked. "Between all the wounds, battlefield terrors, and plagues of God-knows-what during my tour in Afghanistan, I came across write-ups on dozens of neurological puzzlers that were simply stashed away in a forgotten database."

"Perhaps because they merited little else."

"No, it wasn't because they were insignificant; more like it was far more convenient to sweep the cases under the rug, especially when answers were in such short supply. The infectious nasties alone could fill a doorstopper volume, and the medical officers were constantly warning us about the mosquitoes in particular. They were vectors for malaria and a host of encephalitis viruses, along with a catalog of unknown maladies for which we never found a satisfactory explanation."

"Actually, that was my first thought as well," said Tim, frowning. "A bacterium or virus, or some other microbial source. I broached it in the Q&A with the Oak Ridge team this morning."

"And?"

"Negative."

"Then maybe some shell shock from the battlefield flooding back in? The vets were in the dark for years, then suddenly the outside world came blazing back in through their eyes... Must be triggering all kinds of ghastliness their brains had locked down before."

"They said they'd ruled that out, too."

"But there must be some common point of reference," Ernie protested, swirling his wine glass with a measure of agitation.

"Occam's razor can't cut this one down to size," Tim said, pinching the bridge of his nose. "I surveyed them on every tidy explanation—all the plausibles and maybes that make for digestible cover stories and press releases. Rachel's team has systematically picked them apart, without exception, and come up snake-eyes each time."

"I don't know, Tim. This whole affair smells fishy to me. I'd say they have their genuine reasons for dragging you out there, but you haven't begun to hear them yet. They just pushed enough of your buttons to get you to bite. I see a bait-and-switch coming."

"That thought's crossed my mind more than once, I won't deny it."

Tim picked up his wine glass, about to take another deep drink. He caught himself, however; he took a tentative sip and sat back on the sofa, gazing out the living room window. Drizzling rain continued to strafe the glass of the cozy Colonial Revival home, while a gossamer-thin fog obscured the front yard.

"Call me crazy," he said, "but my gut says Rachel's giving it to me straight. At this point, there's no doctor from here to Honolulu who'll touch the case. I'm not sure what kind of epiphany I'm supposed to have poring through their logs, but I can tell you this: The presses are revving up for an old-fashioned scapegoating, with Rachel first in line for the skewer. Calling me was a Hail Mary. For some reason she thinks I might be the answer."

Ernie studied his cousin's face intently, still skeptical but sympathetic almost to the point of pity. "Fair enough. Regardless, whether the details are confidential or not, I know you're not telling me everything. That's fine, though. I'm just trying to guard your flank after—after all the ordeals you've... after everything you've been through lately."

Tim glanced at the ceiling. He had to force himself to look his cousin in the eye. "I know you mean well, Ernie, but—there are times when all the damn hushed tones and eggshell-walking are more maddening than just blurting out the unpleasant truth."

"I don't believe that. And neither do you."

Tim set his glass down on the coffee table with a touch too much force, sliding it on its base to the center of the table. He looked at his lap.

"Tim, look, I won't patronize you with any half-cocked attempts at consolation; you've had more than your fill of that. But I know something about dealing with the memories of sudden deaths. Our squad in Afghanistan was paired with regular units full of kids who were still flashing fake IDs in the bar districts back home. Not to mention all the villagers and locals in the towns. Those frightened eyes, people cowering whenever a shell or a bullet whistled through the air. And the mortars and the mines—they don't discriminate when they spray their shrapnel, nor do they care who witnesses the carnage."

Ernie paused, waiting for his cousin to meet his eye again.

"We saw it happen a dozen times," Ernie continued, "and we were hardened warhorses. Yet we found ourselves grieving like grandmothers for fallen strangers a world away, and the images have never entirely left us, however much we try to push them back. You've never had even that small luxury, Tim. You never found a way to grieve. Don't imagine that you'll get over it, whatever people say. But you will learn to cope with each day in spite of it. And that's all you can ask of yourself."

"Then I'm afraid I've fallen short. Cope," Tim said hoarsely. "Three years gone by, and I'm still numb. There are so many things that I can barely remember, whether from the shock or the impact...or when I had to tell Chloe and Mark in that God-awful hospital room. Every time I try to revisit that day, even around the margins, there's something deep inside that pushes back. Violently so."

Ernie listened to his cousin intently, but in a manner more perplexed than perceiving. He cleared his throat as if to air a thought, but stopped himself.

"It may be of slight comfort for whatever faces you tomorrow, Tim, but you're not the only one who's been answering mayday calls at Oak Ridge lately."

Now it was Tim who looked perplexed.

"But I thought, after the Reckoning—"

"I've been working as an independent contractor of sorts. All those years monkey-wrenching and repairing the data networks across venue after venue..." Ernie chuckled. "This guy I worked with, you know what he called me? Quote: 'a walking museum of knowledge.' Guess I am that—at least on all those customized pre-Internet computer systems at Oak Ridge. 'Ernest Verini Shoemaker, electronic handyman and antiquarian extraordinaire'—how's that for a business card?"

Tim nodded.

"Not bad. You do have a rare combination of skills. They must have been ready to canonize you out here."

"Oh, they were," Ernie said, "especially since they rarely had the budget to do anything more radical, like paying me for a day's work. I was fine with it, as these things go. Connie and I had saved up enough over the years, even with all the hits from the Reckoning, and the house calls kept my skills fresh. But a little over a month ago, I learned my limits in a hurry. One of the engineering departments called me in to combat a virus rippling through the networks across the campus. Couldn't produce even a faint hint about its origin."

"A virus?" Tim asked, recalling the TV news spot he'd seen at the gas station earlier that day.

"I ran every diagnostic I had. Nothing—zippo. I'd never been stymied like that before. Then the virus pulled a disappearing act two weeks ago. Just a few sporadic visits since then and nothing destructive, as best we can tell."

"I made a quick pit stop on the way to Kingston, and the local newscaster had a segment on a computer virus no one knew what to do with. It overran the brain imaging department at a local hospital, of all things. Bizarro name, too, they were calling it, uh—"

"Chakana," Ernie offered.

"It was at Oak Ridge too?"

"No, and that's why it's such a head-spinner. The timing's suggestive enough, but we couldn't establish a firm link between the viruses. Every unwelcome intruder into a data network has a code signature that specifies its taxonomy, and Chakana seems to occupy a different subclass from the one at Oak Ridge. Yet there's a qualitative resemblance between them, if nothing else in the sheer ferocity of their computations."

"Interesting choice of words."

"And apropos, for anyone who's seen them in action. Their algorithmic density and mutation rate—their sheer sophistication, for both viruses—are off the charts. Even with all the diamond-gilded industrial espionage they've been using to liquidate what's left of their opposition, I doubt the Triantarchs' own hired guns could match such a feat."

"I wouldn't be too sure of that," Tim said, glancing away and quietly seething at the thought.

"Anyhow, even the crack mathematicians and code-breakers laid off from the security agencies lately can't pin down the significance of the calculations. The working consensus is that all the feverish number-gnashing is part of a rapid-evolution system, to adapt and quickly hop across security firewalls and network architectures. But that's equivocal at best. The Oak Ridge virus seems to be transcending the bounds of any objective we could readily identify, as if it's giving us a demonstration."

"The Leonardo da Vinci of computer worms."

"Let's just say that whoever these hackers are, I'd like to invest in whatever heist they're about to pull off."

"The timing of it all," Tim mused, grimacing. "You said the virus hit the scene a month ago?"

"Give or take."

"Then there is some overlap with my own mission, at least based on what they told me earlier today. Rachel's assistant singled out a period in February as the start of all the troubles, but she said it was a little over a month ago when the research team completely lost the reins. That's around when the soldiers in the trial began to slip into this bizarre group psychosis."

Tim sat back on the sofa, thinking. After a few moments' silence between the men, he addressed his cousin.

"Ernie, when you took the Oak Ridge assignment, did you make any rounds in the Biomedical Engineering and Prosthetics Sector?"

"Funny you'd ask. It was expressly verboten for me or my comrades to go within a country mile of that division."

"They tell you why that was?" Tim asked.

"Something about a rash of incidents that had been decimating the contracting teams of late, and even that little tidbit I had to pry out of a systems administrator over a few drinks. Oddly enough, the incidents weren't clustered in that sector per se, but somebody in the know must have suspected a link, for reasons that were duly hushed up. One of the Triantarchs apparently has some stake in the goings-on there, and he didn't want outside contractors going around blabbing inconvenient details."

"When you say incidents, you mean accidents?"

"So it would seem; I wasn't able to glean anything more specific. But I will say this."

Ernie set down his glass with an uncomfortable sigh.

"I've happily taken jobs in some hard-core locales, Tim. The kinds of places most people wouldn't touch for a year of hazard pay and a Benz in the driveway. I've told you some of the war stories: troubleshooting data nets that snaked their way through abandoned sewers, fixing wires around toxic waste dumps, squeezing between the walls and crawlspaces of condemned buildings. Yet I was kissing my wristwatch every time it showed I'd finished a shift on my latest gig. You couldn't bribe me to work full-time around there these days."

"Why?"

"There's something about that Oak Ridge complex that gets under my skin. I can't quite put my finger on it, but I can feel it. It's in the air. It's like a rustling in the background. You catch it in people's eyes. You'll want to stay sharp while you're working there. Keep your guard up, Tim, because something's wrong with that place."

Tim grabbed his glass and raised it to his lips, forcing himself to sip rather than gulp the merlot. As he drank, he noticed an odd, peach-shaped flask of white wine perched on a nearby counter.

"That one was a rare prize, from a tiny vineyard off the Loire River," said Ernie, following his guest's eye.

"Yes, you mentioned something about that yesterday," Tim said, relieved to shift to another topic. "Glad to hear the wine cellar's finally up and stocked. Though I presume your treasure from the Loire didn't quite fit in with the crowd, literally speaking."

"The vineyard's owner was new to the scene and hadn't partnered with a distributor yet. But she was descended from an old family of blacksmiths and glassblowers; that bottle there was a family heirloom. Speaking of the wine cellar and family heirlooms, I promised you a guided tour. Now's as good a time as any, no?"

"Uh, sure," said Tim, mildly flustered at the dual reference invoked by his cousin.

7:57 P.M.

"Finely-aged cabernet, straight from the Rhône Valley," said Ernie, proudly raising a cask from the lower reaches of the cellar. Its cramped quarters were filled with an eclectic assortment of wooden compartments mounted carefully on cinderblocks. A cool, moist draft percolated through the cellar, carrying vestiges of the merciless rain outside.

"This was years ago," Ernie continued, "before the Reckoning had all but devoured our travel budget. Connie and I must have broken about a dozen French laws to smuggle this beauty out from the vintner's auction in Lyons."

As he surveyed his cousin's handiwork in the cellar, Tim's attention was drawn to a lattice-like framework used to hold some of the smaller bottles. Its edges were bowed outward, and each compartment was capped by a flexible metal seal inscribed with initials Tim recognized all too well: MGS.

"So that's what Uncle Mitch did with that hardware when his business went under, all those years ago," Tim said, shaking his head at the recollection.

"All that excess stock at the warehouse, and not even the scrap dealers were interested," Ernie forced a smile. "He and your father naturally weren't on the best of terms when their venture went down in flames, so I guess all your cousins relieved him of the inventory."

"Speaking of our dear uncle, Ernie, how's he been holding up since his latest trip to the emergency room?" Tim asked without looking at his cousin. "I got a heads-up last week, along with the rest of the Shoemaker clan, but I know you and Connie have had his ear for a while."

"Last I heard, Mitch's true grit was winning the day again. The doctors haven't been taking any chances since he had the pacemaker installed, and there was some concern about a dip into early-stage heart failure a couple days into his admission. But the worst-case scenarios have already receded, even if he'll be an honored guest in the coronary unit for a while."

Vague thoughts flashed in Tim's mind, but he stopped short of giving them voice. Frowning, he turned fully away from his cousin and fixed his gaze upon a conspicuous bottle of Riesling to his right side. The bottle was perched precariously on the edge of a compartment still under construction. His thoughts were like stuttered words, half-formed, as they concerned matters Tim had but half-acknowledged, deliberately, for some time. Finally, he could no longer hold his tongue. Turning to face his cousin, he did not even attempt to conceal his resentment.

"I suppose it would be good manners for me to send him a get-well-soon card," Tim said, "which I'd do if I sincerely gave a damn how he fared."

Ernie seemed genuinely taken aback by his cousin's outburst.

"Tim, for God's sake, when are you going to let go of this... rage that consumes you every time the subject of Mitch comes up?"

"Call me in a hundred years and I'll give you an estimate. Till then, to hell with him. Frankly, I'm embarrassed that I share ties of kinship with such a scoundrel."

"All that bad blood coursing through your veins—it's poison."

"Please don't belittle what you plainly don't understand," Tim said through clenched teeth. "It was bad enough that Mitch had been playing fast and loose with the company's finances, including Dad's seed capital. That alone nearly cost us the house. But then, when Mitch's creditors pulled the plug, he went underground and put us all at risk. My mother was in tears for a week when the loan sharks made their first visit, brandishing Dad's picture and threatening to return. When they later took him away, Dad came back with a few bruises but otherwise barely a scratch. And I'll bet you can guess why."

Ernie looked at Tim in stony silence, waiting out his cousin's tirade.

"It was because they had a far more effective way of torturing him," Tim added. "They simply revealed the truth about his brother, and all the ways Mitch had found to royally screw up everything he touched, keeping Dad in the dark the whole time."

"There was more to it than that, Tim. One of the executives had absconded with a tranche of the company's funds, and the police couldn't track him down. Mitch didn't want all of their efforts to collapse on account of that. He had to make a terrible choice."

"He didn't have to do it alone. But rather than trusting his own brother with the ugly truth and working it out together, Mitch misrepresented the state of affairs at every turn."

"A mistake he regrets to this day."

"And then," Tim continued, oblivious to the interruption, "he frittered away whatever was left on that fool's errand with those... 'saltatory superconducting wires' or whatever fancy name he slapped on the damn things."

"That fool's errand, as you call it, eventually became the touchstone of a multibillion-dollar enterprise."

"Yes, eventually, as in fifteen years later."

"A new business is never a pristine affair, Tim. And because Mitch had the courage to stick it out through all those trials, he built a port in the storm, one that sheltered the jobs of quite a few good folks when the Reckoning came barreling through. Even the Triantarchs have kept their grubby hands off Magister Engineering, at least for now. Nobody could replace Mitch at the helm, and this is one golden goose they have yet to throttle."

"Of course it is. He had only to sacrifice his own kin to consecrate his temple."

"I wish you could hear yourself." In spite of his exasperation, Ernie's voice was firm and composed. "Maybe Mitch was right all along."

"About what?"

"The 90/10 Conundrum—that's what he called it. The ninety percent of who we are inside is always suffocated by the ten percent that others actually can see, and all the misunderstandings that come as a result. Mitch was painfully aware of how he was seen by those most important to him, in all the wrong ways. That includes you and your father, and it burned him up inside."

"I'm well versed in Mitch's forays into pop psychology," Tim retorted. "His favorite with Dad was the Septego Rule, supposedly something he garnered from a few months of his morning diaries. I was at the dinner table when Mitch launched into one of his characteristic bouts of insufferable bombast."

Tim stepped back and affected a mien of pedantic enthusiasm, his exaggerated gesticulations further mocking his subject. "'The minds that we consider our own, these solitary and unitary vessels of behavior, are more like a committee of roughly seven different personalities that make decisions in collaboration, each an independent person in itself. We rarely appreciate our own septet, let alone those of others, thus all the misconceptions that have begotten everything from frayed marriages to ruinous wars.' It was all so endearing, at least in that self-serving kind of way Mitch was so keen to cultivate."

"Sometimes I think you're never so eloquent as when you're being grossly unfair. Especially when it comes to Mitch. He wasn't expounding on all that to rationalize away his deficiencies, in fact quite the contrary. It's part of what kept him level throughout all the letdowns, backstabbing, and heartbreaks he endured while raising Magister Engineering from the ashes."

"So now he's showing off his little pearls of pomposity as part of a self-help routine for aspiring businesses? Is that how he ladled out the idea to you, Ernie?"

"He always called on a different phrasing with me, but it never failed to ring true. The mind inside each of us is like a mosaic of distinct people, with often conflicting thoughts and motivations and sometimes even violent contradictions. Yet somehow, these inner persons all link up to forge the sense of self we identify with. The catch is that someone on the outside might perceive different facets, different persons within that mosaic in a given circumstance."

"I suppose there's a point here?"

"The point is that Mitch understood this intuitively, well before articulating it to either of us as the Septego or mosaic of inner persons or what have you. He knew it well enough to appreciate another side of even the estranged partners and investors with whom he'd sustained the bitterest of quarrels. It's why he was able to patch up the burnt bridges that almost anyone else would have abandoned and gain financial backing for the brainstorm that finally launched Magister as a success story."

"Then I sorely wish he'd realized such masterstrokes when he was partnering with Dad," said Tim, his indignation only hardening. "Besides, it's not like Mitch came up with the Septego notion all by himself. Hegel offered up a similar dish a couple of centuries ago, only with far greater authority and fluency than our Uncle Dearest could ever muster. Oh, and Hegel also arrived at a conclusion that Mitch's own horn-tooting on the subject seems to have missed."

"Which was?"

"That at the end of the day, all those contradictions have to be reconciled and integrated enough for a unit to actually function. Doesn't matter whether it's the government of a whole country or a single pretentious, self-absorbed tech entrepreneur like Mitch—if you indulge your excesses and lurch to the extremes of your inner poles, then your whole ship sinks and you drag down everyone around you."

"Mitch sought to strike that balance."

"No, Ernie, he categorically did not. He never could steady his ship amid all his manic promise-making and hyperventilating about his Next Big Thing or the still bigger and bolder thing that was always supposed to follow soon after. Then, when his best-laid plans predictably went belly up, Mitch would launch into all that pop-psychologizing to cover his tracks. All that bloviating about his Septego was also peculiarly well timed; it was barely a week later when we discovered that the company was insolvent. I guess one of the people in Mitch's head wasn't with the program."

"Tim—"

"His true self never shone through, we just misconstrued his intentions as recklessness and corruption, he really wasn't the calamity on two legs he appeared to be... Yes, Mitch would have been delighted for us to gulp down that snake oil. The last time I saw him in person was at a ceremony for his supposed largesse as an angel investor and philanthropist, after his ballyhooed 'breakthrough' at Magister Engineering. I paid him a visit backstage after his address."

"I know. Mitch told me."

"No, you don't know what matters; that I'm sure of. Mitch would have made sure to edit out any bits that didn't 'harmonize' with the image he was busily cultivating for himself. What he didn't tell you, I suspect, is that we nearly came to blows back there. I confronted him, demanded to know if he ever realized how much he'd hurt Mom and Dad. And I asked him, point-blank, where his sense of charity was when it came to things closer to home."

"Tim, no, you don't understand—"

"You know what he did, Ernie? He stumbled around a bit at first, got defensive, tried to cover for his actions... So I got in his face again. I dared him to man up and own up. To all of it. He started to say something and then—he backed away and walked out the door. No admission. Not even a lame defense. Just silence and a quick exit. Mitch didn't even have the spine to trouble his precious thoughts with a trip back to the world he'd created for the rest of us. It was as though he'd been paralyzed, so afraid to say anything that he opted for nothing at all."

Ernie stood aside to impart a perfunctory twirl to the bottle of cabernet, presuming to inspect its label.

"Did you keep all those letters you received?" he asked, scrutinizing the bottle as he spoke. "The ones from the Young Schweitzer Fund?"

"Of course," Tim said after a pause, thrown off by the abrupt shift in tone and topic. "That fund has been underwriting me since my freshman year. My scholarships, the apprenticeships after I graduated, even my starter grants in engineering—the lion's share came from the YSF. I owe them everything."

"I'm curious. Did they ever hold an awards banquet or invite you to one of their colloquia?"

"They held a schmoozefest every two years where we chatted up the latest harebrained ideas we had to revolutionize medicine and engineering. Or whatever catchphrase was *de rigueur* to keep the subsidies flowing."

"But those meetings were for the Young Schweitzer *Institute*, not the Young Schweitzer Fund. Check the letterhead on their correspondence."

"OK, so then the Institute funded the Fund," Tim replied, rolling his eyes and holding up his hands in exasperation. "Anyhow, what does this have to do with anything? How did you know—"

"You were inducted into the Institute as well, on your own merits. But its grants maxed out at $2,000 per year. A valuable disguise, in any case."

"A disguise?"

"Tim, the Young Schweitzer Fund was a shell organization incorporated by Mitch specifically to be a benefactor to you. It sounded similar enough to the real thing, so he figured you wouldn't check its source. He wanted me to continue the charade even now, but in light of this... bottomless hostility you still harbor, I figured you ought to know."

Tim's stunned eyes spoke for him as he absorbed the implications of the exchange. His initial reaction was defiant.

"So now he's swindling you too, Ernie? Do you really buy that fish story? I started college years before Mitch's initial public offering at Magister, in fact it was around the time that he was sleeping in that banged-up Mustang, dodging the repo man wherever he went. Besides, there's no way in perdition or purgatory that Dad would have allowed him into our lives like that, not after what he did to us."

"Tim—think for a minute. That's *why* he was living out of his car. He worked triple shifts and sold most of his assets to pay off the debt and keep the company afloat. He finally broke even with some of his early forays, the year before you started at the university; whatever he had left after reinvesting in the company he set aside for you. It took him the better part of a year to gain your father's assent, and even then, it wasn't your father's idea to keep the real sponsor anonymous. That was all Mitch."

"A pixie-dust salesman could cop a more plausible story than that," Tim growled, extending his hands in a gesture of incredulity. "Heck, Mitch probably ripped off the idea from Charles Dickens. It's *Great Expectations*, with Mitch casting himself in the guise of the secret benefactor. That would make me Pip, wouldn't it? However contrite Mitch might have been, he's far too enamored of his supposed gifts to have prostrated himself like that. Besides, if he was so distressed by this 90/10 Conundrum and all these misperceptions of his character, then why not solve the problem by outing himself as my patron over all these years?"

"Because it wasn't atonement Mitch was seeking. At least, not in the main. He didn't want his actions construed as penance, by you or by him. Nor did he want you to feel beholden to him after all the misery he'd caused you. So he simply choked down the agony of unspoken truths and thwarted reconciliation, all for the greater cause. For decades."

"What greater cause?"

Ernie stepped back from Tim and took down a colorfully labeled bottle of white wine from what appeared to be a specially constructed compartment. He uncorked it in a fluid motion, then poured it into a pair of tapering cocktail glasses produced from a locked cabinet nearby. A light, fruity aroma sweetened the fusty air of the cellar.

"There's an unwritten rule against enjoying the wine in one's own cellar," he said, "so we'll skip the toast to keep it unofficial. But one good red deserves a white."

"No argument from me on that."

"Remember, sip—no gulping, please."

They savored a few sips in silence before Ernie spoke.

"You probably don't remember, Tim, because you were too young. But the drawings you used to pump out of that same young child's mind, along with miniature schematics and even 3-D models of the world around you, seen and unseen—you imbued them with a sublime power in their precision, dimensions, and detail."

"Ma used to talk about that stuff from time to time. I supposedly sketched out a layered blueprint of a busy intersection, down to the wiring diagrams for the stoplights."

"Yes, you did—as a kindergartener. I have a good ten years on you, so I well recall the gasps your fledgling efforts elicited from visitors, including a local news anchor."

"Those fledgling efforts of mine also very nearly burned down the family home. More than once."

"But they were your basic training, Tim, the source of the raw material that became the basis for your subsequent miracle-working. The cardiac muscle-remodeling implants that have saved so many heart failure patients, the perivascular monitors to measure blood sugar and regulate insulin levels for diabetics, the mechanical catalysts for improved liver regeneration in hepatitis victims—where do you think the kernels for all those ideas came from? You may not even remember your very own journals from those clumsy tinkering sessions, but you were sketching out the earliest outlines for all the lifesavers you've since brought into the world."

"I think you're reimagining Young Timmy Shoemaker in a much warmer light than Older Timmy Shoemaker now remembers him."

"And now as always, Tim Shoemaker is his own harshest critic. I'm not embellishing any of this in the slightest; you were the real deal, even as the greenest of greenhorns without a day of formal education to your name. So it was scarcely surprising when you went on to finish your high school and university studies at such a tender age that you had to sit out the toasts that were always being offered in your honor. It's why you were steered to become the man that you are."

"I'm hardly the first of our clan to blaze that trail, Ernie. I've never been much for our musty family lore, but as I recall, generations of Shoemakers have cut their teeth as artisans, mechanics, designers, engineers. It's simply how we're wired."

"But once every couple of generations one of us takes a giant leap further, acquires that capacity to discern all the hidden fibers that join up to weave the world we see and to represent that rich detail for others. Thaddeus Weingarten Shoemaker, for instance."

"I heard of him, uh... apprentice to John Augustus Roebling, wasn't he? On a little project called the Brooklyn Bridge?"

"In 1868, when Thaddeus was all of sixteen years old. He was a prodigy, and the story goes that Roebling recognized our ancestor's raw and unpolished talent in the young man's concept drawings. The master engineer agreed on the spot to groom the teenaged Thaddeus as one of his most gifted prospects. But John Augustus died in an accident the following year, and poor Thaddeus fell out with his successor before losing everything in the Panic of 1873."

"What a waste," said Tim with a shake of the head.

"A recurring theme, sad to say. There were a few exceptions. Lydia Shoemaker Cole, for one."

"That's a more familiar name—first woman engineering professor at Carolina A&M University?"

"One of the first at the institution, period; she helped found the department at Carolina A&M. But most were like Thaddeus. Or Denton Shoemaker, special assistant to George Washington Goethals at the Panama Canal. So much promise, before his epilepsy ground him down."

"Odd that you'd mention that. They thought I was epileptic as a kid. Temporal lobe epilepsy, with complex partial seizures—that was the diagnosis. I was practically eating Depakote sandwiches and who knows what other icky medications for three years. But then the condition up and disappeared."

"You weren't the only one in the family to chart such a course."

Tim tilted his head curiously, thinking.

"It's Uncle Mitch, isn't it?" Tim said, none too pleased with his own deduction.

"Same early childhood history, same uncanny gift, same juvenile epileptic fits or whatever they were. You and Mitch were fortunately spared whatever caused poor Denton Shoemaker to succumb, but otherwise, all three of you shared that link. What makes you and Mitch different from the others is that you're only a generation apart, and still firing on all cylinders—relatively speaking. In the past it's usually taken two or three generations for it to appear again, and the Shoemakers so gifted were too often cut down well before their full talents could blossom."

"'It,' 'the gift'—" Forgetting his cousin's instructions regarding the wine, Tim threw back the remaining contents of his glass. He shook his head as he set it down. "Ernie, the way you refer to this as something so...specific, a little voice in my head is telling me that it was Mitch who filled your head with such fantastical fables."

"That's a clever little voice." Ernie smiled and poured them both a refill of the fragrant white wine. "Shoemaker genealogy has been a consuming interest for Mitch, especially since he stepped down as CEO at Magister. He's done more in a few hectic years than our forerunners managed in the past three centuries."

"Regarding what?"

"Mitch dredged up scattered records on the Shoemaker clan," Ernie explained, "stretching back to the colonial period. From the available sources, these alternating spasms of genius and spectacular flame-out have been a family trademark since at least the American Revolution."

"We were headquartered in Pennsylvania then, if I'm not mistaken."

"Mostly jammed into the towns and villages lining the Ohio River, scraping out niches as craftsmen and salaried tinkerers. Every so often, the town elders would sing hymns of gratitude for miracles that took earthly form in a humble peasant girl or knave—a savant capable of mapping a forest after a single glance at the tree line, or constructing a fort robust enough to weather decades' worth of barrages from nature and enemy armies alike. These marvels in the flesh bore several surnames, but one kept recurring as surely as the snowdrifts from Lake Erie."

"Do I get three guesses?" asked Tim, arching his eyebrows as he sipped from his glass.

"You'll break my heart if it takes more than one. The moral of the story is that this generation-hopping gift of the Shoemakers was heaven-sent, as best the locals could tell. So the town-dwellers eventually baptized it 'the Sacred Sight.'"

"Then, of course, our oh-so-humble ancestors made sure to adopt such an overwrought epithet for their own purposes. At least now I know whence Uncle Mitch derived his self-promotional excesses."

"Careful with such thoughts, Tim. That instinct probably runs in your blood just the same."

"One shudders to think. So this Sacred Sight is what Thaddeus Shoemaker was said to possess? And Lydia, and Denton?"

"Along with you and Mitch. There's a distinctive pattern in the way it announces itself to the world, and Mitch spotted it in you after he'd come to recognize it in himself."

"Which, I'm presuming, he claims as his impetus for taking me secretly under his wing?"

"And at such sacrifice to himself. He wanted the Sacred Sight to blaze in all its glory through you—and this is a verbatim quote from Mitch—'without being snuffed out by the cold gusts of a world so often indifferent to what it could offer.'"

Tim nervously finished off the remainder of his wine, more to slake his agitated mind than an actual thirst. Well-worn beliefs and conclusions, securely ingrained since the formative days of childhood, were being ruthlessly assailed in a single potent salvo.

"I still don't understand why this hyped-up handyman's knack would merit such obsessive attention," Tim said, "even by a headcase like Mitch. So a peppering of Shoemakers in past generations were blessed with an extra helping of engineering aptitude. It's not like we were creating artistic milestones for the world to ooh and aah over. The Dumas family had a flair for the written word, the Strauss and Bach families for music; others produce generations of painters and sculptors. What's so special about our Sacred Sight?"

"It goes well beyond a mere talent passed down the generational tree. It's more distinctive and pronounced than that—as though anyone possessing it enters the world with a rare power that can be recognized by others, but not replicated. I realize how tall tale-ish it all sounds, but we know of no genetic factor or other ready off-the-shelf explanation for it."

"Fine, Ernie, but regardless—why is all this so crucial to know?"

"Because that Sacred Sight is all wrapped up with an even more mystifying secret in our heritage. One with a far darker tinge, I'm afraid."

"The heirlooms?" asked Tim, vocalizing amorphous thoughts. "It was right before we made our descent into the cellar, Ernie. You made an odd reference to wine and... heirlooms down here, and I didn't follow you then. But that's what this is about, isn't it? It's why you've been pressing me so much to visit over the past few months."

"There's something Mitch urgently needs to pass on to you. He thinks there may be some as-yet-undiscovered historical strand connecting the mystery of this remarkable power to a still more daunting puzzle, one we don't have the luxury of ignoring."

"And he signed you up as a go-between to make his case, didn't he?"

"Please, just hear me out, Tim. The findings that Mitch has dug up... they boggle my mind and shake my soul with every idle reflection. Vastly more than any other riddle I've ever dreamt up in my career. What's even more important—whatever the link between his discoveries and our family tree, their significance extends well beyond us alone. I can show you, right here in the cellar."

Tim's breathing had taken on a rhythm of deep discomfort, ineffably rattled as he was by his cousin's intimations.

"This isn't the best time for it," Tim said.

"It's been so long since you were here—don't let this opportunity rot on the vine. Give me a few minutes to hash this out with you, it's all I ask."

"Ernie, I know you mean well, but my plate's already full with whatever monsters I'll be facing down at Oak Ridge tomorrow. It's been taxing enough to process all this hidden history between me and Uncle Mitch. I simply don't have the reserves for anything more right now—certainly not for enlisting in yet another of Mitch's lonely battles against the mythological beasts of his own mind."

"But Tim—"

"I'm sorry, but I have to go. The hotel shuttle will be arriving in about ten minutes, at the bus station on Martin Street a few blocks away. I'm all checked in, but I'd prefer not to get stuck in this drizzly mess waiting for the next shuttle to lumber on by. I'll be passing through Kingston on my way back from Oak Ridge on Sunday. Maybe we can revisit all this then."

"Okay," said Ernie with a dejected slump of the shoulders. "Just watch the roads on your way out there tomorrow, and I'll say it again: Watch out for yourself in that place."

"I'll be sure to do that," replied Tim, warily restraining the fitful wanderings of his own unsettled thoughts.

Wenn die Welt gefallen wäre

ohne Hilf' und Hoffnung mehr,

Wohnen drin verlorne Seelen,

Geister, die nun leiden sehr.

Wofür kämpfen sie noch fort,

durch Not und Tod, Krieg und Pest?

Spüren sie geheilt die Welt,

wenn der Schöpfer steht nicht fest?

Chapter Three

Epicenter

Tim's first heirloom

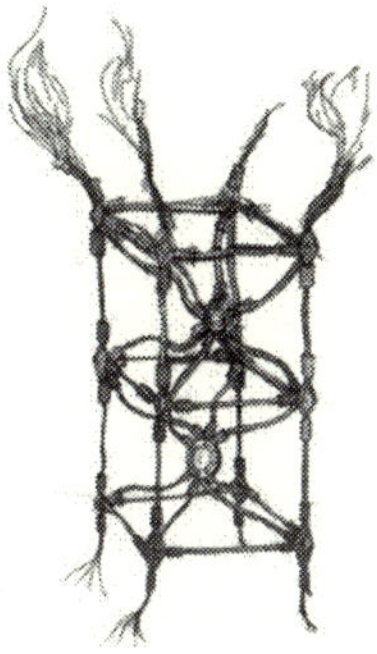

SATURDAY, MAY 17, 5:25 A.M.
VISITORS' RECEPTION
TRASK BIOMEDICAL ENGINEERING INSTITUTE
OAK RIDGE NATIONAL LABORATORY, OAK RIDGE, TENNESSEE

A biting gale assaulted Tim's cheeks as he huddled in the predawn dark outside the gates of the tightly guarded facility. He attempted to shield himself from the unseasonable weather with his thick tan overcoat and charcoal-brown fedora. The stylish outfit, a sartorial legacy of a summer job he'd held long ago, in which he'd supplied technical advice to local detectives and prosecutors, offered no protection to his ears. Clutching a tattered dark gray briefcase in his right hand, Tim winced as his ungloved fingers stiffened in the relentless chill.

Although the rain of the foregoing night had abated for the moment, residual clouds blocked the first tentative rays of the Southern springtime sun. Meanwhile, the dewy air and saturated soil concentrated the hostile wind currents that harassed any soul unfortunate enough to be trapped outside. In this, Tim was joined by a pair of guards shivering at the front gate, their impassive expressions pierced on occasion by a tangible agitation that drove them to frequent cigarette breaks.

"Don't know how you guys do it," Tim murmured to himself, gazing with sympathy at the two men stuck out in the cold.

A recent addition to the hallowed research complex, the lofty edifice housing the Engineering Institute had an ominous aura that disturbed Tim more than he cared to admit. Its architects had designed its imposing tower in partial imitation of a coiling spiral pattern, apparently inspired by the interlocking strands of a DNA molecule in a human cell. This imaginative design, however, was incongruously framed against a background of sparse reflected light from the persistent cloud cover.

The tower was set off from the main entrance by a gently sloping, unusually long foyer, and the net effect—a chalky gray chiaroscuro limning a distant, eccentric structure from base to roof—imparted an uncanny, alien feel to the complex. Aside from the faint hues afforded by a row of multicolored fluorescent lamps, Tim's surroundings were nearly pitch black beneath the mist-shrouded crescent moon. The lamps tacked in the wind like inverted bowls from an awning by the entrance, lending a disorienting, dreamlike illumination to the darkness.

"Rachel, of all the mornings to leave me dangling out here," he grumbled through clenched, chattering teeth.

Tim's grievance was as much a venting of inner unrest as a lamentation of his host's untimely lateness. He was disgusted with himself for the resentment he bore toward Rachel and his cousin Ernie; no matter how often he chided himself for harboring such adolescent feelings, he simply could not shake them. He knew their appeals were heartfelt, yet he could not overcome the grating sense of feebleness that seized him amid such impossible demands. Aggravating the matter was that these pleas for help had emerged from people who knew his history, and the exertions he had made to regain a fragile equilibrium.

All the same, he was soon quivering with even greater discomfort, and not merely on account of the icy gusts that froze his ears and fingers. He had become keen to a faint resonance rippling in the background, inserting itself between bursts of the building's on-site backup generators. Suggestive of a distant howl from a wild dog, yet higher-pitched and mixed with a smoldering roar, the peculiar sound was barely audible, as though taunting Tim's senses. The rest of the site was quiet but in no way serene—like a ship in a twilight calm spell, just beginning to sample the listing waters of an oncoming typhoon.

The silhouette of his host approaching finally appeared in the darkened glass doors at the building's entryway.

"About time," Tim muttered. He removed his hat, watching as Rachel gained the attention of a guard inside the building. One of the sentries near the outer gate spoke into a two-way radio, then motioned Tim to come forward. As he neared the entrance, the doors swung open, and, for the first time in over two years, Tim found himself looking upon his former trainee, friend, and colleague Rachel Bloom.

She was of medium build and height, her eyes at about the level of Tim's chin. She had auburn-colored, shoulder-length hair, her tresses marshaled downward in parallel streams beneath an arched black clasp at the top, and she was clad in a floral-patterned blouse with matching skirt. Her locks framed a pair of dimpled cheeks, a slightly prominent nose, and a soft, rounded chin.

She came to him as he ascended the steps to the entrance, opening her arms in a friendly embrace. It was a quick hug, however.

"I'm so sorry, Tim," she said, pulling away. "As usual, I got caught up in putting out more fires upstairs, mere moments after you'd called in. It feels like the arctic out here."

"No big deal. It's like going sailing off the Outer Banks," he replied with a shrug, choking back his true thoughts on the matter. "A frigid blast at first, but it grows on you soon enough."

A guard near the entrance handed Tim a notepad to sign in. As he scrawled in his bona fides, he shot peripheral glances toward Rachel's face, hovering mere inches away. Her apprehension and frustration were palpable in her wide brown eyes that were at once warm, meditative, and evidently fatigued from chronic wakefulness.

"We're off to the VRRC," she said, as he puzzled over a blank on the notepad requesting his destination for the day, "or the 'Verc' as everyone calls it here—the Vision Restoration Research Center."

"Ah, I remember now." Tim nodded, methodically working his way down the form. "Your assistant reminded me of your former attachment to the Neurosciences Division." He pivoted on his heels as he spoke, turning to face her more directly and exchange a familiar smile. Her appearance was somewhat frumpy yet also comely, in the sweetly unassuming manner of an attractive young woman too engaged in her daily battles to overly fuss about first impressions.

"I was just a wee pup around these parts," she acknowledged with an ambivalent expression. "The Director for Applied Sciences Research was against the move until a certain well-connected authority figure prevailed upon her to greenlight it."

She cast a glance toward a garishly adorned bronze bust of a mustachioed man against the back wall. Light and dark patches subtly alternated on the sculpture's surface to impart a peppery, mottled character to the man's hair, like the speckled feathers of a wise owl, while his wide eyes beamed out with supposed benevolence.

Yet on closer examination, his apparent wisdom and beneficence were clearly affected, dissolving into the marks of a slow-marching corruption. It was as if the sculptor had been consciously mocking his subject in the model of Dorian Gray's portrait, betraying the venality and pompous self-regard that lurked beneath. The effect was reinforced by a ludicrously ostentatious nameplate resting against the wall itself, its letters drawing exaggerated inspiration from the Latin inscriptions on neoclassical public buildings:

METACELSVS

"Yes, a certain well-connected authority figure," concurred Tim with a sardonic grin, the guard himself smiling cynically. "If what you told me on Thursday is any indication, I'd say he and his ilk can be quite . . . persuasive."

Tim completed the form and returned it to the sentry, who busily scanned its scattered fields into a handheld computer.

"You're good to go," confirmed the guard. Tim thanked him and followed Rachel.

"Stay close by," she cautioned him. "This complex doubles as an incubator of new toys for the Domestic Counterinsurgency Department. You'll wind up being interrogated behind a two-way mirror if you drift off unescorted."

"Good to know," said Tim. He followed his host forward into the maws of the darkened edifice, but not before a meditative final glance at the bust of Metacelsus, spurred by the ghosts of an insight that never quite materialized in his conscious mind.

As the pair traversed the cavernous halls of the foyer, Tim was struck by the curious geometry and architecture of the building's interior—an amalgam of mundane functionality and surrealistic style that played tricks with the eyes and mind. Classical patterns mixed with paradoxical forms in two and three dimensions as though lifted straight out of a mind-bending Magritte painting.

The walls about them shortly narrowed into arched corridors etched in marble, like those in an old Roman pavilion. They were capped by an array of skylights that marched up the slope of the gabled roof, as if consciously grasping the heavens.

"Since when did you all import Minnesota into Tennessee?" asked Tim with a lingering shiver.

"I assure you it wasn't our idea. Sometimes I wonder if the sky itself isn't sending us a signal that we've worn out our welcome around here. For two weeks we've been enduring all this rain and then a cold snap out of nowhere to rub it in for us early risers. The hours we've been keeping lately, we're usually pounding away here long before dawn. So I've had the regular privilege of savoring this weird winter-ish spell on the morning commute."

They were now well past the visitors' corridor, striding through more spartan surroundings that signaled their proximity to the research tower. Their path was flanked by muscular bulwarks of reinforced concrete and steel, divided into sections by a jet-black, foam-like substance at the walls' edges and between rooms. The material was a functional addition to dampen vibrations for sensitive laboratory measurements, but the faint lighting and dark edges conspired to engender a beguiling illusion. It was as though the walls were floating within empty space, untethered to anything around them.

They halted at a segment between two large rooms and leaned against the soft padding to rest. Both of them looked sleep-starved.

"What sort of interior theme the architects were shooting for," Tim said with a panning gaze about his environs, "I couldn't hazard a half-witted guess."

"Thereby hangs a woeful tale," answered Rachel in an affected tone, each syllable trailing languidly after the other. "Metacelsus contracted a pair of rising stars in the architectural world, Li Wei Tan and Martin Nimitz, to forge plans and construct what's become the Trask Institute whose halls we're now haunting. Li Wei handled the general design and exterior, while Martin took the inside. I befriended both of them at the tail end of their terms here."

"I know both those names... They were straight out of architecture school, weren't they? Collaborating on those prefab mini-cities in the rundown old industrial parks?"

"Yes, that was them," Rachel said.

"One would hope they had more inspiring projects elsewhere to showcase their talents; the mini-cities initiative didn't do them justice. I had to trudge through one of those monuments to misery en route to a public health powwow in Detroit last year. 'Clockwork Orangevilles'—that's what one of the conference attendees dubbed them. A fitting name."

"I agree. But there wasn't much else on offer when Martin and Li Wei finished school—and they were the leading lights in the field. Oh well. If nothing else, it gave them a chance to launch their careers."

"Speaking of launching," Tim asked, "didn't the two of them eventually jump ship to, uh—"

"Belgium. Another drop in the brain drain. The chattering classes were shocked at first, but it emerged that Metacelsus had been secretly photographing Martin's blueprints, shipping them to a shell company to claim the designs as his own. Martin somehow got wind of it and knew that a Blacklisting was in his future. So before he and Li Wei were secreted out of the country, he recouped some of his losses by using the Institute as his personal sandbox, thus the experimental touches you see around you."

"An inspired bit of revenge; I hope I could be half as clever if I ever get mine."

"A shortcut for your troubles—this way." Rachel led him through a curiously-placed opening on the right wall through a meticulously decorated hallway.

They soon found themselves in an interlocking series of corridors bridged to each other by domelike rooms, exotically framed mirrors lining their walls and replicas of Italian Renaissance paintings bedecking their vaulted ceilings. The midpoints of opposing mirrors had been situated at a finger's-width displacement from one another. The image on each slab of silvered glass, in turn, was reflected at a slight remove by its counterpart on the opposite wall, giving rise to a bizarre gallery of regressing images.

Tim found himself inexplicably perturbed as he walked through this particular hall of illusions. Those images in the mirrors... It was as though they were harboring something that whispered its presence in the corner of Tim's eye—only to vanish, phantom-like, whenever he stared directly at the glass.

SATURDAY, MAY 17, 5:45 A.M.
CENTRAL SUPPLY TRANSFER CORRIDOR
TRASK BIOMEDICAL ENGINEERING INSTITUTE

"Tim," Rachel said with a hint of anxiety in her tone, "I never got around to asking you this, but where did you disappear to that week six years ago? You were...you were different when you finally made your way back, and I never had the courage to ask you why."

"That week? Six years ago?" Tim shrugged, still marveling at his surroundings as they continued their march to the research tower.

He craned his neck to peer at a shallow angle above and just behind his host. A beefy pair of sentries was posted there, this time in full military attire and bearing automatic weapons, guarding a sealed-off chamber near a sign that politely advised against trespassing.

"You know," Rachel added after a fruitless pause. "*That* week."

"Oh. You mean the one that began on August 26, 2019. Day One of the Reckoning, which I got to witness live in Times Square. I still remember the headlines blaring out in that blood-red lettering on the news tickers."

Tim held out his hands and opened his palms, sweeping them slowly from left to right in awkward mimicry of a side-scrolling digital display.

"'Markets Plunge, Triple-Dip on the Way,'" he said. "'Bureau of Economic Research Announces Third Recession of the Great Malaise Since 2007.' Then the bubbles popping, the dams crumbling one after another: $2.1 trillion in student loans sliding into insolvency, the auto and mortgage defaults, the derivatives markets crashing down and taking half the world's savings with them..."

"So you were there after all," she interrupted him. "I went looking for you, you know."

"Looking for... So you were still in New York that day? I had thought you'd taken off before dawn."

"My flight was grounded; ultimately had to hop a few trains to make it back home. From our previous trips to the Big Apple, I had a hunch you'd be skulking about Seventh Avenue that Monday morning, so I was hoping to meet up at one of the coffeehouses while I was stranded. But I wound up having to rely on my sketchy psychic powers to track you down; the cell phone towers were overloaded once the news broke."

"Well, to answer your question," he said with a slight stammer, "you were lucky you gave your research talk on Sunday, because the Rockefeller Conference had degenerated into a mass panhandling session by the time I gave mine two days later. Dozens of hospitals and labs were drowning in red ink, and then I found out my own grant was on thin ice—right as Mark's college tuition fund was going up in smoke before my eyes, and the scholarships for military service were being cut back."

"That's right. Your son had taken time off after high school to enlist in the army, if I recall?"

"Yeah, and in fact, his squad had been called up for duty, coincident with the war fever conveniently being whipped up against all those little resource-rich countries. Nobody knew who was pulling the strings back then, but regardless, I wasn't about to let my son become cannon fodder. So I pulled some strings of my own to have him honorably discharged before deployment. He never knew the whole story and never forgave me for it, and that's when... when the troubles for me started. I decided to finish out the week in New York, to come to terms with it all. I guess I never fully did."

By now they had arrived at a spacious food court just shy of the tower itself, its dormant chandeliers and skylights shimmering with muted menace amid the spare fluorescent lighting and fragments of dull moonlight that flickered their way inside. Office windows of multicolored translucent glass, a different color for each section, faced inward, while an array of shuttered gift shops and food kiosks stood interspersed within an eclectic forest of exotic plants.

"Is there a pianist finishing a graveyard shift here?" Tim asked, tweaking his ears at a soft, lilting sound stirring from an unseen corner. It bore a range of improvisational melodies pleasing to the ear, punctuated on occasion by jarring chords in minor keys.

"I'll show you; follow me," Rachel said with a pained expression Tim didn't see in the low light.

She led him to a semicircular enclosure behind an inactive fountain amidst the foliage, reminiscent of a shallow orchestra pit without the conductor. From a sun roof were suspended planet-like orbs that gently oscillated in distinct, elliptical orbits about a central basin. On this platform was stacked a pyramid of climbing cubes from which the music emanated, the notes and rhythms somehow traced out by the ensemble of hollow spheres hovering above.

"Half a million families in North Carolina and Tennessee, all with a cardboard box as a return address," Tim remarked, contorting his face at the thought. "Yet the brave budgeteers at Oak Ridge are lavishing God-knows-what on a vanity project for some well-connected faux visionary. Another little prince in the House of Metacelsus?"

"Not this time." Rachel directed his attention toward an inconspicuous plaque at the base of the exhibit, bearing the imprimatur of its sponsor: the Defense Advanced Research Projects Agency.

"DARPA!" exclaimed Tim, dumbfounded. "The Internet inventors?"

"More importantly, one of the few agencies to shield its discretionary budget from the Ruling Clans and their figureheads in high places. It exploited a turf war among the Triantarchs some years back, so its engineers here are on an independent payroll."

"But what prompted the DARPAnauts to fatten that payroll for the sake of this overgrown music box?"

"DARPA's real estate here is a glorified playground for artificial intelligence researchers. Especially the quirkier types divining how complexity evolves spontaneously from simplicity, cognition and consciousness from a primitive nervous system—"

"Or music from a potpourri of random sounds."

"The exhibit is called MOTS," explained Rachel, pointing toward a smaller plaque to the right of the first one. "It stands for Music of the Spheres."

"A name with panache, in a classical civ sort of way."

"That's no accident, Tim. The ancient Greeks believed music was an evocation of unadulterated mathematical beauty. So the DARPA engineers devised an AI that could learn, create, and savor that beauty in a pattern of sounds. Whenever the spheres swing about, the electromagnets within them tug on synthesizers in the blocks below, resulting in a sequence of notes and chords. The listeners nearby have buttons by their dining tables to rate the aesthetic appeal of the sound, so the programmers can collate the wisdom of the crowd and feed it back into the neural net of MOTS."

"Learning by recursion, I see. So the ghost in the machine picks up on the arrangements that are pleasing to the human ear, then attempts to build on and reproduce them, assembling its own symphony piece."

"And also goes treasure-hunting throughout its tunes for mathematical surprises—like those musicologists who sniff out the Golden Ratio in a Bach concerto, but this time discerning patterns that have yet to be specified. It's that old idea from Eugene Wigner, the quantum physicist: Advances in pure mathematics stem from arguments of beauty and elegance, and yet they've happened to correspond mysteriously to the empirical workings of physical laws."

"The Unreasonable Effectiveness of Mathematics in... whatever the rest of it was. I had to read that in college, followed by a convincing enough show to fool the profs into believing I fathomed a word of what the good Dr. Wigner was saying."

"You weren't the only one," Rachel said with a knowing smile.

"If I at least understood the gist of that tract, then the gadgetsmiths behind this wonder before us have earned 10 out of 10 from the judges for dual-purpose ingenuity. Based on your description of it, they've created an AI that can internalize the concept of musical harmony, then use it to ferret out new mathematical gems with potential physical significance. Musical beauty to mathematical elegance to the frontiers of physics. Maybe it *is* money well spent."

As he finished, the contraption again slipped into one of its brief, discordant sequences in minor tones, an ugly clash with the silky smooth tracks that had been playing mere moments before.

"Then again," he added with a sidelong glance, "maybe not. That's where I lose the plot. If MOTS was cobbled together to appreciate some of the aesthetics in music, then why does it veer into a five-second funeral dirge out of nowhere like that?"

Rachel turned aside, watching forlornly as the spheres bobbed and weaved about.

"Rachel? Did I say something wrong?"

"No. It's what you heard... and when we all began hearing it."

"I—I'm afraid I don't understand."

"The vision trials. They'd filled us with so much hope, and then... It began mere weeks after we'd activated the soldiers' retinal implants.

But several days before the first manifestations in the veterans, MOTS began doing exactly what you're hearing now. It was rare then, like the occasional slip of an apprentice steadily internalizing his craft."

"What caused it?"

"No one knows, Tim. But it soon became far more frequent, every day and then every hour. We realized it had been the first sign."

"Of what?"

"This sickness." She now faced him head-on, the chords of the machine still chiming resolutely in the background. "And not only in the soldiers."

SATURDAY, MAY 17, 5:53 A.M.
VISION RESTORATION RESEARCH CENTER, 22ND FLOOR
TRASK BIOMEDICAL ENGINEERING INSTITUTE

"Here we are; feel free to drop your coat and bags on any free table space you can salvage from this disaster area," Rachel said. Her tone was muted and self-conscious.

She had led Tim through double doors, into a spacious but cluttered chamber housing rows of experimental apparatus, detectors, and customized equipment to churn through the reams of data being incessantly generated. Hissing tanks of liquid nitrogen flanked fields of lasers in painstakingly constructed arrays. Save for a lone half-shuttered, wide pane in a forgotten alcove that peered out onto the frosty expanse outside, the room was nearly windowless to protect the delicate optical work conducted inside.

Perched on a wide platform near the center of the room was a large black rectangular box. It had a distinctive emblem emblazoned on one of its faces: a stylized version of the Eye of Providence, as rendered on the Great Seal of the United States, but with geometrically rigid lines twisting in a fractal pattern within the pupil of the eye. Its lashes, meanwhile, spiraled outward in conscious evocation of expanding vision, literal and figurative alike. The overall design, rife with the stirring symbolism of an all-seeing eye emerging from blind precursors, carried a significance that was all too familiar for Tim.

"The Simitalis," he growled, glaring at the box and unconsciously clenching his fists. The reaction lasted just a moment, however;

he shook his head as if to shake off the anger that had taken hold of him.

"I knew this wouldn't be easy," Rachel said consolingly. "I used to get a sick feeling every time I entered this room."

"I still get a sick feeling thinking of how callously these bastards ruin decent people, all for their own aggrandizement. Zach above all, even more than the two of us."

"Zach Choi? Your student?"

"The one and only." Tim sighed. "He's the only one who could ever remotely fill your shoes."

"So Zach was also part of the Simitalis project?" Rachel asked. Her tone was scarcely above a whisper.

"Zach came up with many of the recursive algorithms at the kernel of the Simitalis; they're the key to all its miracle-making. He'd stay all night, cranking out pages of drab and dreary code, yet somehow he never burned out. He was a Michelangelo behind the keyboard, and the Triantarchs must have been in the audience to witness the fine sculpture he was carving. Each baby step forward by the vets in your trial, every time they locked onto a visual pattern and chained it to a memory or emotion, the Simitalis itself was learning and rejoicing with them."

Tim halted awkwardly as he remembered his protégé, his gushings more bitter than sweet as they taunted him with mocking mementos of what he had lost.

"Every image meeting the eyes of those soldiers," he continued, his rousing words at odds with his deflated tone, "was grist for the magic spun by that black box now on your platform. Every visual embrace by their gaze would feed the process forward, allow the veterans to make out their world ever faster until they could resolve an object on a first-time viewing. Zach and I crafted that masterpiece with such a progression in mind, like a language that leapfrogs to fluency once a speaker masters the basics. It's on account of him your veterans could see."

"So Zach became the man who knew too much," Rachel said. "Just like Martin and Li Wei. Metacelsus—"

"If the Triantarchs have their way, Zach will never work again."

Hearing this, Rachel could have cried; indeed, she wished she could pause time to go somewhere alone to cry at the injustice done to Zach and so many others. But she was too practical for that—and too self-protecting. She forced her thoughts back upon the task at hand.

"This is where we've uploaded the lion's share of technical data and patient records," she explained, guiding Tim to a nearby computer workstation engulfed in a tangle of thick cables. She hurriedly tapped in an encrypted code at the workstation, which obligingly opened up to a screen crammed full with multiple overlapping windows.

"Because of the classified document restrictions," she added, "we can access it only at this terminal or the backup mainframe, so you'll have to work your wizardry here. You've been authorized to access all the confidential files on this system."

"Anything I should be ready to pounce on?"

"I can't offer much in the way of specific guidance. Be on the lookout for nuances and needles-in-haystacks in the files or folders that could pinpoint what went wrong, where, how..."

"What about the time range of the events?" asked Tim.

"Use your judgment as you go. We currently have only a choppy timeline of things falling apart, and we can't begin to fathom what brought on the mass psychosis. The records include daily logs from before and after the first wireless link-up of the AP-278 retinal implant with the Simitalis, all annotated and filed by date. There are also hourly summaries of the outputs from the Simitalis itself. None of us has the expertise to interpret the evolutionary steps in its neural net, but our collective hunch is that this data set may reveal what sent the project off the rails."

"Have the engineers modified the source code in any way?"

"They've played around with the files created *de novo*, the ones that are formed and serially modified as the visual learning algorithms mature for each patient. But the source code? Whatever you and Zach first loaded to steer the Simitalis the team here has left intact, outside of a little experimenting around the edges."

"I guess I should be flattered," Tim said sourly.

"The AP-278 interfaced perfectly with the guiding protocols as you set them up. The only changes were some minor upgrades to beef up the firewall systems after that virus paid us a visit."

"The virus?" Tim's ears perked up.

"It was a rare bird as these intrusions go. Broke in out of nowhere, carpet-bombed our networks enough to cause a minor panic. But then it left with little harm caused and barely a trace remaining: no programs compromised, no evidence of stolen data even after the most exacting diagnostics. So we never paid it much heed outside of a few tweaks to the system's guard dogs. One oddity I still remember, whenever the virus announced its presence, was that the screen would fill up with these—"

"Calculations," interrupted Tim, eliciting a startled look from his colleague.

"How do you know that? Was it in the briefing?"

"Not exactly," Tim answered. "My cousin Ernie out here is a professional troubleshooter, and he'd worked several stints at other departments in Oak Ridge, battling a similar but more aggressive strain of computer virus. That's the same picture he painted: screenfuls of intricate computations, full of complex numbers and exponentials broken down to binary arithmetic, before the little bugger simply up and vanished."

"Ours was the first to hit the research campus, but the system administrators insisted the other digital plagues were unrelated when they checked into them."

"That's what Ernie said, more or less. His virus supposedly gave evidence for a different taxonomy, compared to the Chakana strain that's hit the broader community in this corner of Tennessee. Still the same basic M.O., though."

"I wonder if they're all variants from the same source," Rachel suggested, "maybe digging up classified secrets in a way we haven't yet figured out?"

"But the prime offenders in the recent rash of network intrusions have been the Triantarchs themselves; it's why the guilty parties in these digital burglaries are rarely prosecuted. It also explains how the Ruling Clans pilfered much of the operating software Zach and I developed for the Simitalis, even before their hired goons had dropped by uninvited to make off with the hardware now in this room. Why would they hack into a system that's already built on their own stolen goods?"

"Perhaps a new outbreak of factional warfare, rending apart the alliance among the thirty families. They've already purged each other twice on a large scale, so maybe their latest truce is off."

"One can dream... But this all has the whiff of a different flavor; the connections are too tantalizing to ignore. Chakana was even targeting data from an assortment of brain studies—neuroimaging scans and the like. It's a tenuous lead and I can't imagine what it means, but at least it's a start. Can you take me to the logs from the first day of the virus attack?"

"Gladly," said Rachel, introducing a pair of impossibly long passwords on either side of a split screen. A nested tree of windows sprouted up before her. She had soon ventured deep into the heart of the Simitalis, replete with inscrutable file designations and code assemblies that elicited a knowing nod from her partner.

"That's your cue, Tim. A friendly heads-up that you may incur some file-access problems here and there, apparently a side effect of the new firewalls. Otherwise, this workstation is your playground."

"Then I'll be sure to leave an unholy mess dredging it all up."

"Please do," she answered playfully. "Could I make you some coffee?"

"Is there a menu?"

"They really have spoiled you out there in the Doghouse, haven't they? No menu needed, as we happen to possess the ultimate concoction in caffeination. We call it The Oak Ridge Rocket," she said, making her way toward a kitchenette tucked into the east wall of the room. "Four shots of espresso, two teaspoons corn syrup, and a tablespoon of a classified energy-drink combination the engineers keep around to fuel their all-nighters."

"Thanks, but I think I'll pass; can't be of much help if I stroke out from your largesse."

He swiveled back to the gargantuan workstation and immersed himself in the esoterica before him. As he pressed ahead, he broke on occasion to take in his surroundings. Amid the background hum of the ubiquitous machinery were the unpredictable chirps of mainframe computers used to digest oceans of data.

As he listened more earnestly, however, the seeming spontaneity of these digital coos gave way to a rhythm that was something more than random—like the subtle taunting of mechanical sprites that would emerge and gleefully frolic in the open, once curious eyes and ears had left the room.

9:14 A.M.

"It would appear the Oak Ridge Rocket didn't quite work as advertised." Tim stood at the entrance of the kitchenette, his outstretched right hand against the door frame, eyeing Rachel with a mixture of pity and amusement. She was out cold in her chair, her head reclining against a side wall.

"Uhh—" Rachel rubbed her eyes. "Tim, oh...how long have you been working?"

"Three hours and change. Between this and your ten-second catnap waiting for the elevator downstairs, I was worried that waking you might get me rung up on charges of torture."

"Yet you went right ahead and did it anyway," she said between a yawn and a smile.

"Well, it was for a good cause. Come with me. I've found something."

Rachel's fatigue vanished as if she'd been given a shot of adrenaline. Tim dragged over a nearby chair, pulling it up to rest alongside his own. He then flipped the cover on a laptop that had been squeezed in awkwardly, resting atop an unoccupied section of the central platform housing the facility's workstation.

"I'd long ago backed up the seminal mission-critical files of the Simitalis," he began, "from the prototype Zach and I had first constructed. Some of the file headings and descriptions seemed a little out-of-place in those data logs you mentioned, so I ran a line-by-line comparison wherever possible between the originals and the current version of each critical file."

"Why are you holed up in the Typeface Fonts directory?" Rachel asked, puzzled at the inconspicuous folder in both machines that was absorbing so much of his attention.

"It was a precaution," he explained, clicking on another artfully hidden folder, itself tucked away in a nondescript file grouping within the directory. "The source code for a leviathan like the Simitalis is forbidden fruit for young cowboy engineers; it brings out the hacker instincts like nectar to a bee."

"Speaking from experience?" she said with another yawning smile.

"You'd better believe it. We had rotating teams assigned to the project, so Zach and I hid some of the core files in those forgotten directories that never register on the radar screen. Incredible to think that even after these vultures in the Triantarchy swiped the heart and soul of our work, our foresight's been shielding them from their own shortsightedness."

Tim laughed maliciously.

"What's this monster here?" asked Rachel, singling out a file with a size several digits longer than its neighbors.

"Tunica Retina—yes, that's one of them. It governs the feedback between the Simitalis and the optic nerve interface of the retinal implant, implementing one of the visual relearning algorithms Zach devised for the neural net processor of the Simitalis."

"Anything unusual about it?"

"For one thing, I can't access its content on your workstation for even a peek under the hood. We did establish additional security parameters to hide Tunica Retina two years ago, in the event someone noticed enough peculiarities in the Typeface Fonts folder to start sniffing around. Still, it shouldn't be under such tight lock and key, even to its very creator."

"Then how can you be sure it's been altered?"

"For the same reason it stood out to you."

He promptly twisted his laptop to place the screen before her, highlighting a file with the same name.

"It's more than quadrupled in size," Rachel said, alternating between the laptop and the workstation. "Roughly 18 megabytes in the original, 73 on our server. Might it merely have been accumulating new facets as part of the neural net? Growing up, as it were, as the vision trials proceeded?"

"Not Tunica Retina per se. We designed it to be a general on the field, tweaking other control files but staying unchanged itself. That's critical to the system's function; in fact, it shouldn't have worked at all once altered. Tunica isn't the only example, either."

He navigated through a series of congested screens, quickly arriving at another hidden directory.

"This file, Nightowl," he said, tracing a line with his finger. "It's a cousin of Tunica Retina; it steers the data stream for the rod cells in the eye implants, the sensors responsible for night vision as in a normal retina. Nightowl is also a critical file, stashed away with the background color settings for the monitor. It's difficult to find, and there's scarcely any reason to screw around with it in the first place. But look, just like Tunica—nearly tripled in size."

"So you think these altered files are associated in some way with this . . . spreading madness in the vets?"

"That's the rub. It would help if I could peer inside the files themselves, but even so, I can't see how a few hacked programs within the Simitalis would give rise to such a corroding of the mind. At heart, they're nothing more than coaches to speed up the vision learning curve, to modulate the guidelines for interpreting the light that strikes the retinal implant and the patient's nervous system."

"What about the computer virus, Tim? Do you still think there's a connection?"

"Given what we've just seen, we're on even flimsier ground there. You said yourself that the Simitalis had registered no functional deficits, and the soldiers did recapture their power to see, at least for a tranquil spell before the storm. Why would the hackers design a worm that would expand, and presumably enhance the critical files of the neural net, while exerting no observable effect on its performance?"

Rachel placed her index finger on her lips, mulling the question intensely. "The dates, Tim. Have you checked the dates?"

"I scoured samples from the daily data log files that you mentioned; couldn't find anything much amiss."

"That's not what I meant. These alterations to the critical files like Nightowl—can you narrow down when they occurred?"

"It's a thought," he murmured, accessing a small data bubble next to one of the files. "That's odd. It says that Nightowl was last updated on May 14, at 22:43 hours."

"Only three days ago," replied Rachel, her voice softening to an incredulous whisper. "What about Tunica Retina?"

He accessed the relevant file and repeated the process. The answer sent him leaning back in his chair, turning to Rachel in disbelief.

"May 16, 21:39 hours," he said.

"Last night? That can't be right. Even with this insane push to a 24/7 schedule lately, this place is deserted on Friday night. Nobody would have been here to make those changes, and the workstation can't be accessed remotely."

Tim furrowed his brow, stewing over their recent findings before breaking in with a request.

"Rachel, can you access backups of the files on these servers?"

"That shouldn't be a problem. The system's on a 24-hour backup cycle, with the last 120 days' worth maintained on site; that'll bring us back to January. I'll need to step in and unlock a few doors for you again."

Tim pulled aside as she moved in, watching as she entered a series of access codes on several screens of the workstation. Her actions invoked a window featuring a stack of digital folders, one atop another.

"Here they are," she said, "the backups for the past four months. The name of each directory is posted aside the date it was created, arranged chronologically from top to bottom."

"Let's survey the field from the 20th of March," he suggested, accessing the pertinent files.

"Any significance to the date?"

"My daughter Chloe's birthday," Tim answered pensively. "A decent place to start. There it is, the Nightowl file. Take a look."

"The first modifications must have been in place well before then; it's still almost twice the size of your original."

"When did you say the virus began flitting through the networks?'

"It was definitely after that, so someone must have been wreaking mischief long before the virus showed up."

"I just hit upon something," he said, leaning forward. "Can we run a simultaneous search of all the backup directories?"

"Sure. What do you have in mind?"

"I can set the parameters in a filename query, to select out any directories containing the two files at their original size. Let's see, Tunica Retina at 18.2 megabytes, Nightowl at 9.7 megabytes, and let's take a look behind Door Number Three…"

He pushed back from the keyboard with a flourish while awaiting the result. When the outcome appeared on screen, he was jolted by the audible gasp of his partner.

"Rachel, what is it?"

"That date."

"February 5th? What about it?"

At first she merely shook her head feebly as she studied the seemingly innocuous parade of numbers staring out from the screen.

"Rachel?" He gently pressed her hand. "This is what I'm here for. What does that date mean?"

"We call it 'El Día del Diablo.'"

9:37 A.M.

"The Day of the Devil?" asked Tim. "How did you come up with—"

"It's the date we flipped the switch," Rachel said, "when the wireless uplink between the retinal implants and the Simitalis went live. Something was off about that day. We knew it from the moment we established the link."

Tim paused and breathed in slowly, gathering his thoughts.

"It was originally a playful quip," Rachel said. "An honorific, in fact."

"An honorific?"

"Our Patient Zero," she explained, "the first to regain sight—he's a 36-year-old former Marine Lance Corporal from Arizona, by the name of Pablo Acevedo. He lost his brother late in the Iraq War, so he enlisted to fight in his honor, serving multiple tours in Afghanistan. He rose quickly through the ranks and became something of a legend: Purple Heart, Silver Star, more decorations than even some of the experienced officers."

"I take it that his service led to his participation in the vision restoration trial."

"In every way imaginable. His platoon was on a mission in Ghazni Province, in the southeast. They were clearing out a weapons cache in a safehouse that was booby-trapped with C-4 explosives, and the place was blown to shreds when his unit entered the house. Pablo was standing guard outside, and the blast launched him into the air. Despite being bruised and bloodied, he picked himself up and darted into the safehouse to save the others in his team—three fellow Marines and two civilians."

"A good man to have in your trench," Tim said with a light nod.

"His squadmates thought so: They affectionately dubbed him 'Pablo el Diablo' for crawling into that inferno, and the name stuck even after his discharge. Unfortunately, it would also be his last engagement. As he was dashing to assist a wounded colleague, an artillery shell detonated about ten feet before him, sending shrapnel point-blank into his face. He barely survived; the tissue reconstruction alone required a half dozen surgeries, and his vision was believed gone for good."

"I see. A fitting pioneer for the trials."

"And a courageous one. We ourselves were unsure about the AP-278 implant for the very reasons you broached on the review panel, even though the suits in the Triantarchy were promising us a rose garden after their contracting firm got its hands on the device."

"I presume you're referring to the modification that the higher-ups were so intent on keeping you in the dark about?"

"That's the one," Rachel confirmed. "For obvious reasons we placed little stock in their judgment, but Pablo volunteered anyway. The surgeons introduced the AP-278 prototypes into his artificial eyes in November of last year. We did some trial runs with the uplink, adjusted a few of the visual field algorithms in the Simitalis, and then convened everyone for the big day."

"February 5th."

"Only moments after the stroke of midnight."

Rachel drew up her lower lip, her eyes misting slightly as she remembered.

"If you could have been there, Tim... It was that rarest of treasures, soaking up the sweet aura of a shared miracle. Simply establishing the uplink itself was a feat, and then Pablo's recovery exceeded all our expectations. Barely a week had passed before he could recognize colors, contours of nearby objects, even basic shapes from a distance. Soon he was resolving simple structures, then more complex designs. Within three weeks, he was navigating the world as he had before that shell exploded before him, and in his honor, we later red-lettered that day as El Día del Diablo."

"But as you said, you'd sensed there was also something off about that day."

"At first it was nothing more than a ... a vague weirdness in the immediate aftermath, certainly no forewarning that the effort would come so completely undone. I can't quite nail down the sensation, to be honest, but about a minute after we'd activated the link, the whole complex registered what we thought was a blown transformer."

"A blackout?"

"Not entirely. The power waxed on and off and the monitors flickered. I could have sworn there was a sort of... faint crackle in the air, not unlike the way you can almost smell and taste the sky before a thunderstorm. And then it started."

"What—what started?" asked Tim, nudging her past an unexpected pause.

"A sound on the Public Address system. It was barely audible and I wasn't even convinced I'd heard it initially; still a struggle to attach words to it. From the get-go it reminded me of those childhood ghost stories about the spooky voice on the record played backwards. It began as a distorted howl, slow and creepy, like a cross between a wounded cow and a wolf, but drawn out in the replay. It gradually morphed into a human cry, agonized and throaty, then two people, three and four, distorted again. Then it turned thoroughly surreal, ghastly—"

Tim's expressive eyes, hemmed in by dark circles of fatigue and stoical detachment, were at once perplexed and suffused with dread.

"Imagine a dozen condemned souls in a war zone," Rachel continued, "wailing in rage and sorrow. Now imagine bundling their cries one on top of another, then stripping away the texture in their voices, distorting their length and range, and you're left with a ... pure, raw scream. Like the very first scream on earth, before there was even a voice to project it, echoing and feeding upon itself until it was everywhere at once."

"This sound—how long did it persist?"

"Thirty seconds, give or take."

"I would have guessed more like thirty hours, given the mark it's since imprinted in your mind."

"But it didn't, at least not immediately. In fact, everything I just described—it took weeks to register, slowly oozing into my subconscious in those moments when I was unoccupied and vulnerable. On the day itself, I remember being creeped out, but I set the feeling aside as we soaked up the moment. It was like those stories you hear about people who witness a grisly sight in the distance, somehow ignoring it at first—only for it to sneak up and ambush their peace of mind in the weeks that follow."

"What was the source of the sound?" Tim asked.

"We never could trace it. The engineers eventually chalked it up to a mischief-maker in their ranks."

"Doubtful. Did any of them strike you as the kind to do something like that?"

"No. I think the engineering team didn't want to think about it at the time. Everyone had worked so hard, the corks were popping and the champagne was flowing...A few drinks tend to alter one's perspective on life's little oddities."

"Or not-so-little oddities."

"Hindsight," she said with a shrug and a defiant though tentative grin. "There was another quirk to that sound, though. Sanjit Khan, one of the software engineers on the team, had recorded the festivities for the history books."

"And perhaps to blackmail you someday. I learned that the hard way in college: Camcorders and alcohol are the match and gasoline of social presentability."

"He enshrined many an incriminating scene for posterity," she acknowledged, "but he also nabbed footage of those mystifying thirty seconds. I've revisited them several times, but the voice—the recording couldn't capture it."

"It was absent from the tape?"

"No, it was there, but nothing like what I later recalled. It was a dull shadow of itself on Sanjit's video."

She braced her left jaw and temple upon a triangle of splayed fingers, softly shaking her head. Her mood had notably dimmed again, sinking into a telltale mixture of melancholy and bafflement that hung heavy in the air as she spoke.

"Think about it, Tim. In any courtroom, what's the gold standard of memory for the past? How can the defense or prosecutors irrefutably demonstrate that an event transpired as they claimed?"

"By an external reference, objective and trustworthy. Like signed documents or—yes, I see, an unaltered video recording."

"That's right, because it leaves nothing for the mind's whims to splice and edit into an embellished narrative. But here it's the opposite. We could all independently remember the horrid dimensions of that voice, yet it never made it onto the tape. The footage did jog my memory, yet it's as though a dumb recording device couldn't faithfully relay the tones and cadences of that frightful whisper, let alone its character. Those became lodged within our minds somehow, at first submerged, but invariably surfacing throughout this ordeal."

"I can't lay claim to much expert cred on this topic," said Tim, thinking aloud, "but could this collective psychosis in the veterans have arisen in the wake of a ... planted notion of some sort?"

"Planted? By what means?"

"Your assistant specified that your team had ruled out an obvious biological source, like an encephalitis virus or a prion protein directly striking the brain."

"Or a chemical agent," added Rachel. "We must have run every tox screen on file, yet turned up nothing in the soldiers' blood or tissues."

"So what if the point of entry for the causative factor is through the eyes or ears? Like a stimulus that introduces an *idée fixe* straight into their minds?"

"I suppose all those cordoned-off military research stations can stoke the imagination at times."

"Actually," clarified Tim, "that particular brain wave was courtesy of an old friend in marketing."

"Oh."

"Seriously, though, how else could the same psychotic behavior grab hold of so many distinct individuals in a cohort, at the same time? There must have been a common vector to deliver the conceptual content of their delusions, filtered in through the old-fashioned five senses. Maybe that's the link with the weird voice on El Día del Diablo, or at least your perception of it. It may also explain the modifications to those files in the Simitalis; perhaps they were exploited in some fashion, as if to sensitize the veterans to the source of the madness."

"But why? Your theory sounds plausible enough, Tim, but what's the motive to begin with?"

"Maybe it really is a brewing factional split among the Triantarchs, exactly the prospect we'd been bouncing around before. Metacelsus and others in Clan Argentus—they like to imagine that they're patrons of the arts and sciences in the old Roman model, even to the extent of burglarizing others' work to maintain the appropriate façade. Their enemies must know this, so what better way to humiliate them than to sabotage their crown jewel at Oak Ridge?"

"There's still a gaping hole in your reasoning," countered Rachel. "Clan Argentus would always have powerless scapegoats on hand if their plans went awry, so their adversaries must know that Metacelsus and his bagmen would deflect such public embarrassment anyway. Besides, if this really were the design of Clan rivals, why put such an elaborate scheme in motion?"

"Why not? To paraphrase F. Scott Fitzgerald, the Ruling Families are different from you and me. They have virtually unlimited resources to engage in such extravagant escapades against each other, not to mention anyone caught in-between. Corruption is like theater to them, so why not confer some epic grandeur to the proceedings?"

"I don't buy it, Tim, and I think even you know you're reaching here. The Triantarchs have plenty of blood on their hands, but the events since the 5th of February simply aren't their style. It's not merely the fact of this marching madness that defies explanation; it's the nature of the delusions themselves."

"What was it the soldiers claimed to see or hear? Your assistant gave me the basics, explained the fact of their shared horrors, but I never got the story on what those actually were."

"Auditory hallucinations at first—the classic voices-in-the-head of chronic schizophrenics. But then their chants and recountings became bizarre even by the standards of schizophrenia—cut loose from their experiences, shared myths and legends, or any belief system to which they could have possibly been exposed."

"Isn't that the definition of psychosis?" asked Tim. "A disconnect from the world outside?"

"Yes, but there's still usually a cultural context involved; and even schizophrenics from opposite poles of the earth tend to share common features. Our medical team has seen thousands of cases, yet the soldiers' manifestations are *sui generis*, utterly divorced from anything documented in the medical literature. Their delusions were vaguely apocalyptic, but the doctors couldn't begin to pinpoint an inspiration for them, let alone account for the fact of their presence among so many of the veterans."

"But I don't understand why you ascribe such hefty significance to their specific delusions."

"We're not sure ourselves, but there must be a reason the same themes recur in one soldier after another. What matters is that their source, whatever its nature, can't be explained. It's a riddle we've chewed on for months. We called in a crack psychiatric team to evaluate the situation and supplement our internal assessments. The top people in the field. Yet not one could unlock the hidden meaning behind the veterans' strange visions."

She reclined momentarily, ruminating as to the best way to explain the situation to her still-skeptical colleague.

"This phenomenon began with Pablo," she said, "like all the other sleepwalking nightmares since February. He'd lost his little sister Esmeralda in the avian flu pandemic of 2021. It was all the more devastating for him since his brother had already been killed in Iraq, so his psychotic delusions were initially tied in with the memory of his siblings, Esmeralda in particular. But then they careened off in unexpected directions."

"Like what?"

"Dreamlike meditations that would last anywhere from a couple minutes to a few hours, promptly followed by sketches which he seemed compelled to produce. Pablo kept fixating on some sort of... omnipresent force; I can't quite do it justice. His drawings became increasingly morbid and horror-filled, and then there was that number."

"The number?"

Rachel sighed and promptly rose to her feet, evidently distressed at the inadequacy of her efforts. She turned to her left and went to a sterile-gray metal bookcase stuffed with notebooks haphazardly lining its shelves. She retrieved one of them and removed a small, red-tinged compact disc from its side pocket, quickly inserting it into an external disk drive perched next to the workstation.

"Colonel Alan Simms is the chief medical officer here," she explained, "and he assigned himself personally to Pablo's case. He supplied us with copies of their recorded sessions one-on-one, with Alan struggling to assemble some skeleton of a medical history. Our superiors have waived the confidentiality rules internally to aid our investigations, so you're cleared to listen in. This was from an early session when Pablo was still speaking coherently, back when the staff had first begun to chart his mood derangements and the first of his freakish diagrams. You'll hear Dr. Simms' voice first on the tape."

She activated a playback button on the workstation's monitor, precipitating a low-pitched droning in the drive that housed the disc. A steady, unflappable voice in a deep baritone coalesced in the surrounding speakers, launching gently into a familiar line of inquiry.

"Pablo, please tell me again when and where you last saw your sister."

"Ay, mi hermanita— "

The second voice was poignant and soft, barely breaking a whisper. Yet it had a latent potency, like a tightened spring that might release at any moment.

"She was here this very morning, Dr. Simms. I felt her arm on my shoulder as I sat for breakfast. I turned and she was there, to my left, asking if I still had the quilt she wove for me when we were both niños pequeños."

"What did you tell her?"

"I said that it was never far away, that I used it as a channel to glimpse the world by touch, ever since I lost my sight."

"Do you still remember visiting her after the flu pandemic, Pablo?"

"Yes, Doctor. I remember losing her from this realm, wondering if I would one day arrive to see her at the same place in heaven. But I no longer have to wait. He brings her to me now, every day that I'm here."

"He? Who is he?"

"Él que recuerda todo, Doctor."

"The one who remembers all?"

"He remembers Esmeralda."

"So he is . . . a friend, Pablo?"

"He is our life and our death."

"Vaguely religious imagery so far, nothing out of the mainstream—relatively speaking," Tim interjected, pausing the recording. "Pablo's speaking as if in a language sprung forth from his own heart, imagining a force that can resolve a deep anguish. I can easily relate."

"If only he'd remained on that course," Rachel said grimly, girding herself as she resumed the playback.

"Pablo, can you tell me about the numbers you've been jotting down for the past week? 1,311—2,372—520—899—800. What do they mean? What about this sketch? I see you've drawn several figures here: a tall building, a pyramid, the foundation of a home, all with a mathematical equation below them. That's truly remarkable, and I was hoping you could tell me the significance of these expressions, especially the one in the center."

"An expression?" asked Tim and again paused the recording. "What is Simms getting at?"

"This," answered Rachel. She inverted the notebook that had held the disc, exposing an index card that had apparently been annotated as a reference. At its top was an equation familiar to Tim, inexplicably so:

$$e^{i\phi} = \cos\phi + i\sin\phi$$

"That's Euler's Formula," he observed, his puzzlement now spilling over into aggravation. "What the hell does that mean?"

"I was hoping you could tell me."

"The formula was a steady-enough crutch for troubleshooting, at least back when I was rigging up AC electrical circuits for extra cash in college; but otherwise I never gave it much thought. My math professors would always gush about its beauty and elegance in their lectures, an association that never quite registered with college sophomores snoozing off their last hangover."

"In retrospect, though, they had a point," said Rachel. "When the AI team first tuned MOTS to fish out mathematical gems with music, that formula was among the first that the device 'rediscovered.' It's precisely what the programmers had in mind."

"But what does this have to do with Pablo's condition? And what were the other numbers that Dr. Simms recited on the tape?"

"Once Pablo had listed more than a hundred of them, their meaning became transparent. Or, at least, easier to look up. They're the first ionization energies of hydrogen, helium, lithium..."

"Maybe Pablo was rattling off random bits of his training. The psychosis must have done a fine job of scrambling his mind."

"Tim, he supplied accurate numbers for all the elements to at least two decimal places, and there were many other such examples. As far as his training and occupational experience are concerned, Pablo had worked as a mechanic and short-order cook to support his family as a young man."

"Maybe he took a few engineering courses outside of the service, or gained some exposure through his technical training in the Marines."

"No. He was a good student, but he'd barely finished high school by the time he enlisted with the Marine Corps, and there are no records of such specialized training once he was in the service. It was a history that he shared with most of the other veterans, yet soon they were manifesting the same patterns, without anything in their backgrounds to explain them."

Tim groaned.

"Rachel, you're saying that these soldiers, out of a clear blue sky, acquired an aptitude for mathematical analysis, that they precisely enumerated physical constants—"

"And then lost themselves to the madness."

She resumed the recording at a forward point, the interchange between doctor and patient having shifted to even more dizzying territory.

"Pablo, there's one number that appears consistently on all your depictions. Can you tell me more about it?"

An uncomfortable minute of silence followed, the doctor's once indomitable voice yielding to an audible twinge of anxiety.

"That number, Pablo; can you tell me what it means?"

"The sacrifice." The young soldier's voice was now stern, that of an authority figure about to disseminate an urgent warning.

"You're saying that the number represents a... tally of sacrifices to come?"

"I will be the first," replied the soldier with chilling determination. "I will not be the last."

Just then, Rachel's pager went off—its tone was jarring. She stopped the recording.

"Not again," she said, cupping her hand to her forehead.

"What is it?" Tim asked, startled by the interruption and still shaken by the recording he'd just heard.

"Follow me," she said, closing out the workstation and collecting her things into an open knapsack nearby. "It's time we met El Diablo."

Wenn wir die Idee aufdecken,

die um Kopf und Körper greift,

Dann wird sie ein Teil von uns,

der immer stärker, klarer reift.

Was ist doch zuerst gekommen,

wenn Idee im Geiste wächst?

Schafft der Geist Gedanken oder,

schafft Gedanke Geist zunächst?

Chapter Four

A Sinister Inspiration

The nightmare of Cpl. Acevedo

SATURDAY, MAY 17, 10:14 A.M.
DEPARTMENT OF CLINICAL AND INVESTIGATIVE NEUROPSYCHIATRY
OAK RIDGE NATIONAL LABORATORIES, OAK RIDGE, TENNESSEE

Rachel and Tim stood before a drab, six-story brick building ringed by a bluish-gray wooden portico dulled by decades of exposure to the elements. Its façade consisted of a cast-iron gated entrance set within a crumbling sandstone arch, the keystone carved in a loudly incongruous flower motif. The entire structure was situated in a vast, withered tomato patch cordoned off by a rusty electric fence overgrown with ivy.

Aside from the armed guards manning each point of entry, the complex had the dismal feel of a 1930s-era sanitarium. Studying its grim exterior, Tim imagined sterile patient rooms with chipping paint, basement amphitheaters with white-coated men swarming before lobotomy stations, and icy metallic tanks used for primitive electroshock therapy. A series of pillbox-shaped storage warehouses stood behind the main building, arranged in cornrows like fortified bunkers in a bitter trench war.

"And they wonder why these old warriors were driven to madness," Tim mused, shaking his head as he drank up the building's aura of shuttered misery.

He stood at a traffic circle's remove from the entrance while his colleague engaged in a vehement exchange with two of the guards at the fence. She was pointing frantically at her pager, following with a suite of impassioned gestures directed toward the entrance. Yet the guards stood unmoved by her pleas, tipping the muzzles on their semi-automatic rifles as they advised against further progress.

For once, the day's weather offered a measure of relief. The air was moist but not oppressively humid as it often was that time of year. A light breeze carried the sweet scent of honeysuckle from a grove near the road. Yet, the sunshine was inconstant, as the billowing clouds were growing thicker and darker with each passing minute.

"Unbelievable!" Rachel exclaimed, approaching Tim from the midpoint of the footpath that traversed the traffic circle. "There's been a security breach, and they're saying they can't allow a guest through the gate without the explicit approval of Dr. Simms. Which would be fine, except that he's stuck giving a talk in Grand Rounds for the next half-hour!"

"What exactly was that page about?" Tim asked. "Seemed pretty urgent."

"It was, but unfortunately it wasn't too specific aside from a request to meet outside Pablo's room. So I don't know enough of the gory details to talk the guards into letting us in."

"Then what should we do?"

"Hopefully, she can help."

Rachel steered his attention toward a young woman with shoulder-length, dirty-blond hair, approaching from just outside the opened iron gate. She stood barely over five feet tall, a stethoscope slung haphazardly about the collar of her ragged physician's uniform.

"That's Diane Mellon," Rachel explained as the woman addressed the guards. "She's the chief neurologist on the campus and collaborates directly with Dr. Simms. Diane's the only one besides him powerful enough to open these gates for us."

"Not sure if I should be pleased or nervous," Tim said, staring blankly at the building behind the gates. "This place looks straight out of the night terrors that used to haunt my childhood."

"These days, it's hosting plenty of nightmares for the grown-ups too."

"A comforting thought." Tim glanced at the pair of sleek, modern towers that sandwiched the building before them. "Whatever's awaiting us on the inside, looks like the Neuropsych Department missed out on a long-overdue makeover."

"Metacelsus' largesse didn't extend to the clinical divisions; we've had to make do with what was available. This building had been slated for condemnation before it was re-assigned to its current function. It's a relic from the earliest days of the Oak Ridge facility, and it hasn't aged well, needless to say."

"I'm surprised the staff don't lose their own sanity, being cooped up here every day."

"Who said they haven't?"

Tim eyed her briefly before turning his attention back toward the rotting fence that surrounded the Neuropsychiatry Department. Diane Mellon turned away from the guard and waved them over.

"Diane," Rachel began as they approached, "this is Tim Shoemaker."

"We meet at last," Diane said as she and Tim shook hands, then she led them to the gate. "The fabled knight from lands afar, come to slay our beast."

"We'll see," Tim said. "It's a tall order to slay a dragon that you can't find in the first place."

"Well, hopefully, we can light the way," she said and smiled at him. Tim could see the tiredness in her eyes, and hear it as she spoke; yet he also detected a whisper of Southern twang in her voice that made him feel at home—along with a proud defiance in her smile. *This one's a fighter,* he thought.

"This way, to the right," she continued. "The elevators are on emergency status in the wake of recent events, for patient deliveries only."

The group entered a stairwell with slatted windows and mildewed walls. Metallic clangs from footsteps above echoed all around them as they made their way upward, and Diane filled Rachel and Tim in on the latest developments.

"My colleague, Dr. Grijalva, was covering Pablo's ward through the early morning, and she was nearly shaking when she signed out to me this morning. El Diablo awoke from a nap in the early hours, more coherent than we'd expected from his recent baseline. But he was also more disturbed, reporting delusions even more perplexing than usual. When Nurse Patterson came into Room 305-C to check on him five hours later, she found he had somehow fashioned a cutting tool out of a plastic utensil. He made several deep lacerations to his arms and torso."

"There goes our lone consolation," Rachel said and, turning to Tim, explained: "We've all been telling each other, 'At least they're not cutting themselves.'"

"It was true until today," Diane said. "Though I'm afraid it didn't stop there. When Nurse Patterson sought to draw Pablo's attention, he ignored her until she came too close, at which point he knocked her out cold and appropriated her reflex hammer. We don't know how, but he somehow removed the wire grate shielding the window, then used the hammer's metal handle to smash the glass."

"I don't like where this is going," Tim said.

"Indeed you shouldn't," Diane said matter-of-factly. "Pablo used the shards from the broken window on his limbs; he came within a hair's-breadth of nicking his left femoral artery. We were understaffed to begin with, and many among the remaining personnel were tackling a Code Blue after an opiate overdose upstairs. Several minutes passed before Pablo was discovered."

"I take it you had him sedated to keep him from doing himself further harm," Tim said bluntly.

"Sedated, yes, and fully restrained," Diane confirmed. As the trio ascended to the third floor and exited the stairwell, she used an ungainly cruciform key to unlatch the stained, dented metal door before them. "But it's what he'd already done beforehand—that's what we're still coming to grips with. Come, see for yourselves."

She led them toward a guarded chamber, waving a pair of ID cards to open a path into the room. Rachel and Tim steeled themselves as they crossed the threshold into the chamber.

"Jesus," Tim said in a raspy voice.

The room's dreary vanilla walls had been transformed into a bloody canvas. Absent from the blood-inked messages, however, was any overt statement of malice. Instead, there was merely a workmanlike display of the mathematical arcana Rachel had referred to before: a bizarre array of equations and numerical constants, their connections and overall theme utterly impenetrable to observing eyes. There was also a heart-rending plea in Spanish scattered here and there throughout the display: *"Esmeralda, ¿dónde fuiste, hermanita?"*

One feature of the nightmarish canvas stood out: a number that clearly did not belong with the others. Its impropriety was exacerbated by its awkward insertions amidst the otherwise well-demarcated numerical constants on the walls, like a child's scribblings on a parent's neat array of documents for an office presentation. Yet it was also the most frequently appearing motif issuing from Pablo's wavering, blood-drained hand.

"Four-six-one-one-seven," Tim said.

"It's the number Dr. Simms alluded to on that recording," Rachel explained. "It's cropped up in all manner of settings—and not in Pablo's work alone."

"The other vets, too?"

Rachel nodded.

"Mostly in their sketches; this is the first time we've seen it on the walls."

"I'd hope this is the first time you've seen anything like this on the walls!"

"These freakish incidents always begin with El Diablo, Tim," Diane said, "but they metastasize soon enough to the rest of the group. There are shared attributes among them, and based on Pablo's own deterioration, I doubt we have much time left. The budget here is threadbare, but we've already placed the other veterans under 24/7 watch."

"Much time left until what?" Tim asked.

"The complete deterioration of the soldiers' minds. Before you ask, I have no idea what form that might take. It's part of why Rachel asked you to come here; we were hoping you could identify where all this is leading. All we know is that the physical signs and symptoms—not to mention horrific displays like this—seem to be telegraphed somehow. They're always preceded by progressively more disturbing elements in the veterans' personal sketches."

"Those drawings again," said Tim. "Dr. Simms on that tape... Rachel, you—every one of you shivers like a mouse each time the subject is broached. What is this power you think exists in Pablo's scribblings?"

"It's from a dark corner of his soul, whatever it is."

"That's helpful," Tim said, however, he immediately apologized. "Sorry, Diane. Didn't mean to snap at you like that. It's just that you called me out here for my expert input, yet all I can muster up is this slow-motion deer-in-headlights impression, ever more so with each new bit of bewilderment this place serves up. Can you give me anything more specific than 'a dark corner of his soul'?"

"I'm sorry we're not able to be more helpful, Tim. None of us has held anything back from you. It's because I…Rachel…we don't know what we're looking at."

"Imagine M.C. Escher," Rachel interjected, "René Magritte, one of those artists specializing in paradoxes and impossible geometries. Now imagine their most horrid nightmares, committed to canvas when they awake."

"You said Pablo's been rendering… shapes, polygons of some sort?" Tim asked.

"That's right. Along with the limbs of humans and animals," Rachel added, "ears, eyes—those hideous, God-awful eyes, twisted around in patterns that stare out at you a little differently, every time you shift ever so slightly in your perspective. And those are only the items that we can—somewhat—recognize in Pablo's drawings. It isn't clear what he or the others have been depicting—not at the outset of the crisis, not now; and it's obviously incomplete, like a work forever in progress. One thing we all agree on is that it must be linked to all those mathematical oddities, the physical constants that he sneaks in out of nowhere."

"Not to mention whatever that five-digit number signifies," Diane put in.

"Then it might be advisable to lower your expectations," Tim said, struggling to keep a lid on his frustration. "I'm sorry, but I can't fathom what any of this has to do with the Simitalis. At its core, it was nothing more than a neural network to guide the patients back to sight. Who knows why its files have been changing since February, but regardless, how would that bear on the events that have been tying you in knots around here? No matter how nerve-rattling Pablo's personal horror show might be, where do you see a possible connection?"

"Perhaps you could see for yourself," suggested Rachel, glancing imploringly at Diane.

"I suppose it's my turn to dampen expectations," Diane said with a sigh, "but the critical-care team snagged all of Pablo's personal effects when they shuttled him off to the PIT. It's restricted access from now on; not even I can authorize Tim's passage."

"That's not what I wanted to hear," Rachel said.

"What does that mean, 'The Pit'?" Tim interrupted.

"It's an acronym: 'Personal Intervention and Treatment,'" Rachel explained, "though it might as well be a bottomless pit for anyone stuck there with a 24-hour shift. It's the unit that houses patients with frank suicidal ideation—minute-by-minute monitoring while awake, no windows, no sharp objects or anything that could be made into one."

"To be fair, going helter-skelter with one's own blood isn't normally indicative of an upbeat personality."

"It's more than just that, Tim. Cutting behaviors and even self-mutilation aren't sufficient, in and of themselves, to gain approval for a PIT transfer. Pablo must have been airing thoughts that the staff members interpreted as suicidal."

"I'm not sure they knew how to interpret what they were seeing and hearing," said Diane. "Pablo was apparently chanting a litany even more disturbing than usual—'this world soon to vanish from our eyes,' and other doomsayings to that effect."

"He was doing the same on the taped interview that Rachel played for me," Tim said.

"The way the overnight medical team signed out his case to me," Diane added, "I'd say they were more traumatized than their patient. Once word had spread of Pablo's latest masterwork of madness, Dr. Grijalva rushed into Room 305-C. Yet she found him to be almost placid in his demeanor."

"Placid, or about to pass out from loss of all the blood he'd used for asylum room graffiti?" Tim asked.

"Placid—I chose the word deliberately. He wasn't fading yet. He was present but he was calm. No acute distress whatsoever," Diane said, "even with his heart rate hitting triple digits. Then there was the paradox of his strength; it took three orderlies to disarm him, along with Dr. Grijalva and Nurse Patterson once she came to."

Diane's account was interrupted by the shrill urgency of her own pager.

"Speak of El Diablo," she said dryly. "I guess I'll be paying a visit to the PIT myself; Pablo's sedatives don't seem to be doing much sedating. Please excuse me."

She promptly left the room while issuing instructions into a mobile phone, at which point Tim, as if seized by an impulse, took off close behind her.

"Tim," Rachel called out, following on his heels, "you heard Diane. The PIT's off-limits."

He didn't answer. They rounded a corner and traversed a long, increasingly dreary corridor, its ambient light progressively tapering down to the dim haze supplied by a flickering yellow bulb. A few steps ahead of them, Diane took her key ring from her white coat, and unbolted the metal door below the failing light source, pulling it outward in a semicircular sweep.

Tim positioned himself so as to be able to see inside: four uniformed personnel quickly joined by Diane, all huddling over a supine figure strapped to a gurney below. The man on the gurney clenched his fists and held them tightly, then released them for a second before clenching them again. His face was turned aside, fixed away from most of the observers about him; all Tim could see was that the man had dark, wispy sideburns. There was a stack of opened notebooks on the opposite end of the room, half-hidden behind a masked physician who appeared to be supervising the efforts.

"From a war hero's chevrons to a straitjacket," Tim muttered as the door closed before them.

"Diane shouldn't be too long," Rachel whispered. "This sort of thing seems to clog her schedule every other visit I make here. Pablo's on an atypical medication regimen, and the other doctors need Diane's input whenever they tweak it."

"I can scarcely imagine what 'typical' would constitute around here."

Tim's attention was drawn to an anomalous mark on the wall to the right of the door jamb. It was hard to identify in the dim light, but as he examined it more closely, he was alarmed to discern a series of stains in a distinctive droplet pattern.

"Dried blood. Was this from Pablo's transfer?"

"No," Rachel answered. "One of the orderlies cut his wrist with the equipment he was moving, right as he'd been opening the door."

"Another of those unexplained accidents?"

"Not this time—just plain old carelessness. The accidents so far have been mostly outside the VRRC, so we ourselves haven't been directly affected nearly as much as—"

Rachel caught herself mid-sentence, alarmed.

"Tim, I never told you about the accidents, and I'm fairly sure my assistant hasn't, either."

"I had an outside source for that particular scoop. My cousin Ernie learned of the incidents while working one of his rotating shifts at

Oak Ridge; your team isn't the only one chasing ghosts. What exactly's been going on here?"

"These unfortunate contractors...They were brought in for renovations and installations throughout the campus. One was nearly paralyzed while maneuvering to retrieve a pair of pliers. The shelf above collapsed straight down upon him. Another was trapped in a cold room when a nitrogen tank sprang a leak; we couldn't save him."

"Good God. So how long have these incidents been—"

"And those are only examples of the mishaps within the Trask Institute building itself," she said, her speech hurried as she cut off his query. "There's been a rash of incidents elsewhere in the complex over the past three months, and our teams have run diagnostics all over the map. We've detected structural flaws in places, and glitches in the control software for some of the systems. Regardless, the programmers and hardware designers insisted they weren't at fault."

"Were there investigations?" asked Tim.

"If you could fairly call them that, since the inquests were politicized and corrupted as usual. If the contracting firm owners were stateside, Metacelsus' lackeys couldn't resist taking advantage. They'd use the findings as a pretext for scapegoating, imprisonment, or outright theft from the targeted companies."

"True to form."

"To a point. This time, Metacelsus himself expressed doubts upon viewing the results. He even personally pardoned officials in several of the design firms."

"You've got to be kidding," Tim responded, scratching his head. "I figured unicorns would be winning at the tracks before a Triantarch would be caught in an act of mercy."

"We were shocked at the time...but there is a certain consistency to his behavior. We've been barred from reviewing the full investigation records. Nevertheless, besides his appeal to you for aid, in general his actions suggest there's some other factor that Metacelsus can't account for, and it's getting under his skin. We suspected that all along, since our own diagnostics have been inconsistent with mere human error."

"I don't know, Rachel. Ever since the Reckoning, quality control's gone straight to hell for software and precision tools. The Triantarchs have gutted our domestic sourcers; it's all about cheap labor and cronyism for them. For our own projects, in fact, Zach and I either smuggled in the parts from overseas, or personally customized the components for the Simitalis, lest we spend half our time debugging all the mistakes from suppliers."

"I agree with you, I wouldn't defend them for a second; but the Ruling Clans at least had the sense to cordon off a pool of competent supply firms for their own purposes. What matters is that the case file excerpts from the accident inquiries we were allowed to see showed no hard evidence of errors by any of the contracting partners. It's as though whatever toxic cloud has overwhelmed the veterans has been affecting our machines as well, altering their very design specs since El Día del Diablo."

Tim briefly chewed on this. He frowned.

"Rachel, why did you react like that?"

"Like what?"

"The way you did just now, upon realizing that I'd already been apprised of the recent spate of accidents. You didn't tell me about them before, nor were you particularly pleased when I brought them up."

Rachel returned a pained, distraught look, stung by the subtext of his inquiry.

"Tim, I know you know this, but I can't tell you how much it haunts me that the Simitalis was stolen from you... and that they put me of all people at the helm of the project. But I have never tried or wanted to take advantage of you or lead you astray, then or now."

"Take it easy, Rachel, I didn't mean—"

"I'm already strung out as it is," she added, verging on tears as if protesting an unjust charge. "Dealing with the mistrust of a mentor who meant so much to me, it's more than I can take. Please don't go down this road."

"I don't mistrust you, Rachel. I never meant to imply that."

"Yet here comes the 'but'."

"But," he answered firmly, "I know that the Triantarchy has you on a tight leash, which you feel unable to slip. I want to help you with every tool at my disposal, but I can't do it if you're not completely frank with me. This trust deficit cuts both ways; it's bad enough that Zach's begun to—"

Tim stopped himself abruptly; no need to go there now.

"I just want it to be like it was three years ago," he said, "when you and I and Zach could all trust each other unconditionally, before... events robbed us of that luxury."

A latch stirring from inside the sealed-off room startled them both. Tim lurched backward from the door as it swung open, further obscuring himself within the shadows of the dim corridor. A quintet of uniformed, barely recognizable figures emerged in a gaggle outside the room, congregating to chat for a moment. But before the door had completely shut, Tim slipped into the chamber; the strangers were too engrossed in their discussion to notice. As he vanished behind the frame, Rachel threw an uncomfortable glance his way before quietly deflecting the team's attention away from the entrance.

SATURDAY, MAY 17, 10:45 A.M.
PERSONAL INTERVENTION AND TREATMENT FACILITY
3RD FLOOR
DEPARTMENT OF CLINICAL AND INVESTIGATIVE NEUROPSYCHIATRY

Tim took in his surroundings. The back and side walls of the PIT chamber were of brick and mortar, burnt and stained over so many years as to resemble the interior of an abandoned crematorium. The enclosed room, deprived of amenities and even modest portals to the world outside, was lit by three dull-green fanned lamps dangling from frayed wires above.

The ceiling was of decaying, faded-white stucco gnawed away by water damage. A brass water jug in a corner and a series of unframed, Winslow Homer-style paintings of lakes and seasides furnished the room's spare decoration. Tim quietly but briskly made his way to the far side of Pablo's gurney, glimpsing the soldier's countenance for the first time. It was clear the man had once been handsome, but was now a shadow of his former self. His face was wan, with slightly sunken eyes pressed shut in apparently deep sedation. His cheeks and forehead were scarred: a warrior's mien, lately emaciated by an unseen, unrelenting enemy.

Pablo was shackled tightly to the stretcher, an IV in his right arm. His limbs and chest were covered with bloody bandages and a yellow-brown antiseptic salve. Telemetry equipment and a pulse oximeter ticked and chirped softly in the background. His breathing was mostly regular but subdued, occasionally broken by a convulsive inhalation that shook the metal rods of the gurney. Immediately to his left, atop a portable drug dispensary, was the stack of notebooks crammed with reports, test data, and other sundry records of his case.

"Page extension 91937 in case of Kussmauling," Tim murmured, reading aloud the contents of a dull yellow sticky note tucked beneath the rubber band that sealed the first of the notebooks.

He impatiently tugged off the band to peek inside, only to be greeted by a web of charts and tables with numbers culled from Pablo's respiratory therapy, blood tests, and a panoply of other clinical lab data. Tim worked his way through the bulging notebooks below, past reams of medical reports, diagrams, and staff notes, before arriving at an anomalous member of the group about three-quarters of the way down.

Unlike the other notebooks, it was encased in transparent cellophane, and instead of binder rings to hold loose leaf documents, the organizer featured a fluted backing designed for file folders, each containing photographs or other loose articles.

"So this is where you've been hiding," Tim said as he took up the notebook for examination. He removed its wrapping and scanned its contents: an assemblage of hand-drawn designs, apparently encouraged as an outlet to sort through the flood tide of images newly available to the formerly-blind soldier. The folders were organized thematically and chronologically, with a mixture of line drawings and watercolors evoking memories of open fields, amusement parks, household pets, and battlefield camaraderie with fellow soldiers.

But there was a crimson folder near the bottom that featured altogether different subject matter, clashing with the halcyon scenes in the sketches above. It began with depictions of common shapes and polygons, drawn with the precision of a master draftsman: tight angles, matching faces, ingenious perspectives. The sketches rapidly increased in complexity, with fractal images and ramifying chains of beads that folded and cavorted into ever more intricate structures.

These structures, in turn, gave way to distorted shapes apparently derived from the cells and tissues of plants and higher animals, interspersed with surfaces repeatedly twisting about one another. Each successive image eventually culminated in an unfinished tapestry that somehow tied into whatever narrative was being spun by its predecessors. Mathematical equations and numbers—either unimaginably large or impossibly small—appeared in the pictures' margins from time to time, like witnesses to the fiendish apparitions at the center.

In the last half-dozen drawings, the infolding, membranous surfaces began to unlatch and swing about, spiraling outward toward the borders of the page. The net effect was an eye-teasing hyperbolic pattern with a series of menacing eyes—some human-like, others of a far different inspiration—trailing along the membranes. The eyes and the strange surfaces that bore them seemed to melt away in an infinite regression as they approached the edges.

"Pablo," Tim murmured, glancing at the wounded man, "what is all this supposed to mean?"

In the last few sketches, the perimeter of the drawn-in region was vaguely elliptical yet asymmetric; randomly-placed inpouchings at the surrounding border alternated with ridges and blebs that pinched outward. Skeletal outlines of what appeared to be organs and limbs were also manifest at the edges, hinting at structures that had barely begun to assume their forms.

Even more unsettling was the center of each image. It had initially featured a half-filled orb that gradually, with each new rendering in the stack of drawings, took the form of an eye that was alarmingly dissimilar from those hugging the rims of the infolding membranes. This one was not only far larger than the others, but eerily piercing and hostile, as though consciously marking its observers from the page in which it had been rendered.

"Doctor!"

Tim startled at the voice of the man on the gurney—and at the firm grip of his hand on Tim's wrist. Tim set down the notebook and glanced into the eyes of an awakened Pablo Acevedo. The man's pupils were distressingly wide, and his heart rate jumped on the monitor as he stared up at Tim. The oddness of Pablo's stare rattled Tim to the core, as it seemed directed at but not quite upon him.

"How can I help you, Corporal?" Tim said, instinctively playing the calm doctor.

"El sueño que acabo de soñar, me entregó un recado; finalmente lo entiendo."

"I—your dream? It bore a message of some sort? I'm sorry, Corporal, I don't quite understand."

"The memory, Doctor. The memories that I drew when my eyes first awoke again. Now they are his memories, too. Soon, he will glimpse what you see and dream, what all of you see and dream."

Pablo's words sent a shudder through Tim, as if tweaking a primal chord buried inside him. He gingerly loosened Pablo's grip and rested the soldier's hand back upon the gurney. But before he could slip away, the crescendo of Pablo's heartbeat breached a threshold. An alarm began to sound. Tim clenched his teeth, watching as the door's latch was slipped by the turn of a key from the other side.

"You're not supposed to be in here, Dr. Shoemaker."

A tall, prematurely gray-haired man stood in the doorway. He had a slight stoop. His voice was admonishing yet mercifully calm.

"My apologies," Tim said as a nurse quickly entered and sedated Pablo, sending him back to sleep to ponder his peculiar thoughts alone.

The tall man entered the room, followed by Diane and Rachel with anxious looks on their faces.

"I'm Dr. Simms—Alan to everyone here," said the man, now sounding more exhausted than upset. The whites of his eyes were badly bloodshot. "I regret that our first meeting has occurred under such...unpleasant circumstances."

"I agree. Though if circumstances had been pleasanter, I wouldn't be here for us to meet at all," Tim said bluntly.

Dr. Simms grunted.

"All the same, we can't allow you to barge into Pablo's quarters like this. His condition's too fragile and—"

"I saw his drawings," Tim interrupted.

"What's that?"

"Pablo's drawings. The ones in the red folder stashed at the bottom of the pile—that evolving image with the intertwining surfaces. What does it represent?"

Simms hissed through his upper teeth, grasping to answer a question that he could not simply brush aside.

"I don't know. The rough consensus is that Pablo is rendering a kind of metaphor in his drawings."

"As in...a birth of some sort?"

"And its prior gestation. The involutions of those membranes are mimicking gastrulation and early limb formation: the first stirrings of a human embryo in a mother's womb. All the abstract forms, the geometries, those grid-like structures in the early images...we're at a loss as to their significance. But the subsequent layering seems to represent a high-res view of a human brain and all its convolutions."

"That must be why Pablo was saying all those things about memory and seeing."

"He spoke to you just now?" Dr. Simms asked, intrigued.

"Something about how 'he'—he didn't say who, just 'he'—how *somebody* is sharing Pablo's dreams and visions, and how he'll soon be doing the same for you and me."

"A consistent motif," Rachel said, "always something about this unknown whoever-he-is, remembering those important to us."

"That's possible," added Dr. Simms in a dubious tone, rubbing his stubbled chin. He nodded in gratitude to the nurse as she left the PIT. Rachel and Diane quickly followed, beckoned away by news of yet another crisis pealing from Diane's pager.

"Still," Simms continued, "this is the first time that Corporal Acevedo has portrayed 'him' as looking specifically through our eyes. Pablo's speaking in symbols, and I can't begin to decode them."

"These themes and imagery—" Tim mused. "As I understand it, the veterans have been reciting from the same basic script since the onset of their symptoms."

"In essence," Dr. Simms concurred, "though Pablo is the unfortunate bellwether in this march. His condition is markedly more advanced than that of his brothers- and sisters-in-arms."

"So I've heard. Listen, while I have your ear, there's a burning question that I never got around to asking Rachel. When her assistant briefed me on Friday, she let it slip that you'd conducted a trial run of a sort—a simple experiment to test if you could cure their ills by undoing the vision restoration."

"We disconnected the Simitalis from the soldiers' implants for varying intervals, to see if their manifestations would subside. In short, they didn't."

"But what about the implants themselves?"

Simms' jaw twitched.

"You're suggesting," he said, "that we remove the AP-278 from the soldiers' eyes?"

"It's the only other component shared by each and every one of the veterans. I'm no expert when it comes to their delusions—heck, I'm still a newbie stumbling through his first day on the scene. But perhaps we could at least track down the source of this sickness of the mind. Whoever's behind all this, saboteurs or cultists or whoever else—they must have exploited a common vector to seed all this misery."

"We did extract the retinal implants from one of the patients: an Army chief warrant officer named Cassius Gaines, though for reasons unrelated. Cassius had developed an inflammatory reaction to a synthetic wafer, integral to the casing and overall assembly of many prosthetic devices. Yet he continued with the same constellation of symptoms as his fellow soldiers, implant or not."

"But what if the AP-278 was merely a delivery vehicle?" Tim asked.

"For what? We've screened for every possible causative agent, even biopsied their neural tissue itself, and nothing's turned up. What could we possibly have missed?"

"That I can't answer, but perhaps the implants could light the way for us. I was on that review panel, Dr. Simms, the one that decided the initial fate of the AP-278 implant."

"I'm aware of that."

"Then you're likewise aware that I argued categorically against human trials three years ago. The AP-278 in those days was an intriguing but thoroughly untested bundle of vision sensors and signal integrators. It was scarcely competent enough to feed a stripped-down message to the optic nerve, much less rekindle the magic of a human retina. You're trying to tell me that in a mere three years, amid the ongoing mass bereavement of the Reckoning and Triantarch misrule, and with the spigots of both public and private R&D drained of their last drops—that this misbegotten little piece of mechanica gained the power to pierce the veil of blindness?"

"Where are you going with this, Tim?"

"Hopefully to the same place you are. We must have collided with a technology that's well beyond the documented capabilities of retinal implantation, quantum-leaping past what both you and I had presumed to be the state of the art. Rachel told me herself: The AP-278 was altered in accordance with unknown specs somewhere in your supply chain, before your surgeons ever took the vets into the operating theater. There must be more to that history, Dr. Simms. Can you provide me with one of the implants that you isolated from Cassius Gaines?"

"With all due respect, even if the modified AP-278 were somehow responsible, I can't allow it to leave the premises. That's a commandment from on high."

"Of course it is," acknowledged Tim, exasperated. "This is where I throw up my hands. I can't take another teaspoon of this bureaucratic castor oil."

"Of what?"

"This caginess that's shackled you like a death row inmate! Why can't you understand that you're choking off whatever wisp of a chance I have to lead you out of this mess? You drag me out here in desperation, yet you won't let me copy the files from my own stolen creation, you won't permit me even momentary access to your Patient Zero, and you won't allow me to follow up the only tenuous thread we could use to begin unraveling this."

"You know as well as I," Simms replied, lowering his voice, "who gives the orders around here."

"Indeed I do. I also know that he's come prostrating himself before me, of all people, because he knows he's in way over his head—even to the point of cowering behind Rachel, relaying his fears to me through her."

Dr. Simms let out a sigh, exhausted by his powerlessness.

"We don't have to tell him everything, you know," Tim said, lowering his voice to a near-whisper. He put a hand on Simms' shoulder. "Frankly, I doubt he even wants to know."

"It's not that easy," Simms murmured, shaking his head.

"Then I dearly wish you luck, because you're going to need it. I can't help you if you won't let me. I'm not doing this to bail out a coward like Metacelsus in his sorry attempt to save face. I'm here for Rachel—for all of you, to shield you from becoming scapegoats. And if you won't act in your own interest, then reflect for one inspired moment on what everyone among your team has endured for this God-forsaken project, about the fires that Pablo and the other vets had crawled through to make it necessary in the first place. Don't debase their sacrifices by abandoning them to the madness caused by this reckless project."

Dr. Simms carefully surveyed their surroundings before gazing intently at the man strapped on the gurney. Pablo's eyelids were pulsating together in a rapid-fire, irregular rhythm that resembled an unbroken seizure, as the telemetry apparatus chirped calmly in the background.

"Even if I could do what you ask, Tim, you've admitted that you're no closer to a solution than any of us. Are you sure you could put such assistance to productive use?"

"No, I'm not," Tim answered firmly. "But I know someone who can."

SUNDAY, MAY 18, 7:19 P.M.
HOME OF ERNEST AND CONNIE SHOEMAKER
KINGSTON, TENNESSEE

The sweet, contrasting fragrances of Ernie's wine cellar were a refreshing change from the musty stairwells at the Trask Institute.

"Glad you managed to make it back here," said Ernie, manifestly relieved to see his cousin again. "Connie's already preparing the guest room for you to catch a few winks before you head back east. So how'd things work out at Oak Ridge?"

"I'll tell you when I have the faintest clue what I encountered there," replied Tim. "You weren't kidding about that place. Even on a good day, it feels like a prison for staff and patients alike. And I wasn't there on a good day."

"I'd hoped that my warnings would prove overblown."

"Hardly. They were dead-on."

Ernie reached for a wine tumbler and poured out a glass for his cousin.

"Here you are, Tim, another serving of the same goodness you sampled before decamping from this place on Friday."

"Sorry again for having bolted off like that, Ernie. I'd already been ground down by a tough week."

"I'd have done the same in your shoes. Never ceases to amaze me that anyone can handle a schedule like yours, even without the surreal surprises that seem to have greeted you over the weekend."

Tim paused to indulge a prolonged sip of the white wine, exhaling with satisfaction at its lingering scent and aftertaste.

"Don't you want a glass for yourself, Ernie?"

"I'll be fine. I already had so much at dinner, another cup and I'd be drinking away what's left of my sobriety. So what ultimately persuaded you to make a repeat visit out here in Kingston?"

"I hardly know where to begin. To boil it all down, I'm wondering if the day's finally come to break this code of silence I've been bound to on all matters Uncle Mitch. Though I'm not much enthused about the prospect. Some of the things I encountered this weekend... I feel like the rat in the proverbial maze."

"Think Mitch can help lead the way out?" Ernie inquired subtly.

"I don't know... but his is the sort of eccentric genius... He can think outside the kind of boxes I keep getting stuck in. Even I can't deny him that. Anyhow, I shouldn't just walk away from the olive branch he's extended. I figured you and I could pick up where we left off."

"I'll be happy to oblige."

"What did you mean by what you were saying on Friday, Ernie? About all those secret-shrouded heirlooms Mitch supposedly has, and their connection to the Sacred Sight? After I'd begun threading my way back to Oak Ridge, I realized I'd heard about those curiosities as a kid, but I've never actually seen any of the damn things. How did you get involved in all this, anyway?"

"The answer is in what you're drinking now, Tim."

"In the wine?"

"In what it represents."

Tim's cousin carefully set the bottle down on a sturdy platform between them and turned it around to display the label. It bore a choppy, faded cursive script on a gold-tinged background, with pirate-themed images flanking a collage of scurvy quotations in Portuguese.

"It's an award-winning muscatel," Ernie said, "that we bought from a local dealer in Porto Alegre, Brazil. It quickly became Mitch's favorite, and not on account of its sweet bouquet alone; turns out that he found a more personal treasure on the way to the vintner."

He glided toward Tim's left and unlatched a wooden cabinet fastened to the wall in a sizable clearing between the wine racks. He flung open its slatted doors with a showman's flair, revealing a series of photographs from sunny venues straddling the equator. They were laid out in a crooked circle, centering on a single striking image that dwarfed the others in both its dimensions and its apparent significance.

"Speak of the devils," Tim remarked, examining the picture of his uncle and cousin in a crisp outdoor setting. The lighting of the setting was at once brilliant and somber. The grinning figures at its center were situated on either side of a heavenly fault line between daylight and shadow, straddling sun-kissed doldrums to the left and the brewing tempest of a tropical rainy season to the right. Towering structures, arching outward and upward with a strangely sidewinding geometry, loomed in the background while a gale-force wind apparently gusted through the scene, ruffling the men's outfits and bending the surrounding foliage to and fro.

"What brought the two of you to Brazil?" Tim asked.

"The official story was that Mitch had linked up with partners in Brazilian architectural outfits, to supply tutorials on his 'evolving designer' software. We snapped that photo at the Largo dos Açorianos; it's a park in Porto Alegre, near an enterprise zone for the design firms. Brazil escaped the worst of Fisher's Reckoning, and it certainly didn't hurt that the site visit doubled as a chance to frolic in a South American playground. So Mitch invited me and Connie along for the festivities after his lectures."

Tim's eyes went to an unfamiliar figure at the picture's center: a tall, imposing bald man flanked by Ernie and Mitch. Unlike his two partners, sporting Panama hats, sandals, and the casual outfits of beachgoing tourists, the mystery man wore a designer vest and wingtip shoes. There was a steely determination in his ice-blue eyes.

"Did you two hire a bodyguard during your little jaunt?" Tim joked.

"We could take care of ourselves just fine, thank you," answered Ernie without missing a beat. "But in the rough-and-tumble neighborhood where he grew up, the local clubs did make regular use of Rodrigo's services; he had a steady weekend gig as a bouncer."

"I'll bet. What's his connection to you and Mitch?"

"Among other things, his full name: Rodrigo Schumacher."

"Schumacher... Shoemaker... a family reunion of sorts, I take it."

"Yes, about 250 years in the making."

"250 years, eh?" echoed Tim. "Puts my own tardiness into perspective. How did Rodrigo and his kinfolk wind up in the Southern Hemisphere to begin with?"

"Our ancestors began emigrating from Germany more than three centuries ago, setting sail for Canada, Australia, and South America as well as what became the United States. Rodrigo and the rest of the Brazilian branch are descended from one David Wolfgang Schumacher or his elder brother, Gerhard Michael. Gerhard Michael was a soldier of fortune, eventually making his way to join a war raging in the Caribbean. He served as a mercenary in the Battle of Cartagena de las Indias, in 1741."

"For which side?"

"Both, actually."

"Ah," said Tim. "The enterprising, can-do spirit of the Shoemaker clan in action."

"Gerhard was a ne'er-do-well in other ways, too. His notoriety didn't reflect too well on the family name, which is probably why it was only seven years ago that Mitch discovered we had a Brazilian branch at all. When he signed up for battle, Gerhard first fought under Lord Vernon in the British service. He soon took up the Spanish standard, however, when the tide turned in Admiral de Lezo's favor—and when the Colombian coffee plantations beckoned for the victors."

"What can you say? The man had his priorities straight," Tim said with a crooked grin.

"Priorities, yes; competence was a different matter altogether. Gerhard suffered from the slight drawback of knowing next to nothing about agriculture. So he made a royal mess of the plot he was granted for his service, and crossed into Brazil to flee his creditors. That's when David thankfully tracked him down, eventually settling in the country himself."

"Tracked him down? For what?"

"When Gerhard left the Old World, he stole some valuable family heirlooms. He'd intended to pawn them off for South American land until, as luck would have it, the Battle of Cartagena solved that problem for him. David knew it wouldn't be long before Gerhard fouled up another scheme after his fiasco in Colombia, and he couldn't let the heirlooms become a bargaining chip in his big brother's debt negotiations."

"Starting to see where this is going."

"So the younger Schumacher mortgaged virtually all his hard-won possessions in Europe to purchase the articles from Gerhard. David couldn't even afford a return trip, and he was forced to start over as a pauper in the New World. But he'd safeguarded those treasures for the generations to come."

"These heirlooms again," Tim said quizzically. "I don't get it. What could have been so valuable that David would sacrifice his very livelihood for a ... a collection of family baubles?"

"You're looking at it," Ernie answered decisively, shepherding Tim's attention back to the curious photograph.

Sitting inconspicuously upon a shadow-strewn concrete slab, resting at the three men's feet, was a pair of unique objects. Tim couldn't tell what they were. One vaguely resembled a crude mini-typewriter, set within the frame of a small but elaborately adorned gyroscope. To its left was an even stranger instrument shaped roughly like a wire sculpture: a kaleidoscopic assemblage of tiny color-coded cables, nestled within protective tubing, that centered on a rectangular matrix of fourteen distinctively shaped, colorful crystals.

The tubes of the second device ramified outward like the stems of a flowering plant, tapering to diamond-shaped extremities that opened at their far ends, forging a fan-like ring of copper brushes. The centrally placed crystals, in turn, were anchored on their collective underside by an intricate lattice that projected its labyrinth in three dimensions. The crisscrossing lines of the lattice teemed with miniature components, like the solid-state electronics of a radio circuit, that culminated in an array of zinc-coated tips lining the grid's irregular surface.

Tim leaned forward to examine the objects more closely, his face puckered in a strained attempt to make sense of them.

"The item on the right from our perspective," Ernie explained, "is engineered to etch messages, or maybe a code of some sort. It apparently transcribes its text onto a soft wafer, some malleable material that can be held and moved around between a pair of widely-spaced jaws."

"Jaws?"

"They're visible if you zoom in on the photo—heavily stylized, thin metal rods resting against a roller, much like the platen of an old-fashioned typewriter."

"You said this gizmo was rigged up to spit out messages, Ernie. What does that mean, exactly?"

"Nobody knows for sure, but Mitch thinks that when regarded as a whole, the device's output constitutes an instruction set."

"For what?" Tim asked with narrowed eyes, grimacing as Ernie answered his question with a resigned shake of the head. He returned his attention to the snapshot on the wine cellar's wall.

"What about the other contraption," Tim said, "the one with all the twisting metal and crystals? Looks like an artist's fever-dream version of an *avant-garde* flower sculpture."

"But with function to go with the form. That bundle of bizarreness commanded nearly a year of teeth-gnashing and hand-wringing, before Mitch's team of wizards began to unlock its most elementary secrets. Even then, they could ascertain no more than the bare outlines of what it actually does. Turns out those are piezoelectric crystals at the center, bobbing and weaving whenever you run a current through the wires. The same as they would in their usual haunts, within the diaphragms of microphones or stereo speakers."

"So those sparkly gemstones aren't just for show. If I had to guess—they're integrating electrical signals, perhaps? Fed in through those copper brushes at the periphery?"

"That's the idea. From there, the crystals transmit a weak electric current into the grid below, which modulates this input to generate a secondary signal in... who knows, whatever that gadget links up to. Rodrigo Schumacher is a practicing physician by trade, and he said the device reminded him of a distorted, scaled-up version of a human nerve cell. Or maybe even the relay system of the inner ear, encoding the sounds that traverse our eardrums. Both those heirlooms had long been handed down the branches of Rodrigo's own family tree, ever since David Schumacher first set foot in Brazil."

"Then the bottom line, I take it, is that those objects in the photo are geared to process information," Tim reasoned, chewing over the curious thought.

"To process it, and to program it. According to Mitch, these are both peripheral devices."

"Peripherals? As in... for a computer?"

Ernie nodded.

"Believe me, Tim, I was no less dumbfounded when Mitch first gave me his spiel. But he's been studying these things for quite a while, filling a couple dozen notebooks with all the data. He's onto something here."

"Yeah, he's onto something—yet another sidetrack into looney-land," Tim retorted. "I'd gotten wind of Mitch's preoccupation with the grand inventors of antiquity—Archimedes, Hero of Alexandria, the abacus-makers in ancient China and the Indus Valley. He was obsessed with all the mythologizing about their early stabs at mechanical number-crunching, that maybe they amounted to more than history's seen fit to record."

"Not only the ancients; he'd also read extensively about Pascal and Schickard in the 17th century. Their early calculating machines evolved into what became our computers today."

"But the operative term is 'calculating machine,' Ernie. From Archimedes through Pascal, even the most fiendishly determined trail-blazers could fashion only crude devices at best—nothing approaching what we'd regard today as a programmable computer."

"Fair enough. But don't you think that some of them may have been at least implicitly aware of the revolution whose seeds they were sowing?

That they were fashioning tools capable of measuring and precisely quantifying the world, to engage in the rudiments of what only our minds had been competent to do before?"

"Frankly, no," Tim said. "All those advances were painfully incremental, so I doubt any of the early tinkerers had a damn clue where their work was leading."

"You sound so certain."

"Look, I'm no expert by any stretch, but the sheer scale of computing history filtered in when I was cutting my teeth as an engineer. If there's one impression that clung to me amidst all those half-remembered lessons, it's that dozens of great minds had to sprinkle their own ingredients into the mix. The hardware of Jacquard and Babbage in the 1800s, the mathematicians and logicians like Frege, Weierstrass, Boole, Hilbert…"

"And then the grand leaps of Gödel and Turing in the 20th century. I may not have the fancy letters by my name, Tim, but I've taken my wrench and pliers to machines that still run on vacuum tubes from the 1920s. I know a thing or two about this line of work."

Hearing Ernie's defensive and slightly indignant tone, Tim realized that his cousin was in no way free of his own doubts on the matter.

"Then maybe you'll agree with me," Tim added, softening his voice, "that Mitch's story isn't remotely plausible. If our ancestors brought these devices from the Old Country, then based on Mitch's own genealogical scavenger-hunting, they must be at least 300 years old. They couldn't possibly have boasted such sophistication back then."

"Mitch has hired a team of world-class experts, working under strict confidentiality aside from Mitch's own family and inner circle, to verify their origin—the same folks who document archaeological finds. The dates held up under scrutiny."

"Then he must be pulling a P. T. Barnum on you, the way he talks up their capacities. I know he's had too much spare time since stepping away from day-to-day operations at Magister Engineering, but he's outdone himself here. This is pure craziness."

"You should also know," insisted Ernie, "that Mitch ran imaging and technical studies of their craftsmanship. Not only for the devices he received from Rodrigo in Brazil, but others he's long had in his possession."

"There are more of these?"

"The seven wonders of Mitch's world, as he calls them, and those are only the ones he deigned to show me. They all display exquisite craftsmanship even by modern standards. If we could rev up a time machine and return to the heady days before Fisher's Reckoning, arming ourselves with the most state-of-the-art machine tools and laser-guided equipment, we'd still be hard-pressed to match their precision."

"But there's no possible way that—"

"To top it off," added Ernie, "even after three centuries of ocean-hopping and tropical weather for the gems from Brazil, these devices have shown only the most minimal corrosion. Their designers knew enough about layering and plating technologies to give them a protective finish that would test the mettle of even the best materials scientists today. Then there are the real bafflers—objects with these impossible geometries, spirals and kinks all over their surfaces. You've barely seen a sample of Mitch's treasures."

"I've seen enough," Tim countered, his jaw tensing. "Maybe it was a mistake for me to follow up on this after all. I don't know what Mitch is cooking up here or how he did it, but it pains me to see that he's managed to draw you of all people into this foolishness."

"I hope you change your view on that, Tim, because he needs you to become a part of it as well. From what you were saying earlier, you must have heard some of the same tales I did as a kid."

"Yes, but I never knew what all the fuss was about, or what those damn hand-me-downs actually were to begin with. I certainly never linked them to whatever crock Mitch has been trying to force-feed you about their origins."

"Forget about Mitch for the moment. Forget the connections he has to all this. Think back to all the stories from Grandma and Grandpa at the family reunions, duly passed along to each new generation. The ones about how the Shoemakers of yore rescued these precious creations away from the onrush of the Johnstown Flood in Pennsylvania."

"I know, or how they were spirited from house to house in Missouri during the Civil War, when guerrillas from the Border Ruffians and Jayhawkers were spilling each other's blood in the streets. Oh, and how every possessor of the trinkets was somehow grandfathered into this generation-jumping vow to guard their secrets. I can imagine the reverence that Mitch showers on that old family campfire lore, but do you know what those stories tell me, Ernie? They tell me that our forerunners didn't have their priorities straight."

"Our ancestors guarded these objects as if they'd been handed down straight from the angels above; there must be a damn good reason for that. Mitch is trying to figure out what that reason is, but he can't pursue the mystery of these heirlooms at the same intensity as he used to. They're destined for your hands, Tim."

"Then they're also destined for a padlocked crate in my attic!" Tim exclaimed. "Because my uncle happens to be nuts, I have to pick up the family lunatic baton? Is this really why you've been nudging me to drop in for so many months? Why doesn't he just sign the heirlooms over to you?"

"Because Mitch deciphered the messages gouged into some of those creations, and while he has yet to gauge the full breadth of their requests, there is one refrain that's belted out with stentorian clarity. The heirlooms must be in the possession of someone blessed with a rare vision, the ability to see the world that lies beyond our immediate senses. The capacity that—"

"The Sacred Sight," Tim interjected with an exasperated nod. "Yeah, I get it."

"Good, since only you fit the bill."

"Ernie, I'll say it again: I'm not about to be drafted into Mitch's private war, even if he's twisted your arm to handle recruitment."

"That's where you're mistaken, Tim. I'm not doing this for him, or for myself. I wasn't convinced at first, and to be honest, I still can't pinpoint any concrete tipping point that brought me over to Mitch's side. But when he has that uncanny read on things...you'd lose your shirt betting against him. And in this case, he seems to have stumbled onto something far greater than the tangled history of our clan alone."

"Then what? Why is this so urgent?"

Ernie exhaled through a partially closed voice box, producing a hollow, rustling sound that seethed discomfort. With shaking hands, he poured them more wine, holding his cousin's glass out to Tim like a peace offering.

"For that," Ernie said, "you'll have to talk to Mitch yourself."

Die Geschichte uns're Welt

ist von vielen Händ' geschrieben.

Voll von Leiden, voll von Leisten,

voll von Freud' und Sorg' und Lieben.

Was bleibt denn in dunklen Schatten,

unentdeckt und unbekannt?

Gibt's in Annalen, die noch fehlen,

Geschichte, die noch nie genannt?

Chapter Five

Legacy of Puzzles

The Cereceph

MONDAY, MAY 19, 11:23 A.M.
PARKING LOT C, PEGASUS ATLANTIC BANK
CHARLOTTE, NORTH CAROLINA

Tim wheeled his car gingerly onto the rain- and grease-slicked asphalt of the bank's parking structure. His bloodshot eyes were ringed by dark gray circles, vestiges of the grinding, seemingly fruitless weekend in Tennessee. He had spent the balance of his assignment with Rachel Bloom in the drab laser lab of the Vision Restoration Research Center, combing through cabinets full of data and vexing reports about the mysterious ailment afflicting the soldiers.

In spite of these heroic efforts, Tim found himself irked by the sense that precious little had been accomplished after his awkward run-in with Pablo and Alan Simms in that dreadful inner chamber. Even the altered program files of the Simitalis had remained stubbornly inaccessible. At least there was a glimmer of progress in obtaining a prototype of the retinal implants, he reminded himself, to perhaps smoke out the trail of whatever curses they had borne.

Yet his spirits slumped every time he recalled Rachel's expression of helpless disappointment, unmistakable in the rear-view mirror as he pulled away from the Oak Ridge campus on Sunday evening. It had tugged brutally at his psyche, far more than he could justify by reason alone. Was he abandoning her in a time of dire need? Was he doing the same to Zach? Was it all happening again…

"At last," said Tim with a fatigue-filled groan. "Was wondering if I'd ever reach this place."

He pulled into the reserved spot near the bank's entrance. Even at his destination, he hesitated to step out. His cousin Ernie had supplied a rough blueprint of what to expect: a vault deep inside the bank, housing the bizarre heirlooms his estranged, eccentric uncle so desperately wished his nephew to possess. Tim had demurred at first; even after entertaining the prospect of a truce, he left his cousin's home early Monday morning nearly as embittered as before.

For years, Tim had remained determined to spite the man who—by intention or carelessness—had hurt his father so badly. Yet his reflections on the enigmas at Oak Ridge had begun to chip away at those plans. For all his flaws, Uncle Mitch had a dead-on intuition when it came to solving seemingly insoluble puzzles. If he could manage to swallow his pride and do as his uncle had asked, maybe he could convince Mitch to help Rachel. Then maybe, for once after all those dispiriting years, Tim could respond with a solution instead of mere soothing words and feckless hand-wringing.

"Still wonder if I should be doing this," he muttered, swiftly emerging from his car.

He chided himself as he struggled to unfurl his umbrella, his inner tussles having distracted him from the relentless salvos of gusting rain. As he neared the bank's entrance, he was surprised to see a smartly-dressed manager standing beneath a protective awning, her eyes fixing in anticipation upon his own.

The woman—tall, attractive, early 40s—wore a tannish-gray business suit with a pale green blouse underneath, a necklace with a double ring of smoky topaz, and matching earrings.

"Dr. Shoemaker?" Her broad smile was disarming.

"Tim," he answered, shaking her hand. "Pleasure to meet you. You're Ms. Jemison."

"Tonya. The pleasure's mutual."

"Glad to hear it. I must say that your customer service department is on top of things. Don't know many banks that personally chaperone their new customers on such short notice."

"I'm afraid we can't take credit for that. Your entertainment today is courtesy of one Mitchell Shoemaker."

"I see," said Tim with an icy glance aside.

"Your uncle insisted on a personalized greeting. He reserved and funded everything you'll see today. He's a good friend in any case, used to coach my son's Little League team. I'd have pitched in even without his financial support."

"I suppose even a jackal has his virtues," Tim mumbled.

"What's that?"

"Nothing. So we're off to the vault, no?"

"Our highest security. In fact, you're among a privileged few to be granted access, again at Mitch's request. It's that important to him, and he's been fanatical in his preparations. I think he wanted to impress that upon you at every turn."

"I think Mitch is too impressed with his own cleverness."

Tonya's eyes narrowed.

"Sorry, Tonya. I didn't mean for that to slip out."

"Not a problem, Tim, we're at your service. Your candor needn't be a source of unease."

"It isn't that. I'm not sure how much backstory you've been treated to so far, and I know you must have rehearsed for this encounter, so I'm sorry if I seem less than enthused. Mitch and I haven't exactly been on the best of terms. We have something of a business relationship, and a frosty one at that. Nothing more."

"I understand. We'll try not to overcomplicate the task."

"OK, I'm ready," he said and collapsed his umbrella. Tonya took it and his overcoat to a nearby rack.

"Follow me, and make sure to stay close," she said, navigating her way past the armed guards and caged-off corridors nearby. At an inconspicuous keypad she punched in a code, and guided Tim into the bank's restricted premises.

"Why all the security? It's been six years since the Reckoning, and a solid four since the Great Default."

"There's been no respite for us, I'm afraid. After the Deposit Insurance safeguards were revoked by the Federal Emergency Committee in the Default, our district was among those most devastated by the bank runs and Rio del Fuego Riots in early 2021. Our parent company's H.Q. nearly burned to the ground. The local economy's been stagnant since then, and despite all the public assurances of restored protections for their assets, most people around here aren't buying it."

"Restored protections," Tim mused with a thoughtful glance aside, chuckling grimly. "Now I see. The news bulletins never did get the full story straight, did they? Despite all the happy talk about secured deposits and bond guarantees after the Default, something tells me the Ruling Clans didn't follow through."

"They never planned to," Tonya nodded. "That goes doubly so for the independent banks and credit unions, and to any promises from the central authorities to back up whatever's held in our trust. Pegasus Atlantic is solidly in that group. In theory, we're one poor investment away from another rendezvous with chaos."

"In theory. What about in practice?"

"Though it's been studiously kept off the front pages, fact is the independent banks are the safest bets around—I'd say so whether I wore this badge or not. It's also the reason I've never feared the 'repercussions' that supposedly await bank staff who dare to air such inconvenient truths where they could be overheard."

"How so?"

"Small-fry banks like us took it upon ourselves to do what the Ruling Clans wouldn't: We set up independent regulatory bodies, watchdogs to police our own members. We've erected a more reliable line of defense against disaster, even building up enough trust to muscle away some business from the institutional juggernauts under Clan control."

"That's the very reason the Clans won't touch you, isn't it? They know the patchwork of failsafes in the indie institutions is worlds better than anything they have in their own. So whatever confidence remains in the financial system, it's on your account, and they'd best not tamper with it if they want to continue to free-ride on it."

"You've said it better than I could. Still, with all the media obfuscation and misery around here, people don't know what to believe. I can hardly blame them. Tempers and triggers are constantly on edge. Even a stray rumor could provoke a mini-run, with all the mayhem that vultures along in its wake. I'll admit the armed security may seem like overkill, but I view it as just as another bit of insurance against a repeat of the debacles in 2021."

Tim's mind had drifted while Tonya was still speaking, distracted by a curious spectacle ahead. A rigid sheath of translucent plastic walled off the main lobby and restricted zone from a capacious structure outside. At first glance, it resembled a poorly-sealed, neglected aircraft hangar, its threadbare roof powerless to withstand the assaults of the pounding rain above.

As the two of them approached the plastic barrier, the scene beyond the bank's confines became jarringly visible through a series of hollowed-out nodules where sewed-on hand grips were apparently intended. On a ruined foundation, patrolled by another pair of guards, was an assemblage of blank-staring souls in tattered clothing, lining up at makeshift counters to claim their meager possessions.

"That's Limbo City, isn't it?" asked Tim. "The tent complex—never believed it'd wind up right outside the bank."

"Many of these people had been depositors at local banks before the Reckoning. Mostly working-class. They lost nearly everything when the Deposit Insurance provisions were canceled in 2021. Now they're mostly bartering and taking on odd jobs. We've organized a low-tech account system for their assets since then."

"What kind of system?" Tim asked as they walked.

"You're looking at it."

They soon rounded a corner and entered a lavish corridor. Its contrast with the scene just outside was stark, mixing brisk digital-age functionality with the sumptuous visual pleasures of Belle Époque décor. Elaborate wall carvings and glass sculptures teemed with the curvilinear elegance of art nouveau, complemented by furnishings in shades of soft maroon and violet. A feast of coveted financial data streamed in on high-security computers, strategically placed to blend in with the surroundings.

Tonya and her guest then made their way through a spacious and even more extravagant lobby, building on the *fin-de-siècle* designs of the preceding corridor. The architecture fused an eclectic mix of eras into a rich synthesis, tailored for the eyes of an exclusive audience: Neoclassical themes etched in staid marble, exuberant Corinthian columns, walls festooned with paintings full of lush Pre-Raphaelite imagery.

"I take it that this section was cordoned off for the tender eyes of Mitch and your other VIP customers," said Tim, his spirit still roiled by the scene outside. "And something tells me they weren't so adversely affected by the Great Default."

"Not necessarily; a fair number of our priority customers lost a great deal, too. The last few years have been terrible for nearly everyone but the Ruling Families, and your Uncle Mitch wasn't spared. In fact, his trials inspired him to become one of the founding contributors of the service you just saw outside by Limbo City. We call it the Lifeline. Mitch's generosity and organizing skills have helped keep countless people afloat."

They came to a stop before a tightly sealed metal door bolted on all four edges. Tonya swiped a coded card and then spoke into an intercom mounted beside the metal door. Then she turned intently toward Tim, her imploring eyes intensifying the emotional appeal in her voice.

"I realize it's not my place to intervene in family squabbles, but I wish you'd give your uncle a chance. I don't know the full history of the bad blood between the two of you, but on many occasions Mitch expressed regret for whatever harm he caused your father. He always spoke of you with tremendous pride; he had great hopes for your future. Take it from someone with plenty of her own family issues: You can't carry an arrow in your heart forever, Tim."

"If it's wedged in deep enough, maybe you can," Tim said in a muted, colorless voice. "I don't know if I'll ever forgive Mitch; but I'm here, am I not? At the very least, I'm willing to hear him out, no matter what's inside that vault."

Tonya nodded.

"I understand," she said.

"For now, that's all I can give."

A buzzing sound heralded a slow withdrawal of the bolts surrounding the door. A pair of stony-eyed security officers joined Tonya inside the gate. The three escorted Tim through another pair of locked hallways and into a rounded clearing with a high ceiling and an immense, brick- and steel-encased vault nestled into the back wall. The officers punched in their security codes and, simultaneously turning a pair of keys, spun the vault's handle and yanked back on the door. It opened silently as it turned on pristine hinges, giving way to a subdued hiss of chilly, climate-controlled air.

Tim watched in wary curiosity as Tonya and the officers retrieved a pair of marked-off crates, each topped by a hermetically tight, color-coded plastic lid. The items inside had themselves been bagged and labeled—an amusing bit of overprotection, Tim thought, for articles that had been haphazardly stored and shuttled across the Americas for centuries. The group briefly diverted its attention to the vault's entrance, where another attendant was wheeling in an oversized cart of shelves meticulously annotated on each crossbar.

Tim looked on with a measure of bewilderment as the team stacked the items in designated locations on the cart, painstakingly checking off a list on a notepad resting on a nearby counter. A guard in the group focused his attention on the item furthest to the left, scrutinizing it with exacting attention.

"Item 589, seal unbroken," he called out in the crisp and unwavering syllables of a military inspector. He yielded his position to a second guard, who repeated the action and the declaration at the end, followed by a third who did the same. They moved on to the other items in succession, completing their tasks with regimented precision.

"Why all the fuss?" asked Tim. "Ten minutes from now I'll be tossing all these things in the trunk of my car."

"Because there's something that Mitch wanted you to see before leaving the site," replied Tonya. "It's a GuangPan broadcast, pre-recorded by Mitch himself about his bequest."

"Great," Tim muttered to himself. "First he dumps his white elephant in my lap, then he makes me listen to his loony bombast in a damn bank vault."

"Not in a bank vault—in a conference room upstairs. Your uncle wanted it made clear that he spent many weeks preparing his message to you, to the point of uploading alternate versions depending on the level of foreknowledge you'd received from your cousin or other relatives. In fact, he must have planned the presentation in a sequence, given his precise instructions to our team on how to arrange the articles on the cart."

"Vintage Mitch, all the *i*'s dotted and *t*'s crossed. He's a thorough S.O.B., I'll grant him that."

"Speaking of dotted *i*'s and crossed *t*'s," Tonya said stiffly, handing Tim a well-organized clipboard, "we'll need your signature on these two release forms. You'll then have free rein to transport the items however you wish, though we suggest you make our upstairs conference room your first stop. Room 250C; you can't miss it. Your uncle's GuangPan presentation is pre-loaded onto the projector there, and the premises are all yours for the day. You'll also find a written information packet on the cart, specially prepared by Mitch. It's full of summary documents, explanatory diagrams, and follow-up contacts for which he's already briefed me and Russell Edinger, my assistant. We'll both be around if you have any questions."

MONDAY, MAY 19, 11:58 A.M.
TELECONFERENCE LOUNGE 250C
2ND FLOOR, PEGASUS ATLANTIC BANK

Tim hauled the cart over to a plush sofa situated at an awkward angle near an oak conference table. He put aside his uncle's recording for the moment, carefully unsealing and examining the objects that comprised his surreal inheritance.

"Mitch, what the hell are you getting me into..."

The first few items were reminiscent of small, fine tools lining the shelves of a Swiss clockmaker's workshop, yet with eye-teasing, spiraling geometric forms and a decidedly modern standard of craftsmanship. A quartet of other items, carefully grouped together, resembled parts of a tool-and-die assembly to fashion high-precision devices. There was a series of perforated thin metal wafers alongside oblong, tapered rods used to punch their holes in oddly specific patterns, followed by the baffling objects that Tim had viewed in the picture in his cousin Ernie's wine cellar.

Then there was a curious confection that vaguely resembled a scale model of a cathedral's organ: an intricate network of tiny pipes surrounded by delicate, double-sided panels in brass and bronze. The panels had been crafted to align themselves precisely, their dance choreographed by an unknown force. Tim rubbed his groggy eyes and stepped away from the cart. He helped himself to some warmed apple cider and pastries from a serving tray on the conference table; whether it had been left for him or simply left over, he cared not.

His fatigued mind had begun to rove again. He remembered Pablo's ghostly pallor, the numbers on the bloody wall and the drawings in that notebook within the PIT. Tim had merely glimpsed the last sketch it contained, yet the ghastliness of the imagery had been seared into his mind. Its surreal geometries, nightmarish shapes, and the eyes, above all that monstrous orb in the center, full of rage and some incomprehensible horror—

"Stay on course, Tim," he admonished himself.

He shook his head and returned to the cart, removing several of the more baffling contrivances from its lower levels. He was drawn in particular to a pair of twinned devices that defied straightforward characterization. Boasting exemplary craftsmanship even to contemporary eyes, they both featured a system of interlocking bars and chains that culminated in a pair of rotating drums, each forged by a marriage of fine copper matrices that could unite in a spectacular variety of patterns.

Tim was able to discern a myriad of 2- and 3-dimensional shapes among those patterns-in-waiting, along with eerily evocative pictures that resembled cave paintings, bizarre and often occult-like symbols, and etchings akin to written characters. Some of these inscriptions displayed kinship to a variety of scripts—the Greek and Roman alphabets, Runic carvings, ancient Chinese ideograms—but most were glyphs of an unknown provenance. Tim found himself ineffably unsettled by the strange contraption and whatever messages its creations were conveying. They seemed to embody a lost history, its source and nature hauntingly out of reach.

"What have you been aching to say?" asked Tim, inspecting the devices. "What secrets have you been holding onto, all these years we've been blindly handing you down?"

He lifted his hands about his temples in a gesture of addled consternation, as though to dampen a noise that had begun to ricochet inside from ear to ear. He promptly dragged out another trove of items and gently placed them on the nearby table. Instead of examining them, however, he dimmed the lights and activated the presentation that had been loaded onto the room's projector.

There was no screen to house the image that soon took shape. Rather, the projector's initially faint light manifested in a whirlpool-like swarm of illuminated dots about five feet ahead, coupled with a whooshing sound akin to wind rustling through reeds. The swirl soon expanded in all directions to beget a maze of colored sand grains, which gradually organized themselves into a three-dimensional outdoor scene, in which appeared a face that Tim knew all too well.

"So we meet again, Uncle Mitch," he muttered.

"It's been an eternity, Tim."

The background milieu had been rendered in jarring, hyper-realistic detail. It was dynamic and fluid; as Tim moved about, his uncle's projected visage responded to him, adjusting its perspective and gesticulations in kind. The display had been endowed with a remarkable interactive technology which, despite the pre-recorded presentation, enabled Mitch's digital ghost to respond to its environment, even answer with a few choice phrases to his nephew's cautious tenders.

Tim's uncle was surrounded by a chaotic open-air locale recently buzzing with purposeful activity, apparently a rusty-roofed junkyard warehouse-cum-electronics workshop. He was seated in a souped-up armchair framed by rows of work benches in the background, each covered with assorted gadgetry and draped by overhanging wires. The heirlooms were arranged carefully on a platform to his side, at hand for live illustrations.

Mitch himself was heavy-set, and shambolic in a mismatched suit jacket and slacks that seemed to have been plucked willy-nilly off a table at a garage sale. A green paisley tie hung loosely from his neck, its fat knot partly covering the right-side collar of an equally ugly paisley shirt of an indeterminate red. He was also turning pale in his hands and slightly ashen in his face, a foreshadowing of the heart condition that would soon consign him to a hospital bed. Yet his robust baritone voice boomed with authority when he addressed his nephew, as if uncannily aware of the younger man's presence.

"I know there's plenty unresolved between us, Tim, and I won't indulge the fantasy that I could dispel even a sliver of your anger with my huffing and puffing from afar. But if you're here listening to my soliloquy, then we've at least taken a halting step forward. As your cousin has gracefully done some of the preliminary briefing for me, I'll get right to the point."

Tim abruptly stopped the playback, took a deep breath and exhaled.

"A halting step forward," Tim murmured and hit the play button.

"The heirlooms that I have bequeathed to you have been in our family since our first migrations to the Americas. Some bear Latin inscriptions, for the most part repeated urgings of discretion for reasons largely unknown. It's as though their creators had enjoined us to conceal the existence of these charms and talismans until the outside world... until everyone else had caught up, somewhat, with the technological prowess these things embody.

"That admonition to remain silent has long trickled throughout our family's lore. I suspect some of our kin may have shown them to outsiders, or at least to an inside circle of fellow secret-keepers connected to whoever created them. But if so, there's no record of such an encounter—remarkable considering how far they've traveled and all the hands they've passed through in our family. For my own part, as a precaution, I've opted to honor that original admonition, and swear myself and my associates to secrecy."

"Does that include me?" Tim said, chafing at the overwrought intrigue.

"I'm sad to say that such historical amnesia is a recurring pattern with these artifacts. Their origin amongst our clan has been lost to the mists of time, as has their purpose or the outsize importance that our oral tradition has long attached to them. I've spent more than a decade unraveling this tangled web, even employed some of my best talent from Magister Engineering to help decipher the mystery.

"Any satisfactory answers remain shrouded in a corner of oblivion, but we've assembled enough of the pieces to know that their significance extends far beyond the confines of our own kith and kin. If you succeed where we've fallen short, the earth will tremble at what you find."

Mitch's charisma was infectious. Even his firmest detractors could not help being swayed, if only for a passing moment, by the man's peculiar amalgam of forceful exposition, swagger, and intrigue that fired the imagination of his audience. Listening to him, one heard faint traces of a lisp, the ghost of an old speech impediment thoroughly subdued but never killed; paradoxically, this slight sibilance imparted a scholarly potency to every phrase Mitch uttered.

It was a cursed gift, Tim thought, enabling his uncle to attract and reliably squander venture capital from countless investors even after innumerable false starts and unmitigated disasters. Yet it had also conferred the wholly irrational perseverance that finally bore fruit in the form of Magister Engineering.

"The first marvel to behold," continued the voice from the hovering image, "as I trust you already have, is the workmanship itself. We couldn't resist doing some polishing-up and restoration here and there, and we've updated the protective layers and veneers where needed. But the original designers made these things so hardy that there was little more for us to do. Nearly all of what you see here is a product of their mastery alone."

Tim squinted incredulously at the heirlooms, his bewildered gaze alternating between them and the almost giddily enthusiastic figure on the air screen.

"That's right, Tim: These objects have scaled the world's hills and sailed the seven seas, yet their fabrication and protective coating have largely spared them from corrosion. Likewise with the machining of the gears, the angles, the dimensions... The techniques and precision are 21st-century, yet whatever hands forged these devices, they achieved the same mark hundreds of years ago."

Tim paused the playback to lean over the items before him, more carefully surveying their uncanny design and finishing. He then poised himself against the armrest of a nearby chair and resumed his uncle's pre-recorded musings, still guarded yet less confident that he could so readily dismiss or discount what was coming.

"We've run every archaeological dating scheme from here to the Great Wall of China: archaeomagnetic techniques, thermoluminescence, even those experimental solar neutrino patterning and cosmic ray capture measurements, fresh from the labs in Uppsala and Hyderabad. It's the same old song-and-dance every time. For most of the heirlooms, the date of manufacture converges on one little bite of history's early-modern annals—sometime around the mid-1600s, each item forged by a forgotten workshop somewhere in the European heartland."

"Forgotten, Mitch?" Tim leaned toward the digital ghost before him, bristling anew at his own frustrated attempts to understand. "That would imply that somebody actually knew about these mythical workshops of yours to begin with."

"Ernie has hopefully filled you in already on the apparatus that I tracked down in Brazil. If the good souls at Pegasus Atlantic Bank have honored my request, then the items in your cart should include a series of molds and frames for casting tools and fine metal objects. That's the first clue: These heirlooms, taken together, all add up to a masterpiece that is decidedly unfinished.

"The hands that forged them must have intended to craft new components that would somehow plug into the inventions that we've been tending through the ages. For example, focus in on the bottom and side panels of the contraption that resembles a miniature church organ."

Tim duly paused the playback to inspect the curious creation again, pulling it slightly forward before resuming his uncle's narration. Mitch, pointing and parsing throughout the strange anatomy of the heirlooms, became more and more animated as he spoke.

"The panels' *raison d'être*," he explained, "is to marshal a high-fidelity auditory signal through the pipes. We couldn't pin down the input until one of my assistants spotted tiny slots sawed into the frontispiece. They're precisely the right size to fit razor-thin metal cards with a potpourri of distinct patterns punched and carved out of them.

"It's these etchings, Tim, that guide the gears which move the panels. In turn, it's that typewriter-like device I found in Brazil—the one you would have glimpsed in Ernie's cellar—that fabricates the command cards. The whole system is structured like those old player-pianos with the sheet music running the instrument. But it's vastly more complex, and the sound output itself is a feeder for another piece of machinery that must have been lost across the ages."

"To do what, exactly?" interjected Tim, throwing up his hands in exasperation. "This is all complete speculation on your part."

"As for the tandem device with the chains and spherical drums...When those plates unite to form the barrels, they trace out a logic statement with the symbols and images inscribed on the drums' interior. It essentially amounts to a string of commands with a meaning that we've never deciphered. Take a closer look. Each drum acts as a stencil or a mold, like a master document for a printer or the die used to mint currency.

"You fill the molds with a molten slurry, let it congeal inside, and *presto*. The walls of the drums imprint images for a virtually infinite variety of spheres, each boasting a unique combination of symbols on its surface. The spherical casts, in other words, are a higher-level version of those punch cards I mentioned earlier, with all manner of commands and codes emblazoned by the symbols that surround them. The makers must have conceived them as a programming array to run still another device, like those old Jacquard looms that spun cloth in 19th-century France, only more—"

A discomfiting pause interrupted Mitch's narration. He succumbed to an enfeebling coughing spell and shortness of breath, the pallor of his hands and forehead more pronounced in the sunny setting where he'd made the recording. His lips were fading to an alarming dull gray. A pair of nearby assistants appeared at his side as the tape continued to roll.

Tim used the interlude to look through the remaining heirlooms spread before him. Their enigmas teased with a veiled menace, even more so than the strange glyphs of the drum-and-chain device. An austere triptych in fired clay prefaced the new series, its hinged components folding out to reveal three distinct diagrams, likely inspired by anatomical sketches of the human body. Each depiction was in turn juxtaposed above a disturbing motif, with various limbs and sense organs of the body stretched in wildly exaggerated proportions.

"Creepy," Tim muttered to himself as he meditated on its meaning—another indecipherable code, perhaps, or a warped 17th-century conception of human physiology.

Still more bizarre was the largest object in the collection to that point. It was about the size of a ripe pumpkin—an irregularly-shaped labyrinth of thin metal plates and fine wires. It teemed with twisting loops and planes, all centering on a compact nest of infolding surfaces that endlessly contorted themselves. The structure was braced across its perimeter by an equally peculiar scaffolding: a web of ribbed metallic tubes and hollowed vertical beams with a grayish-purple shading, like a skeleton ripped from a hellish creature not meant for earthly eyes.

Tim half-covered his mouth with a trio of curling fingers, gripped by a nerve-rattling sense of *déjà vu* that sat uneasily with the alien unfamiliarity of the device. There was a concordance with a place in his recent memory, he thought, something about the wiry matrix at the object's core…

"Those drawings," he murmured, struggling to channel his frothing thoughts into a coherent stream. "From Pablo el Diablo, in that folder. That's where I've seen this sort of…Dammit, what was it in those drawings?"

Again Tim focused on the central meshwork, occasionally shuttering his eyes as if to unmoor his imagination to bound about the sinuous, interlocking configurations of the device. His mind dizzied at the motley variety of curving shapes that continuously curled in on one another, coupled with hollowed-out, convex lens-like structures suspended at the tapered ends of what appeared to be horns. The lenses, or whatever they were, sported more engravings of eerie glyphs and geometric symbols, like those carved inside the drums, that continually miniaturized themselves from the periphery to the center.

This baffling theme of infinite scaling and recursive infolding appeared everywhere Tim looked. An unsettling chill crept up the nape of his neck. It was as though the device had been birthed from the fevered imagination of a medieval mystic or alchemist, seeking inspiration in an arcane sacred geometry for his vain struggles to convert base metals into gold.

"My sincerest apologies; the soul may be willing, but the flesh is woefully weak." Tim startled as Mitch's distinctive baritone boomed out again from the projection. Tim looked up just in time to see his uncle's vigilant attendants stepping out of frame as Mitch eagerly resumed his narration. A tray of medication bottles had been left within close reach of his left hand.

"Now, Tim, I'm about to toss a curveball from this air screen. You're probably thinking that all these obscure wonders of Shoemaker yore have clad themselves in the same garments: what we'd today call software or signal processing, then unbeknownst to the wider world and anticipating its technology by centuries. But all that's a mere prelude to the marvels these artisans were patiently incubating in the shadows.

"The next two objects have a different timestamp from the first group. They were made about fifty or sixty years after the other creations, and those metalworkers broke a world of new ground in that time even by their own lofty standards. Drag out that triptych and the weird, snaking wire device with the lenses and horns."

Mitch lapsed into another, mercifully brief bout of labored breathing before enthusiastically picking up his narration.

"Let's first tackle the triptych. So what, you ask, is being rendered on its trio of panels? The answer is that all three are depicting homunculi: the mapping of our body's tissues according to their degree of nerve penetration, albeit in a format you won't find in any textbook. The face, tongue, hands, and feet are all rich with nerve endings, so they get disproportionate representation.

"Now, here's the kicker. The two diagrams on the triptych's left and right sides represent the sensory and motor homunculi of our cerebral cortex—the way the brain maps our body to sense and react to the world outside. True to form, both exhibits are many years ahead of their time, certainly as 'their time' in the late 17th century has been reckoned in the historical annals."

Tim silenced the newly vibrant voice on the air screen, stealing a moment to confirm his uncle's claims. He probed the first two panels intently. A murky pool of half-remembered lessons gradually cleared in his mind.

"He's right," Tim said, more aggravated than relieved by the acknowledgment.

He shifted his attention to the middle panel on the triptych. It was a freakish piece of work, he thought, whatever it was intended to represent. Its upper half was dominated by a mystical-appearing third eye motif, yet rendered with the exacting precision of an anatomical drawing. The bottom half featured a more seemingly familiar depiction of human brain regions, and Tim closely studied its contents. His exertions bore little fruit, however. He grudgingly returned to the message on the air screen.

"Now, Tim, feast your eyes upon the homunculus in the middle of the triptych, because you won't find its peculiar anatomy anywhere else. That's right—it doesn't exist in the human nervous system, at least not in its extant form."

"No wonder it didn't register," Tim muttered, thankful for an explanation for his prior befuddlement.

"We spent months working with a team of neurologists, attempting to grasp the significance of the unknown homunculus. All we know at this point is that it exaggerates circuitry in the brain's parietal and occipital lobes, both involved in visual perception and interpretation of the environment. The homunculus seems to be amplifying select regions within those lobes and within the temporal lobe, associated with memory and emotional experience.

"The weird triple eye imagery at the top symbolizes 'sight beyond sight' as imagined by the devices' creators, yet quite differently from old notions of telepathy or extrasensory perception. There's probably a link to the 'Sacred Sight' that's run in our family, and thus with some of the legends surrounding our stewardship of these objects, but we have no firm answers. This extraordinary power of mind somehow maps to the distorted brain lobes below... toward what aim, we don't yet know, but it must have a connection to that tangle of wires and surfaces alongside the triptych."

Tim paused the playback. He returned to the second object that had captured his attention before, scrutinizing its mysterious construction and gingerly tracking its loops and turns with his fingertips. It was almost impossibly exquisite in its ramifying variety and detail, and he took great care to not disrupt a single aspect of its delicate design.

"And here, Tim, is where all our gumshoeing merely gets us stuck in the mud, because we know even less about this marvelous monster of coils and plates. We've consoled ourselves by using the little we do know to at least christen it with a suitably ridiculous name: the Cereceph."

"The... say-ra-sef?" Tim repeated, sounding out the syllables that had so effortlessly rolled off his uncle's tongue.

"If it resembles anything at all familiar, it's the meandering convolutions of the human cerebrum and other regions of the brain, but peeled and unraveled like a sweater yanked out into yarn. There are literally thousands of tiny solenoid coils inserted all throughout the columns and tubing—a cloak of weak electromagnets, in essence, that are themselves coupled to magnetometers and data relays. The solenoids activate in a coded sequence that we could never crack, and only when the ambient magnetic field oscillates in the range of about 0.2 to 0.8 Gauss; anything stronger and the whole apparatus goes kaput."

Tim gritted his teeth, struggling to extract a meaningful fragment from the cold technical precision of his uncle's last sentence. Again his efforts fell short. He shook his head and returned to Mitch's narration.

"The Cereceph's designers have also equipped this strange beauty with solid-state electronics and a device akin to a computer's motherboard, all shielded from the magnetic fields. But despite its complexity, it's been sturdy enough to handle all our poking, prodding, and floor-dropping on a great many occasions.

"It's also a paragon of energy efficiency. We were able to run it for weeks using one of those nanotech, proton-gradient 'MitoCon' batteries modeled on mitochondria, the tiny motors that run our body's cells. In case you're wondering, the MitoCon is a robust yet decidedly unproven power source, still barely in the beta phase of industrial development."

"Well, aren't you clever," Tim muttered irritably. Mitch by now had poised himself to cradle the edges of the odd device, carefully bracing his legs as he leaned over its left side. A manic look came over him as he swept his twitchy right hand back-and-forth across a tightly-packed triplet of what appeared to be electrical switches.

"In your case, Tim, we upgraded to a Buckyball LFS battery. It's installed in a pocket beneath those horn-like projections, and it has enough juice to run this mechanical wonder for months on end. When you flip this switch on the right as shown here, the battery feeds in a low-amp current that streams through the Cereceph's entanglements.

"This primary current activates the motherboard, most of the solenoid coils, and what appear to be the core functions of the device.

The second switch, in the middle, sends electricity through the remaining electromagnets, while the third—on your left—circles the current through the lenses and pours it into the helmet—"

"The helmet." Tim paused the playback and scowled in consternation. He knelt before the cart, impatiently scanning the lower levels. Earlier, as he had hastily transferred the items from the cart to the oak table in the dimly-lit conference room, he had missed a pair of objects occupying the bottom shelves. Each object had been sealed in a Plexiglas-like protective sheath and labeled with an explicit instruction: "Handle with care." Curious, Tim thought; the other items might as well have borne the same warning.

"What's this for?" Tim asked, grasping a bulging plastic bag that had been placed beside one of the sheathed objects. He rolled back the plastic to expose its contents and saw what looked to be nothing more than a trio of lengthy extension cords or computer coaxial cables, bound together and tightly compacted. He placed the cables and the first of the Plexiglas-covered items on the table next to the Cereceph.

He gently unlatched the seal on the container that shielded the mysterious head covering to which Mitch had referred. The item was ugly, Tim thought. Its frame appeared to have been inspired by the grim, ghostly war helmets of the Anglo-Saxon sea pirates or Vikings who invaded ancient Britain. Its most prominent feature was an inverted bowl that surrounded the top half of the head, joined to draping metal flaps which descended to cover the sides and back of the neck. A phantom-like visor in the front likewise branched downward to shield the cheeks, jaws, and nose of the helmet's wearer.

There were wide incisions at eye level in the mask, yet these were no mere eyeholes. They had been cut with exacting precision, and were lined with a series of what appeared to be tiny, multicolored embedded beads. Sections of the helmet's rear, meanwhile, had apparently been torn off, exposing tangles of naked wires and complex circuitry.

"Some of these wires look new," Tim said to the helmet. His uncle's digital specter soon confirmed those suspicions.

"As you can see, not all of the work is original," said Mitch's image. Tim rolled his eyes at the strangeness of this quasi-conversation with his absent uncle. "The electrical circuits in both the helmet and the Cereceph had frayed over the centuries, so we reconstructed what we could. About six months ago, we finally went live with these two devices, restoring the nexus between them. It's staggering, Tim, even the mere bits and pieces we've managed to deduce thus far.

"That helmet is equipped with a pair of holographic projectors that synthesize a parade of numbers, letters, symbols, and complex images, right before your eyes. The projections take shape from the collective action of those little beads that ring each eye opening. The beads receive an electrical input which they convert into the light signals, and on this front, the designers of this thing even get style points as a bonus. There's a small switch near the right temple, and you can literally flip the projections up and away from your view by toggling it upward, without shutting off the device."

Tim traced a finger about the headpiece to locate the switch, before directing his attention to the back of the helmet, losing himself in awe at the endless intricacy of its fine wires and circuits.

"As for those electrical inputs into the beads," added Mitch's voice from the air screen, "the helmet features thousands of miniature electromagnets in its own right, even tinier than those of the Cereceph. They're tuned to faintly detectable field fluctuations: on the order of about a millionth down to a billionth of a Gauss."

"I really wish you'd explain why these electromagnets are such showstoppers in the first place," remarked Tim, scorning his absent conversation partner as he walked back his own thoughts. "As if you know barely half of what you're pretending to know."

"So in less than fifty years, the artisans behind all this progressed from rudimentary software to neural nets and cortical modeling."

"That seems to be the case, yes," Tim muttered, still studying the helmet's tortuous wiring.

"I've been keeping up with your work in biomed engineering, Tim, so this is a conclusion you'll appreciate: The fabricators of these devices were striving to replicate an ocean of algorithms—those that steer the human brain."

Mitch briefly halted his account once again, this time to temper his excitement; he took several deep breaths before carrying on. He stood awkwardly beside a work bench, his posture bent, and placed the heels of his hands firmly together. He then parted the fingertips of his opposing hands to form an open wedge, as if arrested in the act of applause, using the odd pose to sweep across the length and breadth of the Cereceph. It was a clumsy gesture to highlight some component deep inside the object, but Tim quickly stifled a mocking chuckle as his uncle started back up.

"There's a nest of black boxes buried within the Cereceph," Mitch explained, "embedding its instructions and conveying a... message, is all I can think to call it, a string of symbols that crops up every time we go prying under the hood. The helmet interfaces with this instruction set through a triad of data cables that we've customized to the Cereceph, like so."

Tim repositioned the two objects in a rough spatial imitation of his uncle's on-screen display, grasping the connecting cables and carefully joining the artifacts as they were linked on the air screen. He then stood to their side as Mitch continued his demonstration.

"Together, Tim, these instruments seem to be involved in measuring and recapitulating our mind's synaptic connections, all the biochemical bridges from one nerve cell to another. But these heirlooms of ours aren't satisfied to merely poke around the trees without glimpsing the grand forest that's created. It's clear that, somehow, the helmet and the Cereceph unite to translate this raw data into thoughts, emotions, various flavors of higher-order cognition. These inventors certainly weren't thinking small.

"Beyond that thumbnail sketch, we know next to nothing about precisely what the pairing does or how it pulls it off. Members of my team have donned the headpiece on a few occasions and sifted through an Everest or two of data. But outside of some compromising photos of helmeted techies and a little radio interference here and there, we have nothing to show for it."

"Then what, may I ask, do you expect *me* to discover?" Tim said as he paused the playback. He stewed on the matter, collapsing briefly into an introspective bubble of ambivalent intentions and pretexts for inaction. He soon relented, however; what else could he do but comply with his uncle's appeals? Was he going to stop now? After all he'd just taken in?

Tim took a moment to pantomime and practice the steps that Mitch had illustrated on the air screen, then carefully put on the helmet.

It was an unwieldy contraption by any estimation, clunky and asymmetric throughout; yet its inverted bowl, at least, was adjustable enough to fit snugly upon Tim's pate. Mumbling the remainder of his uncle's instructions to himself, he moved to enable the three successive switches that would awaken the twinned devices from their mutual slumber.

The first two activations were straightforward affairs, yet he balked at throwing the third switch. Despite the dismissals of concern from Mitch's projected specter minutes before, Tim felt a knot in his stomach.

He took a deep breath and, gathering his courage, flipped the third switch.

Nothing happened.

"False alarm," he concluded, relieved and disappointed in equal measure. Perhaps Mitch was right after all. Whatever gears were churning in the Cereceph, they were doing so quietly and invisibly; the helmet, for its part, seemed little more than a passive and clumsy fashion accessory. The holographic projections before its eye holes pulsed with the occasional flicker of red-tinged static, but otherwise displayed nothing of note or concern.

Tim groped for the switch by the right temple and flipped the projections up out of view, as if they had rested on an imaginary thin film that could simply be raised up at a 90-degree angle. He shrugged as he edged back toward the paused air screen. Before resuming his uncle's breathless tidings, however, he fixed his sights back upon the table of strange and wonderful objects, clearing space for the last item of Mitch's collection.

Tim had earlier caught sight of a bulky object on the cart's bottom shelf, beneath the menacing helmet, yet he had ignored it. The item appeared to be little more than a thin, rough-hewn slab lifted from a nearby quarry, yet it had been painstakingly shielded within its own transparent case. Taking it from the shelf, Tim was surprised by how light it was. Even with the added weight of its Plexiglas protector, it was no heavier than a stowable suitcase. Carefully, he turned the case over to inspect its face-down side...

MONDAY, MAY 19, 12:29 P.M.

"Gah!!"

Tim flinched in nauseated horror at the collage of images that flashed before his eyes. The stone tablet had sprung from a more gruesome creative impulse than its fellow travelers across the centuries. It was headed by a grisly rendition of a human skull outfitted with a pair of eternally frightened eyes. The fissured ring of white sclera in each eye had been nearly obliterated by a dilated pupil. A sickening sense of doom shivered through Tim's body as his own eyes returned to scan the engraving beneath the staring skull.

One emblem of the dreadful carvings he recognized instantly: the Four Horsemen of the Apocalypse, riding in lockstep, on a rectangular block attached to the bottom of the slab. Their perspective had been rendered as if nearing the viewer from the background, a symbolism that Tim suspected had been deliberate. To the right of the Horsemen was a confounding motif: a distorted, cat-like eye that peered out in a menacing stare, its lashes upturned and a diffuse streak resembling a lightning bolt filling the pupil.

"What the hell is it with the eyes on this thing?"

As his nerves settled from the initial jolt, Tim surveyed the remainder of the tablet. It was replete with messages in various guises, indecipherable yet somehow proclaiming a desperate urgency to their audience of one. The most consistent motif was neither an image nor an obscure symbol, but a series of declarations in an alphabetical script, filling the center of the object. The writing struck him as a corruption of ancient Greek in some sections, yet he could otherwise deduce nothing of its provenance. Whatever its origin, he thought, it was screaming out for translation.

Then there were the eerie rubrics carved in at varying intervals about the periphery, their effect—and their inscrutability—reminiscent of the cryptic visual narratives lining the ancient walls of a pharaoh's tomb. Most of them mixed renditions of celestial bodies with mythological beasts, like the template of a medieval astrologer issuing divinations for his rapt audience.

The midpoint of the bottom margin was anchored by an emblem, perhaps a signature to the macabre masterpiece. At its core was a sort of labyrinth with regular walls, forged from a single line twisting out counterclockwise from the center. A trio of spindly curves then projected outward from this central grid, each culminating in a stone shaped like a half-oval. The three objects in the periphery had been placed with exacting precision, their connecting lines and geometry evoking the cryptic character of the bent legs in a triskelion symbol.

"Allow me to guess: signs of obligatory dabbling in the occult for a society of gifted 17th-century freaks and...whatever else you all are supposed to be?"

Yet Tim had spoken halfheartedly. The symbol of the tablet's makers, whatever its true significance, could not simply be dismissed as evidence of pre-modern necromancy or occultism. Its design had been too disciplined and rigorous for that, embodying a centuries-old narrative that Tim was ill-equipped to comprehend. He glanced aside and walked away for a moment, as if to physically shake off the pall that was clouding his mind.

"Something more specific—" Tim murmured to himself.

He pivoted gradually back around, his interest ignited by an element to which he'd given only passing attention before, yet which his subconscious had somehow assimilated into an orderly motif. The sequence of several key rubrics, the ones marking the four corners of the stone's main segment...

"They're telling a story," Tim said.

It was the first semblance he could detect of a coherent pattern (or, at least, an attempted one). The top left was dominated by a pedestrian depiction of a night sky, with uninspired renditions of stars and a crescent moon. Strangely, however, the heavens themselves appeared to be twisting and gnarling, to the point of projecting the darkness—in the form of an indistinct limb, like an arm or a wing—about the lower half of the moon.

"Van Gogh's *Starry Night*: the six-year-old's nightmare version," Tim mused in a faintly facetious tone, a halfhearted bid to quell the nauseating dread still stirring inside him.

The imagery on the lower left was badly eroded by contrast, much of it effaced completely by a wedge-shaped gap that had been scored away from the outside border. Tim could discern little more than the scarred ridges of a rocky heap enveloped by an eerie, storm-like expanse—like a violent, flame-filled churning of the air about the pile. Yet somehow, for reasons that escaped him, the design seemed connected to whatever fearful tale had been first intimated by the living, seething night at the top left.

"Now I see. The eyes—they're evolving, aren't they? Across these panels in the corners?"

Tim briefly shifted his frazzled attention back toward the top left, settling upon an inverted arch that he had ignored before. Amidst the swarming darkness in the rubric was a closed, slumbering eye. It was so amateurishly rendered as to be almost childlike, yet the protruding lashes left little doubt regarding what the artist had intended to represent. Its sterner counterpart on the bottom right was half-opened and confined within the enclosures of a ceramic vessel or earthen jug.

"What the hell is that supposed to be?"

Tim was disturbed by the fleeting, elusive whispers of his subconscious as he wrestled with the symbolism of the inscribed scene. His attention was being unduly consumed, he thought, by the oddly-proportioned container housing the awakened eye. The sinuous edges of the vessel undulated in a manner unbecoming a humble product from a potter's kiln, and were flanked by even more bizarrely-shaped, looping handles on each side. These hand-grips, moreover, seemed grotesquely outsized relative to the vessel's core, each of them bulging inexplicably as they branched out.

To the right of the container was a mysterious woman facing forward. She had been portrayed in the hallowed yet impersonal style of medieval saints, devoid of any identity save for a line of redacted letters at the top left, apparently rubbed out by exposure and the callused hands of intervening generations.

"What are you trying to say?" Tim muttered indignantly, feeling as if the makers of this inanimate object were taunting him from across the centuries.

He gradually pried his attention away from the dark enigma, narrowing his sights to focus upon the corner above it on the upper right. It, too, featured a sequence of arcane symbols, which nonetheless seemed a world apart from the others on the periphery. On this panel's right half was a large sphere, perhaps depicting a planet in the archaic style of ancient Greek Ptolemaic texts.

The orb in question was bordered on its immediate left by a disturbing motif: a trio of deadly spears, converging at three angles upon the sphere. On the panel's left half was a vignette: an erupting volcano, its rivers of lava devouring helpless villages in the valley below.

Yet there was something else in that corner…

Too rattled to pay much heed to the helmet still awkwardly strapped to his head, Tim activated the playback again, this time forwarding past the next installments of his uncle's message. Tim eventually halted at a point that seized his restless attention: a frame of Mitch standing beside a converted countertop with the unsealed tablet perched upon its surface, resting at a steep angle against a back wall.

"Now, Tim, for the grand finale, and not the kind that ends on a rousing note, I'm afraid. This tablet has shown some serious wear-and-tear, for reasons I'll get to soon enough; even with all the work we've lavished upon it, we were able to restore only a fraction of the original. But its declarations are very much intact, in all the terrible awe they inspire.

"Though incomplete and as yet largely indecipherable, this slab boasts a wealth of information that may eventually explain why the other artifacts were created. It's significant enough that my team has snapped a series of high-resolution photographs, in visible light as well as under both UV and X-ray imaging. I've duly scanned and included them as data files in the packet that Tonya Jemison will have provided you."

"Tonya's packet?" Tim froze the playback to go back over his conversation earlier that day with the bank director. "Oh, yes—the packet." He hit play on his uncle's message and Mitch returned to the screen.

"I was hopelessly mystified by this slab's strange proclamations and origin," Mitch said in a hurried tone bubbling with fresh intrigue, "up until I took a sabbatical in Oregon two years back. The script at the core of the tablet was a riddle unto itself, but I had a hunch about its source, based on our own family history and all the Runic inscriptions scattered about the other heirlooms.

"So I did some inspired loitering after a lecture by Magdalena Petrovic at the Oregon Institute of Technology; she's *the* authority in North America on anything involving Germanic languages and literature. Sure enough, she confirmed that the script originated from that linguistic family, but from an East Germanic branch that had long since fallen from the tree: the Gothic language. Aside from a few isolated villages and other scattered pockets of speakers, it's been extinct for nearly 1,500 years."

Tim briefly halted the presentation again, indulging another incredulous glance at the writing that scrolled with such vehemence across the middle of the tablet.

"Magdalena came through for us, Tim. She traced the script on that tablet to the same variety used in the *Codex Argenteus*, a manuscript dating all the way back to the 6th century A.D. It's linked to the Ostrogoths, one of the Germanic tribes with a kingdom in Italy after the Fall of Rome. Here's the catch: We'd already performed archaeological dating on the tablet, and it indeed stretches back far earlier than the other heirlooms, with their wellspring in the 1600s.

"But it doesn't hail from the 6th century, either. We narrowed its origin down to around 1050 A.D., give or take 60 years—long after the Gothic script had fallen into disuse. So the sages who forged this tablet were using a defunct language to communicate. If the gadgeteers behind the later artifacts stemmed from the same group, then they must have been employing the Gothic idiom as a kind of cipher, to conceal efforts that they knew were centuries beyond the powers of the rest of the world."

"If all you've said about these mechanical miracles is true," Tim observed dryly, "then we slackers are still playing catch-up today."

"Such a hunch is reinforced by the symbolism centered at the bottom margin. That distinctive grill-like design with the three tube-like outcroppings, spinning outward—Magdalena determined that it was in line with the badges adopted by medieval craftsmen and their guilds. The trio of stones, surrounding and fused to this guild emblem, apparently symbolized a font of knowledge that taught the metalworkers their craft. Unfortunately, there are references to other carvings that seem to have been lost, so we may never fully know what this iconography represents.

"Regardless, the unifying theme is clear: a team of extraordinary artisans originating in the Middle Ages, somehow in possession of a technology that we can barely fathom even today. They labored in the shadows, unknown to history as they passed down whatever fearsome wisdom had empowered them so. We've yet to fully divine their motives, but the tablet tells of something horrific that must lie at the heart of the riddle."

Tim felt his own pulse skip to a heightened tempo as his uncle re-positioned the tablet, tracing a jagged circle with his left index finger to encompass its four corners.

"Now the eyes," Mitch resumed, offering a prescient nod of acknowledgment to his solitary audience. "Yeah, I noticed them too, and they and the assorted grisliness surrounding them have done a right job of haunting those scenes that fly through the darkness whenever I shut my eyes. But they're definitely telling a story, albeit one with a vast trove of missing pages. Take a moment to browse the rubric on the tablet's top left, then follow the corners counterclockwise to the top right. What tale springs forth as you make your way around?"

"You're asking *me?*" Tim demanded scornfully, mocking his uncle's screen apparition in the planned interlude that followed Mitch's question.

"It's a metaphor, Tim, impenetrable save for one unambiguous, desperate shout that issues forth from its etchings. The rubrics are spelling out the notion of night itself awakening, coming alive, watching us with intent from above. Notice how the eye in each picture is sequentially rousing itself as this strange parable marches along. The general arc is implying that the wakening darkness proceeds in stages, somehow catalyzed by specific circumstances or events. The message is reinforced by the cat-like eye with the lightning bolt, on the segment welded to the tablet's bottom margin.

"In some of the medieval Scholastic circles, this was a variant on the All-Seeing Eye of the Heavens: a menacing spirit glancing down with nefarious plans, poised to pounce at an opportune juncture. Unfortunately, we're at a loss as to what specifically is being implied by the scenes in the first three rubrics, and the rough condition of the tablet hasn't done much to help our investigation. The second panel, in the bottom left, has been half-obliterated by mechanical damage, and we haven't done much better gleaning information from the one that follows."

"Get to the point, Mitch," Tim said, his impatience fueled by the oppressive sense of menace steadily overpowering whatever remained of his internal calm. The two panels on the tablet's right side were harassing his psyche for reasons he could not firmly pin down.

"The writing on that third rubric, to the left of the pottery and the mysterious woman, initially consisted of a trio of Greek or Gothic letters that were deliberately chiseled out. The reasons, I suspect, may be best left to the imagination for now. My archaeological team thinks that the third character is a lowercase *eta*, the seventh letter of the Greek alphabet, but otherwise we haven't the faintest idea what those carvings spell out.

"It's on the fourth panel that we finally began to unearth some answers since, for once, we have a more concrete reference to decipher the scenes upon it. Taken together, they relate an allegory and a dire warning, one intended to ripple across the centuries. Both of these tie in closely with the skull imagery at the top and the Four Horsemen at the bottom."

Mitch adjusted his shirt collar and turned his attention to the center of the tablet.

"This interwoven tale is explained by the Gothic text, a miracle in itself since the language has never been fully reconstructed by us benighted outsiders. No doubt this enhanced its appeal as an exclusive *lingua franca*, in the service of whatever underworld hosted the workshops that gave birth to all these marvels.

"Notwithstanding this mantle of secrecy, Magdalena Petrovic was able to marry contextual clues on the tablets with references from other ancient texts in Gothic, as well as in Latin, Greek, and Hebrew. It's consumed the better part of two years, but she worked her magic. It is to her great credit that, despite the magnitude of her discovery, she has agreed to honor my wishes for the moment and hold back from any public pronouncements."

"Which would mean I'm now bound up in this little ring of secrecy, too," Tim said. The thought of this vexed him. "I'm already bottling up enough damn secrets from my weekend at Oak Ridge."

"Here's the abridged version of our findings to date, Tim. The skull at the crest of all these engravings is gazing out in a terror which it can never shake, as if trapped in an unceasing scream. The spears descending upon the orb at the top right, in turn, together constitute an occult symbol representing an apocalypse. The Four Horsemen from Revelations may thus strike you as a natural progression on the same theme, yet if anything, they were included more as a foil than an elaboration.

"The text, you see, warns of a phenomenon distinct from the Armageddon scenarios in the religious scriptures of antiquity. The volcano at the top is the key to this portent, and it's a metaphor deliberately chosen. The depiction is of an extraordinarily violent eruption modeled after Vesuvius, and the way it swallowed up Pompeii and other seats of civilization in the days of ancient Rome. The volcano motif, in fact, embodies the proximate cause of the calamity to its right, symbolized by the spears targeting that orb."

Tim peered in again at the mystifying sequence, his eyes resolving the outlines above the volcano into a plume of smoke, rising as if from a pillar anchored in the crater.

"It's a mushroom cloud, Tim. Our shadowy band of sages was hacking away at this stone in the Dark Ages, a thousand years ago, yet they knew what awaited us. Not only in the mass destruction of Hiroshima itself, but in another shatterer of worlds, one that took shape in the bomb's wake."

"In the bomb's wake?" Tim protested as if offended by the sheer incomprehension newly washing over him. "You're saying something rose up with that mushroom cloud?"

"There's a passage," continued the voice on the playback, "within the Gothic text that lines the central block, scribed in verse as though to highlight its omens for posterity. It reads roughly as follows: 'When the kingdoms transform the smallest speck into the mightiest of fires, His thunder will shake the world.' This excerpt is saying that the atomic bombing, or however those medieval savants conceptualized it, would be the catalyst for a force—that's the only way Magdalena could think to translate it—that would make the world tremble before it.

"To be more specific, this 'force' would be responsible for the apocalypse presaged in the rubrics that crawl along the edges of the tablet. Therein lies the most baffling twist to these omens. There are symbols of an atom bomb and its threat to life on earth, but it's not a nuclear Armageddon that they're auguring here. It's some other horror, ushered into existence when Fat Man and Little Boy exploded over Japan in 1945."

"Maybe it slipped your attention, Mitch," said Tim, pausing the tape and sneering at his uncle's breathless tone, "but if this thing reared its head in 1945, then its apocalypse is about eighty years behind schedule." He indulged an odd sigh of relief, confident that his uncle had sunk his fortune into yet another shipwreck of foolish naïveté. At least, so he told himself.

"Now for the wrap, Tim, because there's a fervid plea buried within that Gothic text. It's the only remaining hint about precisely why these artifacts have been among us for generations, and what's now incumbent upon us as we explore them further. The script exhorts us with a single, unequivocal recommendation: 'Seek at once the counsel of the Ancient Others, or all shall succumb to the web He weaves.'

"We know even less about these 'Ancient Others' than we do regarding this monstrosity that rose on the plumes of the mushroom clouds over Japan, but my hunch is that these devices were created with them in mind. Somehow, they're supposed to forge a link with the knowledge of these Ancient Others, whoever they are, which we'll need to fathom this apocalyptic force, whoever 'He' is. That, Tim, is where I need you to seize the reins."

"I knew it would come to this," lamented Tim, bracing himself with a drawn-out sigh.

"As extraordinary as our ancestral collection may be, it's nothing more than a scattered remnant of the legacy left by the artisans at the source of all this; and we need the rest of it to understand where to go from here. I've spent years reconstructing our clan's records and recollections, which were lost amidst the various calamities they endured since the first Schumacher left Germany for the forests of Pennsylvania.

"Much of the family was wiped out in the Philadelphia yellow fever epidemic of 1762, the one that Dr. Benjamin Rush wrote all his historic monographs about. Then the smallpox epidemic right in the middle of the American Revolution, fires and wars after that."

"I'm well aware of all the family lore," Tim remarked impatiently. "Hurry up and make your pitch."

"The bottom line is that too many of our kinfolk were cut down before they could transcribe their wisdom about this peculiar inheritance, which has made our task all the more difficult. But we've determined that the other pieces aren't in the US, or Canada or even Brazil. They're in a long-forgotten sanctum of lost treasures, somewhere back in the Old Country. It's up to you to find them."

This time, Tim powered down the recording with no intention of paying it a revisit, grimacing upon finally removing the helmet that he had all but ignored amidst his prior engrossment.

"You should have quit while you were ahead, Mitch," he said, his voice bubbling with contempt. "I can hold my nose to waste a morning on your ludicrous windmill-tilting, but I'm not heading halfway across the world on your behalf." Despite his tone, Tim was bothered by the sense that his scorn was forced or even contrived altogether. As if a part of him had manufactured it to attack his own whispering fears and bafflements from recent days, far more than an estranged uncle who was standing in as the purported target.

He prepared to disconnect the power source still feeding the helmet, but as he reached for the switch, Tim froze in his tracks. The diverted projections by the eyeholes of the headpiece were subtly flashing, inundated with streams of text swarming across. A quiet hum came from the Cereceph, along with a modest but regular pulsation of the tubes housing its electromagnets. Most curiously, there seemed to be a slight flicker in the air about the device, like the wavy, air-looping refraction above a heat vent.

Tim cautiously took up the helmet and slipped it back on, restoring the projections to their rightful place before his eyes. A dizzying sensation intruded as his mind staggered before an onrush of messages mysteriously coursing across the two screens. A gnawing ache began to harass the back of his head and the space above his ears, aggravated with each relentless tick of the clock.

The pain gradually lessened, however, and his conscious faculties themselves followed suit, falling into numbed senselessness. He leaned back in his chair, his eyelids narrowing without fully closing, and gave in to the slithering, sinister dreams that had begun dragging away his troubled inner being.

MONDAY, MAY 19, 1:35 P.M.

"Tim! Tim! Oh my God. Russ, where are you? I need you in here now!"

Tonya Jemison had been coming to check on Tim when she heard a clatter from within the conference room. Bursting into the room, she found her erstwhile client's unconscious nephew reclining lifelessly with his back to the near wall.

"I'm here, ma'am. How can I help?" the young man panted as he entered the chamber, his ponytail and sideburns oddly complementing his crisply tailored professional attire.

"Russ, switch off that thing on the table, whatever Tim had running and... call an ambulance on the landline phone behind you, immediately!"

He acted at once, yanking back on the toggle that linked the helmet to the Cereceph. But before Russ could call for help, Tim's eyes flashed open, startling both the young man and his supervisor cradling her shell-shocked guest by the wall.

"Tim!" exclaimed Tonya. He was looking toward her but not at her; his stare seemed eerily vacant and undirected. "Are you all right?"

"Tonya?!" he called out with a terrified shudder, like a child fleeing a monster in a dream.

"Can you tell me what happened?" she asked, trying to sound calm for her own sake and to reassure the jittery, now fully awakened man seated before her. She was further discomfited by his strangely mime-like motions and insistent gaze toward the ceiling.

"Tim?" she added after an unresponsive pause.

"I can't see you," Tim answered, a sickly pallor marching across his cheeks and forehead. "I can't see anything."

Russ froze. Tonya was about to tell him again to call an ambulance when Tim grabbed her arm.

"Wait, wait... that's odd, the light's streaming back in, opening up from the center." Tim angled back toward her, blinking his eyes and tracing out her face with a tremulous finger, before calming himself and gazing back out at the breadth of his surroundings. His surveys of the outside lasted barely a moment; he quickly buried his head in his hands, as if to rub away a throbbing headache that was pulsing in.

"Can I... get you an aspirin, Tim, or maybe a Lysalgium tablet?"

"No, it's—it's not pain as much as... Actually, could I borrow a pen? And a—a notepad?"

"A what?"

"Just something to draw with."

"Uh... OK."

She nodded toward Russ, who took the hint and disappeared from the room, quickly returning with the requested *accoutrements*.

"Here you are, Dr. Shoemaker," offered the young man in a sharp, punctuated drawl.

Tim snatched the materials from his hand. He sketched with manic determination, mesmerizing his two onlookers with a mystifying image that coalesced with impetuous vigor. Finally, after mere minutes of the exhausting burst, he set down the pad and rested his head back against the wall, his eyes still adjusting to the cascade of sights once again pouring in.

"That's... quite a piece of work you've brought to life there," Tonya said with a nervous smile. "A good sign, I presume. So you can see again?"

"That's funny," Tim replied, gently shaking his head. "Everything's still a fog; I could hardly make out what I was drawing."

"You couldn't see your own—"

"I could have sworn... it was like a scene out of a violent dream, but nothing I can recall in the slightest. It's as though the images were all transferred straight to my wrist, onto the drawing pad."

"Tim, are you sure we shouldn't take you to the hospital for a quick work-up? You just had transient bilateral vision loss. I worked as a paramedic in my past life before the Reckoning, and if there's one red flag I still remember, it's that a shroud descending before your eyes is always trouble, even more so when it traps both of them in the dark."

"But you'd have to have monkey wrenches in a few other gears to be in real danger from it," Tim said, gently rebuffing her. "Mitch had fleeting episodes of vision loss when he was chain-smoking through those 100-hour weeks, and the docs wound up scraping inch-long plaques from the carotid arteries in his neck. I've never been one to follow in his footsteps, least of all his self-destructive habits. I had some nasty bouts of epilepsy as a kid; maybe it's nothing more than that, like a return visit for old time's sake."

"A return of your childhood epilepsy?" Tonya asked him incredulously. As she scanned Tim's nervous eyes, she could tell he was as doubtful as she was about the throwaway explanation.

"Tonya, I honestly... I don't know what just hit me. All I can remember is fiddling around with the helmet and that contortion of surfaces next to it... then I was laid up next to the door. But I'm fine now."

He brushed his head against the wall and glanced up at an oblique angle, cautiously pushing off and lifting himself to his feet. Russ and Tonya instinctively rushed to his flanks, bracing him as he rose. He alternately shuttered and opened his eyes with exaggerated might, peering into the pupils of his two impromptu caretakers. A look of relieved familiarity was materializing in his face, his vision again revealing a world that had vanished for a brief yet frightening interlude. He dug a cell phone from his pocket and grimaced as he gazed down at the keypad. He motioned to Tonya for help.

"I can't quite make out the keys," he said, groping for a pull-down screen on the phone. "Will you lend me a hand? My cousin in Tennessee loaded a contact number onto this phone last night. It's the direct line to the suite in St. Basil's Hospital, where Mitch is convalescing. It's listed simply as 'Mitch St. Basil' on the quick-dial list."

Tonya hesitated, then took the phone and scrolled to the number, tapping it twice to initiate the call.

"Cell phone towers these days," she mused, shaking her head at a failed attempt. She repeated the process, this time nodding as she heard the line begin to ring. She handed Tim the phone and he eagerly pressed it to his ear, sliding back down the wall to sit on the floor. Even now he felt the impulse to hang up rather than speak to his uncle. However, his hand had been forced; he had too many questions, too many unresolved doubts. He stared ahead and saw the conference room blurred through his still-glazed eyes; yet the details were clearer than they had been a minute ago.

"St. Basil Recovery Suite," chirped a voice on the other end, "how may I help you?"

"May I please speak with—" Tim nearly bit his tongue. His resolve had quickly shambled into a bracing indecision, a volley of imagined conversations assaulting his confidence and sapping his will.

"I... Sorry," he said. "I'm afraid I dialed the wrong number."

He cut the connection and hung his head, dispirited.

"Just not the right time," he said feebly, stealing a fleeting glance at the cell phone before tucking it away. His eyes had corrected themselves enough that he could make out the text on the phone's display.

"Is there anything else we can do to help?" asked Tonya.

"No," he replied with a sigh. "I should be getting home. My eyesight's back, and it'll take me a decent spell to pack away whatever Mitch has dumped in my lap."

"Sure," she said, locking her hands behind her waist. "We'll have a team ready to help you bundle it all up for transport. Just give us the word."

"Will do."

"Oh, and one more thing."

Tonya handed him a dark gray, hologram-emblazoned rectangular card.

"A SnapBio card?" Tim said curiously. "Haven't seen many of those lately. I... I've not been much for official elbow-rubbing of late. Who does it belong to?"

"Someone that I suspect you'll come to know quite well," said Tonya, motioning for Tim to hand over the cell phone still on the floor by his side. "I noticed that your phone was the OmniHua model from two years ago, so this old digital business card should be a splendid match."

She tapped through a series of menus on Tim's mobile device to convert its display into a darkened surface, permeated only by the infrequent pulses of a diamond-shaped pattern that burst and splintered outward from the center. With Russ's help, she then methodically scanned the holographic card across the surface until a cache of data flashed on-screen. She handed the phone back over to her guest.

"Ezra... Gordon?" Tim asked, still straining to make out the letters on the display.

"Both Mitch and I count him as a longtime friend," Tonya explained. "He also happens to be your uncle's probate attorney at the Marsden-Kyle law firm downtown. It was Ezra who spearheaded the genealogical research on the inheritance that brought you out here, and his reports are contained in the information packet I alluded to earlier. Your uncle has in effect recruited him to be the general manager of his efforts to track down and demystify your family artifacts."

"My sympathies for the poor sap," Tim remarked with a crusty laugh, yet only partly in jest.

"His full contact information is now on your OmniHua phone," she continued. "Mitch excepted, Ezra knows more than anyone else about the secret history surrounding these heirlooms. Given your... ongoing issues with your uncle, I think you may find it advantageous to direct whatever questions you may have to Ezra."

"I appreciate that," said Tim, and he meant it.

As Tonya and Russ left the conference room, Tim gradually got to his feet, pushing off again from the knees and bracing his back against the wall. Before he had fully arisen, however, he caught sight of the sketchpad that had consumed his attention minutes before. He knelt down in a stable upright stance, finally having regained command of his twitchy joints and muscles, and picked up the pad. He held it at normal reading distance, but his vision was not yet fully restored. He steadily brought the pad closer to him until he could see what his hand had so feverishly committed to paper.

The drawing featured a surreal milieu, demarcated on four sides as if to signify a confined space, and with perspective lines sprinting toward an unclear vanishing point far in the distance. There were arching curves and discursive markings strewn about; they did not condense into anything recognizable, though a smattering of vertical columns hinted at poles or pillars supporting a roof. The outlines of a gateway were evident in the foreground, as were the space-filling contours of a stony floor.

There was something more distinctive at the center of the scene, however. A frenzied series of lines and shadows abounded near the nascent roof, with unfamiliar shapes—like smoky tendrils—pushing out from the midpoint. Arcs of circles seemed to ramify outward and somehow melt into the periphery, stemming from a source that Tim strained to make out. He gradually teased out the patterns, and as he resolved the central focus, a visceral horror welled up inside him. The image was anchored by a nightmarish eye teeming with fury—the same one Tim had seen depicted by another's hand just two days before.

Wenn die Liebe eines Herzens,
die ein andres Herz erfühlt,
Könnt' dies' Band für ewig sein,
eine Kraft, die ewig blüht.
Was dann, wenn eines dieser Herzen
nicht mehr auf der Erde schlägt?
In welcher Welt schlägt diese Liebe,
welche Luft und Kraft sie trägt?

Chapter Six

Thunderings of an Immortal Echo

Organ of a lost priesthood

TUESDAY, MAY 20, 6:11 A.M.
FACULTY AND STAFF PARKING STRUCTURE
DEPARTMENT OF ENGINEERING, SCIENCE DRIVE
DALTON UNIVERSITY, DURHAM, NORTH CAROLINA

Tim sat quietly in his car, his shoulders slumped and his eyes glazed from fatigue and indecision. It was early and the parking lot of the engineering department was nearly empty. Tim's pre-dawn meetings with Rachel at Oak Ridge, coupled with the chilling tide of events that soon followed, had wrenched his daily routine out of kilter.

Each night when he lay down he tried to clear his mind, but memories of his recent disorientations crept into his consciousness despite his efforts, starving him of sleep and sanity. Yet those eyes of his also twinkled with a glint of defiance. It was a reflex he had cultivated over the years—if not quite smiling in the face of adversity, then at least snarling, cursing, talking back to it, then kneading that resolve into the raw material that fuels insights and solutions. Even when any solution seemed a world away—even for a riddle that hardly seemed anchored in this world at all.

Pablo's bloody walls and cryptic statements haunted Tim's thoughts. There was the stone slab... that God-awful tablet. How could its creators have dreamt up such horrid imagery? What were they trying to say? Then there was Tim's own unwitting voyage into a foggy sea of altered states: the strange spell in the bank conference room, his blackout and the blindness that followed, the ensuing sketch, the font of rage at its center... What did it all mean?

He switched on the car radio and lay back in his seat, hiding in the cold anonymity of the lonesome morning.

"It's been a banner day for the Brothers Crassus," piped up the voice on the radio, *"with dual milestones in the worlds of politics and finance. Gerald Crassus scored an overwhelming victory in the North Carolina by-elections called in the wake of the still-unsolved disappearance of Governor Shirley Rossdale. He garnered an 83% vote share on the heels of the most extravagant gubernatorial campaign in history, with over two hundred million dollars spent. The new governor-elect has nevertheless expressed regret at falling short of his 95 percent target, warning of 'untoward consequences' for his staff if shortcomings are not addressed.*

"Governor-elect Crassus wasted little time advancing his agenda. A press release from his minister of policy implementation has confirmed that another branch of the Carolina State University system will be closed for good, followed by steep hikes in fees for primary, secondary, and postsecondary tuition elsewhere. Crassus supporters and fellow Clan members were likewise cheered by the governor-elect's apparent nod to a closed-door auction for public assets as the first act of his new term in the statehouse."

"Just perfect," mumbled Tim, lightly rapping the radio console to dispel a cloud of static. "So now they'll be squeezing even more blood from us stones."

"On condition of anonymity," added the voice from the speakers, *"a Crassus staffer has specified that state parks, museums, libraries, and health and pension funds would all be up for bidding. When reached by an undercover reporter for confirmation at his sprawling vacation complex in the Virgin Islands, the governor-elect refused to substantiate the rumors. Nevertheless, he decried would-be critics of the auction as 'work-shy spongers whose free ride would be over.'*

"Meanwhile, Mark Crassus announced his takeover of Appalachian Consolidated Utilities today in a celebratory news conference and

ribbon-cutting ceremony in Asheville. With the acquisition, he solidifies his control of power and water supplies throughout the Southeast sector. Unfortunately, customers in the Carolinas and Tennessee likely won't be celebrating with him, as their rates are expected to rise by 40 percent over the next three months. This is Jenna Silver with Carolina News Unfiltered, and remember, while the call number changes by the hour, we'll never leave your dial."

"Can't take any more of this," Tim said and, switching off the newscast, exited the car.

The dewy air lapped at his cheeks and forehead below the brim of his hat as he walked to the building. The stairs to the third floor were an unusually exhausting trudge; his briefcase felt as if it were loaded with lead shot instead of papers. Winded from the climb, he dropped the case unceremoniously at the foot of an entrance in the ensuing hallway. The doorway's arch was headed by a familiar sign in multicolored block lettering, with depictions of barking Doberman pinschers and Rottweilers poking through the open letters:

WELCOME TO THE DOGHOUSE

Tim's first instinct upon turning the key was to stumble into his office and collapse in a heap. Instead, he shuffled over to a dimmed corner and leaned uncomfortably against a laboratory bench, too drained to walk yet too agitated to sleep. He marshaled another burst of defiance to collect his thoughts, attempting to make sense of recent events. But the gears weren't turning; best to give it a rest for now, he thought. For a second he thought he might be able to fall asleep where he stood, like a horse in its stall, only a noise jarred him to attention: someone was rattling the lock of the door to the lab. Tim drew back further into the shadows and waited.

A tall woman—just slightly below Tim's height—made her way inside, doffing a cream-colored beret and scarf to reveal dark, curly hair and an alert, observant demeanor that brimmed with gregarious energy.

"Shelley? Shelley Delorea?" he called as he stepped into the light.

"Good morning to you too, Tim," she answered, amused at his gawking astonishment. "Didn't remember you being such an early birdie when I was here, though I'd hazard to guess you're equally surprised to see me."

"I thought you were still in Europe. We all got the news in early May that you were planning a return trip but... didn't know you'd follow up so quickly, I guess. Not that I'm in any way disappointed, of course."

"Ah," she shrugged, sporting a wry grin. "Warming up that mind-reading superpower of mine, and it's telling me... you didn't get my email. I came in from Dublin last night. I knew Zach was having his red-letter day on Thursday and didn't want to call. I was surprised when I didn't hear back from you, but presumed you'd seen it and just forgot to reply. Figured you were too busy with whatever medical marvels you've been dreaming up of late, and you do look kind of, well—"

"Like hell?"

"I was going to say 'worn-down' but 'like hell' works just as well. You do look it, really—worn-down, I mean."

"I've had a rather... atypical weekend. Yesterday wasn't much easier, so I'm officially in arrears with my in-box."

"Well, it was short notice from my end, too. It all started when I made a few friends and car pool buddies a couple weeks ago, at a conference with the other postdoctoral fellows."

"Carpooling?" Tim raised an eyebrow. "Ah, let me guess—you changed out a few oil filters after the conference posters were taken down. You're your father's daughter, Shel. Your poor brothers."

"Not my fault I got the grease monkey gene and they didn't. Anyhow, I built up some goodwill, mostly resulting in a few free drinks and karaoke tickets to embarrass myself with. But then on Wednesday, one of the other postdocs called me with a free ticket. The poor guy had to forgo his week off back home to fill in for a colleague. It was a slow period for me anyway, so I took the ticket off his hands."

"Can't say he's missing much. The Triantarchs have been hard at work screwing up whatever's left of this country since you left in January."

"So tell me about this wild and, apparently, not-so-wonderful weekend you just emerged from."

"Actually, I'm more interested in hearing about your adventures with Dr. Kearney, 'plying the rapids' in those lipid rafts of his."

"I didn't just hear that," she replied, sardonically pantomiming a hands-covering-the-ears gesture. "Dr. Kearney regularly tortures us with hammed-up metaphors about his strange obsession with those kooky compartments in human cell membranes; figures it makes his zany genius a bit more approachable. And that cheesy 'plying the rapids' gag, ugh—you can't imagine how many times he's launched a talk with it."

"I think he's earned the right to occasional cheesiness. So how's his cancer research going? Last I heard, he was working on that library of human cell surface compartments he'd started up."

"He's about halfway through it. It's impressive. The idea is to help his nanotech Frankenstein monsters pick out the patterns unique to cancer cells as opposed to bystanders. His next step is a 'tensegrity catalog' to help guide his drug-delivery nanobots to..."

She smacked her lips and blinked in ironic amusement at the spectacle before her. Tim's eyes were closed, his muscles slack and his chin bobbing rhythmically off his chest; he'd fallen asleep on his feet. At first she grinned, but her amusement turned to genuine concern—the expression on Tim's face was unsettling.

"Hey!" She gently tapped his shoulder. "Hey, Professor, I'm supposed to be the one with jet lag here!"

"Huh? Ah..." Tim flailed as he awoke, anchoring his dizzied body at a corner of the bench. He rubbed his eyes vigorously, as much to hide his mortification as to jar himself awake.

"Tim, what's going on? Should I be worried about you?"

"Worrying about everyone is my job, Shel. I'm all right. I just fired up on a few too many cylinders this weekend. A couple cans of Hellfire Cola, a nap this afternoon, and I'll be a shiny new Shoemaker all over again."

"Uh-huh, and in the meantime, the classic Shoemaker brush-off technique. It doesn't work with me, Tim; I've mastered the art. Another trick I've mastered is face-reading whenever my students doze off in class. There's a little story that they all tell in the creases around the eyes, the twitches of the arms, the bobs of the head; and yours was shouting out far more than mere fatigue. More like agony. And fear."

He cast his gaze aside, discomfited by her choice of words: *fear*.

"Tim, come on. Quit with the strong, silent act and tell me what's going on."

"Shel, it's—" He kept his eyes down, wary of the unspoken messages they would divulge. "I can barely make heads or tails of it all myself. It began with a calling to help an old friend in Tennessee, then some dusted-off family history, puzzles that are still screwing with my mind, and then—a rude re-opening of some doors to the past. The kinds I've been maneuvering for years to shutter and lock away."

For a moment she observed him silently, slowly prodding him to face her eye-to-eye.

"I see," she eventually said. She was about to say something further, but stopped herself, opting instead for a change of subject. "If I remember correctly from the last time we talked, don't you have a sabbatical in the offing right about…oh, now?"

"It's official in a few days. Classes wrapped up last week, and our research grant still has a couple years of hang time before I run out of juice and have to re-apply." He glanced aside with a wistful look. "To think that going into last Thursday I was counting on an uneventful little interlude to bliss out."

"Why don't you call it a day, then?"

"I'm not home-free yet; slated for a guest lecture at Watts Forest U. on Friday, plus all the housekeeping and form-filling before I skip town. Lots of loose ends—"

"Which you're in no shape to be tying up right now, Tim." She frowned worriedly as she read his face again.

"Look," she said, "I can't pry you away from this self-imposed misery trip you're on. But if you insist on sticking around here, the Kaffee & Klatsch will be opening its doors in about fifteen minutes. I think I'll treat myself to a mocha or two; have to stay awake long enough to grab a few things here, then catch up again with Lionel back home before he clocks in for the a.m. shift. How about I sneak out a latte or mocha for you, too?"

"I appreciate the offer, but I think I'm gonna take a rain check. In fact, now that you mention it, I might as well quit pretending I can hold back a river with my fingers in the dam. I'll do a little protocol-proofing in my office for as long as my eyelids hold up, then let nature take its course, even if my catnap means a date between my forehead and the clutter on my desk."

"All right. But I *am* checking on you before I hit the road, no negotiations or sweet-talking to the contrary."

"Glad to know I have a guardian angel so close by," he said, smiling as he retreated toward a recessed chamber set off from the hubbub of efforts outside.

"Neither wings nor miracles from this angel, Tim; only a watchful eye that can spot trouble from time to time. Whatever rumbled through your world this weekend, just be careful, OK?"

He nodded before pulling the door to, settling into a swivel chair behind his desk. He shut his eyes in brief introspection, ill at ease from Shelley's uncanny insights—or, at least, from the telltale signs of distress that he was unable to conceal. He set his mind to practical engagements, inspecting some pie charts and rummaging through a stack of unexamined data.

Inevitably, however, the exertions of the weekend just past began to take their toll, siphoning his focus away from his work. The Morphean embrace crept ever closer, finally surmounting his resistance, and Tim fell asleep at his desk.

TUESDAY, MAY 20, 7:26 A.M.
LABORATORY OF DR. TIMOTHY SHOEMAKER
DEPARTMENT OF ENGINEERING, 3RD FLOOR

"No . . . oh no, here we go again."

As he spoke, Tim bolted awake, gasping and queasy, with a sickly familiar feeling—the same one that had assaulted him the previous day at Pegasus Atlantic Bank. His mind had traversed a sprawling, vivid, and engrossing terrain, vastly out of proportion to a mere half-hour snooze. Yet once again, the specifics of his dreams were fuzzy. His right arm was trembling while evanescent fragments of an event-filled narrative tiptoed through his mind, their deeper nature frustratingly out of reach. He grabbed a pencil and the nearest piece of scrap paper, then sketched out a collage of images.

He worked feverishly, confounded by the suffocating urge that was impelling him—as though the images were flash-flooding directly out of his hand itself. After several minutes of frenzied penciling, he willed himself to stop and look at what he'd drawn. Thematically, as best he could tell, the drawing followed on the heels of its predecessor from the bank conference room, yet with greater detail and a slightly offset vantage point. To make sure, he took the prior sketch from his briefcase and compared the two drawings side-by-side.

"God, this is getting worse," he said.

He initially covered the grotesquerie filling the center space of the sketch, focusing instead on its surreal setting. The backgrounds and structure of the two renditions overlapped in their essentials: the same yawning chamber, with the same vaulted ceiling underpinned by pillars scattered throughout its expanse. But the roof was populated by its own strangely ordered streaks and etchings this time, whispering darkly of a symbolism that had yet to emerge.

The supporting columns of the mysterious chamber, in turn, had become distressingly elaborate. They boasted incipient forms and features that stirred awake the less savory enclaves of Tim's memory—the ones sealed away with childhood fears of goblins and monsters plying the night-swept streets. The pillars in question were ringed by a patchwork of shapes, mostly diamonds and ovals as best Tim could discern, recessed at regular intervals into their towering stone frames. Each of these polygonal adornments was itself bounded by a cocoon of curling flaps, sharp and twisting like a fan's blades.

"It's like these pillars are... like they're telling a story," Tim mused, still scanning the contours of the baffling support structures.

Interspersed between the columns' basic shapes and geometric paragons, as glimpsed before, was a more disturbing array of ornaments. Some resembled the leaves of plants or the stalks of mushrooms; others conjured up the bones, fangs, wings, and fins of a menagerie of creatures, both terrestrial and aquatic. Still others hinted meekly at limbs and the organs of higher animals, but otherwise seemed the province of beasts from an eldritch realm, unseen and unknown.

The background of the scene, dissolving into a featureless infinity within the first drawing, this time housed a pair of large urns that poured out a smoky fire. They were flanked by an incomplete grid on each side, like the scaffolding for a pyramid that would one day kiss the sky above. Tim struggled to extract a more concretely meaningful fragment from the suggestive assemblage of objects, but, failing in the effort, he finally braced himself to take in the front and center of the image.

"It's only a damn drawing, Tim; keep it together," he commanded himself.

The foreground of his latest depiction was mostly blank, aside from a striking feature that had yet to fully materialize. It had the form and dimensions of a disembodied, outstretched hand, gesturing through the early tracings of an arched entrance toward a focus in the center.

Staring out from that spot was the hideous eye again, surrounded by wisps of smoke and tendrils as on the first sketch, but this time coupled to a cloak of infolding surfaces that further prodded Tim's already frayed nerves. There was an even more bewildering addition to the core of the drawing—a rod or tower rising vertically from the ground near the center, positioned as if to be emerging out of the mass of curling surfaces. "What the hell are you supposed to be?" Tim muttered, newly disturbed by the inscrutable images emerging from his own hand.

The central tower was anchoring a pair of hemispheric basins flanking and slightly behind the fearsome eye, each one held in place by rigid chains suspended from the spire. The tower's apex climbed toward the roof which, curiously, was topped with a terse, scratchy margin note. This last addition stood ostensibly separate from the dream scene itself, yet was it some sort of commentary?

Tim squinted as he held up the page to scrutinize the annotation. As he finished, an audible gasp escaped from his gaping mouth. The scribbling at the top edge would have been meaningless to most any observer, nondescript and innocuous. However, Tim knew better, as he had seen it produced by another's hand—only a few days ago in Tennessee.

7:43 A.M.

"It was right there, Rachel, screaming out from my own drawing. Why won't you listen to me?!"

"Tim, please, calm down. I can barely make out what you're saying. What exactly did you see?"

"The number, that... string of Devil's digits."

"From El Diablo," Rachel said. "On the helter-skelter wall?"

"Four-six-one-one-seven, exactly as I'd seen it in Pablo's blood. It was flush at the top of my sketch. I couldn't recall anything from the dream; I was at a loss to even keep track of the lines that my own hand was scarring into the paper. But somehow it was there."

"I don't see why that should come as such a shock, Tim. You said it yourself: You saw those motifs in Pablo's patient room, and in his own drawings within the PIT treatment chamber. It must have filtered into your dream."

"No. It wasn't like that. Look more closely at the scan I just sent you. I lifted more than a few aspects straight from Pablo's drawings: those weird animal limbs and tissues, the outcropping membranes, and the monstrosity with that eye in the center, from which the other features emanate."

"All of which you saw with your own eyes, when you were badly shaken and dog-tired, and on a day when Pablo had all but bled himself dry to convey his latest frightscapes to the world. The circumstances were shocking even to us, and we've been bottled inside this prison for three months. It's natural that those images would have branded themselves inside your mind."

"But why this fever of urgency to draw them repeatedly?" Tim demanded, realizing how shaky his voice had become. "Why after two little catnaps on two separate days that totaled no more than an hour or two, tops? And why would I be perseverating over them in the first place, not only the number itself but...pouring out the same motifs from whatever hellish inspiration possessed the minds of those veterans? They came from Pablo's visions, in a context that has meaning only to him and the others. Why am I trapped in that same nightmare?"

For a moment there was silence on the line. When Rachel finally spoke, Tim could hear he'd gotten to her—she was afraid.

"The beast in your drawings..." she said softly, "it wasn't what Pablo was dreaming up."

"Not true. I got a mere glimpse of his sketches in the PIT, but that horror evolving upon them—it was seared into my head. I can still see it with every freeze-frame that flashes by when I shut my eyes, when...I get a glimpse of whatever's bubbling up in my bad-dreams-in-the-making. I may have only the barest outline in my own drawings, but it's the same entity, I swear it."

"That's not what I mean, Tim; it's the context. Pablo and the other soldiers rendered that figure in isolation, like a portrait, and even then only in fragmented sections parceled about their various sketches. But for you, the entity inhabits part of a scene."

"You're saying that your team hasn't encountered this before? From any of the vets?"

"The scan from your picture is a bit blurry, but from what I can see, you've embedded that thing in a chamber with several compartments. It's as if you've fused the markers of this beast with—I don't know, some other stream from your own subconscious. There's no such milieu in the sketches by the veterans."

"Fine, but step back from the content of this illustrated dream dump itself, and consider the overall chain of events leading up to it. Can't you see? It's identical."

"I think you're stretching your conclusions."

"No," Tim shot back insistently, "I most certainly am not. Both you and Alan Simms described how Pablo had been compelled to produce the drawings, as if gripped by an outside force, and that the elements and setting of the picture evolved each time. You could fit me into the same thumbnail sketch."

"In some ways, perhaps."

"In every way that matters! For God's sake, Rachel, I was *blind* when I drew the first image at the bank. Yet the urge to give light to that scene, one that I could scarcely visualize in my own mind, was as powerful as anything I've felt in years. I couldn't refuse the impulse; it's as though its content was gushing straight out of my hand onto the sketchpad. And then like Pablo, I was driven—no, *possessed*—to flesh out that scene again before a full day had even passed."

"I understand your concerns."

"Do you?" he asked skeptically, like a whistleblower frustrated at pleas going ignored. "We're getting nowhere with this eggshell-walking, Rachel. I'll admit it, I was guilty of the same with you over the weekend."

"Well, that's progress," she said.

"I had my reasons, as surely as you do now. When you first called me Thursday, I heard the desperation in your voice, and I didn't want to inadvertently press your buttons. But we have to be unreservedly open with each other from now on. These hushed tones and things left unsaid are going to strangle any prospect we have to understand whatever miasma has infected us both."

"Infected us both," she repeated slowly. "That's what I've been trying to tell you, Tim. The contagion has spread only among those who received the retinal implant and were linked thereafter by the Simitalis—nobody but the soldiers in the trial. As awful as this ordeal has been for us, neither I nor anyone else on staff has been infected by their madness."

"A madness caused by an infectious agent that continues to elude you."

"True, but all the same, this disease among the vets has been our unwanted companion for months. You were here for a weekend. How could it have seized you and not a single one of us?"

"Were any of you seized into the belly of Pablo's beast? The one that stalks his dreams, and now mine as well? Damn it, Rachel, just tell me how much time I have before I lose my mind, too."

Rachel sighed.

"Tim, nothing I say is going to... It's all too fresh in your psyche right now, and I couldn't begin to explain these common elements or even why I know what I'm telling you. But whatever bond you now share with the vets in my trial, it's not the sickness that's devoured their minds. I've been breathing its caustic air for months, and those vapors have stung awake every fiber of my senses. I'd know this condition from the crudest of outlines, and you simply don't have it."

Tim bit his lip and put a lid on his anger. Turning this discussion into an argument would get him nowhere.

"If you insist," he said after a pause. "Where does that leave us, then?"

"We're calling in the cavalry tomorrow at midnight. Alan has arranged a simultaneous videoconference with experts across both oceans. Mostly neurologists and other clinicians who've altogether seen about twenty thousand outlandish cases in their own practices."

Rachel's words came to him through a haze of distraction; he'd been staring at his drawings. He packed them away for the moment, putting them in a folder so he could focus on what his colleague was telling him.

"As a bonus," Rachel added, "much of the case experience among the outside experts has also been gained in the context of military clinics and battlefield medicine. From their prior observations, they'll have the know-how to scour all the grimy edges and corners of our soldiers' case histories, and they might be able to shine a light on significant elements that we've missed in-house. It's the closest we could come to fusing the whole neuropsychiatric community into a single mind."

"A global Q&A?" Tim wondered. "I thought your team leaders have all but signed a blood oath to stay hush-hush about any events surrounding the Simitalis."

"That's unfortunately still the case," admitted Rachel, "so there'll be some redaction of the backstory pertaining to how, exactly, we went about retraining Pablo's visual cortex once the retinal implant was in."

"Then I fear that Dr. Simms is merely engaging in a pricey version of institutional wheel-spinning. He must know that, too, especially in light of those altered files I found over the weekend. I'm more convinced than ever that the Simitalis must have some connection to the soldiers' madness."

"The mutations in its operational coding, the ones that you uncovered on Saturday morning... they may have been a canary in the coal mine, yes. Still, I couldn't disagree with you more: I am ever more doubtful that the Simitalis itself bears any link to whatever is behind the veterans' psychoses."

"Whoa, Rachel, hold on—you think what's happening to the soldiers has no relation to our findings last weekend? Did I really just hear that? That's almost a complete one-eighty from your position when we said goodbye on Sunday. Then you were a believer, now you're not—what brought about your sudden change of faith?"

"Not a good time for this now, Tim."

"Not a good time for *what*? Rachel, please, whatever you're holding back, we can't afford to—"

"I have to go."

"Now? What..." Tim's incredulous protest was met only by the cold click of a terminated call. "Ah, no, God d—"

He stopped barely an inch short of an indignant slam of the phone on his desk, straining to divert his anger toward a more productive outlet. He opted to dial Rachel once more. He was in his rights to demand an explanation, he told himself. How dare she do this now, after all he'd done for all of them in Tennessee? After how deeply he'd been drawn in?

But he throttled the impulse at the last moment, hanging up the phone and pushing it decisively aside. Rachel had her reasons, and they weren't for him to know. At least not yet.

TUESDAY, MAY 20, 8:24 A.M.
TORCHLIGHT CAFÉ, DALTON UNIVERSITY MEDICAL CENTER

Tim clasped the cuffs of his coat and tucked his hands inside the sleeves, sheltering himself from the dewy drear of the windy morning. The surrounding chill was hardly overbearing, yet his senses had been rubbed raw, and the fog was an unpleasant reminder of his recent sojourn in Tennessee.

He felt exhausted, as if it were already the end of the day and not still early morning. Shelley had confronted him again as he left his office. His latest dream sketch was still fresh in his mind—and, apparently, that it was had showed to her in his frightened eyes. Her words rattled him as he played them back to himself.

"Something's gotten into you, Tim. I don't know what it is, but it's there. I can tell just looking at you—it's deep inside you, and it's eating you alive."

He turned a corner to slip into an unoccupied wedge of a revolving door, and pushed his way into the welcoming lobby of a softly lit café. It was adorned to conjure up the warm elegance of a Christmastime boulevard in 1950s-era Paris. Posters of Edith Piaf and broadsheets for New Wave film premieres lined the burnt oaken walls, while holly branches, mistletoe, and faux mulberries bedecked the low ceilings between dining rooms. Its ambience provided an illusory haven from the miseries and fears that the Reckoning had visited on the world outside. Tim had been a regular for some time. Until recently, at least.

He made his way to the deli counter. The chef, a broad-shouldered man with smiling brown eyes, saw Tim coming. His face lit up as he reached over the counter, extending his hand to Tim. The men shook.

"Good Heavens, I was beginning to wonder if I'd ever see that fedora again; the prodigal professor has returned home! How have you been, Dr. Shoemaker?"

"Percy Laurence. How long has it been, old friend?"

"Almost a year, *mon ami*, which is one year too long."

"That's not entirely my fault, you know. You had an internship across the pond, I recall."

Percy nodded.

"At a bed-and-breakfast in France. Nine months of bliss for an aspiring pastry chef from bayou country in Louisiana."

"A soupçon of Cajun French in the heart of Provence, eh?"

Tim shot a glance toward the café's entrance as he spoke, prompted by the flicker of a scene that had registered and faded in the corner of his eye mere moments ago. He watched the revolving door as a couple squeezed out of its tight space into the café. They headed left toward the coffee bar, holding hands and laughing at their awkward navigation through the moving wedge. The music coming from the ceiling speakers was quaintly appropriate: Piaf's "L'Hymne de l'Amour," followed by

Oscar Straus and other balladeers of mid-century French cinema, their paeans to romantic love as ambiguous as they were passionate.

"I never lost the accent even after I'd mastered the proper dialect of those parts," said Percy, following a mischievous grin with a feigned whisper. "A good thing, 'cause it was a real hit with the locals."

"As were your kitchen creations, I trust."

"I learned from the best. Those Provençal pastries are so beautiful, I tell you, sometimes I think it's a crying shame to see them disappear into a diner's belly."

"I know what you mean. Back in college, I dumped a year's worth of night-job wages into an extended backpacking trip through Provence, and it was worth every penny. I often wonder why I didn't simply throw down and disappear there. The foods, the wines, the music, the romance..."

"Now you're making me nostalgic, Doc. I fell in love there myself, with the place and—"

"It wouldn't have been Provence if there weren't an 'and,'" Tim said, smiling.

"A shame she couldn't follow me back here, but the aroma and the *amour* of that piece of heaven on earth—they certainly did, and they've kicked up that long-buried poetic instinct inside me ever since."

"Poetic, huh? Didn't you have an R&B album in the works? Around the time you left town here?"

"Still working on it. Seems like every day brings new fodder for the lyrics. In this line of work, it's like being a fly on the wall; I've overheard enough personal drama in these years to fill volumes. Hell, what couples *don't* say to each other often shouts louder than what they *do*. The fine print's always in the silences."

As Percy finished his thoughts, Tim's attention rapidly trailed off, distracted again to the background. He heard something familiar amid the medley of voices and noises about him, indistinct yet strangely suggestive.

"So, will it be a Shoemaker Special?" Percy asked, teasing Tim back into the conversation. "Let's see if I still have it right: tomato and Swiss surrounded by alfalfa sprouts, topped with spicy tahini on rye, with a dash of Dijon mustard and a sprinkle of balsamic vinegar on the other slice."

"Sometimes you scare me, my friend. What a memory."

"Only for food, Doc. I hear the recipe once, it's my specialty forever. A handy knack that is, too, for my new assignment on the weekends."

"Oh, that's right—a sous-chef gig at that French place downtown."

"That 'French place,'" answered Percy in mock reproof, "is none other than the Chez Roland, the finest realization of Gallic cuisine this side of the Blue Ridge Mountains. It survived the Reckoning almost unscathed, and the executive chef and board of directors have agreed to donate a percentage of their prepared meals to the local food banks. So it's a joy for head and heart alike. They even funded my airfare out to Provence and back, figured it would be a decent investment to add some authenticity to my already-dazzling repertoire."

Tim darted his gaze around the lobby again, puzzling over a barely-witnessed scene behind him that again snatched the fleeting attention of his half-conscious mind. He turned back to Percy, maneuvering awkwardly to resume their exchange.

"Congratulations!" he exclaimed with a belated smile, embarrassed by his own oafish attempt to feign spontaneity. "So…while we're on the topic of your personal repertoire, what's this Percy's Palate Pleaser I've been hearing so much about?"

"Just a little touch of Cajun-Creole kitchen magic. Slice up some okra and avocados, dice up a tomato, then steep 'em for ten minutes in a cayenne pepper and Worcestershire marinade. Place on a bed of rice, wrap it all up nice and tight *et voilà, mon copain*: one bite soft, the next bite crunchy, some bayou spice and always nice."

"You know better than to dangle such a masterpiece before me," Tim chuckled. "I *must* have a sample."

"*Mais bien sûr, mon ami.* Give me a few minutes. I gotta run the morning drill with my team, but I'll be right back to fix up a full sandwich and salad for you."

"Sure thing."

Tim made his way to the right, claiming a seat at the first free spot he could find. As he took off his hat and coat, his focus was briefly diverted: The table behind him was jammed with folders and charts spilling out from an opened briefcase whose owner had momentarily departed the scene. Tim shrugged while removing the small backpack he was wearing, taking from it his latest dream sketch and laying it on the empty table before him. He held it up for further perusal, still rattled by its contents and the baffling number that inexplicably hovered over the eerie scene below.

His attention was broken, however, by the clicking of high heels and by an intoxicating, vaguely familiar perfume that wafted toward his table. The woman approaching behind him was talking hurriedly on a cell phone; with his head still fogged from lack of sleep, he couldn't quite follow what she was saying. And yet, he felt his stomach tighten. The woman was behind him now, and her voice went from vaguely to outright familiar.

His gut tightened further as she settled in at the table behind him, still talking on the phone. With her back now inches from his own, her voice was unmistakable. *Priscilla.*

Tim sat motionless with a frozen stare, gaming his chances of a clean escape if he simply rose from his chair and left the café immediately.

The lilting French torch songs in the background were distorting into a cacophony as his mind raced. The film posters on the wall ahead, announcing the premieres of a lovelorn tale by Ophüls or a noir by Malle, taunted him mercilessly, as if the dramas of their scenes were calling out directly to him. His heart bounded remorselessly as her voice drew closer still, his stomach finally knotting into a tight fist when he heard what she said next.

"Sorry, Dr. Hauser, it's been a while and I'm not too well-acquainted with this part of town. I can't trust my address tracker after the fiasco in Charleston last week, so can you give me the street number again? I'll ask one of the locals... OK, got it, just a second."

Tim set his dream sketch close to the table's edge and pretended to study it. Message clear, he thought: *This local is busy, so choose someone else.*

"Excuse me, sir, but do you have a minute?"

He ignored her, keeping his eyes on the sketch. A cold sweat marched across his forehead as his heartbeat ticked up to a gallop.

"I'm looking for an urgent care clinic downtown," she continued, gently tapping his shoulder with her hand. "It's somewhere around Ninth Street, but I always get lost in that corridor and wanted to check the route—"

Tim heard a quiver in her voice, now, and could feel it: Her heart's racing, too. He could practically hear its thumping as she tried to get a better view of him; he could almost hear her thinking. Something familiar here... his attire, his suppressed mannerisms, the hat lying on the table, an accessory to whatever task he had become engrossed in... That fedora. She'd seen it before—*many times.*

"Ms. Lehto?" Tim heard the voice from the cell phone call out anxiously, and could tell from the hard, echoey sound of it that the woman, now focused on him, had unthinkingly laid her phone on the papers covering her table. *"Ms. Lehto, are you still there? Is everything all right?"*

Tim felt her attention briefly shift away from him as she picked up the phone.

"Dr. Hauser," she said breathlessly. "I'm sorry, something just came up. Out of nowhere. I'll have to call you back."

Tim by now had pivoted his chair halfway towards the aisle. Could he still beat a stealthy escape? No chance, he thought, and sighed. Both of them hesitated—he could feel her ambivalence—for another protracted moment before turning to face each other directly. Their eyes locked instantly.

The woman was striking—tall, graceful, with dark-brown hair that fell to her waist. Her eyes were cat-green and piercing, her movements suffused with an effortless elegance. Yet there was something haunted in her expression.

Tim's focus wandered to a necklace that draped down to rest upon her gray-blue business suit.

"Tim," she said.

"Priscilla."

"I... I never expected to run into you again, Tim, not like this."

He nodded and they stared at each other, neither of them sure what to say next.

After an unnerving interval, Priscilla finally broke the silence.

"I got a position with Nan Dao Pharmaceuticals this past March," she said. Tim could detect the quiver in her voice, even more pronounced than before. "Sales mostly, as well as on-site support. Since I've only begun revving up with the company, my team preferred that I cut my teeth in one of their branch offices where we had mutual contacts. It's been three years since I was back in North Carolina, but this was the best they could do."

"That's great. Congratulations," Tim said, fighting the urge to say more—to say so many things.

"How, uh... how is everything with your team? Still humming along?"

"Shelley's back in town from Ireland. Zach nailed his thesis defense last week. He was stellar as always. Unfortunately, seems all the forces of the world are lining up against him."

Why had he told her about Zach? He hadn't meant to.

"The burglary," she acknowledged, surprising him. "I knew about it. I'd stayed plugged in to the grapevine for a while after... Anyway, I'm sad to hear that Zach's still feeling its repercussions."

"He's not the only one feeling them," Tim replied, and again he wondered why in the world he'd said this. The double meaning in his response was painfully evident to them both.

"Tim, there's—there's something I've been aching to tell you for a while. Of course, I've naturally been denied the occasion to tell it to you in person."

Like a reflex, Tim shot a glance at the aisle. He imagined himself getting up and leaving through the kitchen. *What are you, fifteen?* he admonished himself.

"I know you told me never to blame myself for what happened. And I didn't... for the most part. But I mourned all the same in the... the aftermath, because I was still at the wretched heart of it all. And I wanted you to know—"

"Priscilla, please," Tim interrupted. "I can appreciate how dearly you must want to unburden yourself of... all this. Good God, I'd do the same if I could. But I can't. Even three years on, it's all too raw."

Priscilla swallowed and Tim saw she was choking back tears. She nodded to him, turning around and quietly, quickly gathering up her belongings.

Then she turned back to him and tapped his shoulder. Again their eyes locked. For a moment he wondered if she was going to say anything at all.

"Just take care of yourself, Tim," she finally said and stood up. Upon reaching the revolving door, she glanced back at him and simply stood at the entrance to the café, as if entertaining the idea of rushing back into his arms. She quickly stifled the impulse, however. She was crying as she turned away from him and left the premises.

Tim picked up his fedora and held it at a distance, examining it for a moment as if newly repulsed by its very sight, before putting it back on the table and slumping over his drawing. Only a friendly hand on his right shoulder jostled him out of his crestfallen trance. Percy gently placed two neatly-fastened paper bags before him on the table.

"Guess you've got another tale for your blues album," Tim said, barely managing a sidelong glance in the chef's direction.

"I figured you'd want your sandwiches to go," Percy answered calmly. "The tab's on me."

"Percy, you don't have to—"

"Yes, I absolutely must. Save the polite refusals for another day, Doc. I made these sandwiches for a friend, not a customer. Anyone with eyes can tell you've been sailing through some stormy waters this morning."

Tim nodded.

"Okay. Thanks, Percy."

"You got it, Doc. And for what it's worth, I hope you'll pardon me for giving you a side-order of unsolicited advice: Don't pretend you can soldier on with a stiff upper lip—not after a jolt to the soul like that. Call it a day and grab some shut-eye."

"Under normal circumstances, I'd head home and do just that," Tim said shakily, "but it's when my eyes shut that the worst always seems to come."

Wohin gehen Taten, Fakten,

wenn sie schon vergangen sind?

Sind sie nur Nebel eines Raumes,

weit entfernt und taub und blind?

Gibt es wo anders Raum und Zeit,

worin sie sich sehr tief verstecken,

Warten nur auf uns're Augen,

dass sie den Raum ganz neu entdecken?

Chapter Seven

The Siren Call of the Mystic Chords

Susan's gift

At home again. In my own bed. So dog-tired. Eyelids sagging. But shouldn't sleep. No, not now. Not after all that. Dreams before were bad enough. This one, it'll take me to a place I shouldn't . . . Can't fight it. Drifting away. No, stay awake! Don't go there! Not back to . . .

SOME MORNING IN EARLY 2022
SOME MOUNTAIN ROAD IN NORTHERN SOUTH AMERICA

"Treks through exotic Andean mountain passes, sight-seeing in rain forests, day trips to the temples at Machu Picchu. Oh, and a plush hotel on a mountain peak in Suriname to top it off. Heavens, Tim, if I'd known you were getting such perks, I'd have signed up years ago to be your traveling companion."

"I assure you, Susie, this is unusual. The sightseeing on these conference trips is usually limited to a grand tour of the lobby at some cut-rate airport motel. Then again, I don't usually have a traveling partner. Your presence on this particular whirl-through-the-jungle prompted some special arrangements—also something about a wedding anniversary, mysteriously marked on my calendar for tomorrow morning."

"I was afraid you'd forgotten, especially since we've made a habit thus far of getting stuck in the east end of nowhere on a regular basis."

"Actually, my dear, milling about aimlessly in various nooks of nowhere is all part of the package this time around. Suriname was one of the havens for refugees fleeing the US after the Reckoning. It's been largely insulated from the riots and civil war wracking many of the other postcard paradises. So its tourism industry has been busy growing a new infrastructure, though not enough to mar its unsullied landscapes with needless additions like maps or other tourists."

"Intimations of spontaneity? Do my ears deceive me? I was afraid the past few years had sapped away your last reserves."

"Very funny. Just wait and see. This trip will be oozing surprises. The road we're traveling now is barely seven years old, and beyond the halfway point, it's a playground full of detours begging to be explored. We'll have the whole day to get deliciously lost before hitting the summit at Tafelberg tonight."

"Sounds wonderful, Dr. Shoemaker."

"It is; it will be. Enough, I'd say, to rekindle some of those sweet post-teenage memories of cluelessly stumbling about exotic places together."

"Again, am I truly hearing right? Could it be? Professor Shoemaker's romantic alter ego, bravely slipping his chains at last. Maybe even you with all your medical wizardry and marvels are figuring it out: No medicine cures what happiness cannot."

"Ah, the thoughts of Gabriel Garcia Marquez, flowing like honey from your lips."

"So you've been studying up, I see?"

"Figured I had to try. I'm eagerly anticipating the next helping of wisdom from Proust. It's usually served up in the evening, right?"

"Marcel Proust, my dear professor, is a friend for all hours in all seasons. That I *know* you know already."

"I've read through and ruthlessly marked up that copy of *In Search of Lost Time* you gave me. Believe me, Suzie-Q, I've learned my lesson; whatever eye-openers about memory or time or love are awaiting my tender ears tonight, I'll be ready. And it makes you all the more irresistible."

"Not nearly as irresistible as the prankster who would dream up an odyssey like this. I'd hug and kiss you if not for the part about swerving around every 100 meters on a narrow road."

"Not to worry; we'll have opportunities aplenty tonight. The hotel's restaurant houses a secret veranda by a small lake on the premises, which I've duly scouted out to determine exactly when to sneak over there."

"Can't wait. You know, I think this is the first time, at least since Mark and Chloe left the nest, that we have a chance to fire up some of that puppy love we used to know so well..."

"OK, we're about fifteen minutes from the welcome center and the high-altitude souvenir shop, next to those scenic overpasses that the tour guide was raving about. So let's get the camera geared up and—Susan? Honey? What is it?"

"It's, uh... nothing important."

"Hon, I can recognize that look even out of the corner of my eye. The bridge of your nose—it tweaks itself ever so slightly when something's gnawing at you."

"Why'd it have to be a *souvenir* shop? Anything else and it all would've faded conveniently away again, out of sight and blessedly out of mind."

"I don't know what to say when you speak in riddles like that, Susie. Please, talk straight to me."

"At the art museum yesterday, Tim. After we'd split up briefly, right by the souvenir shop, I wandered into the European Masters section with all the Surrealists. Miró, Ernst, and then—there was a Dalí painting. It reminded me of—"

"This again. Oh, dear God, I shouldn't have asked."

"I can't click my heels together and wish it away. I know what you're about to say, all those sessions we did together—"

"The therapy, yes, and the tears, and the days and weeks airing all those dirty linens to figure out... to rediscover what we'd lost. That's why we're here, Susie, doing what you've always helped your patients to do. 'Reconciling our wandering spirits'—it's how you yourself described it. Now it's us, here, on this trip."

"And based on your foot's fervent claim on the brake pedal just now, I take it we're not wandering anymore. At least not on that mountain path."

"In light of what we both know is coming, I'd say a five-minute pit stop in this citrus grove might be well-advised. Susie, after all those errant forays and... all my short-sighted foul-ups, we overcame all of it to find each other again. We don't have to go back there. Wasn't that the message being drummed into us throughout all those therapy sessions?"

"A message you've never absorbed in full."

"Wha—what was that?"

"I'm saying it's not that simple, Tim. And I shouldn't have to say it."

"I'll never defend what I did, and I doubt I'll ever forgive myself for it. But when the Reckoning marched in three years ago, torching everything in its path—I was hardly the only one to lose my way."

"Right, I know. As I did soon after, with Jeff. Don't say you weren't going to say it."

"Actually, no, I wasn't. I meant what I said, Susan; you won't hear any mealy-mouthed excuses from me. I'm not going to defend what I did and I wasn't trying to defend it. When I spoke of 'losing my way,' I was making a specific reference—to the vertigo of a lost self, dizzy and dazed ever since our world began spinning out of control. Not only that but... but blind, too. In all the worst ways."

"Dance, dance, dance. What are you trying to say, Tim?"

"I'm not 'trying' to say anything. I am saying that I let myself stray outside and succumb to all those storms, when I should have gripped you ever tighter as the one solid anchor I had through all of it. I'm also saying... a few other things that both of us have heard before, thanks to... She was a real steady hand, that one. Dr. Miles."

"Was thinking earlier, I wish a bit of Dr. Miles' spirit could have joined us here. She was more than a steady hand, she was a guiding light."

"That guiding light is in what she urged us to do, Susie. She doesn't have to be here for us to follow it. This is *our* mountain today."

"But that future needs a solid foundation, one in which we can both place our trust. And for that, we need to finally dig up and face what wrenched us apart. Because you didn't merely stray with 'someone else,' Tim; you strayed with *her*. If she'd been a stranger without that connection, to me and to you, maybe it would have been less arduous, but of all the people in this world—"

"Susie, please, don't go there again."

"Why Priscilla? Why her of all people? The memory of what followed—it's not a relic that I can just stash away within some padlocked crypt in my mind."

"Would it stay there even if you could? Nothing more than an unplanned stroll to a Surrealist exhibit yesterday, a continent away from home, and all that history comes rippling right back to shore."

"It happens, Tim. It's not something you can help. There are cues that trigger our deepest memories, and they can well up no matter what barriers we think we've put in place to fence them off. They're all wrapped together in a package; loosen one strand, and the contents spill out in their entirety."

"'Sometimes the heart betrays the ramparts that our minds have spent years to reinforce.' That's from one of your articles. Your advice column."

"Does that make what I said any less valid?"

"Of course not. I just... You're right, we can't control the cues that trigger memories."

"I suppose I should be flattered that you read my work so closely—"

"It's yours, Susie. Of course I read it closely."

"But you apparently skipped the footnotes. That sentiment was all Dr. Miles—my own teacher before she became our therapist—even the quote itself. That's how she likes to close out her lessons, by summing up key points with something lyrical. Besides, I'm not saying all this to soothe your ears with psych-speak."

"I never said you were. And I wasn't mocking you, Susan. Your words resonated with me, too, because I've never managed to construct a rampart strong enough to wall away the memory of what happened. I wish I'd never gone to surprise you at that event—if I hadn't gone there, you wouldn't have introduced her to me."

"There's no magic pill to un-remember those things, Tim."

"A lesson I wish you'd learn to heed yourself."

"Does that remark come with a decoder ring?"

"I wish; I could use one myself. I'm not hiding anything, Susie, in fact I'm stumbling all over myself to unearth and confront what's left of that buried past. That doesn't mean that I—we—have to be imprisoned by it."

"But that past is still a prison for me; it's why the Dalí painting brought everything rushing back."

"Then let me free you from it, Susie. Feel my hands right now, the way they're holding yours, the two of us alone here in this patch with nothing—nothing in our past—to keep us apart again. Let this be the key that opens your cell."

"I wish it were that easy, Tim. There's a key to this prison, but I never gave it to you. I've been trapped inside because I could never tell you..."

"Tell me? Tell me what?"

"I was uncomfortable bringing us to Dr. Miles at first, given the master-and-apprentice relationship we'd shared before. But no one else I know can connect the way she does, and it's because of the principle she lives by: To heal their rifts, couples have to be forthright about more than the immediate causes."

"Susie, I was paying attention to what she said, too—about having to 'illuminate all those dusty, shadow-strewn corners' in our deepest being. From the first day we were together. Isn't that what we were doing?"

"No, Tim, we weren't. We never were, because there's another part to it that you didn't hear. Dr. Miles was talking about the days long before we'd met. What she called 'the pillars of our souls'—the contingent events and insights that forge our very identities. We're rarely forthright about those things even with ourselves. That's a whole lot harder to open up about, and I could never do it."

"Regarding what, Susie?"

"The necklace that Priscilla always wore, that you saw when I first introduced you to her at the art exhibition outside my colloquium in Minneapolis."

"What about it?"

"It bound all three of us from the start, in a way that I could never bring myself to express to you. It was a present that I gave to her, originally as sort of a gag gift, when we were roommates at Venetus College."

"That came from you? Then you weren't the only one who kept mum about that. It was also... I mean that I didn't hear it from... Dammit, how the hell can I talk about this?"

"It's OK, Tim. I don't need to know what Priscilla did or didn't say when she was with you, because on this point I already know. Even now, that necklace carries a secret that binds us like sisters, and she never would have divulged it. For the same reasons I never could."

"What are you saying?"

"It was during my junior year. Priscilla had switched her major for the third time to art history, and she was in full bohemian mode. I'd returned to school following Thanksgiving, and by then she'd converted her side of the room into a loft, with Dalí's clocks and Surrealist themes all over our ceiling."

"Dalí? So that's where this began?"

"Naturally, I wasn't too keen on her little stab at spontaneous interior décor. My psych exams were on the horizon and I didn't need the distractions, but this was Priscilla after all, so I made my peace with her latest bout of inspired quixoticism. After a while. I even began manifesting signs of co-ed Stockholm Syndrome, coming to embrace her quirky artistic weirdness in my own way. One weekend, I joined her for some shopping in New York City, winding up on one of those quaint art colony side streets in the SoHo district."

"A side street...That's where you're headed with this, aren't you? Like the one where we first met? In Shanghai, during your senior semester abroad—that concealed alleyway with all the local artists hawking their wares on blankets, where we got into that silly bidding war over that—"

"Impossibly cute little jade obelisk with the calligraphy carved on the faces, the one you and I both had to have. You, the one-and-only Timothy Isaac Shoemaker, hotshot grad student already making his mark in the big bad world outside. There you were, quibbling with a poor little college girl over some kitschy street-side art to send home to Mom and Dad. But then strangely sweet enough to warm my freezing cheeks with hands you'd been secretly rubbing over the hot coals in a nearby barrel."

"And also annoyed enough to go ahead and buy you the damn thing so we could stop quarreling. And then brash enough to ask for the phone number of this gorgeous young lassie whom I'd just spent the past five minutes bickering with."

"You always did have a paradoxical charm to you."

"Yet you never did send that jade piece home to your folks, did you, Susie? It was all wrapped up in that cache of memory you were clinging onto."

"I never told you in all our subsequent meetings in Shanghai, but I'd already spent many a lonely evening street-shopping in those old side alleys, dancing under the Chinese paper lanterns. For a reason."

"Priscilla?"

"She'd quit school before the first day of our senior year, having embarked on that half-decade of glorified global vagabondage, as she later called it. I was having a rough go of it then in Shanghai—my Dad getting the pink slip, my sister bouncing between the hospital and rehab. And me, with a Luce Scholarship that had rewarded me with a lonely stay at a near-deserted campus in east China. One of those times when you really need some girl talk therapy with your best friend."

"Who'd all but vanished off the grid by then."

"Hence those little alleys with all the local artists—they were my sole consolation, Tim. One in particular reminded me of places in SoHo that Priscilla and I used to knock around in."

"Where you first spotted that necklace."

"It all went back to that weekend after Thanksgiving in our dorm. Priscilla had been absorbed in her Surrealists kick—their paintings were all around us, peppering every square inch of her improvised loft. It was vintage Priscilla, and I couldn't resist the urge to tease her about it. Then on that jaunt out to SoHo, I'd stumbled across a blanket with a line of handcrafted items by a talented apprentice jeweler from Milan. He was leaving for Italy in a few days, so he was offering his best designs at steep discounts."

"Steep enough even for penny-pinching psych students, it would appear."

"Barely, but yes. It was his pendants that most caught my eye. They were tributes to his favorite artists: hand-painted replicas of Van Gogh, Vermeer, Dürer, Braque, and especially Dalí. There they were, calling out to me, as if cooing a serenade from their preordained places in the original painting."

"They? Calling out to you from the painting?"

"The melting clocks, Tim—from Dalí's *Persistence of Memory*. They were emblazoned right on the necklace. It immediately made me think of Priscilla. So I forked over some of my waitressing money and surprised her at one of her parties—all her sorority sisters got a big kick out of it. Priscilla took it as a quirky badge of honor, and she's been wearing that necklace ever since."

"So Priscilla and that pendant you snapped up for her—she's the reason we first crossed paths in China!?"

"Yeah. I was overcome by a basketful of sweet memories every time I visited that alley in Shanghai. For a farmer's daughter like little lost me, alone in a vast and dizzying country so far away, a stroll through that alley was the closest thing I had to a home-cooked meal."

"Now I see, Susie. That alley in China, its counterpart in SoHo, all the events and people they were wrapped up with . . . They're little landmarks of a trail we've been blazing for years, you and I. One that began with the alley in Shanghai where we first met."

"Even before we'd met. But it became much more than that on the day we did meet. Then when we were married, that quaint little package of my personal history, going all the way back to SoHo and my adventures with Priscilla—it was the beating heart of that crazy mystique you and I were always busy creating."

"I never realized how important—"

"But now you do understand, don't you? Priscilla was one of the few other souls in this wide world who were central to that narrative, the one that our unique memories could unlock. Her very presence helped define what it meant to us. If it had been someone else that you'd taken up with—"

"Susie, you don't have to do this."

"I see you've started up the mountain again. I get it—the subtle signal, the hint-hint. But I need to finish this, and you need to hear it, because I think you now see what I was telling you before: If it had been anyone else, then at least our special history together would have stayed largely intact. But Priscilla? Her intrusion altered that cherished narrative, the one that defined our relationship from our first meeting in that alley."

"With that Dalí necklace as the centerpiece this whole time."

"Even before I gave you that volume of Proust to mark up, I know you've always understood his little tale about the madeleine cake, Tim."

"One little pastry unleashing all those faded childhood memories for the narrator."

"More than that—the madeleine was a little vessel, with its own unique seal, that held and bound all those interlaced memories together. So it was with Priscilla's pendant."

"And that package of interlocking memories led straight back to the day we met in Shanghai."

"In all its clumsy sweetness. But when Priscilla came between us, then we had a clashing web of memories to contend with, vying for control of that same narrative. Even Priscilla knew it—whenever I'm around, she makes sure the necklace is out of sight. She felt it as much as I do. Memory really does persist."

"Which is why we need to build new memories, Susie, starting now."

"Then it's your turn to break that ground, Tim, by severing the chains still binding you so tightly to her and what she ushered in."

"I don't follow you."

"I think you do. I wasn't forthcoming about Priscilla and the necklace during our sessions. But neither were you about the ghosts haunting you, the ones always seeping out from whatever strange bond you shared with her. I can see them in your face again right now as we speak."

"Susie, prior to your colloquium that day four years ago, I had never met Priscilla. You know that."

"That's not what I mean, Tim. You had never encountered Priscilla in person before, but she meant something dear to you nonetheless. It's part of why I stayed with you when I found out the truth, as much as part of me ached to give up and walk away."

"I don't understand."

"I learned a lot from all those years filling the shoes of Dr. Miles, in my own sessions as a therapist striving to save broken marriages. When the couples did persevere and overcome, there was a common thread I saw over and over. They still loved each other, but there was a hidden sore that one or both of them desperately needed to heal, and it wasn't being healed."

"And that they were unwilling to disclose before."

"So you understand; now you need to follow through."

"Susan, I—I'm just not sure what to tell you."

"Can't you see? You're still failing at the last hurdle. We can't fully revive what we had until you let go and open up that crypt inside you, because I know there's something there."

"Why are you pressing so fiercely on this? Can't we just let it go?"

"Because, Tim, some people read lips, but in my line of work, I've learned to read eyes, especially yours. When I first introduced you to Priscilla, there was a flutter in your eyes. It wasn't lust or even attraction per se; I'd seen that dozens of times in the eyes of other men. The guys at Venetus College used to watch her every move. No, your expression was quite different, the kind of expression that betrays a familiarity close to the heart."

"A familiarity?"

"At first it was more a token of curiosity. But then when things had changed two years ago, when you saw her again at the Montreal conference—that glimmer in your eyes became something much deeper. I know you remember, because I told you myself. It was a desperate yearning, closing in on you, for whatever she meant to you. Look at yourself now, turning pale as a sheet at what I tell you. You were never open with me about what that was. I doubt you were open with her, either, or even with yourself. Even now, you're trapped by that same secret."

"That's because... Dammit, no!"

"What? Tim, what just happened?"

"This route's closed off; we're not supposed to be here. I pulled out of that little forest alcove at a different place from where we went in, but it must have dumped us out past the gate where they sealed off the road. The tour guide warned us to follow the detour sign before the souvenir shop. We must have bypassed it."

"Can't we turn around?"

"It's too narrow on this side of the mountain. We'll have to stop off at a scenic overpass, or maybe one of the stations for the construction crew."

"What was that? Tim, did you hear that?"

"Sounded like—I don't know, thunder rumbling from the forest."

"No, it's getting closer. Tim, we have to pull over now."

"Let's try to find a... Oh my—"

LATER—?

"Peter! Zijn bloeddruk! De Ringer-oplossing, bolus, 500 cc—wij hebben het nu nodig, stat!"

"Ja, maar zijn aders, elke keer dat wij proberen om—"

"Ik weet, Peter, maar hij is nog niet stabiel. En waar is de bloedgas? Hij is nog cyanotisch. We hebben geen tijd om te wachten!"

"What... uh... where am I?"

"Dr. Shoemaker! You're awake? We're—we're in Paramaribo City, sir. I'm Dr. Carl de Groot, of the Suriname Capital City General Hospital. To your left is Dr. Peter t'Hooft, my intern. We're your treating physicians here."

"Hosp... Hospital? How did I..."

"The construction personnel were near your car's impact site. They notified us and we were able to send in a Medevac team. Please, sir, you're on a moving gurney, so try not to stir."

"What... what happ—"

"There was a rockslide on Crijnssen Road, in the Wilhelmina Mountains where you were driving and... You're in the emergency ward now. Try to lie still; we're transferring you to the operating room."

"My, my…wife, where… where is…"

"Dr. Shoemaker, please, you're weak and under sedation now, so try to stay calm and rest. I'll be here the whole time. I won't leave your side until we're in the OR."

"Su…Susan. Just tell me where…Susan…"

TUESDAY, MAY 20, 2025, 2:21 P.M.
HOME OF DR. TIMOTHY SHOEMAKER
WEST CHAPEL HILL, NORTH CAROLINA

Tim awoke with a gasp, drenched with sweat. His neck and shoulder were throbbing with pain on the right side. He had fallen asleep in his work clothes, curled up on his bed far from the headboard, his arms and legs bent into his body in fetal position. He dragged himself to the edge of the mattress and slung his legs over the side, massaging his calves against the bed frame to get rid of the pins-and-needles sensation in his limbs. His dream had become a blur, but his heart was still smoldering at the half-remembered slivers of a scene twinkling behind the fog at the edge of his awareness.

As his mind settled, the memory's lurid embrace drew him in ever closer, its content more unnervingly evident with each flicker of introspection. A sick, nauseating sensation overtook Tim and he buckled over as a storm of images tore through his mind. Priscilla's haunting eyes at the Torchlight Café in the morning. The dark forest of his dream. The road.

Susan's jade figurine.

Shaken, Tim rubbed his eyes with deliberate vigor, as if to dislodge his waking mind from the shackles of its recent subconscious journey. Yet Susan's voice was now in his head, clear as a whisper. The fragile emotional plank he'd been balancing himself on so precariously for the past three years was burning to ash under his feet.

"Dammit, get your head in order," he murmured to himself, trying to banish the harassing thoughts. The effort was fruitless. The whispers inside grew ever louder, ever more cruel.

There were four words in particular that repeated themselves in a torturous, endless loop. Tim stumbled over to the small dresser abutting the bedpost. He switched on the lamp above the dresser and groped for the handle of a tiny drawer, nestled into the side of the dresser and concealed beneath an overhanging quilt. He yanked the drawer nearly off its runners, digging around inside to find a small barrel key. Leaving the drawer open, he strode across the room and opened the doors on a polished mahogany cabinet built into the wooden skeleton of a hulking wall unit.

From inside the cabinet Tim removed a locked photobox. He dusted it off, inserted the key and turned it carefully, then lifted the lid of the container. He trembled upon beholding the items within—a series of wrapped and framed pictures he'd avoided for over two years. The box was filled with a decade's worth of captured moments, but Tim pushed past the majority of the photographs until arriving at a large, stylized frame several layers deep.

"God," he whispered plaintively.

He took the picture and held it up to the light, his still-bleary eyes locked on the image it housed. There were snow-capped peaks in the background of the photo, captured by the astute lens of a fellow tourist's camera at an Adirondack mountain retreat more than six years before. Tim devoured every detail of the scene, before resting his attention on himself and Susan embracing, smiling, posed beside a rustic log cabin.

He pressed his eyes shut and set the picture aside. Then, looking up, he staggered to the bathroom and turned on the sink full-blast. His lungs heaved with labored intensity as he splashed his face with the cold water. He felt as though an anvil had just been lifted from his chest.

Tim stared down at the wash basin for a minute, striving to resolve the flurry of recollections and thoughts still clouding his mind from the dream; he then tentatively lifted his gaze to face the mirror before him. He clenched his jaw, fighting back tears.

"Memory really does persist," he said softly, staring back at the man peering at him from the mirror. A tall man with a military bearing, whose eyes were red and raw.

Tim continued to rinse his forehead and cheeks with cool water, pausing occasionally to stretch his sore neck. Dream images were still frothing like rapids through his mind. As he rose up to exit the bathroom, he was overcome by a curious sense of disorientation that he was unable to shake.

He'd been living there for years. It was the same home, the same rooms with the same sights and smells and the soft whir of the fan in the background. Yet it all seemed to strike him a bit differently now, as though he had become a stranger to the place. A faint glow permeated the hallway, visible within the door frame as reflected in the mirror above the sink. Whispers of muted daylight from the rainy afternoon were oozing through the drawn curtains of his home, but this dull radiance seemed to be emanating from somewhere inside.

"Wake up, Tim," he admonished himself, dismissing the observation as a mere *fata morgana* fostered by the meanderings of his weary, disoriented mind. It was such an odd hour to rest and then to rise again, he told himself; and was there ever a good time to have such a dream as he'd just had?

Tim scrubbed his face dry with a towel and filled a cup with water to slake his parched throat. As he emerged from the bathroom, jolted into an uneasy wakefulness, he tried to familiarize himself again with the contours of his home. He found himself grappling with a deeply disconcerting sensation, like a vertigo of conscious perception that was blurring the unmoored mind of his dreams with the more constrained, reliable world of the waking.

He walked down the hallway, straining to convince himself that he really was home, rather than at a faraway outpost somewhere near the South American mountain passes that had invaded his midday nightmare. A trace of that same uncanny glow still pervaded the hall and nearby rooms, sneaking into the corners of his eyes before seeming to vanish inexplicably if he sought its source.

Back in his bedroom, he lay in supine idleness for several minutes, staring at the cream-colored ceiling. He tried lulling himself back to sleep, hoping for a pleasanter dreamscape to fill his mind—or better yet none at all. But his psyche had been far too rattled to allow it. He sat up again with a rumbling groan, then reached for the framed picture that had occupied his attention before, clasping it to his chest before rising to leave the bedroom.

"It wasn't supposed to be like this," said Tim, looking out wistfully upon the lonely living room downstairs before turning rightward, heading toward his second-floor study. He pushed past the stacks of books and electronic media strewn about the small room and set the picture down upon a wide footstool to the right of the windowsill. His desktop computer hummed behind him in low-power mode, its monitor in blackened slumber.

He sat in a fraying wicker chair and pulled up to a wooden bureau underneath the window, gingerly opening a small, creaky drawer on its top right. He exhaled deeply as if to prepare for a dip into icy waters, then removed from the drawer a carefully protected figurine: a small, meticulously crafted jade obelisk, carved with brief messages in Chinese characters on each of its upright sides. He grasped the obelisk firmly and rolled it across his fingers, prompted by Susan's words so lucidly rendered in his dream.

"You were right, Susie," he murmured in sober reflection. "Everything you said on that mountain—you were right about everything."

The figurine's textures were doubling as a master key to the recesses of his mind, unlocking storehouses' worth of dimly-remembered journeys nestled deeply within the realms of his unconscious and half-formed thoughts. He peered contemplatively out the window of the room toward some nearby woods, their rain-swept treetops and bushes hosting the compact frames of sleeping owls gathering strength to stalk the night ahead.

As Tim drew back to replace the jade obelisk within its cushioned dwelling, the corner of his eye registered a seeming aberration somewhere in his midst. He looked first toward the bookcase on the right wall, seeking out whatever had announced its ephemeral presence in the dimly lit study. His heart then leapt at the sight of a varsity athletics letter from his college days, its glass frame tilting forward at the edge of a shelf on the bookcase—and reflecting something behind him, like an animated light show shifting and weaving about.

He pivoted cautiously around, apprehensive at what his roaming eyes would descry, before finally homing in on the source of the dancing pattern: his computer monitor, supposedly still in screensaver mode. It was projecting an embryonic image on its surface, the pixels busily limning the textures of a distinctive figure on the otherwise darkened screen. To his astonishment, the outline was evolving before his very eyes, gradually becoming more lucid and then vaguely familiar. It was a face, one cast crudely out of visible white lines etched on the monitor, but unmistakably a human visage all the same.

"What . . . what the—" Tim's breathless voice was choked off by a disconcerting, tingling sensation that accompanied the jolt of the moment, coursing throughout his head and chest as if to freeze his muscles and vocal cords in place.

The figure was looking out from the screen, but not specifically at Tim—as though intermittently aware of the world outside, and aiming to express a message from lips that moved ever so subtly and indistinctly amid the fuzzy array of swimming pixels. As the screen dots moved purposefully about, Tim's heart began to pound again. The outline's eyes and cheeks were growing alarmingly more familiar.

"This isn't happening. It's not... no." Tim abruptly switched off the monitor, shaking his head in a pretense of disbelief. With each new installment, the developing image had come to provoke a mixture of lurid curiosity and grinding fear of what awaited him; it was all too much to take.

Tim forcefully slowed his breath, desperate to soothe the shock from whatever it was he'd just seen. He then snatched the picture from the footstool and darted out the door of his study, blazing a path back toward his bedroom and tumbling awkwardly down upon the mattress. He was still shivering, staring at the ceiling, unsure whether to ponder what he had just witnessed or to pretend, at least for a precious few minutes, that he had never seen it at all.

Finally, he mustered up enough initiative to rest the photo on the nearby dresser, his eyes wandering again to peruse its frozen moment. They shortly began filling with tears, this time mixing with the unresolved exhaustion that was swallowing whatever resolve he had left. He sat up to collapse the photo on the dresser, then switched off the lamp and rose to shut the door.

Tim promptly shuffled back to crash onto his bed, coming to rest on his side such that he was facing the now-sealed hallway. As his consciousness slowly drifted away again, he was surprised by the dying embers of a faint light seeping through the cracks of the shuttered doorway. Before withdrawing into whatever world his dreaming mind was preparing to forge, he was arrested by one last coherent thought: The light in the doorway was the same rusted glow as had taunted him before. Whatever his attempts to dismiss it as a mind-molded illusion, it persisted nonetheless—daring him to seek its source.

Wenn man vor dem Spiegel steht,
um das Bild darauf zu sehen,
Blickt das Bild zurück auf uns,
folgt wohin wir selbst auch gehen.
Gibt es denn vielleicht den Tag,
wenn ein so gespiegelt' Bild
Könnt' auch blicken, denken, gehen,
selbst im Freien laufen wild?

Chapter Eight

Shards of Memories Lost

The Triptych

WEDNESDAY, MAY 21, 8:49 A.M.
HOME OF DR. TIMOTHY SHOEMAKER
WEST CHAPEL HILL, NORTH CAROLINA

Tim dug through the scattered notes and receipts in his briefcase, rummaging about for a clutch of genealogical documents that he had haphazardly filed away—treasures amidst the trove hauled in from the vault at Pegasus Atlantic Bank. The records were prominent inclusions within the information packet that Tonya Jemison had prepared for him, and he berated himself for misplacing them. Such a waste to spend the first waking hour of a new day in unproductive disarray. But, Tim reminded himself, it was that—a new day. It was blessed for being that alone.

At least this drizzly, dreary Wednesday morning was lending him a respite from the emotional Inquisition that had lately frayed his troubled psyche, whether resting or roused. He was made of sterner stuff than this, he kept telling himself. If he could survive the upending of his world three years ago, he could survive anything; that had become his armor. Yet he'd never tested it against the memories of the very trauma that had forged it, and lately they had been assaulting from all sides. Especially the previous day, with its fraught reunions, its wrenching dream, and what had followed it after he woke…

He'd spent the rest of that God-awful day in a blur of reflection, restless outdoor strolls, and abortive attempts to prepare slides for his forthcoming research talk. Even his night was lost to the grip of insomnia, save for a few scattered bouts of fitful slumber that had done little to restore his daily rhythms. Yet that didn't matter now, he told himself. If he could find the packet from Tonya, he could absorb his mind in a more concrete task and shield himself from reminders of…of yesterday. Of yet another haunted day among far too many already.

His plans would have to wait, however. At least for the duration of an incoming phone call from a familiar number.

"Rachel! I was wondering when I'd hear from you again. What was all that about yesterday? Did you really believe the things you were—"

"No, Tim, of course I didn't. I know the Simitalis is a culprit in this crisis we've been battling here. And that your input and ideas are indispensable, as much as they were when you first trekked out here. It's probably best that you simply disregard the unfortunate turn our conversation took toward the end."

"So then why did you suddenly go doubtful about everything we'd…Oh, I see. They put another gag order on you, didn't they?"

"When you burst into the PIT room unauthorized and sifted through Pablo's notebooks—that set off red flags. Alan Simms tried to keep a lid on the incident, but it slipped out when he was conferring with the suits upstairs, most likely Argentus Clan operatives or even Metacelsus himself. One of my associates here slipped me a note while I was talking with you; as of yesterday morning, apparently, we were supposed to be giving you an official cold shoulder."

"Which I'm guessing no longer applies this morning," Tim mused cynically.

"Poor old Metacelsus can't seem to make up his mind about you. Safe to say he doesn't want you plowing up too many dirty secrets, but he knows he still needs your expertise. So I guess his desperation for a solution took priority over his fetish for secrecy, and you're back in his good graces. At least up to a point. The international videoconference we have on tap for tonight—it'll still be featuring a sanitized history about, uh…"

"Yeah, that-which-shall-not-be-admitted in polite company. So the Simitalis and the burglary will be conveniently omitted from the program, I take it."

"A bitter pill to swallow, I know, but I hope you can still come on board with us tonight. Even with the limitations, we'll be treading a lot of new ground, and we need another dose of your magic. Or at least your undivided attention."

"What—you want me there tonight?"

"I could patch you through with a live link to the proceedings, the same one being used by the international conferees overseas."

Tim pinched the bridge of his nose.

"Rachel, I'm sorry, but I may have to take a rain check on this. My research talk is on Friday morning, and I haven't exactly been conforming to a normal sleep schedule as it is."

"I realize the past few days have been difficult."

"More than difficult. After I spoke to you yesterday... I got an unwelcome visit, courtesy of some ghosts from my past. And they won't be departing anytime soon. If ever."

"You mean you—" Rachel stopped herself. Whatever he meant, it was probably best not to go there now. "With all the fronts you've been fighting on lately, I wouldn't blame you for skipping out on the conference tonight. But I really think your input could bridge the... gaps in our understanding that are likely to arise."

Rachel's entreaty was more urgent than she had made it sound, Tim was sure of that. But he could respond with little more than an ambivalent silence.

"Please, Tim?"

"All right. Count me in," he said, though he still felt hesitant.

"You're a lifesaver," she said.

He responded with another strained silence, unconvinced of the wisdom of his decision.

"One more request," Rachel added, "if you don't mind."

"Isn't there a weekly limit for that?"

"No cross-state odysseys this time, or midnight séances with doctors across two oceans. Just... your drawings, the ones you called me about yesterday."

"What about them?"

"I think you should hold on to them."

"I've been saving them anyway but—why? Is there some reason you need them?"

"I can't narrow it down to a specific reason, Tim, and there's no obvious purpose that I can yet envision for them; but I have a feeling that may soon be changing."

"Why?"

Rachel drew in a deep breath.

"Even with all their lurid details," she said softly, "Pablo's drawings give you the sense he's keeping something out. Deliberately, and for deep-seated reasons that may be unknown even to him in his current state. I still don't get the connection between what the two of you are committing to paper, the meaning of that recurring number or the... that beast in both of your dream sketches. But I can't shake the feeling that your own drawings may eventually fill in what Pablo seems condemned to leave out."

9:16 A.M.

Tim had helped himself to a halfhearted breakfast of soggy oatmeal and fruit after his chat with Rachel. He was relieved to know she was still on his side, and equally nonplussed by her caginess. By all the things, he was convinced, that she wanted to reveal but was still holding back on telling him.

He soon resumed his search for the genealogical history that Tonya Jemison had neatly assembled for him at the bank. His sharpness of mind from the early morning was fading back into dullness, a victim of the previous night's insomnia and the rough treatment of the day leading up to it. Perhaps some productive immersion in unfinished business would refresh his creaking gears.

Having located and browsed through some of the prized documents, Tim paused to re-order his thoughts. He reached for his cell phone from a nearby shelf where it had been clumsily poised, then scrolled through a listing of its contacts. He halted at the number that Tonya had furnished him two days before.

"Marsden-Kyle Probate Law; this is Ezra Gordon speaking," answered the man on the other line. He had a faint trace of a British accent. "How may I help you?"

"Mr. Gordon? This is Tim Shoemaker, I'm the profess—"

"Dr. Shoemaker!" interrupted the other man genially, his mellow baritone reassuring Tim with the steady, engaging rhythm of an unruffled professional. "No need for an introduction. I feel as though I've come to know you quite well throughout this last assignment, so it's an honor to finally speak with the man himself. Please, feel free to use my first name."

"You do the same, and the honor's all mine. Legend has it that, in a matter of mere months, you've managed to do what more than fifteen generations of Shoemakers have failed miserably at for centuries."

"A legend according to your Uncle Mitch," said Ezra with an affable chuckle. "He hand-picked me for this mission with all the high hopes that attach thereby, so I'm loath to belittle such high praise on his part. But I've also learned well the lesson that the best expectations start as humble ones; I've yet to shed light on the big questions that your uncle charged me to solve."

"The very fact that you've plunged into this gig at all is enough for me to sing your praises, Ezra. Can't think of too many attorneys this side of the Appalachians with such an undiscovered talent for genealogical field work."

"Your uncle's a dear old friend, Tim. I'd have done it for free, but he insisted on a measure of compensation."

"I'm sure you've earned every penny and then some. You've been at this for, what, a year by now?"

"And a few weeks on-and-off; lately more off than on, I'm afraid. The hallmark of this line of work is a most arduous species of waiting: for documents to arrive, for hunches to be confirmed, for a long-deferred response from other parties never quite sure how they fit into one's peculiar quest."

"That's actually why I'm calling. It's about your findings from the Pennsylvania State Archives, and the logs from the Dutch government. Based on your name co-signed to the probate documents, I'm presuming you know that Mitch has legally transferred all his heirlooms into my possession."

"Yes, and the bank notified me that you'd retrieved them on Monday. I have to admit a twinge of relief at the news. I know you and your uncle haven't enjoyed the sunniest of relations, and he was dubious at best that you'd claim this particular inheritance."

"Well, you said it yourself," mused Tim in muted contempt toward his uncle, opting against a more caustic response, "the best expectations indeed start as humble ones. In any case, I've been duly following up on his efforts to track down the source of these items. I waged a mostly losing battle against insomnia last night, and had a chance to leaf through your summary report from a few months ago, as well as the scrapbook that he bequeathed alongside the objects themselves."

"The one with the collages, correct? Full of newspaper clippings, old receipts..."

"And plenty of other relics from centuries' past."

"Glad to hear of it. I was tied down for a separate project when Mitch was compiling that, and never laid eyes on the finished masterpiece. I'm now back to a blessedly part-time schedule here and itching to fill in all those vexing blanks. Maybe you could lend me a hand."

"I was hoping you'd be the one casting first light on these tangled webs," said Tim after a deliberative breath through pursed lips, "but I'll see what I can add. Let's start with that Dutch clipper ship, the one that allegedly ferried my ancestors to the colonial United States in the late 1600s. I'm blanking on the name—"

"*De Ontdekker,* and that segment of the family history is not in doubt. I got lucky in the back-and-forth with the historians in the Netherlands. They happened to be knee-deep in the spadework for an exhibition of the Anglo-Dutch Wars and the era of Holland's naval supremacy. So the archival sources are especially rich, even more so since that was the maiden voyage of *De Ontdekker,* doubling as an exploratory expedition for the Northwest Passage through Canada."

"What do you have so far?"

"A well-founded suspicion that your ancestor was on ship; more of a certainty when it comes to the heirlooms themselves. The shipping manifest contained a mysterious entry that translated roughly into 'items of fine metalworking and exquisite sculpture.' The at-length descriptions, needless to say, turned out to be uncannily familiar. The ship's sailors clearly struggled to describe what they were transporting; there was even a gloss on the manifest, fearing that the objects housed a strain of black magic."

"I wonder if that crew really was on to something," muttered Tim, uncomfortably reminded of the incident at the bank. "So the story I have so far: Old Man Schumacher had been a craftsman, apparently in some quaint German town, about which we're completely in the dark. For some inexplicable reason, he'd been in possession of devices centuries ahead of their time, and then for equally inexplicable reasons, he decided to hop the ocean and make a go of it in North America."

"I've chased down several further leads that turned out to be chimeras," Ezra answered with a sigh, "but we at least have a confirmed itinerary for the Dutch clipper. *De Ontdekker* docked in Rotterdam and Lelystad in the Netherlands, though I recently learned that its seafaring commenced in Bremerhaven. The latter was a common exit point for America-bound emigrants from the Netherlands and the German states of the time."

"Not bad for a start. What about archives from the port itself, maybe with a bit more fleshing-out of the passengers who boarded *De Ontdekker*?"

"Unfortunately, the Bremerhaven archives have been mostly lost amidst the turmoil of the centuries. But there's a twist to the clipper's manifest that may hold a clue of its own. Your ancestor was apparently listed simply as 'C. B. Schumacher,' and his own possessions are documented as nothing more than a locket and a few personal items. There are gaps in the manifest and I don't have a specific name, but your heirlooms were clearly registered under somebody else."

"Why—why is that?" asked Tim, grasping unsuccessfully at an answer to his own question.

"In a word: money. The Dutch funded many of their sailing expeditions from private investors, raising the proceeds via joint-stock operations, but *De Ontdekker* likely fell well short of its target. That's why it was ferrying passengers before charting a course to explore the Arctic. The crew's fellow travelers weren't simply along for the ride; those emigrants were essential to the broader mission. Upon their disembarkation in the Pennsylvania colony, it was they who defrayed the residual expenses of the exploratory voyage to follow."

"But how could penniless migrants have been of any use in funding a high-seas adventure? Unless—ah, they weren't all so penniless, were they?"

"Even in the 17th century, alas, the VIPs had a first-class cabin that paid the freight for everyone else. C. B. Schumacher seems to have enjoyed only limited means himself, so he must have teamed up with one of the well-heeled passengers on board, perhaps in exchange for a term of indentured labor in North America. Or maybe a business partnership if he'd cultivated a good enough rapport with the fellow. Either way, your ancestor would have had to entrust the mysterious objects to his wealthier patron, at least for purposes of the official records."

"Hmm, could you hold on a minute?" asked Tim, setting the phone down as he hurriedly fetched a parchment-coated album nearby. "Now you're ringing a few bells. My uncle's annotations for the scrapbook made reference to a colonial-era archivist, whom the two of you had met up with in Pennsylvania."

"I knew generally of her work, Tim, but I'm afraid I stopped short of meeting her. In fact, that missed connection marked the unofficial start of my own involuntary re-assignment to other tasks for a few months. I never did make up for that lost time, even after I eventually hopped back on board the genealogical treasure hunt."

"Not to worry, because it seems Mitch took it upon himself to captain that particular ship in your absence. He must have contacted that Pennsylvania historian on his own, at least based on what he managed to inveigle into this scrapbook. There are copies of old billboards, shingles, plaques, various species of legal documents—all from slides that the archivist had been preparing for years. According to Mitch's notes, they were for a historical convention that, alas, never got around to convening."

"Swallowed up by the Reckoning," reasoned Ezra with scarcely a moment's pause.

"Yeah, it had a knack for that. At any rate, Mitch was at least able to put the archivist's emphatic preparations to good use on another front. The materials in the scrapbook were lifted from her field work and active research, the kind that wouldn't have been accessible to the lay public. Mitch's running commentary makes clear that most of the legal documentation, particularly the old contracts, isn't even available in the community or specialist databases."

"Contracts, you said? That might be our ticket, at least to sniff out the name of your ancestor's partner in whatever ventures they were mixed up in. Can you find an associated surname in those archives?"

"Let's see. Mitch subdivided the contents into categories and... ah, possibly a bullseye on the first toss: a scanned-in image straight from the archivist's slide collection. It's a facsimile of an old Pennsylvania contract written in German, apparently from 1692. There's a monographed seal in the lower right corner."

"Any luck making out what's on it?"

"Not sure," said Tim, wary of overly raising hopes. "Best I can tell, it's maybe some emblem related to a cobbler's shop. But there's some lettering inserted right above the seal. Having a hell of a time getting a fix on it but...wait, there it is: 'Schumacher and Koenig.'"

"Can you spell out the second name for me?"

"K-O-E-N-I-G."

"Nice work," replied Ezra after a brief but thoughtful intermission. "So he would have been 'König' in the original listing from Europe, the 'o' with an umlaut on top. I have an alphabetized print-out of *De Ontdekker*'s manifest here, so let's see if I can find the name in one of its sections. No...no...ah, blast, not here either."

"It doesn't show up?"

"Not in the primary manifest. Much of it was lost in a warehouse fire at the Dutch archives, and the experts could reconstruct only a portion of the missing sections."

"Might there be a reference elsewhere?" Tim proposed. "If this guy was such a high-roller, maybe he had a direct line to the skipper himself."

"That's a thought. I had some of the ancillary documents translated—captain's logs and the like. Poring through them and...hmm, the skipper makes reference to a certain 'Daniel' who seems to have been a regular guest in the cabin, not one of the crew. Do you have a first name from that contract?"

"It's too mangled; can't make it out. I could maybe try flipping through the—"

"Hold on, we may have a winner here," Ezra interjected, his voice charged with fresh enthusiasm as he pored over a promising find. "The name is in the notes from the ship's surgeon, after a minor accident on deck: Daniel König. There's a detailed social history in the medical chart. It says that Daniel boarded with his wife Sara en route to the port of Philadelphia, that he was a well-to-do merchant and investor who teamed with local artisans in his hometown of...Leipzig, State of Saxony, Kingdom of Prussia. Evidently not the quaint little town we thought."

"Jackpot. Then Daniel must have met my ancestor in Leipzig or thereabouts. Or so we think...Can we be sure that C. B. Schumacher had roots in the same city?"

"Not 100 percent, but I'd ante up in favor of the affirmative. If not roots then at least a solid grounding there. People for the most part weren't too mobile in those days, especially someone of limited resources. For all practical purposes, Daniel König was a 17th-century venture capitalist, so your ancestor must have been at least established enough in Leipzig to have attracted his attention. It's not too surprising when you consider that the city was a manufacturing and technical hub, then as much as now. To the extent we can make any sense out of your heirlooms and their origin, Leipzig would fit the bill."

"Mission accomplished, for now," said Tim with a shrug. "So where does that leave us?"

"I'll have to glean what I can from the archivists in Leipzig, along with any other clues that would point to a business district or even a particular location in the city."

"What I meant—honestly, what gems is Mitch expecting me to dig up in this scavenger hunt he keeps foisting upon me?"

Ezra vented a labored sigh, cognizant of a tough sell ahead.

"He wants you to tread on the same ground that gave birth to these objects, Tim, to breathe the air around whatever house of miracles forged them into existence. He's convinced you'll make a spectacular discovery there. A crucial one, even."

"Crucial for what?"

"That I can't answer, but I'll say this: I've been teaming up with your uncle for years, ever since we were both cadets sailing off for the first time on our strange and wonderful adventures. I was there when he partnered with your father, and when those enforcers from the underground lenders came in looking to break our knees."

"So I see you're also well-versed in the Miseries of Mitch."

"Yes, but in the Masterstrokes as well. I was also there when your uncle stood virtually alone amid his cockamamie plans and blueprints, for those self-organizing grids to facilitate high-temperature superconductivity. That was the core of what became Magister Engineering, and Mitch succeeded because he saw past the blind spots that had snuffed out the vision of everyone else in the field. I see that same twinkle in his eyes for this, Tim, albeit mixed with a sense of... alarm, that I can't quite nail down."

"You sensed it too, huh?" asked Tim, his gruff rhetorical query sprinkled with grim apprehension at its deeper implications. "It shone through like a blaze in Mitch's recording that I glimpsed in the bank. It must be why he's so insistent that I take the reins. I'm supposedly the next in line to be gifted with this 'Sacred Sight' that's run periodically throughout our clan, though to me all this family lore is mostly a smattering of tall tales searching for an author."

"But you've actively followed your uncle's lead, Tim. Why else would you be speaking with me now?"

"Because I may need his help in navigating some treacherous terrain of my own. And also . . . I don't know how to put this, but something freakish hit me a couple days ago. It was at Pegasus Atlantic, when I was in the bank's conference room, fumbling around with Mitch's inheritance for the first time."

"I'm sorry to hear that. Is everything OK?"

"Given all the other ghoulish weirdness I've encountered in the past few days, I'm not entirely sure how to answer that," said Tim, muzzling any urges to build on the riddling remark. "Anyway, I suspect a face-to-face awaits us in the near future to link our respective resources. I'm in my pre-sabbatical doldrums—or at least I'm supposed to be—so I could meet with you practically anytime to hand over this scrapbook."

"I already have some local contacts to help crack open the Leipzig archives, so I'd prefer to start the paper chase right away. In fact, if you have a lunchtime opening today or tomorrow, let's grab a coffee to inspect our mutual inventory."

"What else should I bring to the party?"

"A copy of your uncle's GuangPan recording from the bank, along with a couple of the most distinctive heirlooms in structure and function. They've survived the knocks of several centuries, so they should be hardy enough to haul back and forth, though it wouldn't hurt to pack them up in a box or those protective crates from the vault. If I can then polish off a detailed sketch of your inheritance for our fellow gumshoes in Leipzig, I could buy us a nice headstart for whatever road you elect to take in this investigation."

"Sure thing. I'll have to carve out a couple slots in my daily planner to design some slides for a talk, but I should be able to scrape out an opening somewhere. I'll be back in touch before noon."

12:06 P.M.

Tim spent the rest of the morning sifting through the tasks he had laid out for himself. Tackling them, let alone completing them, was another matter altogether. He was too vexed, too distracted. As noon approached, he treated himself to a light repast of half-eaten sandwiches—it didn't quite amount to a lunch—and readied himself to head downtown. The meeting with Ezra was on.

With a few minutes to spare before his planned departure, Tim seized his uncle's scrapbook and browsed more of its carefully assembled pages, settling on a section devoted to grimy family photos dating from the late 1800s. Their scattered stains and the hand-woven outfits of their subjects lent them an austere, rustic charm despite their gritty authenticity. More than once Tim had to remind himself that he wasn't just admiring old photographs but was looking for clues.

Around midway through the scrapbook, Tim halted at a large black-and-white photo of a pastoral scene set between a shed and a tapering silo. A hastily assembled bench in the foreground supported a gaggle of occupants across three generations. There were six restless children in the front, grandparents on easy chairs to each side, a relatively young woman in the back, and a rugged patriarch with a prominent facial scar directly to her right.

The woman could manage only a tired, half-formed smile, but she evinced a kind of defiant tranquility, as if having long ago made peace with her rough and unforgiving surroundings. The man, for his part, was stiff-jawed and uncompromising, as was the custom for such portraits at the time. Yet his embrace of his wife was tender and protective.

According to the caption beneath the image, the man was Tim's great-great-grandfather, and the resemblance was undeniable. More astonishing to Tim, however, was that the woman bore more than a passing likeness to Susan.

There were her wispy, shoulder-length locks of what must have been red or light-brown hair, her softly-framed forehead, her gentle nose resting above pursed lips set between freckled cheeks. The hues of her irises were a mystery in the color-starved photograph, but their slightly almond shape reminded Tim of the eastern Mediterranean echoes in Susan's eyes, so evident in her gaze on the first day that he had beheld them.

"There's another picture I should be looking for," he murmured, turning and glancing toward his basement door. He snapped the album shut and, inhaling deeply, stood up.

He was in the basement, rifling through a rusted toolbox set on a high shelf. It took some searching, but he finally extracted a sealed plastic container that shielded an old-fashioned skeleton key inside, which he used to access a locked cabinet on a nearby counter. Inside it were more framed pictures of Tim and Susan in a bevy of mostly outdoor scenes.

Unlike the pictures he'd been perusing earlier in the upstairs bedroom, however, these photos included a pair of enthusiastic children—oftentimes joined by smiling young friends or cousins. Tim halted abruptly at the third picture in the stack, and taking a screwdriver from a tool-board hanging on a nearby wall swiftly pried open the picture's frame. A smaller photograph had been wedged into a corner between the casing and the larger picture—a sun-kissed portrait snapped on a visit to an old family farm.

"I knew you were still in there," he whispered in relief, staring at the picture. His eyes glistened as he held it at arm's-length under the toasty illumination of a naked light bulb dangling from the basement ceiling.

The broad contours of the picture were oozing back into a tentative familiarity. Tim's smiling, squinting former self had staked out an impromptu seat on a piled bale of hay, snug together with Susan while their two children frolicked in the foreground. He exhaled contemplatively, stirred by a tide of emotions; he then held it closer to the basement light, methodically gauging its dimensions.

Tim nodded in confirmation of its size and dashed back upstairs, resting the photo on a kitchen counter before changing his clothes and gathering the items requested by Ezra. As he prepared to exit the house, he raised the picture to his eyes again and gazed at it for a full half-minute. He then nestled it discreetly within an unused segment of his wallet, snatching up his keys as he strode out to the car.

WEDNESDAY, MAY 21, 12:47 P.M.
OLD FRANKLIN STREET
DOWNTOWN CHAPEL HILL, NORTH CAROLINA

"How many damn red lights can they pack into a half mile?" Tim seethed, gripping the steering wheel so hard his knuckles began to turn white.

It was nearly an hour until his meeting with Ezra Gordon, but he was craving a longer bite out of the day, itching to rehearse for his upcoming lecture from the slides he'd already compiled. Tim took a breath. *Easy, man,* he told himself, loosening his hands on the steering wheel. The first part of the drive had been smooth, enough to help him rest his roving mind in a coveted valley of clarity and relative tranquility.

But now the dismally familiar tokens of a neglected and crumbling infrastructure loomed in the distance: the dreaded orange cones. A lane had been closed ahead, likely due to a damaged gas line or ruptured water main. Tim eased his neck back on the headrest and clamped his eyes shut in consternation, shaking his head to elicit a defiant chuckle.

He flung open a long-ignored panel ensconced within a gap on his dashboard and twisted a switch resembling that of a small egg timer at the panel's base. A dull green light flicked on, followed by a thin metal gate peeling itself open to reveal a delicate black screen enclosed within, gradually powering itself awake.

He advanced a modest city block before coming to halt again at a drawn-out stop signal encumbered by a mess of slowly merging cars. Tim shifted into Park and focused back on the monitor before him. After adjusting its display, he fetched a plastic-ensheathed booklet from the glove compartment, unsealed it and skipped ahead to a diagram-filled page late in its contents.

"Eureka," he murmured in muted satisfaction, poring through the figure legend on the top left of the page. "Shou Ti Yun Duan Corporation, Version 3B: On-the-road cloud computing local network link. This must be it." The damn cloud was down half the time, but he was up to the last four slides he had thus far prepared for the lecture. If he could snag them from home onto the mobile hard drive of the car, maybe the present detour would be less than a complete waste.

Tim typed in a succession of codes beside a waiting screen prompt. He soon arrived at a visual interface upon which he eagerly traced a zigzag with his index finger, stopping it at a telltale address for a folder on his home computer.

"Home sweet home," he said, highlighting a quartet of digital files. "Liver regeneration, digital nephron, muscle, spleen, and—"

Tim's heart sank. The data transfer from his home computer had stalled in its tracks. An error message protesting a newly choppy connection with the source appeared on the screen.

He waited in vain as the system persisted in its fruitless exertions. After a couple minutes he switched on the car radio, maneuvering its tuner to home in on a local news broadcast.

"Good afternoon, North Carolina," cooed the voice from the speakers, *"this is Kayla Su filling in for Jenna Silver at Carolina News Unfiltered. Our top story: Hundreds have been reported killed and thousands more injured amid fresh rioting in New Kansas City. The unrest erupted following the abrupt closure of the Hidalgo Springs electronics plant and the cancellation of employees' unpaid salaries, pensions, and municipal food assistance, justified under the Federal Fiscal Emergency Act passed late last year."*

Tim shook his head as he brought his car steadily forward toward another bottleneck.

"Workers had already been striking in the wake of layoffs, wage cuts, and other austerity measures approved despite the record $300 million payout awarded to the company's departed CEO, Steven Vedius. Mr. Vedius had resigned his post in the wake of corruption and embezzlement revelations that had dogged his two-year tenure, and his exit package prompted furious accusations of nepotism and a 'golden parachute' from community and business leaders alike."

"$300 million for two years' worth of stealing from your workers and running your own company into the dirt," Tim spat at the radio. "Guess I've been kissing the wrong asses all these years." Well, he thought, at least this latest outrage was fairly tame—by Clan Vedius standards. He shook his head at himself—how sick, how disgusting, to be thankful for a mere robbery.

"Nevertheless," added the voice on the radio, *"Acting Governor and Ruling Families representative in the Kansas-Missouri District, Margaret Vedius, closed the investigation of her brother's activities upon denying any meaningful wrongdoing. She also dissolved the City*

Council and warned that there would be more 'belt-tightening' for New Kansas City residents on the heels of a recent downgrade of the city's financial credit rating.

"One of our reporters trapped amidst the riots quoted Governor Vedius as threatening to 'personally burn the city to the ground' if the uprising continued. The Governor herself has neither confirmed nor denied the claim. In other news, a second shark attack was reported today in the vicinity of Nags Head, following on the heels of similar incidents at other coastal resort towns . . ."

Tim tuned out the broadcast momentarily as he confronted anew the troublesome data transfer on the dashboard monitor. He threw up his hands and cancelled its stalling attempts to connect, before maneuvering a second and then a third time to download the lecture slides.

"That's a start, at least," he murmured in a subdued tone, as the first of the four files finally streamed in. He was less fortunate with the others; the infuriating acrobatics of a spinning hourglass icon signaled a still-abortive transfer for the remaining three.

He moved to cancel the transmission again but stopped himself at the last moment, hoping that the small breakthrough with the first file would be repeated if he kept his patience. He crawled through another hindered intersection before halting yet again at a roadblock, this one imposed by nearby construction workers who appeared to have no intention of resuming the traffic anytime soon. Tim rolled his eyes and sank his forehead into the steering wheel, passively absorbing the ongoing radio broadcast.

"Municipal authorities in several towns across eastern Tennessee's Anderson and Roane Counties continue to be mystified by the so-called digital trances that lately have been snarling computers at a number of financial institutions in the region. According to bank officials, their machines appear to shut down for brief periods lasting for as little as one or two minutes, performing detailed calculations of unknown significance before coming back up again with their screens intact."

"What the hell?!" exclaimed Tim in alarm, jerking his forehead away from the wheel and boosting the radio's volume as the broadcast pushed mercilessly ahead.

"Following complaints by customers at ATMs during the affected periods, bank representatives have disclosed that the unexplained event

has occurred roughly twice a day for the past week, and has affected more than a half dozen banks and credit unions. Officials have taken steps to assure the public that no customer data has been lost or stolen, but they are as of now unsure about the origin or nature of the incidents.

"Authorities have not ruled out a virus or hacker attack, and some have speculated on a connection with the so-called Chakana Virus, which began infecting databases at several local hospitals two weeks ago. It subsequently invaded a number of biotech and electronics firms as well as other targets with no apparent connection, including libraries, museums, and even zoos and aquaria. However, Chakana has not resurfaced since late last week, and experts have been unable to corroborate suspected links between it and the current developments."

"Sounds like this thing's breaking out of its cage," Tim mumbled nervously, reminded of a bank he himself had visited two days ago. It was far from Tennessee, but still...

"At present," continued the radio-voice, *"neither the responsible party nor the motives behind the disruptions are known. Sources within neighboring Tennessee counties and other states have denied any related incidents. In international news, officials at the Grand-Fleuve fusion reactor in Limoges, France, have reported modest but encouraging gains in power output for—"*

"What does it mean, dammit?" Tim asked himself insistently as he switched off the broadcast. Ernie, Rachel Bloom, the filling station en route to Tennessee with the grainy TV image and the dogged reporter—they had all made reference to a kindred phenomenon. The spreading virus, those bizarre calculations... the calculations. Wasn't Pablo rendering them too? On that blood-encrusted wall of the patient room? And the other veterans? Posting numbers, or computations, or—"

Tim nearly punched the steering wheel amid his thwarted ponderings, but halted himself just before making contact with the horn. He shook his head, sensing a link yet troubled by the as-yet unconnected dots in the larger picture. Amid the unsettling distractions, he soon realized that he had ignored the progress on his car's dashboard monitor: Success! His conference files were now fully available.

With the traffic ahead still grinding slowly forward, he accessed the lecture slides and proceeded to scrutinize their contents, reviewing their structure and rehearsing his talk aloud. He grimaced as he worked his way through the material. By the time he reached the last slide, his brief oasis of tranquility had dissolved into a demoralizing quagmire of uncertainty, frustration, and vague unease.

"Now we're in business," Tim said—a contrary dose of positive thinking seemed his best hope for now.

He heaved a sigh of relief at the scene on the road ahead. He was now one block from the clearing that would liberate him from the early-afternoon snarl on the broken road. He paused at the stoplight and reclined upon the headrest, rolling his neck from shoulder to shoulder and stretching the small of his back. He tipped up the panel slightly to deflect the monitor's glare, seizing an opportune moment to close his weary eyes and breathe deeply. As he drifted off into a shallow meditation, his mind bounded about the vistas of recent events hazily remembered.

A thought seized him. Tim opened his eyes and removed his wallet from the breast pocket of his coat, carefully unfolding its flaps to access a protected compartment inside. He gently teased out the photo he had found in his basement only a few hours before. He ran a finger across its surface, limning the contours of its subjects: the barn in the background, the grazing livestock at the edges, and the family seated atop the baled hay.

Tim traced an imaginary halo about the wind-tossed hair and gleeful grins of his children. The two were mugging for the camera with a youthful insouciance that had yet to be shackled by the manacles of doubt and self-consciousness. He leaned against the driver's side window and tilted the photo before him. Susan's sweetly smiling face beamed out angelically from the picture, channeling the affection and protection of the man who stood beside her with his arms draped tenderly about her shoulders.

"Oh, sorry," Tim said sheepishly, jarred out of his daze by the blasts of car horns behind him. The light had turned green. He hurriedly laid his wallet and the photo upon the passenger's seat, racing through the crosswalk and into the freedom of the unobstructed road. He pressed forward with some urgency, blasting through a chain of curving intersections followed by a pair of turns that eventually sent him down a long, soot-encrusted industrial thoroughfare.

He frowned at the sight of a yellow light switching to red as he approached, applying the brakes and pushing back against the headrest as he had done before. He shut his eyes to indulge in another brief spell of restless contemplation, pressing himself to leash his drifting mind and gear up mentally for the meeting with Ezra over the next red light or two.

Less than a minute had passed before Tim opened his eyes once more, readying for the imminent flash of green on the stoplight ahead. Yet Tim found himself feeling oddly out-of-sorts with what his eyes were taking in. The tenor of the neighborhood seemed to have shifted inexplicably; the outside appeared darker and gloomier than before. His pupils were adjusting to the dreary illumination of the overcast sky, he thought, his surroundings further dimmed by the grungy neglected factories to each side of the road.

There was another intruder into Tim's comfort zone, however: a residue of the same unexplained glow that had taunted his senses at home the previous afternoon. At first he disregarded it, but he felt more unsettled with each city block that he cleared. He paused at a familiar stop sign, glancing about the car's interior as if to lure out the faint radiance around him, only for it to flit maddeningly in and out of his ken.

"Why won't you just come the hell out?" he growled.

He shrugged forcefully as if to dispel the vexing sense-teaser from his awareness, heading rightward as a trailing vehicle rushed toward the intersection from behind. Tim groaned at the sight of yet another freshly-turned red light in the distance, straddling the crossroads of a heavily trafficked artery within the city. The upcoming delay would be protracted. He tipped the dashboard panel back down to reveal the monitor, preparing to dig in and finish rehearsing the last of the four slides...

Tim gasped and recoiled at the spectacle that greeted him on the screen. The diagrams of his slide had faded into insignificance and were overshadowed by a figure that was drawing itself right before his eyes. It was that face once again, the same one that had transfixed him the day before. Yet it was far crisper and more coherent in its currently-emerging rendition—alarmingly so.

The outlines of a nose and mouth were already evident; the cheeks were smoothly delineated yet slightly asymmetric, as if to highlight the characteristic ridges, peaks, and valleys marking the mien of a unique individual. Waves of soft hair were softly caressing a shapely neck and gentle forehead, while eyebrows and lashes grew more apparent above a pair of distinctive eyes. Tim stared at them helplessly, barely managing a breath as they inched ever closer to the fullness of a human countenance.

"Ah, God, no!"

He was shocked from his trance by the frantic honking of a truck's horn directly ahead. Tim's car had drifted past the chipped yellow midline, perilously close to an oncoming pair of vehicles that had turned on from the main route before him. He veered back to the right in a panic, gritting his teeth as he slammed down the brakes.

To his horror, he realized that he had overcorrected his position: The car skidded into a series of spins that brought him lurching toward a culvert bordering the road. He crossed his arms to shield his face, bracing himself for impact as the car shot forward, plunging down into the ditch.

BACK ON THAT HIDEOUS DAY THREE YEARS AGO...
AROUND 4 IN THE AFTERNOON
THAT SAME DAMNED HOSPITAL IN SURINAME

"Dad? Dad!! Oh my God, what happened?!"

"Uhhh—Chloe? Sweetie?"

"Dad, what's wrong? Why are you so out of breath? Why can't you talk?"

"A little groggy, that's all. The docs have me pretty well knocked-out. I got... banged up bad out there."

"Aunt Sophie called us in the middle of the night, she said there was an accident but the hospital down here couldn't answer any questions. She put us on a plane straight here to Paramaribo."

"Mark's here, too?"

"He's outside in the waiting room. He's terrified, Dad, but he can't face you. He's afraid of what you'll tell him."

"It was like a rockface splitting in two and collapsing right on the car. We were driving in the passes through the Wilhelmina Mountains to the south, and I took a wrong turn. Then there was a sea of stones, and a boulder. I—I couldn't stop in time."

"Where's Mom? Is she in one of the other patient rooms here?"

"Chloe, Mom, uh—"

"Dad, where is she?"

"Chloe, please don't cry like that."

"I want to see Mom! Where is she, Dad? Where's Mom?"

WEDNESDAY, MAY 21, 2025, 1:19 P.M.
RUST BELT LANE, NEWCOMEN INDUSTRIAL PARK
OLD CHAPEL HILL, NORTH CAROLINA

Tim groaned as he lifted his blood-smeared nose from the steering wheel's air bag. He pressed a pair of fingertips into the hollows above his drooping eyelids, massaging out the pain there. Yet his senses were otherwise dimmed from the car's collision. His ears were straining to break through a disorienting tomb of silence while his eyes slowly dragged themselves back to an outward focus from his brief spell of unconsciousness. His dulled perceptions had muted the initial shock, but he dreaded it nonetheless, like a man awaiting the onrush of throbbing from a stubbed toe.

As he came to, he groped instinctively for the door handle, yanking it open while he snatched the keys and unfastened his seatbelt. He staggered out of the car in a daze, landing at the top of the roadside culvert and shambling back against the vehicle's frame, his shoulder blades nestling into a crevice left by the slightly-opened window on the driver's side. He cradled the back of his head atop a ridge that ran between the door and the roof of the car, heaving and gazing skyward.

Tim clamped his eyes shut and leaned back, sucking in the cool ambient air. It was filthy, its drizzly wisps permeated with soot and the grotty miasma of chronic industrial neglect, but he wasn't thinking about the air quality. Each breath brought his half-drowned senses bounding back to the surface, culminating in an unwelcome signal from a belt-buckle pager that duly assaulted his eardrums.

"Chloe," he remarked, his face twisting in a pained grimace upon glancing down at the message on the pager. He texted a perfunctory promise to call soon, buying himself a few minutes to craft a delicate response. He then tipped his head back again and shut his eyes, viscerally dreading the frightened voice that would surely greet his call.

His anxious stupor was shaken only by the cautious pleas of another voice. This one was asking Tim to grab hold of an ice pack hastily wrapped in a pair of dishrags.

"This is actually for your forehead," the man advised. "But you should probably choke off the bleeder in your nostrils first. Pinch the cartilage against the bone, lean forward for a couple minutes, then transfer the ice pack to your nose."

"Wha—oh, dammit." Tim flinched in dismay at the sight of his clothes, splattered with the blood still trickling from his nostrils and abraded skin. "So much for any epiphanies with Ezra Gordon this afternoon," he murmured to himself in frustration. Following a brief spell of fruitless introspection, he took the man's advice, dabbing his cut and bruised forehead as he stanched the bleeding from his nose.

"You sure you're OK, buddy?" asked the stranger, worried as much by Tim's persistent state of distraction as by his wounds. "I've seen more than my share of accidents on this broken-down road, and you're lucky compared to most. Looks like your car straddled a bit of the upslope from that gutter after plunging in, so you may have escaped the worst. But you—and your wheels—still absorbed one hell of a blow. You really should go to the hospital to rule out anything serious."

"I'm afraid that'd merely dredge out still more layers from the hole I've already dug myself into," Tim replied nasally, twisting back to scrutinize the damage to his front bumper and hood.

"No insurance for the hospital or the sick wagon to get there, eh? I've heard the whispered warnings, too. They say the bill from a three-day stay might as well be a second mortgage."

"If only it were so straightforward," said Tim with a strained, sardonic chuckle. "The problem's more a matter of me being a reliable fuck-up in everything I touch these days."

The man's jaw quivered slightly as he took this in.

"My name's Giuseppe," he said after a few moments' silence. "Giuseppe Galieri. I'm a restaurateur; my café's across the street."

"Tim Shoemaker." The two nodded in place of a handshake, Tim tilting his head slightly sideways in curiosity at the kindly man behind the mottled, pasta and sauce-stained smock. "From Joe's Pizzeria Tesoro, right? 'La mia casa è anche la tua.'"

"Good to know my name precedes me."

"It had a familiar ring to it, or at least your ad jingle did. But I'd never approached your restaurant from this trajectory, needless to say. I'm a professor down the 15-501 Freeway. I used to stop by or order in your Pizza Pretzels all the time. They were a Godsend for my round-the-clockers during grant-writing season. Though honestly, I never saw you there before."

"I wasn't there much to be seen, until last month. I have a more upscale place out in Carrboro; my custom was always to hunker down in the kitchen there while my team took the reins at the pizzeria back here. But then those thieving Crassus Brothers got their hooks on all the public utilities. They've already jacked up the electrical and water rates while the service shrivels away, and now that they've locked up the region as their personal fief, it's all about to shoot up even more."

"So I've heard."

"I've had to lay off half my staff and split my time between the two operations. Say, what's that sound? It's a chirping noise, like a pager."

"CC," Tim said with a dispirited sigh, torquing the belt loops of his pants to eye his beeper again.

"What's that?"

"A page from my daughter—Chloe Carolina Shoemaker. I have to switch off my cell phone all the time for lectures and professional glad-handing, so the beeper stays on for her to reach me in case something goes amiss, for her or for Dad."

"So—she knows when you're in harm's way?"

"Nothing specific," Tim answered matter-of-factly. "It's a variant of the Hawk's-Eye Tracker the military developed for embedded combat zones years ago. I was actually one of the civilian engineers roped into its early gestation, before . . . other matters soaked up my attention. Anyway, some fishing boat captains later adopted it to rescue their men overboard. I got it from an old pal who trawls for shrimp along the Outer Banks."

"I've heard about that. Some watertight microprocessor under the wristwatch, right?"

"Measures pulse, pore diameter, ambient and body temperature, all these proxies of the sympathetic nervous system."

"Ah, the fight-or-flight response in the thick of danger. I was headed for medical school myself years ago, before the price tag lent a more appealing sheen to Mama and Papa's restaurant biz."

"Seems like you haven't missed a beat, regardless," observed Tim. "Anyhow, this gadget is fine-tuned to crunch all the data into a magic algorithm, to detect whenever its owner is in physical danger or otherwise having an all-around bad day. It then links up to a satellite from the GPS or the ESN network from Europe, and beams a location to the contact person. Chloe and my son Mark insisted that I all but implant this thing surgically under my skin."

"Can't fault them for lack of vigilance."

"Let's just say this isn't the first time I've had a rough go of things behind the wheel," Tim replied with a sigh, unclasping the pager and powering on his cell phone.

"I suppose you have a couple calls on your agenda," mused Giuseppe, discarding the used ice pack from Tim's hand.

"Just one, actually. Chloe's in an oceanography program on the opposite coast at Puget Sound, a three-hour time lag though nothing insurmountable. But Mark's half a world away in Abu Dhabi, and never very eager to interrupt his day for trifles like father-son talks."

"I feel your pain. I have one son in Qatar and another in Helsinki. It was such a trial for them to snag those exit visas, I doubt they'll be visiting home anytime soon. The Reckoning's been like a mythical wind for the young'uns these days, scattering them across the globe. They've gotta be firing on all cylinders to retain their work permits, which I guess means that calls to Dad don't always figure high on the priority list."

"Yeah, I guess," said Tim with a forced grin, rankled by the insincerity of his reply.

"Well, I should head back to the kitchen. As for your car, call me crazy but I wonder if it might still be roadworthy. The front grille's clearly had better days, but it looks like you fell into that drainway on a straight enough angle to spare the tires and chassis from anything debilitating. My old business partner runs a towing company; he could have a truck out here within the hour."

"I'd appreciate that, Giuseppe. Thanks for lending a hand."

Tim clutched his cell phone with ambivalence as Giuseppe left. He paused for a moment, puzzling at how the device on his wrist could have remained silent during his previous emergency, when he'd been shell-shocked and momentarily blinded in the conference room at Pegasus Atlantic Bank. He quickly shook off the thought, however, and entered the number from his pager. He hesitated once more before completing the call, wrestling with what to say. He came up with nothing, sighed and hit the Dial button.

"Dad!" His daughter's voice bore a potent mixture of breathless apprehension, gnawing resentment, and tearful relief.

"Hey, CC."

"What took you so long to call? And please don't make up some excuse. I know this game; that text you sent me was to buy time, wasn't it? You didn't want me to hear you speak, and I know the reason isn't good."

"Well, I guess I can't make up any excuses now," Tim said with a contrived chuckle.

"What happened?"

"It's kind of a long story, sweetheart."

"Well, then you should start telling it right away."

Again Tim forced a laugh. "It's nothing to be upset about, CC—just a comedy of errors and miseries out here with my pre-sabbatical preparations."

"Try again, Dad. I read the manual on the Hawk's-Eye Tracker from cover to wrinkled cover. I know what it means when that signal's triggered. It doesn't go off just because you're having a lousy day."

"Well, today's been plenty lousy. Not in the life-threatening sense, though. I was—packing away some old lab equipment into storage while making my plans to ditch town next week."

"Please, I really—"

"And the moving company," Tim said, speaking over her, "they mixed up the orders and shipped everything to the wrong side of town. I had to track down and verify all the items, then spend half the day fighting to convince them that my invoice matched the goods they'd delivered to the switched-up site. I guess it got to me enough that I...blew my top out here arguing my case, very nearly brought the warehouse down on my shoulders."

"Must have been one hell of a dust-up," Chloe replied, still unconvinced. "What happened to 'winning battles with calm persuasion rather than rage and confrontation'? You and Mom must have repeated that refrain to Mark and me a million times from...from when we were still in the womb, probably."

"What can I tell you, I guess Dad didn't follow his own wise counsel," Tim said awkwardly, seizing the opening she'd given him to change the subject. "Speaking of your brother, what's the latest news out of Abu Dhabi? He and I chat maybe once every three months."

"Actually, that sounds like an improvement over before."

Tim sighed.

"You're right; it is. Even so, conversations rarely breach the surface of the mundane: How's work, how's he getting around in the desert, any new dust storms lately...Mark's...Mark is still Mark."

"Mark is still Mark because he's still *you* in so many ways, Dad. Bottling up his misery; refusing to say a word about what's bothering him—that's your playbook. I don't think you have standing to complain when Mark follows suit."

"I guess that's fair," Tim said.

"Mark's never been able to work out the trauma of that day in Suriname. He puffs up that stiff upper lip of his, yet even he knows it's a sham. It's why he chose to live two continents away from you. And from me. He doesn't want to be reminded."

"I know that sentiment too well because—well, because you're right in what you said. I've been doing the same thing in my own way."

"But there was something else that still frightens him to his core, Dad. He swore me to silence when he told me, but—I think that's only made things worse for all of us."

"What do you mean, CC?"

"It was at Mom's funeral. You were putting on a show of self-assurance for the two of us, so we wouldn't worry about your own state of mind. But Mark had wandered off on his own after the main ceremony, and he'd somehow strayed into one of the sealed-off corridors by the chapel. He wound up outside the double doors of that parlor, where you were speaking frankly with Pastor George and Rabbi Ted. He overheard what you said."

"What I—what I said?" Tim said softly, his memory clouded by a fog of diffuse shame and denial.

"Mark quoted your words verbatim to me, the way you were reviling yourself… that you didn't care anymore whether you lived or died. It's haunted us both ever since. It's why we insisted you get the Hawk's-Eye Tracker. We couldn't trust you to take care of yourself, and we couldn't even tell you why."

Tim bit his tongue and forced down a painful lump in his throat.

"Chloe, Sweetie, it pains me so much to hear that you two were holding that in. I admit it: I've been powerless to deal with Mom's loss myself; I'm nowhere close to it even now. But what I said in that parlor… I don't have that impulse anymore. As Mom herself would have told you, the things I said then—they were the unfiltered cries of a heart rubbed raw."

"But you just said you're still powerless to deal with her loss; your heart's still rubbed raw. Horribly so. You're still tormenting yourself without any idea of how to escape from your own cruelty. Do you really think you're putting *my* heart at ease by pretending—by *always* pretending? I know that trick. I know it all too well."

Chloe's voice was trembling with choked-back tears. Yet it was also paradoxically full of resolve, poignant and incisive in the message that she was conveying to her father.

"Dad, there's something you're urgently looking for even if you won't acknowledge it outright. Something connected to Mom and everything she meant to us. You have to find it. If not for yourself, then for me and especially for Mark. So that one day we can sleep without having to fear that... that one day, we'll wake up only to hear we've lost our father, too."

His cell phone back in his pocket, Tim ambled to the edge of the downsloping culvert, directly to the right of his car, and sat down at the edge of the shallow ditch. He felt numb at first—a coping mechanism, he thought, for the deluge of emotion threatening to wash over him since retrieving that picture from his wallet. But he was soon doubling over, the pit of his stomach overcome by the full force of what had just transpired.

He was sickened by his own dishonesty with his daughter, even as his rational mind could conceive of no alternative to the clumsy lie he'd told her in the pressure of the moment. Rationalizations—yeah, those came easy, he thought. Didn't matter whether they were justified or not; that wasn't what was really getting to him. It was Chloe's revelation itself, and the precocity and unsparing depth of her insights.

Yet to his surprise, he also found her words to be stirring up a long-neglected reservoir of determination inside him. Tim arose with a start and strode up the back slope of the culvert to access the front passenger's-side door of the car. He peered through the window, his line of sight gradually locking onto the dashboard display that had wrested his attention before the wreck.

To his disappointment, however, the fragile screen had been cracked up and down its midline, shattering any chance of replicating whatever had mesmerized him in the first place. He winced and turned around, and rested his back at an awkward angle against the door. A moment later, however, he remembered something else.

"The picture!"

He dug his key ring from his pocket and went to unlock the door.

"Dammit!"

The door was stuck. Tim turned the key gently as he jiggled the handle. After a minute or two of turning and jiggling, he managed to swing the door about a third of the way open. He spotted his wallet, crumpled on a forward section of the footrest, and quickly retrieved it. But the picture was nowhere to be found. He did a sweep of the floor mat but came up with nothing.

"Come on, where are you?"

Wrenching his keys from the lock, Tim turned on a small pocket flashlight dangling from the keychain and did a more thorough search of the car. After a few moments, he glimpsed the edge of the precious photograph sticking out from a crack on the underside of the glove compartment. Leaning into the partly-opened door, he reached inside the car to get the picture. His fingertips came tantalizingly close to it but still fell about an inch short. He snarled in aggravation and, scanning the compartment, spied a miniature umbrella that had been dislodged from its holder under the seat.

He maneuvered the umbrella's steel-tipped cap to press the photo delicately against the surface above it, prying it out, slowly, gently…There! He stepped away from the car to examine the picture in the dull shine of the overcast afternoon, cupping a hand above to shield it from the drizzle.

Tim began pacing up and down the central lane of the culvert, strewn as it was with tiny puddles and coarse vegetation bursting through its pockmarked, fissured surface. As he inched further away from the car, he puzzled at the evocative power of the photograph, its poignant moment reaching out to him from across time. The faces of his children, of Susan, even of Tim himself seemed to be calling out to him, relaying a message he was as yet too blind or fearful to perceive.

"Whoa! What the—"

Tim leapt briskly forward, startled by the sound of gnashing metal behind him. He whipped back around to see the rear wheels of his car now poised precariously over the ditch, having swung around in an arc so that the back right tire spun futilely in the space above the center of the culvert. The drizzle had picked up by now, and the vehicle must have slid on the rain-slicked grass of the gently sloping hill beside the ditch. His own jostling mere minutes ago might have also done its part—when he himself was in the car's path.

He shook his head, shuddering at the thought and pivoting back around to walk away. But he halted in his tracks, as if frozen by the vestiges of a half-glimpsed phenomenon that had lapped at the fringes of his consciousness a moment before. He glanced obliquely upward, squinting his eyes while shuffling through his recent memories. *What the hell was that just now?* Was it real? Or another phantom—a fluttering of an overactive imagination?

No—he'd seen something, he could swear it. He turned back around slowly, looking intently through the car's back window for several minutes. There was nothing behind its glass now, at least not that he could see in the dreary light and nagging cloud-spittle still coming down. But he was sure it had been there: that same elusive glow, taunting him with every revisit of a past that he could no longer lock away.

Wenn sich die Glieder einer Kette
miteinander einigen,
Sagt man nie, dass sie dann sich
an 'was bewusst beteiligen.
Also gibt's auch so eine Kette,
bleibend da hinter die Stirn.
Wieso denn, schafft dies' Kette
das Bewusstsein im Gehirn?

Chapter Nine

Heralds of a Strange Apocalypse

Mother and child, 1945

WEDNESDAY, MAY 21, 4:43 P.M.
LABORATORY OF DR. TIMOTHY SHOEMAKER
DEPARTMENT OF ENGINEERING, 3RD FLOOR
DALTON UNIVERSITY
DURHAM, NORTH CAROLINA

"So, Dr. Choi, word is you'll be at the premiere of a certain much-anticipated production tonight, with a certain special someone headlining the cast."

Matt Hansen unfastened the last snap on his lab coat and doffed his work goggles as he spoke, joining his friend and colleague in the small lounge as a microwave oven hummed behind them.

"Then the secret's out," Zach answered dryly. "Yeah, Renee's playing Cosette in *Les Misérables* tonight. And I thought I'd issued a specific injunction at my thesis defense against ever spouting that epithet in my direction."

"Dr. Choi? Dr. Choi? Paging Dr. Choi?"

"This is your last warning, Matt. One more time and you'll be 'Faceplant Hansen' the rest of the week. Yes, I did hear of your spectacular tumble at the pick-up basketball tournament last month and yes, I will gleefully rub it in if pressured.'

"Aww, pal, no need to be such a curmudgeon about it. You give me something to aspire to."

"Then I pity you already."

The two shared a sardonic chuckle as the microwave's bell dinged. Zach dipped his finger into the bowl of soup inside and set the microwave for another minute.

"So why didn't you tell us?" Matt asked as the two sat at the table in the center of the room. "The Doghouse Denizens would've happily hijacked the mezzanine section to cheer Renee on for the big night."

"She was a little nervous about the debut; her acting troupe hasn't organized anything on this scale before. And assuming they can fix up their rustbucket of a tour bus, they'll be rolling throughout the Carolinas after the show's run is wrapped up here. She was iffy about even me attending her premiere, let alone dragging a dozen of my fellow malcontents in tow."

"Can't blame her for that. I'm surprised we haven't been uninvited more regularly from these sorts of events. Anyway, so long as the production packs in a few weeks' worth of outings in its current run, I figure we'll find our way to the theater at some point."

"Ah, don't sweat it. Give me a headcount here and I'm sure she could scare up a few tickets for us."

"A fine lady you have by your side, Zach."

"I always thought you had the market cornered in that department. How long have you and Melissa had the soulmate thing going on? Ten years now?"

"On-and-off ever since that freshman prom, with the 'on' now having permanently overtaken the 'off.' High school lovebirds and beyond."

"You've definitely got us beat on that score. At least Renee and I have the on-and-off part down, though the latter's had a decided advantage in our case."

"Why are you always so merciless with yourself about that? The two of you drifted apart for a while. It happens."

"Drifted apart?" Zach asked with a mocking laugh. "More like Renee snapped up a one-way solo ticket to Splitsville two years ago. She all but disappeared for six months in Hong Kong, with me an ocean and a world away."

"Well, like what's-his-name said, absence makes the heart grow fonder."

"Um... not exactly, Matt. For weeks after the burglary, I was on a liquid diet of vodka shots and Jägerbombs. Apparently, she felt my drunken deadbeat routine was interfering with our quality time together. Go figure."

"Given that you filled half those six months with the company of Lin Jie, you weren't all too shabby as drunken deadbeats go."

Zach squirmed at the reference. Matt grinned impishly.

"Don't tell me you honestly believed we didn't know," Matt said. "A fellow Doghouse Denizen makes it with a model-slash-nightclub singer? Please. The Doghouse gossip monster was running at full tilt."

"You're knocking loudly on a door with a bright red 'Keep the Hell Out' sign," growled Zach, nervously shaking his head, not meeting Matt's eye. "I'm officially off the market now. Renee and I are back together. That means major demerit points for reflecting on girlfriends past. Even more so for rebound relationships past."

"C'mon, Zach, we're just two guys yapping with each other; the rule doesn't apply here. Hell, what rule does apply in the Doghouse? We're talking sovereign territory here."

"Ah, the Zen of Matt Hansen. If two jerks blather in the woods but their women aren't there to hear it, do the jerks make a sound?"

"Works for me. Besides, if experience has taught me anything, it's that our better halves love us for our contradictions, for which you are truly the peerless archetype. In fact, it's always intrigued me how you pull it off."

"And you, my friend, are truly without peer in the dark arts of twisted banter, especially in your conjurings of such contorted 'compliments'—or whatever it was you just uttered."

"I never disappoint. Seriously, though—what was Lin Jie's gig?"

"You got the broad outlines right," Zach answered with a sigh. "She was a florist back in China originally, who could somehow channel the gamine eyes of Audrey Hepburn with the reincarnated voice of Josephine Baker." Zach shrugged. "At least, that's what they said on her press releases."

Zach studied the lab ceiling with a look that was half-wince, half-smile.

"I realize now," he continued, "it's what drew me to Lin Jie during those Driftwood Days when I'd lost sight of... everything. Beneath all the manufactured glitz and sparkle, she was real. She didn't take herself or her celeb status too seriously, never bought into her own hype. And she didn't stick to just the ritzy nightclubs."

Matt nodded.

"I heard. I remember thinking that was very generous of her, very democratic, lightening the spirits of all the broken shells in the old downtown dives."

"How do you think I met her?"

"Yet here you and Renee are—back together, the old spark re-lit. It's a nice story, Zach."

"The heart has its own playbook," said Zach without hesitation, as if summoning a long-readied response. "It's always gushing with ironies that I doubt our feeble little minds will ever digest in full. My own still boggles at the paradox of it all."

"A paradox?"

"That I got to know and adore Renee more than ever after I thought I'd lost her for good. Whenever another soul captures a piece of your heart, there's usually a looming disaster gift-wrapped with the package—"

He cast an uncomfortable glance toward the entryway of the lounge. Matt swiveled in his chair to eye the same spot. Both men shared an uneasy awareness of the reference in Zach's words—and the absent subject at their core.

"But sometimes," Zach added, slowly turning aside from the doorway, "that other soul winds up stripping away all the pretenses you string together for your own self-deception, unearthing a jewel that's been under your nose the whole time. That's what Lin Jie taught me about Renee. What? Don't give me that look. Don't you know, good bluesmen are always by nature savvy dime-store philosophers. I felt like I had one of those old sad melodies echoing in my head when I came seeking out Renee again."

"Waxing poetic, too? You're beginning to scare me."

"It was the little things, you know... Her idiosyncrasies, even ones I hadn't been so crazy about before. Those were her patented inventions, after all. I came to embrace them only after realizing how much I missed them."

"You know better than to leave me hanging like that," Matt chided with tongue firmly in cheek, breaking up an awkward pause in his friend's reminiscence. "Don't worry, no Guy Credentials on the block for spilling the sappy details."

"It wasn't in Renee's repertoire to sleep in on weekends, even when we were both dog-tired from all the water-treading to stay afloat—back in those first terrible months after the Reckoning. Sometimes I was so zonked out that I'd try to sleep right through to the afternoon; believe me, it was more pleasant to stay in Dreamland. But she was like a bouncing ball all around me that wouldn't stop. She made me greet the morning with her. It had used to drive me nuts, but in retrospect, after I thought I'd lost her, I realized how much her attitude helped make those dismal days... less so."

"Melissa's helped me that way, too."

"I wouldn't doubt it, and like Renee with me, there's probably nobody else on this rock who could do that for you in the same way. Speaking of connecting... Whenever Renee and I were in different cities, I'd stumble out of the shower or simply switch on the phone in the morning, only to discover that she'd already called me a dozen times, urging me into this screwbally, wordplay rise-and-shine routine we'd also happened on together. She had this quirky penchant to push me away for a moment when we were chatting, or glance aside when she talked; it was a little pause she used to gather her thoughts."

Zach took a brief pause of his own then, surprised at the depth and force of his own recollections.

"Renee had this—I don't know what to call it—this sweet vanity to her, the way she'd tease me posing in all the photos we snapped, her diva skills in karaoke. Yet not in a pretentious sort of way... And then there were all her Renee-isms, years ago when she was fresh in from Hong Kong—the way an 'apostrophe' became a 'catastrophe,' or the way she first interpreted a turn of phrase or idiom like 'the straw that broke the camel's back.'"

"'The last straw that killed the camel,'" Matt interjected with a genial chuckle. "I think that one ignited a bit of reverse acculturation; Melissa and I use it all the time."

"Then you grok my vibe. All those eccentricities and trifles... individually they didn't amount to much, but altogether, somehow they defined Renee and framed whatever clumsy self-portrait we were sketching out together. I suppose that's why I'm feeling kind of dark these days. I can't imagine losing her again, and losing all that, now—"

Zach paused again, his attention this time riveted by a shoebox-sized photo affixed to a cabinet in a nearby corner. It had been a humble yet familiar fixture over the past six-odd years, a rousing emblem of teamwork and esprit de corps: Tim and a quintet of his young charges in full-on rowing regalia, posed triumphantly with their medals in a canoe moored to a nearby dock.

"That was from the Lumber River Regatta, right?" asked Matt. "It was before I'd arrived on the scene here, but I remember being bombarded by all the rowing lore during my first week in town: *Doghouse Denizens and Rulers of the Rapids*."

"We came in second actually," Zach said, his gaze dissolving into a wistful stare. "Still quite a feat, given that our sponsoring boathouse probably hadn't updated its equipment since the days of the Civil War Ironclads. The regatta took place after I'd already committed my next five years to the PhD program here, but before I'd formally enrolled. Yet even then, Tim and his Gift of Gab had gotten me paddling oars well beyond the setting sun for his team."

"Before you'd enrolled—ah, I remember now. You deferred a year before disappearing behind these walls, didn't you? I still marvel at whatever dog-and-pony show you must have been hustling, to draw a paycheck for essentially plying the ski routes in a little corner of southeastern Switzerland."

"And in Austria and South Tyrol," Zach mused. "Yes, such an arduous task it was, manning the pristine slopes and ski chalets in a trio of Alpine wonderlands. I wonder sometimes what idiocy convinced me to leave that little outpost of heaven."

His mood abruptly sobered as he studied the picture.

"I remember that afternoon on my shift," he resumed, "when the dam first broke, and Fisher's Reckoning came rushing in like the Flood. My team had been blissfully supervising a slalom course in the Swiss Alps. It was a balm for all of us in the years that followed."

"A balm? What are you referring to?"

"The memories from the day before the news got out to us; we were so isolated out there on the slopes. I clung to those memories for the same reason that Tim once adored the photo on the cabinet so much, doting and fawning over it like a proud father. Like a last gasp of innocence, before the ashes of the Reckoning came raining down to—to smother that happy world."

"Odd that you'd mention that, since I've never seen Tim so much as glance at that picture. For that matter—call me crazy, but every time he pops his head through the doorway of this lounge, I swear the rest of his body almost never follows."

"There's a reason for that, Matt. Like you said, the Regatta took place long before you got here, three years ago."

"Why is 'three years ago' suddenly the magic phrase in all this?"

"She's not in it," Zach explained, "but she was there at the pier by the river. It was Susan who snapped that picture."

4:57 P.M.

After an uncomfortable two minutes, Zach abruptly rose and fetched his soup from the microwave. He sat down at the table and crumbled a cracker into the broth. Matt watched his friend eat for a minute or so, reflecting on what had just happened. The tragedy evoked by that picture was poignant, and Zach must have felt it, no doubt. But not from a comfortable distance. Tim had lost someone dear to him; now Zach was fearing the same was in store for him.

"You know you'll have to tell Renee at some point," Matt began.

Zach dropped his spoon awkwardly into the soup and grimaced.

"It's not a good time for this, Matt," he said with his eyes still on the soup.

"When will it ever be a good time? I'm only being real with you, Zach. I'd hope anyone calling himself my friend would do the same for me."

"With what aim in mind?" Zach retorted indignantly, his ire and irony now aimed directly at Matt. "What could I accomplish by telling Renee now? 'Hey, Honey, I'm on The Blacklist of the Damned Souls with no prospect of gainful employment in the next decade, but on the bright side, I hear they're selling pup tents at steep markdowns over at Joe's Tent City Emporium.'"

"How about we pick up where we left off at the Cantina last Thursday. You said Renee's family has some pull in Taiwan and Hong Kong, and they'd vouch for you there no problem. Don't write off a prospect like that merely because you can't sign your name in Chinese yet. Her family could probably lock down an interim sinecure for you while you're learning the language."

"Acculturating to a world outside the Triantarchs' clutches isn't much use if you can never escape them in the first place."

Matt began to reply but quickly stopped himself, instead further studying Zach's fidgets and gestures to get a better read on what he was thinking.

"Zach," Matt said at last, "what exactly did you dig up?"

"Over the weekend, after what you said at the Cantina, I decided to check back in on the prospects of leaving town. I got in touch with an old friend, connections with the Jacques Neckers..."

"With the Underground? Good God, Zach, I was hoping you'd be proactive about this quandary you're in, but that's a little more than I had in mind. I'm obviously no expert on the rules of the road for Blacklistees, but going anywhere near the Underground—"

"I used back channels, I... Let's just say we communicated through a third party. Not like it matters anyway, because according to them, the noose is even tighter than I'd thought."

"You already knew it was tough getting out, but it has been done. Look, I did some digging of my own recently with the help of a distant cousin—she's a retired army officer with contacts among the intelligence spooks. No spectacular revelations other than what I think you already know: Many of the Damned Souls have slipped the chokehold of the Blacklist; a few have done so without even having to ditch the country."

"Matt, listen to me—"

"Once again, you're clipping your own wings."

"No, I'm not. *Everything's* changed since the start of this year, all of it for the worse. It goes beyond the block on the exit visas. There are probably ways around that, but as of this February, the Ruling Clans have made a database check mandatory at all the airports and other points of departure. It's about the only damn infrastructure that's still functional anymore. I should've seen the writing on the wall when Governor Rossdale was conveniently 'disappeared' right before the Crassus Brothers moved into the North Carolina Statehouse."

"So that's it—you're just gonna give up?"

"Can't you see, Matt? They're no longer content to work from the shadows anymore. The Clans are seizing power and flaunting it right in the open. The Jacques Neckers think it's a prelude to a mass crackdown, like in those old-fashioned dictatorships that don't pretend to go halfway."

"But we talked about this at the Cantina—that's not their style. Much cheaper and more lucrative to let others do the dirty work and lovingly document a few shock-value examples to cow the masses. Networks of informants? A real secret police? Too much trouble and upkeep, too many hired thugs to pay off. I don't see the Triantarchs going full Orwell on us, at least not yet. They're a kleptocracy at heart."

"I don't know their mindset, any more than I know why they put me on their damn Blacklist. But they've decided all those hints and insinuations of despotism aren't enough anymore. There was apparently a lot of chatter among the Underground hacktivists about a military foray into the breakaway regions, or another war on the way overseas... Nobody's exactly sure. But the window's all but closed to make any move now. Even with an exit visa in hand, I'd be detained before I could board the aircraft or ship and what's worse, Renee would be implicated, too."

"Wait, you're saying they'd go after—"

"Yes, that is what I'm saying. And there's not a damn thing you or I can do about it."

"Would you mind telling me the name of this cowering impostor who's taken over Zach's body?" retorted Matt, purportedly incensed by his friend's defeatist tone yet also by the fears he himself was now entertaining.

"Go ask the dirtbags who stole my life away two years ago. I'm sure they'll have an answer to suit your fancy."

"God da—" seethed Matt, choking off his speech. He took a moment to steady himself. "Look at yourself, Zach. More importantly, *listen* to yourself. Giving up so meekly. That kind of death wish-fulfillment will grind down your spirit like a pebble in a stone crusher."

"Which would matter if I had an actual alternative. I appreciate your intentions, Matt, but I'm done stringing up prayer beads for the false hope fairy. I'm not deluding myself anymore."

"No, in fact, that's exactly what you're doing. We don't need to oust the Ruling Clans to beat them. The small victories count, too. When us little folks simply find a way to survive and thrive, without fearing or depending on the Triantarchy."

Zach merely glared at his friend in response, slurping his soup with exaggerated alacrity. His companion frowned, glancing aside as he tried a new tack.

"There's something I never told you," Matt began cautiously, "about my own brush with the Ruling Clans. Most of Melissa's college tuition was covered by a Kepler Scholarship when she first enrolled. But then Clan Argentus, in their infinite wisdom, decided that such subsidies were a waste of the public coffers that they could better pillage instead. So they canceled the Kepler and other grant programs, even as her fees were skyrocketing with each new semester."

"Just say it," urged Zach, bristling with contempt for their implied tormentors. "They were grooming her for the debtor's prisons, weren't they?"

"Hell if I'd ever let that happen. I took extra shifts at the Morse Cannery and chipped in for her any way I could, but it was barely a drop in the bucket after her father was laid off. So she began working nights at the—"

"Troubadour Lounge."

"You knew about that?" Matt asked. His cheeks paled as Zach looked up from his soup, amused at the disquieting thoughts clearly swirling in his friend's head.

"Oxygen is your friend," said Zach with a raspy chuckle. "Don't worry, it's not because I ever patronized the joint myself. Lin Jie had done a few stints at the Lounge before we met, and she saw Melissa by one of the poles that the exotic dancers would twirl around... Anyway, she told me she'd seen Melissa there. Or rather, mentioned it—she figured I already knew."

"It's admittedly on the awkward side. Not sure how the arbiters of etiquette would advise a guy to ice-break on a topic like that."

"Of course I wouldn't have brought it up out of the blue; I knew it must have been uncomfortable for you. Though to be honest, at times I wanted to pipe up about it simply to tell you it was no big deal. It actually reflects well on her—and on you for understanding why she had to work at the Troubadour for a while. Snobs judge people for doing jobs like that, because they don't have normal-people troubles."

"I'm relieved to hear that coming from you... and still a bit surprised, I have to admit."

"Why would you be, Matt? Isn't this what you yourself were trying to say? All the Triantarchs' sneering sycophants in polite society will never have a damn clue about what hounds the rest of us as we plow through their muck—the moral compromises, the tough calls and swallowed pride. Melissa did what she had to with the hand she was dealt, and she had the guts to keep her chin up and carry on."

Zach rested his voice with a reflective pause.

"The pole dancers," he added, "street hustlers, ditch-diggers, day-laborers—they've all got more dignity than any of the black-tie sociopaths or backstabbing flunkies on the Ruling Clans' payroll. Maybe in their own way, their little acts of defiance all add up to those small victories you were touting just now."

"Then you're with me, Zach. So now it's time for you to take the next step, and draw some concrete inspiration from their examples."

"I would. Believe me, I've turned over more grimy, moss-encrusted stones than you could imagine; I've all but begged for paid assignments well outside our field. But everyone's too stiff-scared to invite even a passing association with The Blacklist now. If you think about it, back-alley joints have even greater reason to shun me than straight-up businesses, because they're already worried about being shut down. It really is that bad, Matt. I've gone so far as to consider casting my lot with one of the Underground groups."

"You're really thinking of *joining* the Jacques Neckers?" asked Matt, stirring with a nervous twitch of the jaw.

"Whatever's left of them; or if need be, one of their more radical offshoots like the Wat Tylers. At least I was, based on what I first heard this weekend. Apparently, they all run little co-op industries that at least defray the monthly bills for their crews. But after about ten seconds of reflection... You can probably guess you're not the only one to be driven paranoid by the very thought. Much as I'd like to toss some mud in the eyes of the Triantarchy, the latest news from the Underground—ill winds are already blowing."

"That upcoming crackdown you were warning about?"

"The Clans are sharpening their bayonets. The plan is to liquidate the Wat Tylers and the original Jacques Neckers, along with anyone associated with them. I can't simply slip off the grid with my name already on The Blacklist, and if one of the Triantarchs' lackeys found me so much as dishwashing for one of the Underground co-ops—"

Zach's cheeks were now noticeably ashen.

"They'd show up at Renee's doorstep, too," he continued. "As surely as they would if I tried to cross the border or stow myself on a plane or ship headed for... wherever. Every possible way out of this would place Renee right in the same line of fire."

"So it's true then," said Matt. "Even with all they've done, I used to believe the Ruling Clans wouldn't cross that line, at least not since the

Mayfly Massacre. I figured they were still too divided and, you know, 'This is still America—that can't happen here.' All wishful thinking—we really are drifting into it now, aren't we? Disappearing loved ones of alleged enemies, going after Renee... Hell, that's fascism without the fig leaf."

"They don't need to dress up their ill intentions any longer. Governor Rossdale was disappeared, and she's not the sort of small fry the Triantarchs usually single out. The Clans control nearly everything now: the legislatures, courts, banks, energy suppliers, law enforcement and regulatory agencies. There's not a single check left on their power anymore."

"If Renee's really in such danger, why not tell her? So that you can at least make a stand together?"

"Because she has options that I don't have, avenues that'll disappear if I drag her into my fight. She still has her overseas passports for now; she can get out. But she'll lose everything if I take her down with me, so the only way I can protect her... is to let her go. It's merely a question of whether I burden her with the gruesome truth before I do it."

"There must be another way. You can't capitulate so meekly. Tim's been sticking his neck out for you, and he has his own friends in high places. Isn't there anything else he could do, maybe something we've overlooked?"

"Perhaps," Zach answered with a peculiar expression, his alarmed eyes fixated on the entrance to the lounge, "but I suspect that now isn't the time to sound him out."

Matt turned around and flinched at the sight of the slumped, bedraggled figure in the doorway.

"Tim!" Matt exclaimed, as he and Zach both rushed out of the lounge to assist their limping mentor. "What happened to you?"

"Nothing but a little charley horse," Tim chuckled weakly. "I'll be back on the tennis court in no time."

"You have a gash on your forehead. The blood's soaked through the bandage," Zach said in response to Tim's raised eyebrows. "Your nose? Seriously, Chief, what happened?"

"I had a little fender-bender."

"Those are not fender-bender injuries, Dr. Understatement. Seriously, what happened?"

"What can I say, Zach, you got me," acknowledged Tim with another bloodless chuckle. The gesture had the opposite of its intended effect; Zach saw more than pain from mere physical injury in the expression on his mentor's face.

"I had a rough go of things today," Tim said, "navigating those decrepit alleyways in the industrial park of Old Chapel Hill; went hurtling straight into a roadside drainage ditch. Still nothing major—heck, I can still drive the old lemon, for now at least."

"I'd say you could use a little tuning-up yourself right now," Zach retorted, increasingly annoyed by Tim's downplaying. "Even without the bumps and bruises, you're exhausted. Your sabbatical's already under way unofficially, so why not just sputter your way back home and collapse?"

"That's still topping the agenda," Tim confirmed. "But I have a little engagement tonight; had to swing by for a few odds-and-ends."

"Tonight?" Matt interjected. "You mean for the talk at Watts Forest U. on Friday? Out in Winston-Salem?"

"No, it's a—" Tim held his tongue, choosing his words with care. "Some unfinished business from my trip to Tennessee. Anyway, now that you've reminded me, I have an appointment to drop my car off at the garage early that same morning, so I'll need a lift out to Winston-Salem and back. I'd better transfer ownership of the pass for the parking lot by the main auditorium where I'll be speaking, before I forget and wind up earning you a parking ticket as a souvenir."

"Guess I'm today's lucky winner," Zach offered with a shrug, accepting the crinkled orange decal Tim took from his wallet. "Are you sure you're even in any shape to sit behind the wheel on the way home today? The shadows around your eyes are flat-out grotesque. I swear, you'd personally scare off the zombies if they came swarming into town."

"I realize I'm not fit for a magazine cover, but I'm fine now, really," Tim quipped with a botched wink, sluggishly gathering his briefcase and belongings. "I'll call you from the body shop on Friday, let's say about two hours before the talk. Should allow plenty of time to bully our way through traffic down to Winston-Salem."

The two young men worriedly looked on as Tim shambled clumsily out the door and into the hallway, watching as he disappeared down an adjacent stairwell. They waited for a moment, wondering if they'd hear a crash as Tim fell down the stairs. Matt breathed an audible sigh of relief when the outside door clanked open and then slammed shut.

For a few seconds they stood in the hallway in silence before returning to the lab. As they turned back inside, Matt caught sight of a small, flexibly-encased rectangular wafer lying askew atop a nearby filing cabinet.

"What's that?" Zach asked.

"Picture. It probably fell out of his wallet when he was entrusting you with that parking decal. He was too out-of-it to notice."

As he stepped back to punch a message into his cell phone, Matt handed his find over to Zach, whose expression turned to one of shock the instant he saw what it was. Matt himself had missed its significance.

"Stubborn jackass," scoffed Matt, in a show of gentle mocking. "Of course Mr. Macho Tough Guy has his cell phone powered off. I can't even send a simple text that he left his family photo here. I guess we'll have to... Zach, what's wrong, man?"

"I wonder if this is tangled up with whatever's been eating at Tim lately," Zach answered, still scrutinizing the photo.

"Why would it?" Matt looked over Zach's shoulder at the picture. "Just some classic photo-album fodder, the whole Shoemaker household before a barn with some cuddly livestock to round it out. My folks must have snapped a couple boxes' worth of those when my sibs and I were always roughhousing around the family farm."

"Matt," Zach said, turning to his friend, "Tim hasn't let himself near these kinds of pictures in almost two years. You were just getting your feet wet here back then and probably didn't realize, but... his office used to be crammed with pictures of Susan and the kids. They were on every wall and windowsill. It's what I first noticed when I was interviewing here more than six years ago. Then he began to remove them after the accident in Suriname, until finally, well, you've seen his office—all of those mementos are gone."

"I remember you constantly reminding me and the other fledglings starting up at the Doghouse, 'Don't mention family, not even in an offhand way.' I got the message, don't get me wrong, but I never could wrap my mind around the reason. Wouldn't a grieving widower take solace in family pictures? I know I would."

"He did, for a while. Then he didn't want to remember anything. Funny thing is, though, you could tell he never stopped thinking about it. Sometimes I wonder if banishing the pictures made him think about it more than ever."

Matt considered this for a moment.

"Then maybe this is a halting step in the right direction, if he's gathered up the emotional reserves to finally re-engage with it all."

"I hope so," Zach said, "but I fear otherwise."

"Maybe you could say something to him when you give him back the picture."

Zach shook his head.

"I'm not going to say anything."

Matt seemed to be expecting his friend to expand on his thoughts, but Zach merely stayed silent, his probing eyes locking their gaze onto the picture.

"Tell you what," added Matt, "I'll put the picture in an envelope, and if Tim asks about it when you pick him up at the auto shop tomorrow, just tell him I have it. I think someone should say something to him, and I think I'm a good candidate for the job—no baggage, ya know?"

"Works for me," Zach said, though he didn't hand the photo to Matt straightaway. He was still studying it, puzzling at its meaning and whatever had prompted Tim to put it in his wallet—and equally unsure if he should tell Matt to seek out the answers to such questions for him.

THURSDAY, MAY 22, 2:37 A.M.
JEAN-MARTIN CHARCOT CONFERENCE ROOM
CLINICAL AND INVESTIGATIVE NEUROLOGY DEPARTMENT
OAK RIDGE, TENNESSEE

Rachel reclined her head against the unevenly textured floor-to-ceiling post behind her stiff chair and snaked a hand back to massage an aching knot between her neck and right shoulder. She shut her eyes as the speaker at the podium before her stepped down, followed by a disorganized five-minute pause in the proceedings of that early morning.

While relieved at the conference's forthcoming adjournment, she felt no joy in her relief. Long hours had been spent, many theories had been discussed, yet a resolution remained infuriatingly out of reach. She glanced to the seat on her right, occupied only by a laptop computer situated at an oblique angle toward the front. A familiar face graced its screen.

"Still holding up there, Tim?" she asked with the hint of a groan.

"I slept off much of the evening, so I have no license to grumble. That your team has managed to round up dozens of burnt-out techies for this at such a depressingly ridiculous hour, though—that's a small miracle."

"More like proof of our abject desperation for answers. We barely had to market this thing to the project members after the initial announcement. It's been standing-room only."

"Needless to say, Rachel, your team's set an intimidating bar for organizational prowess. Even with Triantarch patronage financing each step, it's still quite a feat to videoconference experts from six continents and fourteen time zones, all for the same midnight jamboree."

"Partly because it's been midnight only for us; easy to pick out the beggars from the choosers in this exchange. Besides, I can't take credit for it. This has been Alan's baby all the way."

"Speaking of that particular devil, it would appear that Dr. Simms is about to pick up where he left off. I guess this is last call."

"Ladies and gentlemen," Dr. Simms began, projecting a kind of withered authority from behind the dais, "our thanks to you again for convening with us tonight, wherever in the world you've joined in. To recap, all of us associated with the sight restoration trials have undertaken strenuous efforts to attach a verifiable diagnosis to this unexplained neuropsychiatric condition.

"As you've become aware by now, this apparently degenerative disorder has tragically afflicted our courageous group of veterans since the launch of our vision re-learning program in February of this year. Despite extensive consultations, however, coupled with an exhaustive search of previously attested case studies in the neurological literature, we remain in the dark. We are unaware of any documented syndrome or reported clinical correlate that can explain our findings, nor any indication of causative factors."

He gestured toward his colleague seated beside the podium, her eyelids relentlessly drooping from a losing battle against exhaustion.

"This is why my esteemed associate," Dr. Simms continued, "Dr. Diane Mellon, and I have organized this videoconference with all of you from so many countries, as a consultation of last resort. We've heard from many of you, and you have likewise heard from our very best today, from both the engineering and medical sides of this grand effort. We have sought in the process to present a comprehensive story of that effort up to this point, and of the crisis that continues to grip us. We would therefore welcome any final words of guidance or suggestions that you could furnish."

A sprinkling of polite applause was followed by the deflating silence of unmet expectations. Simms' voice was by now conspicuously hoarse, drained of its resonance by nearly three hours of fielding questions amid a medley of translated voices from two dozen countries. Sighing with a resignation to which he had become long inured, he set out to collect his materials from the speaker's platform and bring the session to a close. Barely a moment after he had tugged the microphone toward his chin, however, a mildly accented voice began to boom through speakers channeling in comments from participants the world over.

"Dr. Simms! Hello, I'm Tomoko Miyazawa. I am one of the interpreters for the medical faculty here at Kagoshima Daigaku, a university hospital here in southern Japan. We have something, may be of interest to you. So sorry to trouble you at such a late hour."

"Not at all, Ms. Miyazawa; we welcome any further input," Dr. Simms replied, intrigued but wary of raising his hopes.

"We happened to have a professor emeritus visiting with us this week, Dr. Kunihiko Yoshida. He has been practicing medicine for more than 70 years; he was on our clinical faculty here at Kagoshima and returns periodically for conferences. We briefed him yesterday from the abstract for your symposium, and again prior to his arrival from the clinic a few minutes ago. He believes that he may recognize that syndrome you have been describing in your patients there."

The interpreter's announcement tore through the room like a rousing tonic for the remaining conferees, their somnolent eyes giving way to the rapt attention borne of breathless anticipation. The two hosts by the dais maintained a more impassive pose for their audience, at least overtly. They quietly pined for a breakthrough yet refused to acknowledge it even to themselves, too stung by the lasting venom of past disappointment.

"Please, continue," Dr. Simms invited with an outstretched hand.

An elderly yet remarkably vigorous man moved into view of the cameras in Kagoshima, still transmitting live to Oak Ridge. He grinned reflexively, then held up a framed, poignant image for his audience: an old, sepia-tinged photograph of a young woman swaddling an infant. They were seated, the woman's face partially concealed behind a thick, gauzy mask.

She clutched her infant, also with mouth shielded, carefully to her bosom. The background was blurry, with what appeared to be a cave or a rock quarry behind her. The doctor then turned to the interpreter, addressing her in Japanese while periodically facing the camera in acknowledgment of his audience.

"Dr. Yoshida is saying," began Ms. Miyazawa, "that this woman was one of his first patients when he was working as an army field medic, prior to formal commencement of his medical studies. Her case left a lasting impression upon him, and he continues to carry this photograph. He said that there was a, I suppose you would say, small wave of a disease that struck about 800 people."

"And the photographed woman was one of the victims?"

"She was in fact the first—what you would call the 'Patient Zero.' His team named it the 'Tachibana Syndrome' after Mutsumi Tachibana. She was a nurse at a mobile medical facility, who first noticed and reported the condition in several patients that she was tending to for other complaints. Another name for it—"

"Pardon me, Ms. Miyazawa," Dr. Simms interrupted, "just wanted to make sure that I understand him correctly. So Dr. Yoshida is confirming that his patients presented with a similar clinical picture as our cohort here?"

The interpreter turned and spoke to the august physician, who nodded and then replied at length.

"Dr. Yoshida says, yes, the illness resembled the one you have depicted. The patients exhibited a gradual neurological deterioration. They also—"

She turned in puzzlement toward Dr. Yoshida, apparently nonplussed by the words she was relaying.

"The patients also reported peculiar phenomena," she continued after a corroborating exchange with the doctor, "images in their minds and even the, as you say, apocalyptic messages to which your own patients have been prone. They drew pictures with some resemblance to the ones your patients have sketched.

"Furthermore, although they did not report the same delusions and hallucinations as your veterans, the specifics were uncannily similar from patient to patient. The doctors did not understand how such circumstances could possibly avail."

"So, this syndrome does have a history," said Dr. Simms, looking obliquely toward Diane Mellon as she nodded an acknowledgment. He turned again to address the interpreter. "I'm still mystified, though, as to why this disorder has not been more thoroughly documented in the clinical literature."

"Dr. Yoshida says that the delusions and other symptoms were less severe than those presenting in your patients. There were no seizures, nothing along lines of... the blood messages on walls. Additionally, the patients recovered eventually, although the affliction persisted for several years in worst cases. Since the original population was so small and the disease thought to be spontaneously self-resolving, Dr. Yoshida's team published only two minor case report articles in the literature. This was many decades ago, so the reports may not be available on electronic databases."

"So they did recuperate," Dr. Mellon repeated in a thready voice directed toward Dr. Simms.

"It worries me that the episodes in our population are so much more pronounced in their features," he reasoned, sharing her cautious burst of encouragement, "though I agree it's a good sign."

Simms paused briefly to digest the thought and rest his own aching vocal cords, before quickly directing his attention back toward the interpreter.

"Ms. Miyazawa, I noticed in the photograph that Dr. Yoshida displayed to us—the woman and her child were both wearing masks. Had the doctor's team discerned a means of... of contagion for this disease?"

"They were initially unsure of its method of transmission, Dr. Simms, so they quarantined much of the region as a precaution. They never could elucidate how and why Tachibana Syndrome manifested within the quarantined zone or treatment facilities, so as a further safeguard at the time this photo was taken, both patients and the doctors donned masks to filter out fine particles. Food supplies were likewise isolated while physical contact was restricted."

"Were these measures effective?"

"They may not have even been necessary. The authorities later lifted the quarantine as there was no documented spread from person to person or through contamination of food or water. In fact, most of the cases were diagnosed within nine months of each other, and outside of that initial cluster, there were only sporadic mentions of other such incidents. These were reported mostly within the families already affected as well as among American soldiers posted in or traveling through the region. There were no more mass outbreaks—until the current one, perhaps."

"I doubt they were testing eye implants back in those days," murmured Simms, inclining slightly toward Dr. Mellon.

"Maybe that's why Dr. Yoshida's patients had smoother sailing," added Dr. Mellon in a breathy whisper. "Still can't suss out a nexus to link our two cohorts, though."

Simms frowned in consternation at the still intractable riddle, grasping for a way forward. As he turned back to the video display, he seasoned his ensuing inquiry with a modicum of ambiguity, inviting his partners across the ocean to expound at their leisure.

"Ms. Miyazawa, we were wondering if Dr. Yoshida—if he noticed anything conspicuous about the patient population. Was there a pattern in the people afflicted?"

"A... a pattern, Dr. Simms?"

"A predilection for contracting the disease based on age or gender, for example? Or patient clusters defined by blood type, location, any other correlating factors to link them together?"

"Ah, yes. Dr. Yoshida, he says that the affected group varied by age, blood type, and gender, almost no predisposing factors observable. Statistical analysis at 95% confidence interval supported only a modestly higher incidence of Tachibana Syndrome in pregnant women compared to general population; it was unclear when or how the mothers contracted the disease. It was not observed in pediatric patients, however, some children of the affected mothers, they—Dr. Yoshida says, hard to describe, but they were... unusual."

"Unusual? In what way?"

"They were extraordinarily bright and precocious; normal youth in most respects but rare prodigies in mathematics and often in music and the visual arts. They were also emotionally brittle and unstable, prone to odd outbursts and vaguely-defined terrors that could sometimes cripple their ability to function."

"Does this pattern describe the child in the photograph, Ms. Miyazawa?" asked Dr. Simms, probing for a breakthrough revelation.

"Yes, very closely. In addition, the mother in that picture—she later told the doctors, her son suffered from graphic nightmares that he always seemed poised to act out. Maybe even a vision comparable to those she reported during her own ordeal with the disease. Otherwise, principal connection among the patients was geographical."

"Now that you mention it," said Dr. Simms, "we were wondering about the background of that photograph behind the young mother. Is that... we couldn't precisely make it out, some kind of a coal mine? A stone pit?"

"No, it is—" began the interpreter cautiously. "In the background, that is rubble from a building. That was what Dr. Yoshida was about to say earlier—another name for Tachibana Syndrome, it is Kinoko Kumo no Netsu. In Japanese this means 'mushroom cloud fever.'"

"Mushroom cloud! So you're saying that Tachibana Syndrome was first observed—"

"Yes, after the atomic bombings in Hiroshima and Nagasaki. All of the affected patients were from these cities and the surrounding districts, fleeing the radioactive fallout. Dr. Yoshida was interning as a teenaged medic's assistant at Hiroshima in 1945. It was there that he met the mother and child in this picture."

The remaining conferees in Oak Ridge looked on in stunned silence. The implications of what they had just heard had barely begun to take hold, yet the narrative filled their hearts with a deep and ineffable dread.

"God, what a horrible association," Rachel remarked.

She pivoted toward the networked laptop to gauge the reaction of her distant partner, and to solicit his own thoughts on the potential significance of the discovery.

"What do you think it—Tim?"

He was tilted away from the computer's webcam, wearing a thunderstruck expression while gazing intensely downward, wracking his fogged and jumbled memories.

"Tim, what is it?" Rachel asked intently. "Where is all this pointing? What does it suggest to you?"

"It suggests much more than I ever—" He shook his head, mouthing a silent epithet of agitated disbelief. "Rachel, I... I'm not sure what to tell you."

"But the way you're reacting—it signifies something to you. People haven't left the conference room yet. Maybe they could help you interpret it."

"They won't be of much help because, honestly, I can't be, either."

"With what? Tim, come on. You're speaking circuitously when this is no time to hold back on anything!"

"It's a personal connection, of sorts, and I want to be clear on this: I'm not even sure if it is a real connection. Or if so, how I could possibly draw it all together into a concrete picture. I'm sorry, Rachel. It's almost 3 a.m., and I'm too drained to express myself coherently right now. Especially if the topic involves rummaging through—through those untended back alleys in my mind. I'll have to sleep on it. Tomorrow, once my slides are all assembled for the research talk on Friday, I promise I'll follow up with you."

"Tim, please, wait. I don't need the tale in full. You can't just leave me hanging like this, leave... all of us like this! What did you hear? Why does it matter so much?"

"It's what that Japanese doctor said, like a prophecy that I... I still don't know, but I fear it means Dr. Yoshida may have been witnessing something far more gruesome than he could have possibly known. Probably best to leave it at that. I'll be in touch."

"What does that—Tim? Are you still there? *Tim?*"

Rachel's pleas went unanswered as her computer screen faded out, her exhausted conversation partner having staggered away and tumbled face-down on a waiting mattress. Upon rising from her seat, she startled at the sight of a small crowd of onlookers gathered about her. Her voice must have breached the bounds of discretion—and Tim's words even more so. The remaining attendees stood around her, buried in stunned silence for another excruciating minute, struggling in vain to assimilate the meaning of what they had just seen and heard.

Wenn die Samen einer Pflanze
in den Grund gesät werden,
Wissen sie was bringt die Zukunft,
ihr' Verwandlung in der Erden?
Wissen Blumen, Blätter und Stiele
woher denn sie alle stammen?
Wann sagt die Pflanz', aus Boden steigend:
„Nun weiß ich, woher ich komme."

Chapter Ten

Seeds of an Ancient Provenance

A warning in Gothic

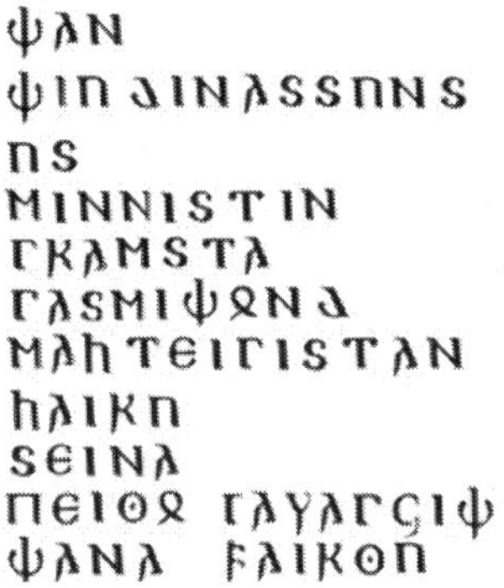

THURSDAY, MAY 22, 7:12 A.M.
HOME OF DR. TIMOTHY SHOEMAKER
WEST CHAPEL HILL, NORTH CAROLINA

Tim awoke gasping and trembling, his left cheek encrusted with the dried remnants of tears and drooled saliva. He rolled over and tentatively opened his eyes. His sleep had been invaded by yet another mind-searing dream scene, the specifics of which faded instantly upon his waking.

The ceiling seemed to be crushing down upon him and then vaulting back up repeatedly—a fleeting hallucination, Tim knew, but the sensation was still jarring. His senses had been thrown far out of joint by recent events. Finally adapting to his surroundings, Tim swung his legs over the side of the bed and planted his feet on the floor, sitting upright and cupping his face in his hands.

"Damn it!" he exclaimed. "Just one night, give me *one* night to rest already!"

He rubbed his forehead in a circular motion and squeezed his eyelids shut so hard they hurt. An onrush of images spun before his mind's eye like paintings hung on the inner walls of a whirlpool, far too quickly and in too great a number for his conscious faculties to process.

"Here it comes," he muttered, flicking on a lamp and yanking open a bedside drawer to retrieve a pencil and notebook. He set about compulsively sketching in the images again, unable to picture them explicitly yet somehow managing to craft them into a coherent scene. He drew with breathtaking speed and concentration, gradually finding relief only as he filled in the picture gestating so violently inside him. Before he had even completed the frenzied oeuvre, Tim swallowed in audible fright at the spectacle that crowned the slowly maturing sketch: that same five-digit number yet again, this time repeated in a spidery scrawl across the topmost margin.

Having finished his sketch, Tim couldn't bear to examine it right away—he needed a break. He leaned back against a bedpost and, taking several gulping breaths, shut his eyes for a few minutes. He hesitated to open them again, yet he was darkly curious about what was on the page he'd filled in with such frenzied drawing. What now had he added to the eerie canvas he'd so inexplicably begun in the bank's conference room on that fateful Monday afternoon?

Only one way to find out.

"Courage, man," he commanded himself, summoning the will to ram through his lingering hesitation. "This isn't the first time you've seen these things. It sure as hell won't be the last."

Tim opened his eyes and took the notebook from the bedside table to study his latest creation.

Yet again, the guiding theme of the previous drawings had been faithfully carried over to this latest one: On the page there appeared an unearthly chamber of unknown provenance or location, held aloft by pillars carved to represent a strange, wholly unfamiliar epic. The ceiling teemed with even more odd shapes and lines, their unifying significance still unclear but as disquieting as ever. Tim felt suddenly queasy. There was something jarring about those broken edges and curves, he thought...

The rear of the scene was scarred by the same smoking urns as before, but this time they appeared to be fronting a gate of some sort. The latter was styled with a sloped lintel at the top and elaborate columns of its own—at least, early hints thereof—oddly reminiscent of the grand design and shape of the road-straddling gateways ringing an East Asian city center. The gate itself was set amongst a throng of arched chambers receding endlessly into the background. Again there appeared the malevolent eye at the picture's center, even more horrid than before.

"Pablo must have been confronting this thing day after day in his own dreams," Tim muttered, comforting his nervous heart with the company of his own voice. "He and the other soldiers in that damned clinical trial. No wonder they all went mad. And now the same pattern for my own illustrations. More detail, a hell of a lot more to the picture each time—"

Tim's observation quickly gave way to a plan. More dream sketches were soon to come, he was sure of it. Better to record his fleeting impressions while he could—while some fragment of the nightmare was perhaps still smoldering in his just-awakened mind, to help compare each baffling new take on the mystery. He activated a recording device on his cell phone and spoke, freely but lucidly, into its receiver.

"Dream Sketch #3, Thursday, May 22nd, 2025. The eye that's anchored the image from the start seems to be... cloaked, I guess, by the same smoky tendrils and infolding surfaces as before. But this time those smoky loops and membranes are set off from the eye itself, like there's a series of concentric rings between them. The outer fringes of this—entity at the center appear to distort and bleed into the surrounding space, curling over themselves with hyperbolic forms in a kind of infinite regression. This is in line with what I saw in Pablo's drawings in the PIT.

"The tower behind the eye climbs to the roof, and it's got a symmetrical form now, something I can make out—like a fountain in a city park or upscale hotel, assembly still at a rudimentary stage yet already active. I can detect... outlines of diffuse streams spurting out from tiny cavities, embedded in the rising spindle at the center of the structure as if a pump had been activated minutes ago.

"Foreground more fleshed out now—only a disembodied hand and arm in previous sketch, now with a muscular shoulder and back, evidently a person yet to take full form. This figure... appears to be singling out an object through a wide arched entrance into the main chamber of the scene. The outstretched hand is apparently directed toward an unseen landmark, or perhaps a nearby comrade yet to be rendered in my drawings."

Tim rubbed his sore, sleep-bereft eyes, their sensitive corneas stung by the ambient light and air, and shifted away from his sketch. He switched off the lamp and lay back down on his bed, pining for the sweet embrace of at least another hour or two of rest. But his troubled mind was too revved-up for sleep. He groaned and clenched his teeth and fists, enraged at his inability to control his thoughts. But what did his rage do for him? Nothing. He took a series of deep breaths over a couple of minutes, then picked up the phone from the bedside table and dialed a number scribbled onto a message pad beside the receiver.

"Trask Institute, Vision Restoration Lab," answered the surprisingly perky voice on the other line. "This is Rachel Bloom."

"Wonders never cease," Tim said. "Have you even been to bed yet? That conference adjourned only a few hours ago."

"Is that why you're calling me at work instead of on my cell? You seriously thought I'd have taken the morning off?"

"I thought it was a possibility. I didn't want to risk waking you."

"Well, that was thoughtful of you—I guess I should say thanks. The little courtesies really do mean a lot these days. Thank you for being so considerate. I'm sorry if I sounded kind of snippy there."

"No apology necessary—and you're welcome. Anyhow, to tell you the truth, I thought it was a slim possibility you'd be sleeping. I hoped you were but figured you weren't. I was calling to get a heads-up on your arrival time at the laser lab."

"What can I say? You figured right. I could barely rest last night after the conference broke up. But what about you? I thought you had planned to sleep in and touch base after you'd wrapped up the slides for your talk."

Tim shrugged as if Rachel were there in the room with him.

"I had planned it that way. Unfortunately, my unconscious mind had other plans. It's been rather uncooperative these past few days. Though I did make another sketch."

"Another dream sketch?" Rachel inquired after a pause. "I was wondering about that, actually. You seemed pretty agitated at the end of our last exchange regarding... that topic. To be perfectly frank, you had me kind of worried there, Tim. I wanted to reach through the phone and pat your head like a little girl does her frightened puppy."

Tim laughed.

"If only I were so cute when scared out of my wits," he said and paused himself. "I've been having some nightmares lately."

Although he hadn't meant it to, Tim's tone had darkened considerably with this last remark. The minute he'd made it he knew Rachel had heard the shift; it would have been impossible for her not to.

"I've never been much for dream interpretation," she said gently. "Not of my own, let alone someone else's adventures in sleeptelling. But we've been gathering the scattered shards of a broader narrative, however disjointed it may nonetheless remain—increasingly from the other vets as much as from Pablo himself. I may even be able to frame some images from the scene you've been constructing in your sketch."

Tim studied the drawing he'd just made.

"If you can pull that off," Tim muttered, "you'll put Freud himself to shame. This latest conundrum-on-canvas is an even weirder jolt to the eye than the last one."

For a moment Rachel seemed to hold her breath.

"Why specifically—what's different about it?"

"There's that five-digit number again, this time sprinkled like snowflakes all over the space above the drawing."

"Four-six-one-one-seven?"

A wave of chills washed over Tim.

"Yeah. The same damn code-to-nowhere as far as I can make it out. It's also one of the few motifs that I can faintly recall from the dream visions themselves, before my hand re-creates the rest of the memory on paper. Those unworldly geometric forms that Pablo somehow conjured up—I'm seeing them now in my own drawings. They're skirting the fringes of that whatever-it-is in the center, that creature that's been haunting him and me alike. And there's something else. Have any of the patients' drawings contained a fountain?"

"A fountain."

"Yeah."

"Like the ones in a public park?" asked Rachel.

"The structure's admittedly incomplete, but I can't conceive of what else it could be. It's situated behind that central monstrosity, and it's multi-tiered, with—basins, best I can tell, wide and encircling like at the Trevi Fountain in Rome."

"If our imaginations roam the prairie without a harness, we could ascribe a small world's worth of shapes to the unexplained objects in

Pablo's pictures—but a fountain wouldn't be one of them. I'm sorry, Tim; I don't know what it means."

"Unexplained objects," he repeated, partly to himself. "That reminds me. At the videoconference last night, Alan Simms made reference to a sampling of other numbers from Pablo's, um, oeuvre. He'd begun elaborating when that question barrage came blasting in from five countries; I suspect he never got the chance to finish the thought later. Do you remember? He was alluding to the figures that were slithering into the margins of Pablo's drawings."

"The numerical constants?"

"So that's what they were. Like the physical constants on that tape you played back for me on Saturday, when Simms was interviewing Pablo after his latest dream-sketch?"

"Broadly speaking, yes, though the numbers Alan rattled off on that taped session were the ionization energies of a few random chemical elements. The three he cited last night had featured in Pablo's earliest drawings, and they boasted more fundamental credentials: the Planck constant, Boltzmann's constant, and the speed of light in free space."

"The Planck constant?" Tim asked, tantalized by a burst of intuition that quickly fizzled out again. "What about the helter-skelter wall? Could you fix any significance to that triad of numbers that Pablo was splattering up there on Saturday?"

"We know the 'what,'" Rachel acknowledged, "but when it comes to the 'why,' we're lately even more in the dark."

"For now," he responded with a sympathetic sigh, "I'll be more than happy to clear a few 'whats' and 'what the hells' off the table."

"8.854 times 10 to the power minus 12," she said in a tone of exacting precision. "1.257 times 10 to the minus 6; 7.297 times ten to the minus 3. Pablo had also scattered those figures along the edges of his earliest depictions, and we dutifully ignored them then."

"I suppose his scribblings were tougher to overlook when the ink came from his veins."

"Sure, but I still can't see why he was so emphatic about them. Pair up each of those numbers with its standard SI unit of measurement, and you wind up with garden-variety physical constants that greeted us in our engineering texts. The first two are gussied up in the usual way for a Very Important Number, represented as a pithy-sounding Greek letter: *epsilon*, *mu* . . ."

"The permittivity and permeability of free space," Tim deduced.

"You got it, followed by the fine-structure constant. I cut it short out to three decimal places, but Pablo was more demanding. He managed nearly a dozen in each case on that bloody wall, all of them dead-on accurate."

"Why on God's green earth is he slicing into himself to showcase electromagnetic constants?"

"That's merely the appetizer, Tim. Pablo and his squadmates have been peppering their pictures with dashes and dollops of other magic numbers both before and since, fortunately with paint or pastel on paper instead of blood on walls. Thus far, we've also catalogued the gravitational constant, the vacuum expectation value of the Higgs Field, masses of the quarks and leptons, the Rydberg constant, and Avogadro's number. They've all been tucked away in the nooks and crannies of Pablo's sketches, most of them with at least one repeat appearance."

"A calling card," Tim mused in a near-whisper, vocalizing a thought apparently not intended for the ears of his listener.

"What was that?"

"A bit of idle brain-wracking," he answered dismissively. "Nothing worth pausing such scintillatingly surreal conversation about."

"Tim, we're well beyond the point of cookie-cutting obvious answers with Occam's Razor, as you always liked to say. Whatever outlandish explanation may be lapping at your thoughts, I'm keen to hear it."

"All right. It hit me yesterday, regarding the uncanny parallels between those computer worms. Both the one surfacing within the networks at Oak Ridge and the Chakana virus that's been striking banks and even biotech companies for whatever reason."

"But we're still not sure if they're truly related."

"I know, but hear me out. My cousin Ernie teamed with a cybersecurity division years ago while freelancing as a code-sniffer for hire. When I met up with him last week and in the days since, he's lifted the veil for me on how the network security gurus seek out a signature in the virus's code or behavior—some distinctive attribute that would yield clues as to its authorship. When it comes to our mischievous digital friends, Ernie found a solid candidate for such a signature. For that matter, so did you."

"I did?"

"You and he both latched onto the same uncanniness," Tim affirmed. "The way these viruses blur the screens on affected machines, spouting out a blizzard of calculations. Meanwhile, Pablo and the vets are adorning their brand of abstract art with numerical graffiti of their own, as if in imitation of the haywire act by computers affected by the respective viruses. We were heading in that direction with our guesswork over the weekend, but we didn't follow our hunches."

"Because we had no reason to, Tim. The numbers offered up in Pablo's drawings, and the weird computations on the infected machines—I'll admit the overlap in their timing struck me as more than coincidental. But I never bothered to pursue that lead since I couldn't begin to explain it."

"But perhaps we could make some headway if, at least for now, we give up on trying to explain the connection and simply allow ourselves to gape in wonderment that it exists at all. We're blinding ourselves by inspecting the paint on the canvas, when we should be stepping back to take in the whole picture."

"How do you mean?"

"As I was hinting at before—by the unique calling cards they're both flashing to the world."

Tim heard little more than a tentative hissing sound from Rachel. She had confined her answer to a feeble grimace, not fully convinced yet equally unable to offer a rebuttal.

"I'm not gonna overstate the case," said Tim, tempering his tone to win her to his side. "I can't conceive of how Pablo and the others could have lost their minds in the same way, and been commandeered to manifest the same delusions. Nor do I know how the Oak Ridge and Chakana computer viruses could have sprouted from the same bud as whatever's causing this mass psychosis in the soldiers. And I'm not sure I even *want* to know how the monster in our compulsive drawings, theirs and mine, fits into it all."

He paused momentarily, drawing out his answer to better hold her ambivalent attention.

"Yet even with all those caveats," he added, "this chain of horrors must have been assembled in the same factory, by the same hands. So what if we don't have a—a mechanism to stitch together all the phenomena? We know they share distinctive traits that have to be more than coincidental."

"Like what, besides the timing?"

"Their M.O., for one thing. Once again we were on the right track on Saturday but didn't follow through. All these anomalies seem to be marching to a similar tune: the progressive seizure of a data-processing device, even one as sophisticated as a human mind, to express the internal world of a hostile external agent."

"Sounds like demonic possession."

"In a fashion," agreed Tim, "but not the kind you'd associate with graveyards or restless spirits. The source of all this is surgically methodical, and more importantly for us, it seems to be telegraphing at least an afterimage of its motives and grand plans. It's an unambiguous stamp, not unlike the personal tags left by sophisticated hackers for their creations across cyberspace."

"The calling cards you were referring to?"

"Now you're with me. When Ernie was working in cybersecurity, his squads were tasked with developing digital bloodhounds, to sniff out defining features in the code content or algorithmic structure of new computer worms. It's how they were able to link different attacks to a single author, and predict which machines were next on the target list. Ernie was emphatic, though, that the digital calling cards of the virus makers weren't necessarily *logical*, at least to outsiders. They could be anything that had meaning to the designers of the malicious code, from cybergraffiti to in-jokes with their fellow hackers."

"To spilling out screenfuls of furious number-crunching on the monitors of hijacked computers."

"Spot on," confirmed Tim with enthusiasm, grateful for even the bare semblance of progress.

"So you think that our veterans' scribblings of impossibly precise physical constants," mused Rachel, still straining to understand, "whether as oil-on-canvas or blood on a wall—might represent the same phenomenon in spirit? A sort of 'human mind virus' equivalent of these computer virus calling cards?"

"I'd say there's more than a passing resemblance," answered Tim in the flat, deflated tone of one sensing a disappointing finish to a promising lead.

"Of course. You don't sound too happy. And in light of your fizzling balloon impressing at the end of that sentence, I'm presuming you're not terribly inclined to elaborate."

"As I said, if you'll forgive me for twisting around your own words—I'm decidedly weak in the 'hows' and 'whys' that would explain the 'whats.' But that's beside the point. The digits on the drawings and the blood-smeared wall, and the computational frenzy on the computers—they're nonsensical *to us,* with our untrained eyes and ears. But it's that very head-spinning nonsense that ties them together. So we should try to dig deeper, to divine where these numbers are pointing."

"I think I follow you," said Rachel, "though there's something I can't quite wrap my head around. Let's say we could ascribe all these disturbances to the same author—both the computer viruses and whatever forces are overwhelming the soldiers' minds. If what you're saying is true, why would the twisted geniuses behind it all toil away like this on such a...stupefying obsession? With a purpose and message apparent only to them?"

"Because their targets, at least, are far less obscure. The operation that you and your team were effectively shanghaied into running, however noble its original intentions—it leads all the way up to the Ruling Families. They've lately been busy consolidating their control over all the country's levers of power, even the judicial and enforcement apparatus. There's little in the way of legal or official sanctions that can tie down their ambitions anymore. So this twisted backdoor assault may be one of the few avenues of resistance still open to enemies of the Triantarchy."

"You think the Wat Tylers or the other hacktivists are behind this?"

"No, definitely not the hacktivists. No doubt their rage burns brightly against the Ruling Clans, but they wouldn't target them in such a scattershot manner, with so much collateral damage for your team and other unfortunate souls caught in the crossfire. Besides, this riddle-within-a-riddle act isn't their style; it's too oblique and clumsy to make a statement in the public commons."

"Then industrial espionage?" Rachel surmised. "Or a rival faction among the Clans?"

"I doubt that too, at least as we usually conceive of such power plays. But the ringleader of all this is probably a big fish with a good reason to sink its fangs into the Triantarchs. Think about it. Despite their pretensions to nobility and culture, the Ruling Families' *raison d'être* amounts to little more than the grand theft of a nation."

"In which they've been largely successful."

"Sadly enough. But there's only so much loot they can extract from the 300 million-odd plebs they're reducing to penury. So they have to reel in bigger prey at home and overseas: corporate rivals, well-funded institutions, corruptible governments riven with their own factions. At some point, they probably crossed someone with the intelligence, resources, and ruthlessness to fight back, and fight dirty."

"But who could pull this off?"

Tim engulfed his bottom teeth with a tensed lower lip, casting about fruitlessly for a plausible-sounding conjecture before shrugging in resigned defeat.

"I fear I'm more Inspector Clouseau than Sherlock Holmes at this point," he said with a self-effacing wince. "But the general tenor of it all might hold a clue. There's a species of thematic unity in the universal constants, the imagery of the soldiers' delusions, even the iconography invoked by the Chakana virus."

"What is the 'Chakana' even referring to? I never did get the backstory on it."

"A local newscast was sounding out an anthropologist about it on my way to Tennessee. Chakana is a tree-of-life icon in the Inca mythology, bridging the mortal realm with the domain of the gods. Chakana and the other symbols taken together—they're conjuring up a mystical landscape of sorts, buzzing with themes about earth and the heavens, some imagined apocalypse, powerful and malevolent entities lurking unseen in the midst. Not only the imagery that's been inflicted upon Oak Ridge, but also on some items closer to home that I myself—"

Tim stopped himself mid-sentence, audibly withholding an outgoing gust of air. Rachel duly took note of the curious interruption.

"The whole ensemble has the whiff of a doomsday cult," continued Tim, "obsessed with channeling deities and animal spirits, the elemental forces they believe to govern the world. That doesn't necessarily exclude an implication of the more humdrum usual suspects, like rival blocs in the Triantarchy or even corporate spies."

"Nothing wrong with that line of speculation. Considering the scale of all this, there are likely more than a few players in this miserable operation."

"No doubt. But whoever they are, they've got a serious grudge against the Ruling Clans. They're vindictive enough to lodge their sick calling cards within the data networks and the very minds of dozens of innocent people—people guilty of nothing more than being mixed up with a project near and dear to the Triantarchs' hearts. It's like a perverse art form, almost. The mastermind probably fancies himself an undiscovered genius, daring us to follow the impossible turns of his twisted path."

"Not sure we have much choice but to follow his lead."

"Which I'd do, if only I knew what path he's blazing."

"Are you sure you don't?"

Something about Rachel's question sliced through Tim's delicate zone of comfort, far beyond its raw content or the undertones that first rippled throughout it. Her words were suggestive without being accusatory, yet he found himself feeling defensive. He quashed the feeling for the time being, earnestly focusing his attention back upon the tangled line of inquiry that had occupied him shortly before.

"Those numbers in Pablo's drawings," he said, "they're tugging at loose strands that the addled mass of confusion between my ears—that it's only begun to knit into a more cohesive tapestry. The figures keep reminding me of... some chimera of an answer that slithers away from me every time I get close to finding it."

Tim grimaced in consternation, galled by a memory that hovered tantalizingly out of reach. He rubbed his furrowed forehead with the heel of his right hand, as if to massage the errant recollection into focus.

"As if it would do one iota of good even if I could remember," he groused. "I doubt it'd amount to anything more than distracting fodder, confusing things even worse than they already are."

"Tim, what do you think all these numbers are guiding you toward?"

"Something I read, or heard, or simply overheard a few years back, right when my world had started spiraling through Hell. I keep getting wrapped up in the same smothering curtain, the one that had been choking off my recollections of events from that period when we spoke last Thursday. Yet I'm sure of it: Pablo's numbers on the wall, whatever they truly mean, were heralded in a sliver of my own experience. Which—at least for now—I'm helpless to recapture."

"Then why not focus on the more recent events you *can* recapture?"

Tim winced again at Rachel's intimations.

"Rachel, where are you trying to go with all this? These aren't idle hints you're sending my way."

"They're not meant to be."

"You think I'm spinning this out of whole cloth?" Tim asked, taken aback by her pointed rejoinder.

"No, but I do think you're grasping at a plausible-sounding proxy for what you're really thinking. You're not the only one capable of elaborate verbal waltzes, to distract and flutter your way around a truth you don't want to confront. Alan Simms himself has been doing it to me for—"

Now it was Rachel who paused awkwardly.

"Tim, please, don't take this the wrong way, but you asked me to be more up-front with you when you stopped in over the weekend, and I'm merely fulfilling your request. Look, it's not only you, and not only Alan. I know what you're trying to do because I've done it myself, far more lately than I care to admit. Your suspicions may be grounded in truth, but your bottom line is an obvious contrivance, which I could maybe prod myself to believe if you believed it yourself."

"I'm not dropping red herrings here," he insisted, bruised by what he thought she was implying. All the same, he kept a tight leash on any petulant feelings and stayed on-topic; this wasn't about him. Or was it? "Again, I'm telling you, I know there's a hint to those numbers on Pablo's wall, and it's embedded somewhere in my own past. It's not that past itself that's important; it's something bigger it connects up to, if only I could nail down the timeline to a more specific event."

"And once again, you're using that tortured past from years ago to camouflage a more lucid hint from the recent past."

"I don't know what you mean."

"Yes you do, Tim. It's whatever took shape as that frightened specter I saw last night, right there in your eyes after Dr. Yoshida spoke at the videoconference."

Tim throttled a gasp that had begun erupting from within his chest.

"I wish—" he began hesitantly. "I wish you could simply forget that you saw all that. My reaction then—it was nothing more than a stroll onto one of those untended planks that a restless mind tends to get lost on. Especially when it's lured by a supposed breakthrough that dissolves into a mirage with even a minute of solid reflection."

"If it's so meaningless and unconnected, then there's no harm in entertaining me with it, is there?"

"Except that it's such an obvious disconnect, you'd think me a fool for even deigning to mention it."

"Tim, I'll lend a fair hearing to almost any seeming outlandishness in light of the wringer I've been shoved through recently. Anything except an obvious canard by you to hide whatever's stewing inside. Allow me to remind you again: You were the one wagging the finger at me and Alan over the weekend, chiding us about holding things back. Now it's your turn to follow your own advice."

Tim ducked his head for a moment, girding himself for an awkward twist in the conversation, before a clanging sound from the other end of the line put his plans on hold.

"Rachel, is anything wrong?"

For a moment there was silence.

"Rachel?"

"I—I thought someone was calling me, but it's probably just a..." Rachel's voice wavered as she spoke and again Tim found himself waiting for her to resume. She seemed to be holding her breath.

"Probably just a what?" he asked.

"What? Oh—nothing. Tim, I'm sorry I'm suddenly distracted, but something's come up and I have to go. Let's talk later today."

"Of course, but Rachel, why—"

But she had already hung up. Tim shrugged in nervous bemusement, seeking to set his darker suspicions aside and focus on more pressing matters.

THURSDAY, MAY 22, 7:26 A.M.
VISION RESTORATION RESEARCH CENTER, 22ND FLOOR
TRASK BIOMEDICAL ENGINEERING INSTITUTE

Upon replacing the phone on the receiver, Rachel gradually slowed her breathing again and froze in her seat, listening for the seething whispers that she was convinced she had heard just a moment before. It had not been from tiredness, she was certain. It had been real. Some presence had inserted itself into the background static while she and Tim were talking. A faint sound that seemed to gurgle and rise with thinly subdued fury. A wordless, static-like whisper that yet communicated something on the edge of spoken thoughts, somewhere between a hazy allusion and a concrete premonition.

And it was still there.

As her senses struggled to home in on the sound, a pattern emerged, barely rising above the deceptively audible static forged by her own roiled imagination. It was like an animal's roar somehow stripped of texture, and mixed with the resonance of a crow's call rippling throughout a desolate landscape.

"My arm! Help! Get me out of here!"

What...Was that part of the sound? She glanced about confusedly at her surroundings, which at once struck her as both perfectly normal yet eerily serene, as if some invisible presence had settled over the lab.

"Help! Please!"

Rachel stood up in alarm at the muffled cries coming from behind a closed door to an adjacent wing of the laser lab. She dashed to the source of the pleas and nearly fell back in horror at what she saw through the solitary windowpane in the door. Josh Mercer, one of the other engineers, was screaming. His right arm was trapped between the horizontal edge of an open, refrigerator-sized centrifuge device and a moving vacuum seal that was pressing to close down upon his imprisoned limb.

"Josh!" Rachel exclaimed and, forcing the door open, tried to push the seal back and away from his ensnared upper arm. "Damn it!" The door wouldn't budge.

She desperately began punching in a series of digits on a nearby console to order the seal back open.

"I tried, Rachel; the damn codes don't work," Josh gasped. "The centrifuge chamber isn't spinning, but this seal's got me in a lock. I can barely feel my right hand!"

Josh was right, she saw: The numerical display on the console blinked a line of red 8's seen in failing electronics. She whipped around her colleague and unplugged the hulking machine. Nothing changed. His arm remained stubbornly pinched in the vise.

"The spring for the seal must have already snapped," he said breathlessly. "You've gotta force it back manually. Please, God, hurry!"

"Alex," she said, airing her frantic thoughts aloud. "He was using an Allen wrench on this machine before; he should know how to shift the seal."

She dashed toward the entrance to find the lab mechanic and quickly enlisted the help of a pair of technicians drawn near by the commotion in the chamber.

"Irina," she commanded them. "I need you to find Alex, immediately—I saw him in the break room about a half hour ago so he shouldn't be too far. Paul, I need you to put out a Code Orange alert under my pager number, get the medical personnel up here with a gurney from the First Floor Infirmary and wherever else they may be scattered. I'll make a direct call for an ambulance. Go, now, get to it!"

As she summoned help at an emergency landline telephone mounted on a wall near the misfiring equipment, she stretched the tips of the fingers on her free hand to support the shoulder of her terrified colleague. He had dropped any pretense of stoical endurance of the pain and was now wincing and moaning in agony.

"Aaarrggh!" he cried out, succumbing to panic as he desperately attempted to jerk his arm free.

"Josh, hang on!" yelled Rachel, slamming down the phone before rushing to his side. She cradled her hands about the back of his neck. "Help's on the way. Try to keep calm. Look at me, OK? Look... I'm staying right here."

The loud whoosh of a swinging door broke their fearful interlude barely a minute later, as Irina returned with a burly young man who swiftly accessed a tool kit from a cluttered cabinet behind the wayward machine. He ripped open a side panel of the centrifuge and coolly but vigorously rotated an exposed cylinder to the left.

Upon hearing a telltale metallic pop, he quickly lifted himself and grabbed the edge of the seal, yanking it back as Rachel helped her shell-shocked colleague to withdraw his injured arm from its mechanical incarceration. The group sighed in relief as they gingerly helped settle him on a nearby chair.

"So... cold," Josh said with a shiver, his voice cracking as he clutched his arm with his unaffected hand. "Thanks... for the heroics. It's an ice box at the... bottom of that centrifuge basin. Another minute, and I swear—"

"Josh, try not to say too much," Rachel urged him, judiciously wrapping his forearm with a clean towel that had been warmed from its perch atop a nearby machine. "The medical team should be here any minute. Can you at least feel your hand?"

"Barely," he said, grimacing at the sight of the bluish-purple skin about his wrist and knuckles. "It's so stiff—ah, God, do I have frostbite?"

"We'll make sure you get through this OK," Rachel reassured him, although she doubted her own words. "Irina, can you lend me a hand here? Gently wrap the rest of this towel around Josh's arm and hand; it'll keep him warm and help the circulation. I need to follow up the Code Orange and brief the medical team on the way."

The younger woman stepped forward while Rachel quickly studied a flurry of messages on her pager, grabbing her cell phone to answer them.

"Josh, what—what happened?" asked Irina, ignoring Rachel's advice for him to rest his voice.

"Not a clue," he said, tremulous as he spoke yet animated by the mere act of engaging her attention. "I'd just loaded some... blood samples, to spin them down and isolate the white cells. Out of the blue... the seal shut right on my arm. There was no warning at all. I always thought the safety catch... the catch was supposed to keep it from sliding down on an obstructing object like... an extended limb of the person using the damn thing!"

"It is," interjected the mechanic, calmly restoring the toolbox to the cabinet and slowly making his way to the exit. "This pricey piece of junk had been acting up since last month, but the company techs were penciled in this week to give it a Monday morning tune-up."

"They did, Alex," Rachel confirmed, frustrated and flummoxed. She accompanied Alex to the doorway as she spoke, having received word of the medical team's imminent arrival. "That repair squad sent by the manufacturer—they debriefed me on their way out. They reported a few minor glitches with the wiring but otherwise nothing too out-of-sync. Certainly not the kind of gross system failure that would track to a breakdown on this scale."

"Yet another installment in the Trask Institute Follies," Alex scoffed contemptuously. He paused briefly to glance back at Josh, who was still quivering yet had reached an island of relative calm, his arm fully wrapped and tended by Irina. "Looks like things have stabilized here for now. I'd better get back to work. I'll try to duck out at noon and snag a dozen jelly doughnuts from the food court for you all. For the rest of the lunch break, I have a feeling I'll be busy with the incident report."

"Don't worry yourself with it," offered Rachel, grateful for his help. "You bailed us out from this morning's mayhem, so let me handle the red tape monster for once. I'll draft the report and you can just sign off on it."

"You and Josh have already endured more than enough mayhem for the rest of us put together," Alex countered as he shuffled wearily through the exit. "And not only with today's fireworks. It's my job to dirty my hands with all these malfunctioning messes hounding us over the past month, including all the damned documentation that attaches to it. I've got this."

As he was leaving, Alex passed alongside a stretcher being rushed into the main laboratory by the five-strong medical team. Unable to maneuver the bed into the room, two of the medical officers rushed inside, promptly examining their patient under Rachel's guidance.

"How does it look?" she asked, kneeling beside a haggard man in a rumpled white coat, his tattered badge identifying him as the chief medical officer.

"I've seen worse," he said. "Heck, this isn't even the worst we've seen today."

"Today? You—you mean there was another accident on-site this morning?"

"You don't wanna know."

"Yet another... reason to get the fuck out of this place!" Josh interjected, rising gingerly from his chair as another pair of medics helped him to the stretcher, carefully wheeling him around.

"We'll monitor his circulation and keep close watch on that hand down in the infirmary," said the chief officer. "The ambulance could be a while. So much for the expedited service we supposedly enjoy here at Oak Ridge."

"Will Josh be OK?" asked Rachel, sidestepping carefully out of the afflicted man's earshot.

"You all freed his arm in the nick of time," nodded the medical officer. "Any longer and there would have been serious tissue damage, with an amputation probably to follow. We've got him stabilized for now."

"Please, tell me," Rachel said, gently clasping the arm of the chief officer as his colleagues finished securing their patient for transport. "You said that today... there've been other accidents?"

"I can't talk in detail about our other cases, Dr. Bloom, but I suppose you'll be hearing about it soon enough regardless. Right around dawn, the pressure locks failed in a hyperbaric chamber two floors below. Two people hospitalized, one critical. Strange thing is, the incident rate is maddeningly scattershot. We'll have bouts of insanity like this morning and then things will be blessedly silent for the next few days. But I'd say we're already past our quota of close calls and outright disasters for the week as it is. I'd better rejoin the team."

Rachel found a magic marker and posterboard to compose a "DANGER: Out of Order" sign for the dysfunctional device. Upon taping it to the top of the centrifuge, she moved to leave the chamber, but halted at the doorway. She glanced warily back around, silencing her own breath momentarily while she listened intently for a few discomfiting moments. Nevertheless, she heard nothing unusual. She departed the room with a drawn-out breath of tentative relief, largely but not entirely convinced that she had merely imagined the low-pitched howl that had baited her senses mere moments before.

THURSDAY, MAY 22, 3:17 P.M.
HOME OF DR. TIMOTHY SHOEMAKER
WEST CHAPEL HILL, NORTH CAROLINA

Tim gnashed his teeth in a rebuke directed sharply inward, shaking his head at the text message filling his phone's screen. He read it again.

> Tim FYI tried to reach u earlier, u left
> photo in doghouse, must have fallen
> out of wallet.

"Unbelievable!" he growled.

> Will bring to u before talk at watts forest
> tomorrow - Matt

"Brilliant, Timmy," he mumbled icily to himself, resorting to a childhood moniker that had generally been reserved for unsavory exchanges with family and teachers. "Two years since you'd glimpsed that picture, and you handle it with less care than a cheap cigarette lighter."

He was aggravated at himself for his fatigue-abetted carelessness, and by the disconcerting realization that his young charges were now likely aware of his recent personal travails. But he was also ill at ease with the inconvenient insight that a part of him was in fact relieved to be temporarily free of the picture—of everything it symbolized, and of the events with which it had been lately associated—or he wouldn't have left it behind.

Tim freshened his face with a moistened dish towel at the kitchen sink, nudging himself further awake before settling in at his usual spot at the dining room table, its surface littered with research papers and reminder memos. The audible notification of Matt's incoming text had jolted him out of a much-needed afternoon nap. On the bright side, at least this one had been mercifully dreamless.

"Last two lecture slides... done and done," he said, checking off a crammed to-do list with a satisfied nod. It had been a reasonably productive day prior to his nap.

In fact, he now had a precious spare hour to ruminate over the baffling exchange he had shared with Rachel that morning. He flipped open a dated but still smoothly-lined blue folder housing a colorful array of contents in professional stationery, alongside a dog-eared compilation roughly the size of the sort of pictorial travel guides sold at airport bookshops. The latter was filled with technical papers, medical research abstracts, and a potpourri of other specialized arcana—an accidental souvenir from a meeting of international minds at a balmy Singapore hotel.

The presentation topics were conspicuously labeled with dates and times from six years ago. Tim quickly flipped through the pages, stopping at a point about four-fifths of the way in. He had dutifully bookmarked the position upon retrieving the book of research abstracts, salvaged from a grimy basement foot locker earlier in the day. He paused to peruse it further, noting the name of a presenter prominently emblazoned at the top of the page.

"Gregor... Chetkiewicz," Tim muttered, narrowing his eyes as he prepared to wade through the relevant content. Before he could proceed, however, his attention was yanked away by the shrill vibration of his landline phone. The number on its tiny, battered screen had become all too familiar by then.

"Rachel," he said after a gust of breath through pursed lips, his reaction more unsettled than he cared to admit. He lifted the phone with some hesitation, mumbling as he pressed it to his ear. "A promise is a prom—"

"Tim, hi. Is this a good time to chat?" Rachel interrupted. She sounded hurried. Her salutation was wholly devoid of enthusiasm.

"The way you got off the phone earlier, I feel like I should be the one posing that question," he offered with a clumsy chuckle. He'd heard the unease in her voice, loud and clear.

"I doubt I'll use the words 'a good time' with regard to anything here," she responded with an equally feeble laugh.

She took a deep breath.

"What happened?" Tim asked.

"It's nothing," she replied, waving away her lingering jitters. "Well, not quite nothing. Just some unexpected speed bumps in the morning routine. No—not speed bumps. How callous of me. No, really, Tim, never mind that. Any updates on that... that buried history you'd been unearthing this morning?"

Tim hesitated. What was that all about? He was about to ask her but then he realized, whatever had happened, she wasn't going to tell him. He knew her well enough to know that.

"Yeah, I guess. Kind of. I dug up an old program from a research conference I attended in the spring of 2019. Even now, I'm not quite sure why my intuition is leading me down this path, but I think it might help cast a brighter light on those troublesome hunches that were dogging me earlier today."

"About the numbers in Pablo's sketches?"

"Yes, and—"

Tim abruptly quenched his instinct to continue, ardent as the desire was. He truly had stumbled upon something significant from that old conference. It was a long-lost jewel, pried out from the black hole of memory that had swallowed up so many of his recollections from those years before the accident on the mountain. But it wasn't what Rachel had called him about. He could hear the disappointment in her voice, in her very breathing, when he mentioned that year, 2019. Her pleas from the morning came back to him. It was time to listen to them.

"I think we should probably pick up where we left off this morning," he said, a slight waver in his voice. "You were right to inquire about my reaction to the revelations from Japan last night, and I suppose I owe you whatever I can scrounge up for an answer."

"I was hoping you'd remember," she replied, clearly relieved.

"When Dr. Yoshida described the Tachibana Syndrome, along with its origin in the atomic bombings of Hiroshima and Nagasaki... It all reminded me of an item that I'd coincidentally received on Monday, the morning after returning from Tennessee."

"An item?" asked Rachel, pressing past a gap of reluctant silence from Tim. "Of what sort?"

"It was—an heirloom. Without drowning you in the details, my family has long been in possession of objects supposedly from the Old World, the source and meaning of which we've never come close to uncovering."

"Wait—an heirloom, you said? Makes me think of old clothes, or quaint family baubles stashed up in musty attics."

"No, these are far more than little antique tchotchkes handed down across the generations," Tim answered emphatically. "No quaint wedding gifts or anything else you'd customarily associate with a family heritage. We don't even have any idea how we came to possess them."

"So what are they, then?"

"They're artifacts of fine construction—baffling objects in every way, which for reasons unknown were clad in robes of frightful self-importance. My estranged Uncle Mitch has been consumed by the history surrounding them. He seems to believe they're the work of some, I don't know, secretive guild that forged them for a grand design of sorts."

"To what end?"

"Nobody knows," said Tim with a labored sigh, "not even Mitch himself. He's concluded that at least some of the artifacts constitute a form of seminal information technology. They may have even served as crude tools for pioneering experiments with grand ambitions, toward cognitive reconstruction or somesuch—except that the devices are apparently not so crude at all."

"They're still functional?"

"Apparently so, as I myself found out the hard way. And that's not the only feat of age-defying magic they pull off so effortlessly. Testing by Mitch's team has conferred a vintage of at least three centuries upon the artifacts, yet most of them have been barely affected by the wear-and-tear of all those intervening years. What's more, Mitch claims they've attained functional heights at or beyond the level of even today's AI technologies."

"I agree, not the usual keepsake to reside within a family treasure chest," Rachel remarked, equally bewildered by Tim's accounting. "But what does all this have to do with the atomic bombings?"

"There was also a stone tablet among the belongings whose primary purpose, as best I can tell, amounts to scaring the daylights out of subsequent generations with whatever twisted imagination created it."

"What was on it?"

"Threats, portents, the usual augurings of the apocalypse. Though not the familiar, warm and fuzzy apocalypse we were all reared on, the kind from old scriptural texts or pulp novellas—"

"Tim," demanded Rachel, "what was on the tablet? What was its purpose?"

"A warning. Its makers were shuttling a warning through time, to ensure that future generations paid heed... that we'd prepare for whatever danger they believed was on the horizon."

"So I take it that you and your uncle have been deciphering their unhappy tidings."

"I wish I could say we were. Unlike the other items, this tablet hasn't enjoyed a gentle passage through the centuries. It's chipped and eroded all over, it's missing a complement or two that build on whatever it's saying, and even the fragment that we do have—it's nothing but a medley of hideous images, text, and symbols that we can't peg to anything more concrete. All we know for sure is that its representation was among them."

"A representation? Of what?"

Tim's jaw tightened.

"Tim? A representation of what?"

"The mushroom cloud from an atomic bomb. It's unmistakable."

"A mushroom—oh," said Rachel, suddenly bereft of words.

"It wasn't that alone," added Tim, clumsily stretching his thoughts. "The carvings on the tablet were teeming with weird omens that we're only beginning to untangle. The other imagery scarred on the surface of that slate—I can barely keep tabs on all the random spookiness it kept spilling out from every corner. But the atom bomb imagery was at the heart of it all. There was some text that fleshed out the warning in more gruesome detail, and it traced his origins or his... imminence, I guess you could say, in the exploding of the bomb. In one way or another, the whole tablet seemed to be about him."

"About *him*?"

"It doesn't say whom exactly. Only 'somebody,' apparently a bigshot for whom we don't want to be rolling out the welcome mat. It said that he would be awakened by the atom bombs dropped in the midst of a catastrophic armed conflict."

"So you feel that this—this tablet of yours anticipated the use of nuclear weapons in 1945?"

"Anticipated," Tim repeated with an unnerving chuckle, like that of a shaman taunting a supplicant with a frightening truth, one that he would reveal only in the most nebulous of koans. "Yes. Definitely."

"Tim? What's funny about what you just told me? Did I miss something?"

"I'm sorry, Rachel, that was inappropriate," he replied, mildly baffled and perturbed by his own inappropriate reaction. "Chalk it up to my dark sense of humor, I guess. Or nerves. Or both."

"Oh. So can you tell me why your humor turned so dark and disturbing on me?"

Tim cleared his throat.

"My Uncle Mitch commissioned a team of archaeologists to attach a precise date to that slab," he said. "They found that it was on the order of a millennium old, etched out in the Dark Ages of Europe."

"A thousand years ago? What prompted them to—how—"

"My thoughts exactly. It couldn't be right," Tim said. "Yet even in the face of doubts coming from his own inner circle, Mitch's investigations have held up with every cross-check. The medieval sages responsible for that tablet were somehow cognizant of nuclear fission and its eventual perversion for use as a weapon of war. So they rang that alarm across the centuries, admonishing us to beware of whatever else would ascend with the billows of the mushroom cloud."

Tim heard a loud metallic creak, telling him Rachel had abruptly sat back in her chair. He could see her in his mind's eye, and he could practically hear her thinking.

"Tim, do you believe this Tachibana Syndrome that Dr. Yoshida was describing... Do you think the omen on the face of this tablet—"

"I can't say for sure they're related; the rubrics carved into the stone were short on specifics. But I still can't see how this 'him' alluded to on the tablet, whoever or whatever he is—if he was indeed zapped out of his slumber by the atomic bombings... I can't see how he would have any link to some poorly-documented psychosis afflicting the survivors in Japan—and a self-resolving one at that. Even less so to a somewhat better-documented psychosis among the Oak Ridge veterans that, for all we know, shares only a few coincidental features in common with Tachibana Syndrome."

"But I think you can surmise why the rest of us came down with the chills and shivers last night, when Dr. Yoshida first mentioned that the Syndrome arose exclusively in the wake of those mushroom clouds."

"I'm well-versed in the history of your patch of ground right now, Rachel. One of my middle school field trips was a grand tour of the Oak Ridge facilities, and we got the solemn spiel about the Manhattan Project. About how the uranium for Fat Man and Little Boy was enriched right there, before they were released over Hiroshima and Nagasaki in 1945. And I'm just as convinced that it's entirely irrelevant."

"What makes you so sure?"

"For one thing, Oak Ridge was hardly the only historical site connected to the Manhattan Project. Much of the development occurred at the University of Chicago, and the initial tests were conducted at Alamogordo and a host of other unfortunate locales in the 1940s. Besides, your mission there today is a world away from its Priority Number One back in 1944; if anything, it's the polar opposite of the Manhattan Project. You're not fabricating weapons of mass destruction. You're fashioning tools to help victims wounded by those very weapons. It's the noblest of efforts, Rachel."

"At least it was, until the Ruling Clans put their stamp on it."

"Fair enough. But I'd exile from your head any straying thoughts about how this could be some twisted form of punishment, with you and the other hapless souls at Oak Ridge somehow paying for the atomic bombs made there 80 years ago. Maybe the forces behind all these weird happenings in Tennessee picked it for symbolic purposes, but all my hunches are telling me that's incidental to what's really going on."

"Then what is really going on?"

Tim hesitated.

"I—I'm still not sure where to go with this, Rachel. That's why I held back last night. The link between Tachibana Syndrome in Hiroshima and the madness overwhelming your soldiers—a part of me is shouting that it's got to be more than a coincidence. That's why the warning on that stone tablet freaks the hell out of me the more I chew on it. All the same, that warning mentioned nothing about a mass psychosis or anything of the sort, so even if the stone is true in what it says—how does Tachibana syndrome, let alone Pablo's condition, relate to what it portends?"

"But you yourself said your uncle hasn't managed to decipher the whole tablet."

"That's true," Tim conceded, "but I still couldn't even begin to guess at how the stone would connect up the atomic bombings to these outbreaks of mass insanity. I can't even connect the two outbreaks to each other. The bottom line is... what, specifically, does the mushroom cloud in 1945 have to do with retinal implants or visual field re-learning algorithms in 2025? There's no rational chain to hitch them together."

"Then perhaps you should revisit your own words from this morning, Tim. All those hunches of yours, whispering hints of a link between the Chakana virus and Pablo's bloody numbers on the wall, however obscure to an outsider. What if it's the same kind of force at work here? What if the connection isn't at all rational or linear, at least as we'd normally construe it?"

"That wasn't intended as a question, was it? You still think I'm rope-a-doping around the truth."

"Look, we've both been shaken by the omens you've been sitting on, even before you spelled them out just now. It's taken me half a day to pry out the backstory from you. Yet you're still downplaying a link that I sense, and I fear, you also believe to be present. I know we've always been trained to keep a professional detachment from our own creeping intuitions. But in this case, Tim, your hesitation is making you deaf to whatever bits of truth all these phenomena are whispering out to you. You have to embrace them."

"You may be right," he admitted reluctantly. "It's because that link would be chained up not only with the atomic bombings, but with me, and to a skeleton buried in my family closet that—that I'm hardly itching to exhume. My uncle and I have a poisoned past to say the least. And now the very thought that our mutual heritage could be cloaked in nightmares, somehow related to all these conundrums enmeshing you and me both—I guess a part of me would rather not deal with it."

"I understand, but all the same, I think you know you have to deal with it. I believed before and now believe more than ever what I first told you when I asked you to come to Oak Ridge: You're the only one in this forsaken world of ours who can help us now."

Tim paused to read between the lines. *She believed more than ever.* There was a reason Rachel had added that. He decided to probe gently at first.

"What makes you say that, Rachel?"

"Having been locked up in this place for months," she said with a deep, throaty gust through her voice box, "you start sniffing out faint hints from everywhere. As if the clues were seeping out through the cracks in the walls around you. It's my sixth sense, and you learn to trust it."

"A sixth sense." Tim replayed her words in his mind. "Are you sure these clues are merely seeping out through the cracks in the walls? Because it sounds to me like you've encountered something more overt to cue you in, readily taken in by senses one through five. No need for the sixth."

His conjecture was met only with a stifled reply followed by an uneasy silence.

"Rachel," he inquired pointedly, "what happened today?"

"What—today?"

"When you got off the phone with me this morning. Something happened."

A chill went through her and her cheeks blanched. Following the shock of the morning's events, Rachel had busied herself with a series of routine tasks, shunning any inconvenient bouts of reflection. But now, after the conversation she'd been having with Tim, she found herself shaken anew by the ghostly murmurs of a deeper menace. The morning's terror had continued to simmer in her unconscious mind, which had then assimilated the forebodings newly issuing from Tim's lips.

"There was an accident," she said.

"Is everyone all right?"

"Barely," she replied, pausing momentarily. "Josh Mercer, one of my colleagues, nearly lost his right arm to frostbite. The sliding lid of a refrigerated centrifuge jammed in on it with no warning, and all the failsafes broke down."

"Good God. Another freak accident. You've had a veritable plague of them at the Institute lately."

"Yeah," she said, hardly enthused at the thought. Tim heard a curious sound after her acknowledgment, like hair brushing against the phone receiver. She must have glanced away for a short spell to gather her recollections, but her thoughtful aside had apparently borne fruit; her voice was newly animated when she spoke again.

"It's starting to make sense," she added. "There's been an X-factor to the latest string of mishaps, one that hadn't dawned on me when I spoke to you over the weekend. It's the pattern of the incidents itself—all hinting at a deeper theme. It's been eluding me the whole time."

"What about them?" asked Tim with heightened curiosity. "Is it the timing?"

"No. Their locations. It hit me just now, while talking to you. Before this week, the accidents were alarming enough, but they all occurred some distance away from the Vision Restoration Research Center and our auxiliary facilities. In fact, they were confined to the other buildings entirely until two weeks ago, when they began to strike the lower floors of the Trask Institute for Biomedical Engineering."

"The mechanical ghosties seem to be working their way up to you," Tim conjectured in bewilderment.

"My thoughts and fears exactly, and that's not the only feature that stands out from the background. Another disaster had already befallen us earlier this week, in one of our adjunct departments two floors below. It houses a microtome apparatus—the ultra-thin knife that's used to slice our biopsied tissues into single-layer specimens. We need it to prep our samples for histological examination by the Pathology Team, to identify cellular abnormalities in tissues of the affected veterans."

"I'm afraid to imagine where this is going. A sharp-bladed tool with a link-up to the broader computer network—doesn't mix too well with a gremlin-haunted laboratory."

"In the course of duty, one of the pathologists lost two fingers when the device activated without authorization. It was a small miracle that the surgeons managed to re-attach them, but needless to say, our examinations of tissue specimens have since been running rather behind schedule."

"As if you didn't already have enough mysterious miseries to contend with," Tim said. Gory images flitted through his overactive mind. "Did you at least have better luck tracking down the defects this time?"

"The preliminary post-mortem was unremarkable. We found nothing off-kilter in the gears, other than some subtle and supposedly inconsequential programming changes in the machine's operational coding."

"The damn program files again. Just like the altered command routines for the Simitalis that we uncovered on Saturday."

"There's a more alarming parallel, though," said Rachel, "which has been screaming out its presence to me ever more since we began talking. The alterations in the code were localized to a program subroutine that links the microtome to a scanner, used for fast-sequence fine imaging of successive tissue slices. The suspicious happenings all clustered around a specific subset of our efforts: data acquisition and analysis of tissue biopsy samples. And there's one particular tissue type that features nearly every time in these grisly narratives."

"Brain biopsies? You mean, from the veterans in the clinical trial—from when you were ruling out an encephalitis or other direct infection of the brain matter?"

"Which we're still doing, in fact. A few days ago, Alan Simms had assigned the Pathology Team to acquire more data for the videoconference last night, using the tissue samples we already had on hand. This was before the microtome incident, but the pathologists were already on edge. I think their collective subconscious had already picked up on the frequency of all these bad vibes, well before any explicit rumors were afoot."

"So you're saying that the accidents have been bunched up with activities having to do with the brain or spinal cord? Or the nerves that sprout out from them?"

"It can't be random, Tim. The preceding spate of accidents in the other institutes had also followed the same instruction manual more or less, originating at clinical and imaging centers that specialized in brain pathology and nervous system function. This weird epidemic of incidents moves on to affect other instrumentation, but it always starts with the brain."

"As was the case for the Chakana computer virus," Tim observed, now wearing his concern more overtly. "You may remember—I mentioned that hallmark of its behavior when we teamed up over the weekend. Before Chakana began infesting the banks throughout East Tennessee, it was infiltrating neuroimaging centers at hospitals and biotech firms, plowing through thousands of brain scans."

"Then I wonder if the accidents may have been a by-product somehow, of the obsession driving whoever's responsible for all these infiltrations. You were getting at this earlier yourself, Tim. The retinal implants and the Simitalis supply a unique conduit between our data networks and the human nervous system. The pattern of the mishaps, Chakana's targets—they all seem to feed into the same tale, of some interloper trying to pry his way into a treasure trove of information locked inside the coils of our minds."

"Your assessment sounds spot-on," agreed Tim, his voice trailing off to a self-directed muttering. "And yet again, Ernie was right there with you."

"What was that?"

"My cousin Ernie. He's the digital exorcist-for-hire, driving out the demons from the informatics networks at Oak Ridge."

"I remember—you were talking about his work earlier today, and when we first met up on Saturday. What about him?"

"He's racked up an ungodly tally of hours repairing these tangles of cables and wires, enough to become something of a Whisperer to the Machines. It's *his* sixth sense, the way he can gear up his mind and all but commune with the ghost hiding out in the electronics. That's why it rattled me all the more hearing it from him. Constantly in the background while he was assigned to Oak Ridge, he said, there was a ... a *presence,* is all he could think to label it."

"Your cousin," said Rachel, pondering aloud. "You were saying he was a contractor, right? Tasked with finding the source of the virus that crashed our gates here?"

"That was his gig. The way these phenomena target the brain and nervous system—Ernie wasn't keen to that specifically, but still he knew something was off about this place. The same vibes you started picking up after El Día del Diablo."

"Is he still posted at our campus?"

"No," Tim said, stammering somewhat as he wrestled with an answer, and how much bitter truth he would infuse into it. "Ernie, he—finished his contract, fixed up what he could and went on to other projects."

"So he did," Rachel shot back. Tim imagined the dimples of her cheeks swallowed up by a forlorn expression; she knew what was up. "Your cousin didn't leave per his original plans, did he?"

"No, he didn't."

"What did he tell you exactly? Let me guess: 'Phew, I couldn't stand another day in that hellhole.'"

"Ernie's as stalwart as they come, and it made my soul ice over to hear him of all people speak in such stark terms. This 'presence' for him wasn't oblique or remote. He said it felt like a shadow sneaking up from behind, only to vanish whenever he turned to glimpse it. I balked at telling you since I know you don't have the luxury of packing up and leaving as he did."

"I appreciate your thoughtfulness, but you could have told me earlier. Ernie's hardly the first hired hand to quit on a day's notice; hell, we've had people walk off the job mid-shift. As I was telling you over the weekend, many of his compatriots have wound up on our accident reports. I'll bet we've managed to scare away an army of contractors from near and far."

"I can believe it. But what matters is that both you and Ernie are arriving at the same conclusion from your experiences there: that we can't pawn these phenomena off as mere high-stakes espionage, or whatever the explanation *du jour* might happen to be. All of these disturbances—the Oak Ridge and Chakana computer viruses, the altered files in the Simitalis, the pattern of the on-site accidents, the psychosis in your patients and the messages they're conveying—they're all part of some hideously grandiose scheme. Whoever's responsible for them, they're not thinking small. And perhaps—"

Tim halted his reasoning for a moment, his composure ruffled by the mere thought of what he was about to say. But only for a moment. Rachel was right—he couldn't keep running away from the unhappy prospects these anomalies were portending.

"Perhaps they really do lead back in some tortuous path," he conjectured, "all the way to the atomic bombings and the Tachibana Syndrome in 1945. And thus ultimately to whatever these family objects of mine have been shouting across the centuries."

"Then maybe that tablet in your inheritance truly does hold a message for us, even if not meant for us per se."

"Maybe it does," Tim affirmed in a perfunctory tone, not entirely clear which parts of her conclusion he was agreeing with. "Rachel, one more thing before I sign off. You said there was a member of your team who videotaped the events once you'd flipped the switch on El Día del Diablo."

"Sanjit Khan, our ex-chief software engineer. Emphasis on *ex*."

"One of the lucky ones?"

"Sanjit had an escape route plotted out well before being press-ganged into our operation—an old start-up firm he once consulted for in Valparaiso, Chile. When it came time to sign off on his exit visa, his overseas contacts vouched for his bona fides."

"And likely paid the requisite bribes," said Tim without a moment's hesitation.

"I don't doubt it. Even before he decided to head back to the Andes, Sanjit had surreptitiously documented every baby step and grand stride in his efforts, with copies maintained on servers at his old company.

It was part of the back-up plan, an extra layer of protection for his hard work that would be several latitudes away from the long arm of the Triantarchs. Video documentation was naturally a part of that, disguised as nothing more than collegial goofing around with his camcorder on big days. His archives are the closest we have to an official record of El Día del Diablo."

"Do you think you could forward him my contact information, maybe even have him send me a copy of the recording from that day?"

"He officially parted ways with the facility only a month ago, so I could probably track him down. Anything you're expecting to find on it?"

"Nothing specific," Tim answered cautiously. "The Simitalis is the very reason I've become submerged in this strange brew from Oak Ridge to begin with; and the more I wrestle with everything we've uncovered, the more I'm convinced that its corrupted operational files may be at the heart of it all. I don't think it's an accident that their first tweak occurred on El Día del Diablo, and I want to see if any incriminating behavior that day—a knowing gesture or other hint of foreknowledge among the attendees—shows up on the video record."

"I wouldn't count on any exposés to add to your resumé. I must have replayed portions of that tape dozens of times myself, whether on a screen or in my mind."

"Doesn't surprise me to hear it," Tim acknowledged. "But I have a feeling the culprit may still be hiding somewhere on that recording. If I view it with the right eyes, maybe I'll find the smoking gun he's still using to hold all of you hostage."

Wenn wir 'n Wasserfall ansehen,
    der die Luft in Wölkchen webt,
Brennt das Bild sehr tief ins Hirn
    und wird zu einer Majestät.
Könnt Natur nicht oft erinnern an
    solche große Grandynthesen?
Ob Bild im Kopf, ob Bild im Wilden,
    sind sie gleich im Kern des Wesen?

Chapter Eleven

The Soul on the Screen

The Helmet of Blinding Vision

FRIDAY, MAY 23, 11:06 A.M.
HANCOCK AUDITORIUM, BAUMANN-GRAY MEDICAL SCHOOL
WATTS FOREST UNIVERSITY, WINSTON-SALEM, NORTH CAROLINA

Tim and Zach heaved deep breaths as they lifted the cumbersome, overfilled box to their hips, maneuvering it up a quartet of rusty stairs before depositing it in the space behind the speaker's dais.

"What exactly did you pack into this lump of mangled cardboard?" Zach asked, his hands on his thighs as he leaned over to catch his breath. "You decide to slip a prop show and comedy routine into your talk?"

"No," Tim answered, also breathing heavily, "I think there'll be enough unintentional comedy when the audience sees the slide animations I couldn't resist tacking on yesterday."

"Every time I get my jibe-thrower geared up to razz you a bit," Zach answered wryly, "you beat me to the punch."

"I believe in acting preemptively to lower expectations," Tim replied, his sarcasm bearing a note of contrivance. "Especially for myself."

"I thought I was the trendsetter in that fine art. Besides—and against all odds I'm switching to a semi-serious frame of mind here—I have a funny suspicion you're gonna wow the crowds today, Tim. Seriously, what's in the box under all the packing paraphernalia alongside that... backup slide projector you're still paranoid enough to drag along?"

"Considering past conference misadventures, I'd say my paranoia is a well-honed adaptation. As for the other contents—it's a rather convoluted tale."

"For you? When is it ever not?"

"They're mostly a few trinkets and—gifts, you could say, courtesy of my dingbat Uncle Mitch. I picked them up at a bank on Monday and was carting a few of them around to a meeting I was supposed to have with a mutual acquaintance on Wednesday."

"Which I'm guessing didn't pan out, based on your little detour into a roadside ditch in Old Chapel Hill."

"Kinda threw a monkey wrench into the gears of my day," said Tim with a sheepish frown, "not to mention my car. Anyway, regarding the acquaintance, we spoke on the phone but haven't met in person. His name's Ezra Gordon. He's an old family friend and probate attorney who's floating around the outskirts of Winston-Salem today. He's in the City of High Point all morning, finessing the handover of some rotting old mansion to a historic society. Even Civil War relics have had a rough go of things since the Reckoning."

"My, my. To think that someone with such status among the local gentry would stoop to pencil in a schedule slot for riffraff like us. Must be a weighty matter."

"It's certainly been weighing on me. Whatever the case, any resolutions will have to wait another day at least. Ezra had offered to swing by here after my talk to meet while we were both in town, then drop me back home on the return leg. But he just FYI'ed me that the clients are getting restless and he'll likely be booked into the evening. Looks like I may have to beg your indulgence for a round trip back home after all."

"You bailed on him, he bails on you."

"Guess that makes us even," Tim concluded with an annoyed chuckle. "In any case, I was stuck with the family trinkets that I'd trucked in for my abortive meeting with Ezra today. The lid on their original crate got torn up in the accident, so I wound up packing them into the box. I figured I might as well use it to haul my backup slide projector out to the auditorium. Lemonade out of lemons, I guess."

"So did you at least wind up rescheduling with the guy?"

Tim nodded.

"It's on for tomorrow around noon. Unfortunately, I just realized that may pose a slight problem. My car will still be in the shop."

"Well, it's your lucky Saturday, then. I'm driving Renee out to Old Chapel Hill tomorrow morning. Her theater troupe has more-or-less declared squatters' rights over a floor in an old tobacco factory there. They're rehearsing some of the outdoor scenes in *Les Mis*, and prepping for their tour dates across the region. I'm not too happy about her working there—the place probably wasn't up to code even before the Reckoning—but what do I know? I'm just the nosy boyfriend."

"I appreciate the offer, Zach. But I've already taken up enough of your time and—"

"And my time is my business. Don't worry about me—it's no extra hassle on my part driving you back. That is, so long as your driving habits aren't contagious."

"You're safe there, I think. I'll be keeping those to myself."

"Glad to hear it, Chief. So when do you take your opening bow?"

"In about twenty minutes. Turns out that I'm the accidental keynote speaker today, for which they're dutifully postponing the announcement until I'm already on stage with nowhere to hide."

"I thought you were the lead-in for the keynote," said Zach. "What happened?"

"Dr. Kasper ran into a random checkpoint on his way from Eastern Carolina University—the latest innovation in highway maintenance from the Crassus Clan. Kasper's an old army surgeon without much patience for bullshit, let alone the latest round of idiocy out of the Triantarchy. Word has it that a mini-confrontation erupted."

"Brave man. Isn't that a ticket to a jail cell nowadays?"

"Not Kasper. When he stares you down with those ice-blue eyes of his, you'll wish you were on the other side of the world. They won't want to deal with him a moment longer than they have to. Still, it slowed him up enough that he couldn't make it here in time. So there you have it: I am now officially the highlight of the morning."

"Professor Shoemaker to the rescue once again."

"As always. Anyhow, Dr. Lagrange will be up here shortly to gush out the introductory boilerplate for me, and probably work in a few jabs at his old friend. Could you do me a favor, Zach? I noticed the organizers shut off the projector for this little intermission after the last talk. Their gear is well past its sell-by date and it can take a few minutes to warm up and connect with the laptop. If you could head over to the AV techs at the back of the auditorium and signal me when they've switched on the projector—"

"On it, Chief," Zach replied, dropping off the elevated speaker's stage and jogging up an aisle toward a locked door straight ahead.

"Hey, Tim!" someone called from a staircase on the opposite end of the stage, his identity obscured amid a cordon of conferees engaged in chitchat and business-card bartering.

"Matt, is that you?" Tim called back, projecting his voice through cupped hands about his mouth. He waved Matt over and the young man ascended the stairs to the podium.

"Sorry," said Matt, panting as he stopped beside the dais. "I wasn't sure if Dr. Lagrange was already on his way up here; didn't want to be caught out with the Klieg lights about to hit the stage."

"Don't worry, I don't foresee too much drama ahead," Tim answered, curiously less than certain about his own prediction. "With the lunch hour so close, I'll be thrilled if half the audience is awake by the time I roll out the Acknowledgments slide and thank them for their patience."

"Enough with the ritual self-deprecation," Matt laughed. "Zach and I both know you're going to kick ass today."

"Of course I will," Tim replied with a sly, confident chuckle of his own, like a clever operator dropping his studied act among friends. "I just try to pretend otherwise before the curtain rises; helps keep me honest. And focused."

"Well, at the very least, you'll have a raucous cheering section from the northeast seats. Almost the full Doghouse is there," Matt noted with a showmanlike sweep of the left hand that ended with it resting on his chest, "including an embarrassingly tardy yours truly."

Tim nodded.

"That should keep them awake," he said. "At any rate, Zach reminded me you'd be arriving separately from the rest of the caravan. So what brings you up here?"

Matt removed a laminated photograph from the breast pocket of his dress shirt. "I know I said in that text message yesterday that I'd bring the photo by before your talk. But I was truly the absent-minded future professor this morning—I left it on the breakfast table in an envelope with the week's mail. I was halfway here by the time I realized, so I doubled back to pick it up. I can't believe I didn't get pulled over on the way here—"

Tim had been eyeing the photo with a stunned expression, largely ignoring and baffling the young man beside him. The shift in his swaggering demeanor was almost palpable.

"Anything wrong with it, Tim?"

"No, uh—I was just astonished that you took all that trouble to keep a promise," Tim suggested with a forced grin.

"Anytime," Matt answered warily as he departed the stage. He looked back periodically to scrutinize his mentor's visage, as Tim was still staring at the photograph.

Tim's trance was broken by a wolf-whistle directed toward the soundstage, issuing from a half-opened door hidden in the back wall of the auditorium. Zach Choi was there signaling a thumbs-up from the AV room. Tim laid the photo upon the dais and connected his laptop to a bulky data cable protruding from a damaged wire panel to its top right. As the projector warmed up, he interspersed sporadic rehearsals and reminders with self-conscious glances at the picture, finally permitting himself a more immersive perusal about four minutes in.

The walls and sounds of the amphitheater began to distort around him, the people and their voices fading and blurring as another world, and its frozen moment, crept in and commandeered his senses. Tim's reverie quickly dissolved away again as the projector's light source flickered on. His first slide now made a double appearance on his computer monitor and a screen behind and to the right of the podium, slowly drawing the divided attention of the throngs still bustling in front.

Tim glanced up toward his right. A tweedy gentleman with a full beard was chatting with two visitors in an aisle. The man held his open hands aloft, briefly interrupting his conversation to apprise Tim of the spare ten minutes remaining until the talk. Tim flipped through his slides to rule out any inadvertent omissions while affixing a small wireless microphone to the lapel of his shirt, gently testing its reception. Satisfied, he stole another precious minute to drink in the contents of the photograph in all its humble grandeur.

"Thanks again for the short-notice keynoting, Tim," rumbled an imposing bass voice from the right of the podium. The bearded man in the tweed suit, heavy-set, resolute in his stride, approached to shake Tim's hand with a robust, muscular geniality.

"Gus Lagrange," smiled Tim in response, his own voice a more cautious contrast both to Gus's and to his own a few minutes ago. "Great to see you, old pal. I was sorry to hear about Dr. Kasper. I doubt I could fill his shoes, but it's an honor even to attempt."

"No need for such modesty; you've never failed to deliver in the clutch, least of all for a masterwork like your talk today. Everyone who's worked with you on it has said the same thing, that you were the only one with the mind and mettle to bring this effort to fruition. I've been making the rounds at the local universities lately, in fact I dropped into Carolina State last week to speak with one of their donors and trustees—"

"Raquel Lapin? My project sponsor there? She and Sharad Dilip, one of the department chiefs at Carolina U.—they were the angels who swooped in to help me secure a new grant two years ago after, uh..."

"The break-in—I heard all about it, Tim. Look, I know you like to keep your cards close to your chest. Raquel said that she and Sharad actually came to you with an offer of assistance rather than you coming to them with a request, but... I just want you to know you shouldn't hold back if there's any way we can lend a hand around here. I can't guarantee I'll be able to help, but with all you've done for the field, for all of us, we'll never leave you out in the cold."

"There actually is something that I—" Tim gazed out toward the audience, his eyes darting to the small section where his team sat bantering with enthusiasm in anticipation of his talk. He was anxious to puncture his own wall of silence, the one in which he had immured a bitter truth. But now wasn't the time.

"After the talk, Gus. I'll get back to you on it."

"I'll make sure to remind you; it's what I'm here for. Well, the hour will soon be upon us. So if you're all set, I'll do the honors."

"Dive right in. I'm ready."

11:30 A.M.

The audience members clustered before the stage returned to their seats as the host assumed his place behind the speaker's dais. Gus's introduction was prolonged by his explanations of the schedule shift, allowing Tim a final glimpse at the photo, its afterimage consuming the attention of his undirected moments. He quickly returned his focus to the slides as his colleague completed the opening flourish.

"And now ladies and gentlemen, it is my privilege to introduce our main attraction and keynote speaker for today's conference on The Merging of Minds in Engineering and Medicine, a good friend and a man who truly can leap tall buildings in a single bound. Many of you here have profited directly from the innovations that have emerged from our speaker's Doghouse, as he affectionately calls his laboratory down the I-40 freeway in our proud state. Years ago when he and I were both graduate students and professional troublemakers, our speaker was as well-known for the audacity of his pranks as for his groundbreaking ingenuity."

Muffled snickers broke out sporadically in the audience and a wry smile creased the lips of the gray-bearded host as he continued.

"Many in our generation still recall our speaker as the mastermind behind the infamous Halftime Holographic Flying-Saucer Invasion, a feat he pulled off years ago in our football conference championship. Despite his mythical exploits of mischief, however, he's also a master of our field, as you'll all have the privilege to witness in his talk this morning, 'Sublime Superficiality: Fine-Grained Digital Replicas of Cells and Tissues as Membrane-Bounded Calculation Domains.' So without further ado, please welcome our keynote speaker, Dr. Timothy Shoemaker."

"Thank you, Gus," began Tim as the applause steadily trailed off, "above all for charitably leaving out my lesser-known and less-well-received pranks in your introduction. If the news ever did get out, I'd be run out of town before the end of the lecture."

Tim coasted on the tentative giggles in the crowd, using the interlude to reposition the slipping microphone on his lapel. As he settled back in, however, he was momentarily distracted by an unnervingly familiar sensation: that of a pale, yellow-brown glow somewhere in the background. Whether it was being perceived or merely imagined, he was powerless to resolve.

"Oh, and by the way," he added in a mock *sotto voce,* "if rumors of those prior antics of mine have already leaked out to the tender ears of anyone assembled here today—I confess to all of it, and so much more."

Tim's self-directed insinuation ignited another wave of sporadic laughter that undulated from one side of the auditorium to another before slowly dying away. Like a street magician adroit in the fine art of subtle misdirection, he exploited the diversion to further becalm his agitated inner sea, shaking off all the cares and conundrums of the previous week. He edged away from the podium to roam with authority across the stage as he spoke, invigorated by a mounting sense of confidence.

"Like so many other walks of our turbulent lives these days," he resumed, more focused but with tongue still firmly in cheek, "success in our field often boils down to the marketing of it all. The buzzwords. The slogans—a pair of which is about to appear in gaudy bold letters on the next slide. That's because there are two such ideas I want to implant inside your minds today like dancing ballerinas, flitting without pause about the stage that hosts your thoughts: logical parsimony, and modularity. It's upon these two simple pillars that we're engineering the artificial livers, the kidneys, and the hearts for patients awaiting a needed transplant.

"First off, logical parsimony. It's one of those scholarly word-weddings that sticks in the head like a catchy Top-40 tune. What does it mean in this context? We're talking here about degrees of freedom: the minimum number of independent data pieces we need to uniquely specify a phenomenon. Even the humble electron that surrounds an atom's nucleus and flows through a wire to power up our latest gizmos—how many juicy tidbits must we mine about each one to know its dirtiest secrets? Anyone?"

"Four!" came a smattering of responses from the audience, coupled with snide glances from his own team in response to the professor's familiar shtick.

"Indeed. Each electron has an address in four parts—what we call the quantum numbers. By the same token, we need a dossier on each of the tissues and organs we're aiming to engineer, albeit a wee bit larger. Nah, scratch that—a hell of a lot larger. Luckily, we're not condemned to specifying the fine points of every single electron inside our tissues, and that's where the logical parsimony bit comes in. Once we've defined higher-order structures—the cells and tissues built up from our molecules and atoms—we can occupy our attention with all the coolness of the higher complexity..."

Tim squinted, gazing back at the screen to advance the slides. There was a static-like crackle about the edges and bottom of the display. In itself, it was nothing unusual for an aged projector in an old facility that had seen better days. Yet, for a moment, he was flabbergasted by what he saw. He turned to the slide to camouflage his amazement—and to confirm that his tired mind wasn't playing tricks on him. It wasn't. There did indeed seem to be something non-random about all that fuzz in the background. Tim shook off the thought and turned back to the audience.

"So we need an army of summary statistics to capture what we'll call the complete algorithm set of the liver. What's that, you ask? It's the instructions the liver follows to do its job and earn its keep: to make and store sugars, to detoxify our blood, to synthesize the biochemical cocktails that clot off our bleeding or give us a fever. And make no mistake, we're talking about algorithms here as surely as we would for the source code of any computer program or electronic gadgetry.

"That's the bottom line, folks: The liver and kidney are peerless information processors, and these algorithms, these rulebooks to govern their behavior, are the key to unlocking their integrated structure and function. It is through them that we aim to reverse-engineer their digital equivalents, the templates from which to design and grow the transplanted organs themselves."

"Oh, not this again," Tim thought as he advanced another slide, fighting to stay focused. The static and swirling on the screen had persisted in the same inscrutable patterning that they had exhibited before, teasing with hints of a more concrete outcome in the works.

"Each level of organization," Tim continued to the audience, "possesses its own algorithm set to forge the powers of the amazing human liver, and that's where the modularity comes in. It means what it sounds like: compartmentalizing an organ to reconstruct it from the ground up, section by section and function by function. When it comes to engineering our made-to-order livers, that means replicating all the things that make the organ so extraordinary—including its ability to regenerate from injury—and making sure it won't be rejected when the surgeons finally transplant it."

Another slide—and there was something different about the loops and static in the background of the projection screen, to which Tim had a split second to devote his attention before moving on.

"So," he resumed, his élan and self-assurance returning as he immersed himself in the topic, "we've armed ourselves with the algorithms for the liver's individual cells, its tapestry of tissues, and the full organ itself. We're now ready to go a-tinkering in the way we inveterate eggheads know and love most. You guessed it: a comprehensive computer program that digitally represents the algorithms for the liver's biology, in the form of source code that we can tune and tweak to get ever closer to the real thing in all its perplexing magnificence.

"At the heart of it all, we're 'translating' a flesh-and-blood liver into a more compacted set of mathematical expressions—the same way a Fourier transform calculation converts a rich, colorful picture from your camera into a vast but manageable series of computations. With practice, we get better at recreating every bit of the liver's texture, from the cells on up to the full organ itself. Since we're not only building new organs but also simulating disease, the million-dollar question is how to best model the tissue conceptually, both when it's working right and when it all goes wrong."

"Could we perhaps make judicious use of the tissue surfaces, my dear Professor Shoemaker?" A familiar voice from a standing audience member interrupted Tim's rhetorical question, affecting the accent of a self-styled Watson to Tim's presumed Sherlock Holmes.

"Yes, Zach," said Tim, shaking his head with an eyes-closed grin and a chuckle at the cleverly-timed interruption, the audience soon following suit in droll laughter.

"I assure you, everyone," Tim added, gesturing toward his protégé as he indulged a rare moment of lighthearted distraction, "that was not part of the presentation; I do not have a straight-man or audience plant to help me along in my talk. However, I do have a smartass who happens to double as a newly-minted PhD in my group as of Thursday last week, even though he'll never admit to it publicly. A round of applause, if you please, for Dr. Zach Choi."

Zach rose again, sporting a sardonic grin as he engaged in an exaggerated theatrical bow.

"Indeed," Tim resumed as the laughter gradually ebbed away, "the guiding spirit for our digital cells, tissues, and organs beckons to us in the form of the surfaces that interact with their environment. It's here that the biological algorithms I mentioned are executed and the calculations take place.

"Consider, for a moment, five distinct disease processes: cirrhosis of the liver in a chronic alcoholic, the diseased kidneys in renal nephrotic syndrome, soft tissue cancers, congestive heart failure, and a lytic viral infection that bursts open its infected cells. Nothing in common, right? In fact, there *is* a tie that binds them, both in what causes these conditions and how they in turn cause misery for the rest of the body. That common bond is the loss of interfacing surfaces in the affected bodily systems, and thus the effacement of the plasma membranes that partition compartments in our cells, tissues, and organs."

Tim's pacings about the stage had followed a roughly figure-eight pattern that returned him to the vicinity of the speaker's podium, and he seized the opportunity to pause and gulp thirstily from a glass of water that had been providently placed atop the dais. His throat had become palpably sore and parched, his vocal cords having been rubbed raw already by an all-too-eventful week preceding the talk.

"The germ layers—the evolving membranes of a human embryo in the womb—boast an ever-expanding surface area that develops into our tissues as grown-ups, in all their form and function. And it's on those surfaces that our organs calculate and recalculate our bodies' physiology and homeostasis—their regular dose of good housekeeping, day-in and day-out. Or, at least, so we hope, because if these surfaces are disrupted somehow, no longer able to tally up and reckon our physiology, then we have disease.

"And that, my friends, is the cue for our job description as tissue engineers: to restore the breadth of calculations that define the organs we're constructing off-the-shelf for transplant. Moreover, to do so in as many degrees of freedom as needed to digitally recreate the computational complexity of the tissue surfaces, the sites where all that biological number-crunching takes place."

Tim halted again, his carefully-timed silence accentuating the importance of the slide to follow: an animated diagram anchored by an anatomical sketch of a human liver, fading into a frenetic foxtrot of digital 1's and 0's that filled the screen. The interlude secured him a precious moment to ponder the once purposeful-seeming static on the computer monitor's background.

Contrary to his fears from the start of the talk, the pattern-forming activity of the curling shadows and wisps had begun trailing off about three slides before, rather than firming to a telltale image. At least, for the time being. He was relieved to be free of the diversion and yet . . . on some level, he felt disquieted by those same confounded expectations.

"This slide encapsulates," said Tim with an ambivalent sigh, "the essence of our digital livers and kidneys. Remember, we can represent a stream of data, and in particular an evolving stream of inputs and outputs, in a variety of physical forms that possess identical information content, however distinct each one may appear to our eyes. And the converse of that principle is equally true.

"So all those compromising images and videos of your friends? You know, the ones you all duly upload onto your favorite social media? They can each be expressed equivalently as a bitstream—a string of 1's and 0's, of binary code. Which we could equally represent as a series of up/down switches in the circuits of your computer's motherboard, or in any other physical correlate of the binary digits. Our eyes and minds then 'compile' this drab bitstream back to the visual richness of the original picture or video. Same basic idea with our digital organs, albeit vastly scaled up..."

11:53 A.M.

"Therefore in conclusion, we have here a still embryonic yet robust tool in our hands: a system to replicate and reverse-engineer our own organs in a digital world, in fine-grained detail. By mapping the information content and algorithms of the calculating machines in our bodies into their digital equivalents, we're able to precisely recapitulate our cells and tissues in the language of information processing.

"With this promising start, we can then express disease in terms of a breakdown in that very processing. We've thereby taken a small but significant step toward quantitatively modeling a variety of pathological processes, in terms of the loss of surface interfaces where physiological calculations occur."

Tim was interrupted by a smattering of premature applause as he moved to finish his talk. It had been barely more than 20 minutes since he flashed the first slide, 20 rousing minutes that had passed in a seeming instant without the intrusions of recent frustrations, or uncertainties, or...

"Diagnosis and treatment of disease in general have benefited lately from high-precision molecular classifications, like genetic and membrane protein markers, that supplement more traditional diagnostic divisions. We've advanced this principle to its logical extreme: quantifying physiological function according to the nature and degree of requisite information processing in a given tissue, then defining and detecting disease whenever processing drops below that threshold.

"As injectable nucleic acid or protein-based 'mini-computers' become more sophisticated, we may even begin to apply new treatments at the level of this physiological information processing. I know we're bumping up perilously close to the lunch hour after an already long day, so I think I'll stop there. My voice is on the brink of departing my vocal cords right now, so let's break for a couple minutes to stretch and schmooze, and then I'll be happy to field any questions."

The crowd erupted into concerted applause, partly in admiration at a job well done and partly in sheer relief that the conference was drawing to a close. Tim returned to the podium to rest his feet and voice alike; but amid the extended ovation, his roving attention locked fiercely upon an item that he had been deliberately ignoring. The photo was there, in the same place and with the same contents as before. Yet it stirred the deepest chords of Tim's being this time, more so even than on the morning a few days ago when he had first rescued it from two years of forced amnesia.

He was overcome by sorrow that Susan was not there to share in the moment, as she had been on many such occasions in the past. Yet there was a resonance between the rhythmic clapping and her figure in the picture, as if she were present after all, smiling at him as he basked in the approbation of the crowd.

"Marvelous job, Tim," bellowed a deep, gravelly voice from a spot below the stage.

"Gus!" Tim exclaimed, shaking himself from a trance of seconds that had dilated into seemingly hours of his mind's devotion. He walked to the edge of the stage, stooping only slightly to shake the hand of his imposing host.

"I wish I could tarry behind and close things out, but I got a page right as you were wrapping up. Looks like I'm needed to douse a fire or two at the clinic. Think you could draw the curtain on the conference here?"

"No problem. Are you sure you can't stay, though? I'll need just a few minutes to muddle my way through the Q&A, and I was hoping we could at least talk a little shop on your way back to the clinic."

"I'm afraid I'll have to take a rain check on that. I doubt it's anything serious, but my staff's in a bit of a tizzy so I'd better hightail it over there within the next fifteen minutes. My apologies, as I know I promised I'd hear you out on... whatever matter you'd shelved right before the talk. If you could give me the condensed version, I could at least chew on it a bit and perhaps join up with you later today."

"It's about—" Tim bit his lip in hesitation, the confrontation at last week's thesis defense still jarringly fresh in his mind. "It concerns Zach Choi."

"The young wisecracker on your team?"

"Yeah, that Zach—a wisecracker extraordinaire. He's also the brightest prospect I've had in years, who's in real danger of being snuffed out by—by the toll of recent events."

"The Blacklist," Gus said. "So they were right."

"God, so you know already?"

"When I was speaking to Raquel Lapin and your other sponsors at Carolina State—she didn't intend to divulge it, it was clearly a slip, but she said something about Zach's plight. I was hoping it was only a rumor."

"Is there anything you can do, Gus? I've tried everything I can think of to get a posting for Zach, to the point of tapping some sketchy back channels even against Zach's own wishes."

"That doesn't sound particularly wise, Tim."

"It wasn't. But this is an outrage, and I was out of ideas. I thought maybe if you... You're about as well-connected as anyone I know."

"It's not my style to sugarcoat these things," Gus said and shook his head, "and you're a friend, so I'll give it to you straight. I'll pull every string I can—discreetly, that is—to help that young man, but I doubt it will change anything. I haven't told you yet, Tim, but the teaching hospitals here lost most of their own public funding toward the end of last year."

"Toward the end of 2024? Oh, don't tell me—another casualty of the Fiscal Emergency Act? The Triantarchs went after you, too?"

"We certainly weren't spared the axe. As for the balance of our reserves, we have to get approval for every light bulb, every damned paper clip that appears in the hospital requisitions, all under the watchful eye of a Crassus official who must be getting paid to make things miserable for us. It tears me up to hear of Zach's predicament, but any connection to the Blacklist would jeopardize what we have left. I'll try to work around it, but I wouldn't get my hopes up if I were you. What you're asking for, you might as well ask for a miracle."

Tim nodded with a clenched jaw, stung by all-too-familiar disappointment as his host exited the auditorium. He watched as the bulk of the audience followed suit. He then turned in shame toward his own young charges—still chatting in their section on the left—embittered by the injustice against Zach and his own fruitless attempts to reverse it.

He shook off the sour aftertaste of the moment and returned to the podium to field questions from the fast-dwindling crowd. The photograph stared up at him as before, arousing a long-submerged vein of stifled emotions as it had reliably done with each prior viewing. And then there was the cold, dull glow out of nowhere, back again yet oddly more pronounced...

"Question! Professor Shoemaker!" A young woman's voice called out from amongst a small throng of raised hands.

"Ah, of course," Tim responded, shaking himself back out of his reverie. "To all the troopers out there sticking around for the Q&A, I welcome your queries, quotes, and quibbles alike. As with the previous talks, please give your name and affiliation. That way, we'll have a headstart on following your illustrious careers, up to the day you're here giving a talk yourself. Let's start with the young lady there to my right."

"Thanks. My name's Kat Gershwin. I'm starting up next fall as a student at the med school, so I have a novice clinical-ish perspective on all this. You mentioned at the end that you were devising a scheme to subdivide diseases into fine diagnostic categories, based on this—loss of information-processing capacity. Could you delve into that a bit more?"

"With pleasure. Soft-tissue tumors and leukemias were once diagnosed, and staged for their spread and severity, according to things you could easily see. At least with a high-powered microscope by your side—the shape of the cells, for example, or any obvious nastiness with the chromosomes that hold the cell's DNA."

Tim edged back away from the dais, but not before a disorienting sensation had impinged upon his comfort zone from the outside, as if creeping in from the corner of his eye.

"These days," he resumed, "our diagnoses are more fine-grained. We arrive at them by taking a sampling of biomarkers—distinctive patterns involving biochemical molecules associated with the cancer cells—that can help predict a cancer's behavior and how best to treat it."

As if compelled by the irresistible force of ancient instinct, like a moth drawn to a lamp, Tim darted a sidelong glance at the now-flickering computer screen. He swallowed thickly. He had allowed himself but a fleeting glimpse at the monitor, yet he could no longer dismiss the impression that was inexorably devouring his divided attention: A specter was hovering nearby, slowly assuming its form on the screen.

"As a clinical tool," he added with a slight stammer, "our own approach channels that same spirit of high-precision diagnosis. But if the promise of our system pans out long-term, it may ultimately provide a more universal metric of disease state and severity—one that would cut across the breadth of human illness, by specifying the nature and degree of lost information processing. Think of it as a data fingerprint uniquely tied to each disease, defined by the degree of disruption in the information bitstream that normally crosses the surfaces of affected tissues. OK, with that food for thought now on the table, let's go to the next question—"

Tim now halted conspicuously in his tracks as he crossed behind the speaker's dais. The final slide of his talk had taken on an oddly translucent character upon the laptop monitor. Its title was still visible as a bold-lettered "Acknowledgments" in its proper location, as were the personal names beneath it. Yet the letters were somehow fading in and out as Tim looked on.

In their place was the ghost of an image that was unmistakably taking shape, and far more rapidly than on prior such occasions: the outlines of a cheek, the corner of a mouth, a wisp of gently curling hair, all of them in jarringly human colors. Tim instinctively entered a key combination on the computer which kept the monitor on, but severed the feed to the projection behind him.

"Oh, my apologies, everyone," he remarked with an awkward step away from the podium. Several hands were still raised in the audience, coupled to puzzled looks on the faces beneath them. "Technical difficulties intruding on the scene here. Didn't mean to ignore you."

He gestured abortively toward another audience member in the back right corner, deliberately steering his attention away from the laptop's screen. *Stay on track, man,* he instructed himself silently, *eyes on the audience*. That had always been a reliable crutch before, using the discipline of external duties to wrest himself away from internal turmoil.

Except that this time, the turmoil wasn't all internal. He tried to convince himself otherwise, that it was all merely some bizarro hallucination, of dream visions somehow intruding in while he was wide awake. But he couldn't deny what his own eyes were taking in.

"Let's get to that question I promised," said Tim, summoning a spell of forced humor to reorient his troubled mind. "There in the back row, from the gentleman wearing the tie-dyed vest."

"Gareth Crane," said the young man as he rose from his seat, "from the electrical engineering side of things. Which I emphasize because I haven't a drop of medical intuition in me, and was curious about how exactly you're turning these info-processing measurements and digital livers into practical therapies. The kinds of things you could put to use in a busy clinic."

"Glad you asked," Tim replied, straining to absorb himself in the topic at hand. "This part is more the province of my colleagues with MDs by their names, but I can supply the broad outlines. We're describing normal body functioning, as well as its breakdown in human disease, in terms of nested layers of information processing in the tissues. We ultimately represent these in our digital livers as binary code, hexadecimal code, or whatever other base encoding you have in mind, then use evolutionary algorithms to match our digital approximations ever more closely to the real thing—"

Tim halted abruptly, visibly startled, as a hissing sound—a whisper of sorts—seemed to emanate from the laptop. His questioner looked on in bafflement and some evident concern at the ill-timed interruption.

"Sorry," Tim continued, his pretense of calm rapidly faltering. "Creating real-world therapies is at heart a matter of heading in the reverse direction: running our digital tissues, and the treatments we've devised to restore their information-processing capacity, through what you might call, uh—adapters."

"Could you . . . elaborate on that concept a bit?" requested the young man in the back row, politely attempting to get Tim's attention after yet another uncomfortable pause.

"Certainly. Adapters, in this case, are translators of a sort, which we develop on the basis of emp—of empirical testing. We use them to convert our digital representations of biological entities back into the biology itself, and thence into macroscopic applications, especially the medical tools we're most interested in developing. Those include—"

Tim clenched his teeth, desperately grappling with his emotions. He had taken another errant glance at the laptop monitor. *Just shut the damn thing down,* he thought, yet some force inside him stayed his hand. It took a substantial effort to control his breathing and compel his attention back to the questioner.

"As I was saying," he resumed, "those include a vast array of investigations and interventions: diagnostic techniques, small molecule drugs, gene and protein therapies to name only a few. An illustrative example would be a biomark—a biomarker, that summarizes the information disruption in cancer cells and thus tags them for selective binding by a toxic molecule. Our digital biomarkers could be quickly converted into their biological equivalents, and vice versa. Remember, the fine-grained digital representations and the molecules they recapitulate are ultimately one and the same..."

Tim's unconscious pacings had taken him to the rear of the stage, from which vantage point he was unable to resist the temptation to glance at the monitor again. The image was now concrete. The outlines on the display were no longer mere white strands lacing the screen, as they had been in the study of his home three afternoons ago. They had fully matured to render a human face.

A woman's face, to be specific.

Light brown hair, curled in a distinctive style with which he was thoroughly familiar, draped down the sides of a hauntingly beautiful visage cast in extraordinary detail, as though burned in directly from a high-resolution snapshot. A gentle forehead, distinguished by an irregularly crescent-shaped birthmark on the upper right side by the hairline, framed the contours of mesmerizing blue-green eyes. The left was a bit lighter than the right, but they both gleamed ever so slightly, as though twinkling from an aroused spirit within. A gently sloping nose sat amid dimpled cheeks with scattered freckles, and rested above full lips that appeared engaged in a fruitless effort to form sounds, to murmur something to anyone who would listen.

Transfixed by the sight, his jaw trembling in a mixture of disbelief and sheer incomprehension, Tim barely managed to make a passing glance at the sparse crowd that remained. The handful of aspiring questioners had by now lowered their hands. Some looked up at him in speechless perplexity or even apprehension, while others whispered to each other.

Yet, Tim scarcely heard or even saw them. He wiped the sweat from his forehead and cleared his throat. Cleared it once, then a second time. His throat was terribly dry.

"My sincerest apologies, everyone, I—I'm having some unexpected issues with my slides here. We're already clear into the lunch hour anyway... I think it's maybe best to cut the Q&A a little short. Thanks again for coming."

The crowd dispersed, followed by members of his own team slowly filtering out through the exit while glancing back worriedly at their mentor. Tim leaned forward with his forehead buried in his left hand, furiously calling forth a haze of recent memories as the thinning remnant of the audience brought him closer to complete solitude. He cautiously peered through his fingers at the dais, once again catching sight of the picture that he had laid there so painstakingly before the talk.

"This photo," he murmured to himself. "Every time it's been a photo, and then the dull glow—"

The auditorium about him faded away as he disappeared into his own recollections, thrusting himself back to that fateful afternoon three days ago in his study. It was a different picture then, but a powerful scene all the same. Then the glow, then the lines solidifying on the monitor of his home computer. He shifted to his car the following day, moments before he'd plunged into the ditch while driving in Old Chapel Hill.

The photo from Tim's wallet, then the glow, then the image growing crisper on the screen of his car's dashboard. He leapt forward in time once again, replaying scenes from his lecture mere minutes ago. The photo on the podium after Matt Hansen had delivered it into his hands, the surreptitious stares at its contents before and after the talk. Then the glow, and now the face and the person to whom it belonged...

"What else was there?" he whispered, struggling to reassemble half-noticed minutiae of the three scenes. "Damn it, I know something else was—"

"Tim!" A familiar call came from the edge of the stage, startling him from his thoughts.

"Zach! Don't come over here!" Tim rushed toward the short staircase on his left, blocking the younger man before he could advance any farther.

"Whoa, Chief—what the hell has gotten into you?"

"Wasn't expecting company, that's all; figured I had my own private kingdom to myself here for the afternoon. I thought you'd gone with the others for lunch."

"I was about to, but I was watching you from the hallway and happened to catch your freak-out during the Q&A. It *was* a freak-out, Tim. I saw the whole thing, and it was as spooky as—"

"Spooky," Tim said distractedly. "That's a fair description of, well—"

"Damn right it's fair. Spooky and then some. Over and above the general spookiness that's been tracking your every move lately. What's going on with you?"

Tim hesitated for half a second.

"I'm fine, I promise you, but there's something urgent I have to take care of."

"You're fine."

"Yes, Zach—I really—"

"Shelley Deloria told me you scared the living daylights out of her when you popped in on Tuesday morning. She said you looked like 'a shambling mess posing as a person.' That's a verbatim quote. The very next day, you drove your car into a culvert and then came into the Doghouse looking half-dead, barely able to spell your name if even that. Then, today, after twenty solid minutes of wowing the pants off everyone with your talk—out of the blue you go all Dr. Tim Jekyll and Mr. Hyde on us. And what's with the Day-Glo prop and the... whatever all that was, the special effects on your last slide a few minutes ago?"

"You—" Tim's pupils dilated wide open, as he flung his gaze in rapid alternation between his young charge and the blank projector screen. "You saw those things, too, Zach? The glow and the—the lines taking shape on the projection?"

"Of course I saw them. We all did! Why wouldn't we have seen them?"

"I... I'm not sure. Whatever this phenomenon is, it weirded me out so much the first time I noticed it—I wasn't certain if it was truly out there or just a hallucination wired into me somehow."

Tim's mind whirled.

"Tim—and please forgive my bluntness—you're sounding totally loco here. A hallucination? What is it that's going on here, what's wrong?"

Tim had twisted halfway around, locked in a frozen stare that stalked the box which he and Zach had set aside before the lecture. He squeezed his eyes shut again, retreating back into the deep well of his firming recollections. His heirlooms from Uncle Mitch—they were there each and every time. He'd placed them back in the crates from the bank, then brought them into his study at home. That was where he'd first seen the phenomenon—the self-organizing pixels on the computer monitor. Then in the car, at Ezra Gordon's request in anticipation of their aborted meeting. Then into the box that was now hiding in plain sight on the stage behind him.

Tim thrust his eyelids back open and ran to the container while his flabbergasted protégé looked on. He threw open the flaps of the box and partially lifted out a sizable item, half-concealed by a layer of protective foam. It was the Cereceph, as his uncle had dubbed the device, purring with a nearly inaudible hum amidst crystalline tubing that trickled out the dying embers of a gold-hued radiance.

"How has it still been churning along like this while—" Tim's mind succumbed to another bout of frenzied backtracking through recent events.

He went back beyond that afternoon in his study. His mind returned to the scene at Pegasus Atlantic Bank, on that fateful Monday after he had retrieved the heirlooms from the safe and sat alone with them in the conference room. Then came Mitch's recorded discourse, then the helmet, the blackout, and the fragmentary scenes when he awoke, his vision returning ever so gradually as Tonya Jemison and her assistant nursed him back to health.

Tonya's frantic voice reverberated in his mind—the first sound that he could recall as he lay helplessly against the wall of the bank's conference room, clambering back into consciousness.

"Russ, switch off that thing on the table, whatever Tim had running and... call an ambulance on the landline phone behind you, immediately!"

Tim knelt down and inhaled deeply as he withdrew from the shallow trance into which he had settled, the blizzard of his remembrances finally congealing into an answer.

"Mitch said this thing could stay activated for weeks on the battery power he'd supplied, that it boasted three separate switches," Tim reasoned to himself, his tone rising well above a whisper. "Russ must have shut down only one or two. He wouldn't have known to do more."

Tim hoisted the enigmatic object clear out of the box and set it gently aside, resting it atop the foam pad that had protected it from above. He then painstakingly inspected its coiled surfaces and grooves, returning to the three toggles he had first turned on while sampling the strange helmet that had accompanied it.

One of the switches had been pressed down, but he'd been right in his suspicions about the other two: They were in the same placements as he had recalled upon activating the device for the first time. He moved to switch them off but hesitated before acting on the impulse, casting his gaze back around to the monitor. The poignant image was still on its surface, its vibrancy diminished yet commanding the screen nonetheless.

"So am I still under a restraining order against crossing this imaginary line back here?" Zach asked. Tim made his way back toward the steps at the edge of the stage.

"Please pardon my disappearing act there, Zach. I was caught up in a... dilemma. Been trying to solve it for days. The answer came to me literally moments ago."

"I'll buy that. Though I'm guessing you're indisposed to share any specifics—not about the dilemma, nor about that contraption that you just lifted from the box."

"I can scarcely understand it myself; no use in perplexing the both of us even more than we already are."

"A curious way to put it, Tim, because the most perplexing facet to all of this is the way you're behaving now, compared to the trip down here or even as you were in the minutes before the talk. You're not yourself, and I'm hardly the only one who'll swear to it under oath. Immediately after your lecture, with the whole crew gathered in that hallway outside the auditorium, Matt recounted to all of us how your mood did a clumsy 180-degree flip before his eyes. And right after he'd delivered that picture to you prior to the... Yeah, that's what this is about, isn't it?"

"The picture?" Tim asked with a nervous glance away.

"Yes, the picture. The kind you've been hiding from your eyes for two years running."

"Okay, Zach," Tim admitted. He was solemn yet also decisive, unashamed of the truth that he was now embracing. "You're right. The picture has everything to do with this. But I couldn't begin to explain it to you now. Please, trust me on this. I'll be fine, but I can't have you privy to this just yet. Go to lunch with the others; I'll fill you in on the way back home."

Zach shook his head.

"I was going to tell you, Renee texted me during your presentation; her ride to the theater had an emergency, so she needs me to give her a lift. Matt agreed to shuttle you back to the Doghouse."

"Then I'll carve out an opening tomorrow, I promise. One more request: If anyone else on the team asks what's up with the boss lately—"

"Fine, I'll be your accomplice—for now. I'll tell them a comforting bedtime story to veil the truth. But only so long as you hold up your end of the bargain tomorrow."

"Thanks for understanding, Zach."

The young man nodded curtly and made his way off the stage, pausing at the bottom of the steps then turning back to his mentor.

"Far be it from me to intrude on your séance or whatever you have planned here. But what exactly is so urgent that you have to hole up inside like this? Why are you turning this auditorium into your own personal bunker?"

"There's someone I have to call," Tim answered with unswerving determination. "It's a reunion I've put off for far too long."

Wenn die Gegenwart vergeht,
um Vergangenheit zu werden,
Entfernt sie sich von uns'ren Augen,
gehört danach zu and'ren Erden.
Ist es denn nur einfach so,
dass „nun“ von allem „vor“ sich trennt?
Doch bleibt das „vor“ ja immer noch,
wenn es mit „nun“ zusammenrennt?

Chapter Twelve

The Grand Liaison

The demon on the canvas

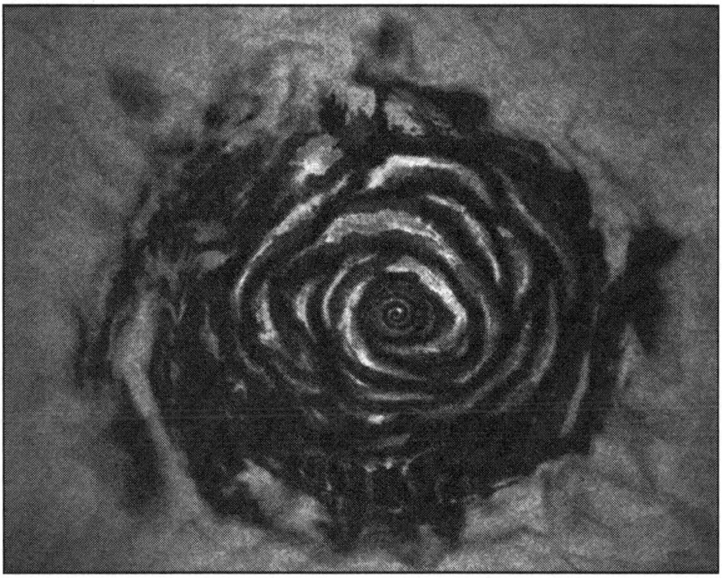

FRIDAY, MAY 23, 12:33 P.M.
HANCOCK AUDITORIUM, BAUMANN-GRAY MEDICAL SCHOOL
WATTS FOREST UNIVERSITY, WINSTON-SALEM, NORTH CAROLINA

Tim scowled with a soldier's resolve as he highlighted an icon for a familiar phone number on the computer screen. He selected a video-dialing option and took a deep breath before proceeding. A faint vestige of the apparition still appeared on his laptop's monitor, but had faded enough that he could access its other functions. Tim was still on the stage of the spacious lecture hall. The audiovisual crew had dimmed the podium lights at his request as they passed through.

A muted incandescent residue bathed the auditorium's maple-lined walls and foam acoustic panels in a ghostly indoor twilight. Tim heaved again as a green bar pulsed on the screen, opening up audio and visual communications with a destination thousands of miles away; there was no turning back now. He steeled himself for a rocky exchange, but was quickly disarmed by the amusing sight that greeted him.

The picture on the monitor yielded a panoramic projection of the other side, like a half moon nearly rising out of the screen, and in this case centered on the ruddy face of a portly man in a state of sustained exertion. His eyes were closed and his telltale moustache flipped upside-down as he balanced his inverted body in an apparent handstand, breathing in a tightly-regulated rhythm to maintain balance.

"Should I even ask?" Tim asked with a disbelieving scoff.

"Wha—" The man opened his eyes and that was the end of his handstand; Tim's Uncle Mitch tumbled to the floor of what appeared to be a private hospital room.

"So many years since we've talked, Mitch, and our long-awaited reunion kicks off with you literally topsy-turvy."

"Tim! My goodness, of all people... I didn't expect you—"

"Sounds like you're less than happy to hear from me," said Tim. "I figured as much."

"No, it's not that at all. I'd been communicating with my yoga instructor on the channel that you called in on, and I'd just presumed she was the one phoning me up. If I'd known that you—gosh, if this little re-connect between us weren't awkward enough already."

His uncle stood up, stacking a pair of pillows by a wall beside his hospital bed and reclining upon them. He then folded his legs upon a colorful cloth mat—a striking, meticulously designed hybrid of a Persian rug and a yogi's wall decoration.

"Let me give it to you straight, Mitch. This won't be a laid-back conversation by any means. I suspect you know that, but I felt it necessary to say it outright. For now, you still have a hospital suite as a return address; are you sure you're really up for this? I won't pretend to like you, but I'd prefer not to give you a coronary."

"I appreciate that. Very gentlemanly. Rest assured, the cardiac function tests all came back roses, so no worries there. In fact, the docs are preparing my discharge papers. One more day in this exalted prison cell and I'll be savoring the springtime air in the Willamette Valley."

Mitch gazed wistfully out an unseen window nearby, buying a few extra moments of think-time.

"I'm more worried," he said wistfully, "about the prospect of us ever being able to carry on like family again. I'm a justifiably proud uncle, Tim. I've been following your career and all you've given to the world for decades. Makes it even more regrettable that our conversations always wind up burdened by a ... by the collective weight of a past we're condemned to bear on our shoulders."

"Such lofty oratory for a personal mess that scarcely deserves it," Tim said with an ambivalent irony that veered perilously close to sincerity. "We might as well skip the soap opera scenes and pained retrospectives. That's not why I've called you."

"The heirlooms," Mitch concluded, his mood suddenly animated. "Tonya Jemison relayed the good news to me after your visit to the bank on Monday. She also said that something went a bit awry as you were inspecting the devices."

"A bit awry?" Tim said. "Mitch, I lost consciousness—and then my sight for more than a few minutes—after I put on that helmet. And that's not even the riddle that's been nagging me since—it's what the helmet was linked up to when it knocked me out cold."

Tim detached his webcam from the top of his laptop, inverting its orientation and panning to lock in on an object he'd placed atop a stool beside the speaker's dais.

"The Cereceph!" Mitch exclaimed. "My team's been poring through the reams of data we collected before, teasing out its nature and function. We've made some progress but nothing spectacular. Have you broken any new ground?"

"That's what you're about to witness. I'll be fixing my camera angle to display the Cereceph and my monitor alongside it. Pay close attention to the screen, Mitch, without making so much as a casual glance away. I haven't the slightest inkling how this phenomenon affects the active programs running on the computer, so you may catch only a couple eye-blinks' worth before we lose the connection."

Tim assembled the various components in their proper positions, mounting the camera on an unused whiteboard to scan the podium and its periphery. He then removed the treasured photograph from the breast pocket of his shirt.

"This may take a few minutes," he explained, "or it may not. The process seems to march along ever faster each time."

He turned and held up the photo in the dim light, studying it intently. His uncle and the surroundings of the empty auditorium progressively faded away, nearly vanishing from his perception. The whistle of the wind through the barn in the picture's background, the giddy shouts of the children about the haystack, the neighs of horses and the bleats of sheep, the rustling of the wind through his wife's hair as he caressed the back of her neck and shoulders—the day returned to him in all its rustic richness. It was no longer a static instant frozen in time, but a moving tapestry whose sights, sounds, and textures echoed throughout his being.

"My God." Mitch's gawking astonishment awoke Tim from the world that his mind had spun anew. "On the monitor, is that—"

"It's her," Tim confirmed as he eyed the screen head-on, his uncle's image and surroundings now fully blotted out by the starkly-rendered image upon the monitor. "It's Susan."

The two men fell briefly silent, riveted by the mysterious wonder before them. Tim swallowed audibly, fighting to keep his emotions under control, then pressed forward with methodical resolve.

"I lost track of the time, Mitch. How long did it take for those pixels on the monitor to assemble into Susan's face?"

"We didn't even cross the two-minute mark, Tim. And—you can hear me right now?"

"I can't see you, but you're coming through loud and clear on the speakers. Whatever the Cereceph's doing, it appears to exert this power only on the surfaces of machines that convey information—computer monitors, tablet screens, liquid-crystal displays of some sort. What's more, it learns and improves with each depiction."

"How many times have you witnessed this?"

"What you're seeing now—it's the fourth such occasion, and the rendering has never been so rapid or high-resolution before. The first two instances were cut short. They were suggestive, but I wasn't even certain that it was Susan on the screen. Yet there's no question now. And it's not only her representation but her very...being, her essence and spirit, appearing there too. The facial expressions, the movement of her lips—not addressing me per se, but it's as though she's there, aware of... I don't know, herself, maybe even the world outside."

"You think the Cereceph is responsible for this?"

"I'm sure of it, Mitch. It's been a fixture in every instance, and it always forecasts the image with the same tell: that dull light emitted from somewhere among all its snaking coils. I was too blind to see the connection at first, until it hit me that only the first of the three switches was turned off when I drove away from Pegasus Atlantic—the one that links the Cereceph to that helmet. The other two remained on, their workings almost imperceptible until—"

"What?"

Tim cradled the photograph in his hand and held it before the camera, shining a pen light on its surface to clarify its features for his uncle.

"That picture—I remember it clearly," Mitch remarked, stirred by his own flash of memory as much as by the external spur that had jogged it. "Yes, it was from that trip to the Wisconsin dairy farm, wasn't it? Your father was behind the camera."

"How did you know?"

"It was the first tentative olive branch in almost a decade that he extended my way—the first tiny glimpse he allowed me of the years I'd lost with all of you and the families that you were creating. It was also in this picture that I saw that glint in your eye again, the one that silenced any remaining crackles of doubt that I still harbored."

"About what, Mitch?"

"That you were also blessed and cursed with the Sacred Sight, just as I have been and as I'm sure Ernie reminded you in Tennessee. Your father's welcome was still frosty at best. He gave me a peek at the photo but never produced a copy, either physical or digital, so that tiny glimpse was also a fleeting one. But it was the only tenuous connection to what I'd lost."

"You memorized that scene?"

"Oh, yes. I committed it so tightly to memory that the date and place of that picture were frozen in my mind. I could pay it a visit anytime I shut my eyes and re-imagined it. I know it must have meant far more to you, the kind of memento you'd revisit every day; but it was significant for me, too."

"Yeah, every day," murmured Tim, stung by the shame that his uncle's words made him feel.

"So that picture was the spark for the Cereceph?"

"It's been the only other constant in this weird tale. The currents that it stirred within me when I finally brought myself to look... They were a riptide, Mitch, tossing me around like a ragdoll, body and soul."

Mitch rested a curled, solitary index finger against the furrowed edge of his upper lip. An anxious minute ticked past as Tim's troubled introspections continued to ferment out of view, mercifully away from the monitor's unsparing display.

"For a precious moment," Tim resumed, "those currents purged away the memory of that damned day in Suriname. They brought me straight back to the dairy farm—the kids tumbling around with the sheepdogs, hopping about the mud puddles. Yeah, I was able to conjure it up, too. Like I'd never left the place. Returned to the scene and breathed its air again. It was always when I corralled that world and forced it back into view—that was the cue for the Cereceph to kick into gear. Its depiction of Susie would always follow suit."

"What happens if you power down the device?" Mitch asked softly, wary of his nephew's delicate state of mind. "Does the image linger?"

"I've never put that to the test. Those two switches have been on since the moment I watched your spiel on Monday, in the bank's conference room."

Tim approached the eye-teasing bundle of cables and surfaces, clasping a pair of toggles between the thumb and forefinger of each hand. He hesitated, plaintively eyeing the face on the monitor once more. Out of seeming instinct, he backed away and dashed back toward the computer screen. With hands agitated from the thoughts swirling in his head, Tim entered a keyboard combination to activate a screenshot capture tool. He promptly enclosed the face on the monitor within a spacious rectangle—its edges born from the path of his own index finger dragged across the screen.

"Why am I even doing this?" he thought. Susan's face, the original, was clearer in the picture which had inspired his poignant recollections as well as the Cereceph's projections of them. There was nothing special about a static image on the screen, anyway; the magic was in the process, in the Cereceph's active sketching before his very eyes. Yet he couldn't let the image simply dissolve away this time, not with the way it seemed to be calling out to him. He needed a reminder.

Tim saved the screenshot and then made his way reluctantly back to the Cereceph, once again angling his hands to close upon its two enabled switches. Slowly, he began to flex his thumbs, finally pushing down to disable the device. The image remained on the screen for a few potent seconds, before dispersing back into the pattern that had earlier occupied its surface—a now dumbfounded Mitch Shoemaker, staring out from the makeshift perch in his hospital room.

12:43 P.M.

"This is your baby, Mitch," said Tim after a long, flabbergasted silence by his uncle. "What the hell did we just witness?"

"I never doubted the genius of the Cereceph's design, Tim, but not even I suspected it was capable of this."

"Then at least we have that in common. I need you to open up to me, now, about everything you've learned. You were saying that your team had made some findings; I have to know what they are."

"I don't want to get your expectations up. I fear that anything I say will fall short. With that said, we have made some strides. The Cereceph is mostly still a black box, even after all our high-priced poking and prodding. But when you said that Susan's pictures may be the impetus for its activation—that may hold the key to at least one of the grand riddles surrounding this device."

Mitch paused.

"Care to elaborate on that?" Tim said.

"Think back to my message from the recording you viewed at Pegasus Atlantic. The Cereceph's essence is all about reproducing the brain's unique faculties, but at the level of its integrated cognitive powers and concept formation, not merely the biochemical circuitry that runs our nervous system. We couldn't advance much beyond such broad generalities, until I joined forces with Goran Filipovich a few weeks back."

"Is that a name I should know?" Tim asked in a flat, colorless tone, as if stripped of emotion by the absence of the haunting face on the monitor.

"He's a neuropathologist from Switzerland who assisted me years ago at Magister Engineering, and I was able to coax him into extending a business trip in Oregon last month. He used the blueprints we've constructed from the Cereceph—our maps and imaging data—to narrow down the cognitive functions it must be mimicking in the human brain."

"Mimicking? I'd say it's tapping straight into them."

"As we now know, yes. When Goran unfolded and mapped out three key portions of the Cereceph, he found that two of them closely parallel known cerebral cytoarchitecture—the fine cellular structure of distinct brain regions—with both compartments somehow linked to memory. One consists merely of tangles of association cortex from the frontal lobes, possibly for long-term storage of events or facts. The other is more distinctive: a compacted representation of the hippocampus and amygdala, central to memory formation and its long-term encoding."

"The amygdala," Tim repeated, his thoughts piqued by the reference. "The center of emotional memory in all its guts and glory—the feelings and fervor that we attach to our recollections."

"You got it. Those two sections of the Cereceph are reasonably faithful representations of the corresponding regions in an adult brain, but the third is a different species entirely. A portion of it does resemble Brodmann's Area 17 in the brain's occipital lobe, and based on your line of work, I suspect that'll be a familiar reference."

"It's V1, the visual cortex—the vision center of the brain."

"Right, except that the rest of that section in the Cereceph doesn't approximate the surrounding terrain of the occipital lobe. Most of it remains indecipherable, but Goran was able to identify a spitting image of a chunk straight out of the brain's parietal lobe, somehow spliced right into the thick of the structure."

"The parietal lobe?"

"The one and only. This tidbit was at the end of Goran's sojourn, so I never got the full story on his find; but he filled me in on a few teasers just days ago. Turns out that his functional scans suggested the structure is singing from the same hymn sheet as the region designated the 'precuneus,' which I confess to knowing not a thing about. Is that striking any chords for you? Tim?"

Mitch halted at the start of an abortive question as he at last beheld his nephew at the center of the monitor. Tim was leaning forward awkwardly on the speaker's dais, thoughtfully massaging his wrinkled brow with the upturned fingers of his right hand. The laptop's microphone amplified the auditorium's eerie acoustics, suffused by an airy stillness save for the oscillating coo of a nearby fan, its blades filling an abnormally extended silence on Tim's part.

"The precuneus—it means everything," he said, in a tremulous tone barely above a whisper. "It's a visualization center, where we picture things of overriding...personal importance, within the temple of our own thoughts. Whatever else it can do, the Cereceph must be externally replicating what we call the mind's eye—our capacity to imagine and internally reproduce an event, a face, or a pattern of any sort."

"And you believe that it derives its input from...from memories of great emotional weight?"

"From the images they summon forth," Tim clarified emphatically, "and which the device can readily gain access to. That must be why it was so obsessed with rendering Susan, and why the photograph was so powerful as a primer. It's as though the Cereceph knew, instinctively, that nothing could shake up my soul as much as the image of Susan and the kids on that day. As though it was seeing and somehow even feeling the same things I was. So it locked in on her very being, as cradled within the shelters of my own mind, and projected her onto those computer screens."

"Then that helmet must have tuned the Cereceph to your specific memories and visual center. Maybe that's why you blacked out at the bank. To have set that device to all the tones and wavelengths of your mind—it would have taken a toll. The technical demands must have been beyond comprehension."

"This is all beyond comprehension," Tim said with a wave of his hand. "Nothing more so than your team's insistence on an origin in the 1600s, for the Cereceph and nearly everything else."

"I never claimed to grasp even a thin strand of that thread, but we can't deny the empirical evidence, and it's been corroborated a dozen times over. Every clue and whispered hint leads us back to the same era."

"I know. I have another meeting with Ezra Gordon to discuss this hidden-away history and make our plans more concrete. Mitch, look, I'm not denying what my eyes took in. But that doesn't mean I can stash it away in the 'Received Wisdom' bin just yet, even if I could divine whatever wisdom is supposed to be crowning me with enlightenment in the wake of all this. And I sure as hell can't wrap my mind around the origin story your team has cooked up for it."

"Tim, what more do you need? Don't lose sight of the big picture. I've been absorbed for years in all the lore of our family artifacts, yet not even I've enjoyed so much as a secreted glance at what the Cereceph could actually do. You discovered it yourself, and it was in your hands that I finally saw it, too."

"But even with the most advanced artificial intelligence at our disposal today, we're nowhere close to achieving what the Cereceph makes routine. A few cutting-edgers in Japan have managed to eke out some semblance of non-invasive brain scanners, or maybe wrench away a murky drop of significance from the magnetic fields about our heads."

"Yes, I've heard. There was some hubbub about all that even before the Reckoning consigned most of the stateside projects to an indefinite deep-freeze—all the buzz about improving polygraphs or mood-readers."

"My point exactly. Here we are in the year 2025, without even a sketchy map to seek out these Holy Grails of the mind, even for limited applications. And I'm supposed to believe that this marvel you handed over to me . . . that it's the handiwork of a guild of metalsmiths from the 17th century?"

"As I said, I'm only the messenger, Tim. I can't explain the tidings I've come to bear."

"Which makes us both equally useless at this point."

"If you insist. But that also makes it all the more vital to heed what little we can decipher and follow the trail it's blazing. These artifacts have been with our family for centuries, conceived and created in the face of whatever horror that tablet was portending."

"The tablet—" Tim mused, his thoughts too scattered to congeal into a question.

"And the answers lie across the ocean in whatever workshop bore witness to that creation, however obscure it must have remained to the world outside."

"I was wondering when you'd ask me," Tim said. "My sabbatical may be coming up, but that doesn't give me free rein to jet off and do your dirty work."

"Must we wage this battle in the quicksand with every encounter?" Mitch lamented, more disheartened than disdainful.

"Maybe we must, perpetually burdened as we are by a past that we're condemned to bear on our shoulders. Your words."

"Then perhaps it's even more imperative that we skip all the soap opera scenes and pained retrospectives. *Your* words."

"Well, touché to you," Tim said icily.

"Fine," Mitch shot back, nevertheless bottling his frustration and impatience with his nephew. "You want me to say it? I dragged you into this originally; I'll cop to that. But ultimately you came to me with this call, not the other way around. You understand the frightful power of the Cereceph now, and by implication of everything else in this thorn-wrapped riddle that it's been our family's curse to unravel. Otherwise, you wouldn't be staring out from that screen right now, alone in that personal mausoleum you've fashioned from a conference hall."

"You fancy you know what I'm thinking, don't you, Mitch? You always did have a knack for excessive self-flattery."

"I can almost sniff that fearful aura around you from 3,000 miles away. There's more getting under your skin than what you've divulged thus far. This would be a decent time to open up."

Tim bent forward to conceal a grimace, grudgingly acknowledging the inconvenient truth in his uncle's plea.

"I didn't mean how that came out," Tim relented. "Ever since talking to Ezra in particular I... I know where this is going, Mitch, and I know it'll be taking me to Europe sooner or later. I guess a part of me is still lashing out. Not at you specifically, but at—what I fear I might find."

"I understand your wariness, but there's something you've already found, and it's scaring the hell out of you as it is. It's what prompted you to contact me in the first place, isn't it? To reach out to me for help? More than the Cereceph itself."

"You're right, there is more to it—far more. I've been drowning lately in a strange brew of events that all began around when I visited Ernie last weekend. It makes even less sense than this freakshow of an inheritance you passed on to me."

"What specifically?"

"Dream visions out of a murky underworld, impossible computer viruses, contagious psychoses with imagery out of... some imagination that hardly seems bound to earth."

"You're saying this all commenced during your trip to Tennessee, when Ernie revealed the heirlooms to you?"

Tim briefed his uncle on Rachel Bloom and the blinded veterans at Oak Ridge.

"They're certain about that?" asked Mitch, struggling to assimilate what Tim was telling him. "So this spreading psychosis among the Oak Ridge veterans—you're saying that Rachel Bloom and her team have ruled out an infectious agent?"

"It's one of the few things they're 100 percent sure about, Mitch. Whatever's causing the phenomenon in Rachel's patients, there's no simple check box for it on a medical chart. Or anything in the medical literature for that matter. We've dredged up some scattered clues, but they've left us even more bewildered than before. Especially the way—"

Tim choked off the thought with a dismayed shake of the head.

"Tim?"

"I don't know how else to put this. Rachel's sensed it too, but... The infections of those soldiers' minds, and the electronic viruses afflicting local computer nets—it's as though they've issued from the same source."

"The Janus Virus," said Mitch cryptically, without expounding on the thought.

"Janus?"

"It's a favorite concept for those of us operating on the more kooky fringes of AI and robotics, as I was before my superconductivity tinkerings finally bore fruit. The thought first crossed my mind with the news of the Chakana worm."

"You knew about that? About Chakana's infiltrations of the medical centers and banks around here?"

"News travels fast, Tim, especially if it travels in the company of a few digits after a dollar sign. It's been amusing to witness the Triantarchs' sudden desperation. They've all but dangled a 'Wanted' sign in select channels, seeking the assistance of us supposedly lesser citizens. They're even offering a reward to anyone who can hunt down and trap the source of the Chakana virus."

"So it's true—they're not behind all this freakishness." Tim savored the thought. "Nice to hear that for once, the Ruling Clans get to share some of our misery rather than cause it."

"Oh, I don't know about that. I'd still bet the lion's share of that reward money that the virus arose from some inter-Clan feud. For all we know, whichever Clan put out that reward did so just to dupe a few of us well-practiced technobabblers into becoming instruments for the inter-Clan wars behind the palace gates. But you think this digital worm is also the culprit, somehow, behind the neurological anomalies among the veterans in that clinical trial?"

"Perhaps. Or perhaps another sprout from the same bud—maybe an electronic analogue of whatever biological agent is causing the mass psychosis at Oak Ridge."

"Or maybe it really is the crazy hunch you had to begin with," Mitch suggested, intrigue building in his voice. "Maybe we really do have a Janus virus on our hands. All things considered, given what we've already seen, it's hardly a stretch to imagine."

"Mitch, what exactly is this thing?"

"It's a hypothetical wad of information, capable of manifesting itself alternately in two forms. The first is a mass of data in electronic networks—the classic computer worm that invades critical files and propagates its bitstreamed being throughout cyberspace. The other, a biological infectious agent—a virus or some other bit of nastiness capable of reaching the brain. A Janus virus would straddle both worlds and likely have an unorthodox means of transmission, able to transfer its essence as biochemical information, from an outside stimulus, into the brain itself."

"Both worlds," Tim repeated, wrestling with the riddle that laced his uncle's words. "I see. So it would originate not necessarily as a microbe or biological agent per se but as a vector, a sensory input that could... squirm its way into the folds of the brain somehow, and reproduce its content in a recipient's mind and memory."

"That's its mark of mastery: an ability to exist simultaneously within digital and biological reservoirs of information, leaping effortlessly between them. It's the Grand Liaison between minds forged from carbon and their counterparts in silicon."

"Then there really is a logic to it, to all those hexes and horrors at Oak Ridge," Tim reasoned, more to himself than to Mitch.

"Wha—I'm sorry, Tim, I missed that. Sounded important."

"Both the retinal implants and the Simitalis provide a unique conduit between our data networks and the human nervous system."

"Retinal implants and the Simi—what?"

"They're tools that bridge human minds with external information processors, much as you were describing in the abstract with this... Janus virus. There's a bit more relevant history to this. Around the same time Chakana started wreaking all its mischief, Rachel's team began encountering an epidemic of on-site accidents. Ernie apprised me of the situation before I'd even set foot at Oak Ridge. He'd had his own run-ins and close calls while doing some contracting on the campus. It's part of why he got the hell out of there with no plans to re-up his contract at the site."

"I know. He told me, too."

"But it turns out that when you parse out the pattern of those supposedly freak accidents, things become even more suggestive of a non-random force at work. According to Rachel, the equipment failures were sparked by electronic beasties within the Oak Ridge computer networks, altering the operational coding of machines that you really don't want to have acting up on you. Oh, and there's another recurring note in this symphony of mishaps: They have an uncanny way of targeting instrumentation used for brain scanning and tissue analysis."

"The same pattern as the Chakana virus," said Mitch, openly surprised at his own conclusion.

"Then you see it, too. Whatever mad genius is responsible for these phenomena, it's as though he's trying to pry his way into a treasure trove of biological information, locked inside the twists and folds of our minds."

"Wait—back up for a moment," Mitch said, his gaze drifting upward as if seeking out the remnants of a faint flash of insight. "The way you were describing this neurological breakdown among the patients in the Oak Ridge trials—it seems like you were saying it hit them all at once."

"Not exactly; there's been a sequence to it, but the dominoes have all fallen in quick succession. What's more—and this is going to sound screwy even given your taste for oddball notions—the veterans in the trial all wound up manifesting the same basic psychotic patterns after they were first displayed in the Patient Zero. Down to their specific delusions and these... drawings they were all but possessed to make. It's as though even the content of the psychosis had been spreading from one patient to another. Like a contagion, perhaps first planted in their heads by this Janus virus, wherever the hell it came from."

"You're sure about that?" Mitch asked, his voice welling with intrigue. "That it was leaping from person to person?"

"Only among the soldiers in the trial but... yeah." Tim paused and took a moment to study his uncle's expression. "Mitch, I may be off-base here, but you don't seem—well, frankly, shocked. Like what I've just described isn't as weird and unfamiliar to you as it should be."

"Because what you've described has been... foretold. And not in a place either of us would expect."

"Foretold? By what?"

Mitch sat back for a moment with a curled fist to his mouth; he appeared to be framing his answer with care.

"The stone tablet, Tim, with all those grisly, apocalyptic inscriptions—"

"It's not like you have to remind me of its contents, Mitch. That thing freaked me out so much from the get-go that I balked at even giving it a second look. Eventually it dawned on me that the carvers of those messages—they must have had a damn good reason for calling us to attention. I took pains to upload that data pack you'd passed on to

Tonya at the bank, the one with the scan and annotation of the tablet's surface at high resolution. Give me a sec."

Tim searched through his files and promptly loaded a digital facsimile of the tablet on his computer monitor, zooming in and out with his attention fixed to a designated portion of the screen. He directed an impassioned gaze toward the image, tracing an unsteady index finger in an S-shaped sweep across its surface.

"The panels!" Tim exclaimed. "What about the one in the lower right-hand corner of the tablet, with the figure of the unnamed woman and that... drinking vessel, or whatever the hell that pottery's supposed to be? I don't know why, but that scene's been creeping me out even more than the others on the stone."

"Uh, the panels on the corners—" Mitch stammered slightly. He had intended to steer the conversation elsewhere, but he decided for the time being to humor his nephew's queries.

"I don't blame you, Tim. I've had the same reaction. There's something especially frightful about the iconography at the bottom right, as though it holds a message more profound than the rest. I'm sorry to let you down, though; I'm afraid we're equally blind to its meaning."

"You've got nothing?"

His uncle's tone sounded like a shrug.

"Just a bit of offhand speculation from a symbols analyst with the archaeological team, after she'd been poring through one of our earlier X-ray images. You may recall, the team's fairly certain that the third letter in the trio is indeed a Greek *eta*, but we have too little to go on for the other two. The analyst noted that the middle character—it looks to be another lowercase symbol that's at least somewhat symmetric on its left and right sides, possibly sloping though difficult to be sure."

"I guess that narrows it down somewhat."

"Too little to bridge the gaps in our understanding, I'm afraid. We still have nothing at all on the first Greek character. It's so puzzling, because those letters collectively are the only part of the tablet to demonstrate such a pattern."

"You mean, the way they've been eroded?" asked Tim.

"The deliberate nature of it, as I recounted on that recording at the bank. Somebody with access to that tablet must have taken a hammer and chisel to scrub out the letters, either to hide them or... I don't know. My gut says the responsible party was panicked by whatever those letters represented."

"He has company. Every time I look at that slab of hewn rock, I get the chills all over again. So many horrors implied, yet so much left to the imagination."

"No argument from me there, Tim. But it's not on account of the panels in the corners that I brought up the tablet again. It's because of the Gothic text in the center. What you said a minute ago, about the soldiers in Rachel's trial being gripped by an unknown force, like a monster invading their minds and filling them with overlapping delusions and nightmares—the warnings in Gothic presaged that."

"But I didn't hear anything of the sort on your recordings from the bank, Mitch. I thought your team had already translated what those stone carvers had to say."

"It's not on *our* tablet, but on others that were linked to the one that we somehow inherited. It was news to me, too. Magdalena Petrovic briefed me based on some textual and archaeological analysis that she's been carrying out over the last couple weeks."

"Magdalena—the Gothic language scholar? The one who helped you to crack all the notations in the ancient script?"

"That's her, the best in the business. Do you remember the omen that had been carved upon the tablet? About how some threat would emerge in the wake of the mushroom clouds, a force even more terrible than the war in which they first appeared?"

"Clearer than I'd like to, actually."

"Good, because Magdalena's been able to clue in on what the warning actually means. She managed to cross-reference the allusions in that portent to a trove of Gothic inscriptions and other texts—in Latin as well as the European vernaculars used at the time—that had stymied scholars across the centuries. Among the links were some Minor Codices in Gothic that had defied accurate translation or comprehension, but her star discoveries were in a Latin medical treatise and an exorcist's handbook, both hailing from the late Middle Ages around the start of the 1400s."

"Exorcisms?" asked Tim, squinting in consternation. "Medical tracts? That doesn't sound too promising."

"Maybe not, but sometimes the most precious of gems come in humble packages. It's a long and rather convoluted tale, Tim, but her detective work revealed that the soul-chaser's manual and the medical text had both transcribed critical portions of the lost tablets. The medieval sages behind the stone slab in our family seem to have begun with the messages about the atomic bombings, the awakening menace, whatever the hell the Ancient Others are supposed to represent...Our tablet was apparently the first. But its creators expounded on it to give more precise forewarnings about exactly what would awaken after Hiroshima in 1945. Or at least, how it would manifest."

"And etched their messages upon other stone slabs that didn't track with our family tree."

"The lost tablets may be out there somewhere; we're not certain. But for reasons unknown, this guild behind all our family artifacts broke its strict code of secrecy when it comes to the messages carved in stone, at least to a literate group of insiders they could trust. The exorcist's instructions and the medical corpus make clear reference to the Gothic inscriptions on our tablet, and then cite the other carvings to hint at what the sages predicted would arise with the mushroom cloud."

"A spreading madness," Tim reasoned, "seizing the minds of the afflicted in rapid succession."

"In essence. The authors from the 15th century conceived of it as a form of contagious demonic possession, or even a *danse macabre* that would spread from one village to another like the plague epidemics. But yes, at its core the syndrome very much resembled the plague of the mind that's been overwhelming all those veterans in Rachel's clinical trial."

"Mitch, is Magdalena sure of this? These aren't trivial implications we're talking about."

Uncharacteristically, Mitch hesitated for a moment, as if trying to bolster the merits of a case that he had thought was cut-and-dry before his nephew's challenge.

"A lot of the evidence is indirect, Tim, and Magdalena's still ironing out the details, but—"

"How so? I need to know."

"It seems the medical text mixed several historical and mythical events into a single allegorical blender. There was a legend about a village that had been overrun during a 13th-century Mongol invasion when troops under Subutai, one of the Mongol Khan's top generals, swept into Hungary and Poland before the Battle of Mohi near the Danube River.

In the panic that followed, one of the local noblemen, a respected warlord, went completely mad, in a manner not altogether different from those veterans at Oak Ridge."

"In what way?"

"In every way that you described Rachel's patients, Tim. Even to the point of being compelled, as if by an outside hand, to draw these... things. I know you mentioned the Oak Ridge veterans were similarly compelled, but what exactly were they sketching out?"

"I'm not even sure where to begin. There's a... beast, of sorts, in all of them as well as in my own drawings, manifesting ever more tangibly with each new sketch. Words alone can't do justice in describing how grotesque this entity is—teeming with malevolence in every damn fold of its being, and full of all these shapes and geometries that mess with your mind. To have depicted this monstrosity—it's as if the veterans had been emerging from a trance-trek straight through some Circle of Hell."

"That's what Magdalena said about the sketches from the Hungarian lord. Filled with hideous, grotesque shapes and contortions that couldn't possibly have sprung from an earthly source, or been conceived in an earthly imagination. It's part of why his contemporaries thought him frankly possessed. Magdalena's still deciphering the details from the old medical tract, but the drawings alone terrified the warlord's retainers so much that they feared casting eyes upon the sketches that were birthed in his fits of madness. His affliction was said to have then spread throughout the village, in a manner closely mimicking the plague epidemic—the Black Death itself."

"Wait—I'm no historian, but I thought the plague came a century later."

"It did, but that's the point. Apparently, what happened to the Hungarian lord in the 13th century was true, based on contemporary accounts in other sources; the Mongol invasion uncovered something in its wake."

"What exactly, Mitch?"

"We don't know, but whatever it was, it scarred the nobleman's mind for good. When the medical and exorcist's texts claimed that the warlord's psychosis spread like a virus through the village—Magdalena said that part was a fiction, tacked on with the hindsight of scholars writing in the 15th century. But why would the authors feel the urge to embellish the nobleman's curious case? Because they recognized hallmarks of his syndrome from the portents on the lost stone tablets, and they seized the opportunity to instruct their readers on how this strange mind-sickness could proliferate—even if it didn't actually do so in the case of the warlord himself."

"And it happened in Hungary, of all places…"

"Uh, yes, that's where the records all lead," said Mitch. He puzzled over Tim's throwaway remark and whatever personal significance had spurred him to utter it, but for the moment opted against exploring it further. "One facet of all this that still confounds me, Tim. I can see the parallels between the nobleman's solitary madness and the contagious affliction that's befallen the Oak Ridge patients. But the tablets taken together are pretty damn adamant that the viral form of this insanity was supposed to rear up right after the atomic bombings. Yet instead, it's taken 80 years to show up, a whole ocean away from Hiroshima."

"Actually, Mitch, it didn't."

"What? How?"

"Two nights ago, while on a videoconference link-up with Rachel's team, I found out that the mind-hopping madness in her patients is the second appearance of this phenomenon. The first was a milder form called Tachibana Syndrome, and it was initially observed—"

"In residents of Hiroshima and Nagasaki in 1945," Mitch interjected, his mind synching with Tim's. "Exactly as the stones had prophesied."

"And now this contagion has commenced its next phase in the heart of Tennessee."

"Then why the interlude of 80 years between the first cases in Hiroshima and the phenomena at Oak Ridge? And what's the point of this epidemic of madness to begin with? What's it all leading to?"

"I don't know what the nexus is, Mitch, but there's got to be a concrete connection between the Tachibana syndrome and the more gruesome outbreak Rachel's been battling at Oak Ridge. An infectious vector we don't yet understand, maybe even a person…That Hungarian noble must have been stricken by some sort of precursor, an irresistible force seizing his mind yet incapable, at the time, of spreading to others."

"Which brings me right back to those nightmare drawings, Tim. Do you think this creature in the sketches from Rachel's patients…Do you think it could be the same as—"

"The horror that sapped away the mind of that warlord in Hungary, or the beast foretold by the tablets? I'm not totally sure, but it can't be a mere coincidence."

"What does it mean though? Why are the soldiers so obsessed with depicting this beast?"

"My gut feeling is that the creature represents whatever was jostled awake amid the mushroom clouds, even if only as a metaphor. Perhaps the veterans are crying out somehow with those renderings, giving form to the source of their madness. And if the sages behind that medieval tablet knew enough to warn us of its advent, then its origin must be at least as old, probably far more so. Which means that what became our heirlooms—"

"Must have been forged to confront this thing," interrupted Mitch, again anxious to air their mutual conclusion.

"Or at least to serve as a... divining rod, to help guide us toward some answers. Hopefully before all these damn riddles drive us mad in the process."

"Drive us mad." Mitch cryptically repeated his nephew's words, visibly dogged by a nagging thought he had been unable to banish. "Tim, you said something in passing a moment ago that I barely caught while chewing on all this. It was when you were talking about the demon sketches by the veterans in Tennessee. You said... I don't know, you implied you were drawing this thing, too."

"That slipped out, but only because it's true."

"Good God. You've been infected by this madness, too?"

"Not the same thing, no. I feared the worst initially, but Rachel was insistent that whatever hit me, it's distinct from the affliction swallowing up the minds of the soldiers, and by now it's clear she was right. My own drawings are dream sketches, almost flooding out of my hand after I wake up from a nap or even a brief doze. I began making them after passing out at the bank on Monday, and since then... I don't know what it all means, only that the sketches and the visions, whatever I can remember of them, get worse each time."

"That's another thing that's been gnawing at me, Tim—the timing of it all. I introduce you to our family artifacts, and at nearly the same time, you're called to Oak Ridge to help decipher an enigma that just happens to be related? We've had these objects in our hands for three centuries, puzzling and fretting over them... and then the key to explaining them emerges from an unrelated distress call right when they're passed to you?"

"Because it's not unrelated," Tim countered. He strayed from the monitor for a brief interval, once more scrutinizing the slumbering coils of the Cereceph, before returning to face the worried countenance of his uncle on the screen.

"I'll spare you the gory details, Mitch. That device I blurted out earlier—the Simitalis—was a marvel that I developed with my star student, a versatile AI designed as an assist device for visual re-learning. I guess you could say that it—that it was a gift of this Sacred Sight that you've said has been hopscotching through generations of our family. I felt like I was in a trance at times while designing its microcircuits and coding its core algorithms, as though I could see every junction and loop in its wiring to replicate the way a blind person would learn how to see."

"How exactly did it wind up at Oak Ridge?"

"Through the hands of very well-compensated thieves, sadly enough."

"The Triantarchy."

"At the behest of Metacelsus, to be precise, some pompous bigwig in Clan Argentus. The Simitalis was stolen from us two years ago by thugs on the Clan's payroll... and promptly made its next appearance at Oak Ridge, right at Ground Zero for all the chaos that's engulfed the place of late. Doesn't matter why it was stolen. What does matter is that somehow, I've been a part of all this freakishness there from the start, long before I was aware of it. I may have even caused much of it, if the Simitalis turns out to be implicated in spreading whatever vector is causing this madness in the soldiers."

"But how—"

"I don't know the why or the how," Tim said abruptly, impatient to wrap up his thoughts. "I can't explain how the Simitalis plays into all this. But Rachel made it clear that everything started going downhill on February fifth, the day the link between the Simitalis and the veterans' retinal implants went live."

"February fifth, you said?"

"Yeah. Does that date mean something to you?"

"I..." Mitch turned aside for a moment to ponder the question, bracing the heel of his right hand against his forehead. "I could have sworn I took note of that day myself for some reason but—damn it, I can't place it. I'll have to dig through my work logs over the weekend."

"Fine. Look, we could spend half the day bouncing more ideas back and forth, but I don't think it'll get us anywhere at this point, at least not without further groundbreaking on the part of Magdalena and your team. We're still missing key pieces. I can't tell you why, but that third panel on the tablet, in the bottom right-hand corner—it's getting right at the heart of what this beast is supposed to be, and how this madness is connected to him. I just know it."

"Tim, I'm not trying to press your buttons here, but based on what you've shown me, there's another cornerstone to understanding all this, and I don't know why you keep pushing it away."

Tim forcefully swallowed a lump in his throat.

"I know where you're going with this, Mitch, but as much as I'd like to believe there was more to it...The Cereceph is like nothing we've seen before, capable of projecting powerful memories from the inside of my own mind to the outside world. But that doesn't mean those specific memories are important to it. The Cereceph was forging Susan's image as a demonstration of its powers; I only wish her face on the screen meant something more, that she herself was central to this."

"What makes you so sure that she isn't?"

ASLEEP AGAIN, BACK IN...DAMN, OF ALL THE DAYS.
EARLY JANUARY 2020, AROUND 8 A.M.
SUSAN'S PROFESSIONAL SYMPOSIUM IN MONTREAL
WHY THE HELL AM I HERE?

"Tim! Over here! Look at you, all gloomy. You promised to enjoy yourself here."

"I am enjoying myself here. I've been stuffing my face all morning. Have you tried the—"

"Apple cider?"

"Yeah. If you haven't, you really should. It's almost as good as the cider your Aunt Mischa served us last time we were in Missouri."

"Aunt Mischa does know her cider."

"Among other things. Who knew my sweetheart Susie was once such a terror?"

"She exaggerates. I liked to play Explorers, just like the boys. Had I been a boy, no one would have blinked, let alone characterized me as a 'terror.' Don't tell me you don't approve of Explorers for little girls."

"I do. You know I do. I love my little tomboy. But I thought it funny that you never mentioned it—I had to hear about it from Mischa. Finally, I learned where Mark and Chloe got their wanderlust from. Thankfully minus most of the scrapes and bruises."

"Like I said, Mischa exaggerates. Anyhow, you know that cider isn't even her recipe—it's from Uncle Konstantinos originally. And you're right, this cider the caterers got hold of kinda-sorta tastes like it. It's brought me back to my girlhood, actually, in quite the Proustian sense. Maybe I should write a multivolume account of my girlhood in Lafayette County."

"That's what Mischa said. Though I doubt she was thinking Proust."

"Nancy Drew, more likely. But I'll stick with Proust. He gets it. Lincoln did, too."

"Lincoln? As in Abraham Lincoln? The tall President-with-the-stove-pipe-hat Lincoln?"

"Yes, Tim, *that* Lincoln. The 'mystic chords of memory'—those are what bind a nation together, he said. They bind us all in fact, the echoes of those mystic chords, across the generations and from sea to shining sea. Proust took the idea further, showed it was universal, powerful. We're all children of Mnemosyne in one way or another."

"Children of… who?"

"You're terrible, Tim. You know this, I know I've mentioned it in your presence. And don't look at me like that—I am *not* reference-dropping this time."

"Actually, I suspect you may be, but for the sake of marital accord I'll take your word for it. I take it Mnemosyne's a Greek goddess?"

"The goddess of memory. She's something of a patron saint to the therapist community, our inspiration to brave all those cold, forbidding catacombs of a patient's mind, secluded away by instinct and habit."

"Cold, forbidding catacombs—sounds about right for the memories I've been crafting of late."

"Tim, you're back at it again. Don't let all that recent noxiousness drag you down. It's why I wanted you to come to Montreal in the first place, to take a vacation from all that, at least for a while."

"This time is different, Susie. My core funding for the project, the key sponsors—they've pulled the plug on everything."

"When did this happen?"

"I found out yesterday. Things were getting dicey even before the Reckoning, but now… I don't know what to do. Gus Lagrange thinks he can secure some interim funding, but if it doesn't pan out—"

"It will."

"It almost certainly won't."

"Tim, the moment you start stewing like this, it's like you're giving a preemptive surrender to circumstance. That's especially dangerous at a time like this."

"I can't detach that easily, Susie. Every time I try, it's as though I drift along and lose my bearings, to the point of forgetting who I'm even supposed to be."

"You don't have to detach, so long as you remind yourself that you're not alone while you carry on the battle. Half of my most decorated colleagues have lost their grants or been laid off since the Reckoning, some even before I was. It's a struggle for all of us."

"There's more to it than that. So much more."

"Tim, whatever it is, don't let it fester inside you; it'll burn away at you from within."

"I just can't get his face out of my mind, when he heard the bad news last month."

"Mark?"

"He busted his hump for four years to win that scholarship. He sacrificed so much, just as… just as we'd—"

"Mark will find a way to make lemonade from these bitter lemons. He's talented enough that he'll have more chances, and there are other avenues of support."

"Susie, I made a promise to Mark. I had to bargain for forgiveness from my own son after…"

"Mark is alive today because you kept him out of this wretched war. These… feudal families, or whatever they're calling the oligarchs behind the insanity in the country these days—they try to hide the body bags streaming in, but everyone knows. Tim, you saved our son. Why are you torturing yourself about it?"

"Because I went over his head to do it, and I stole his dream. That's why I promised him I'd carve out a better path for him. I've never failed him before, and now, at the worst possible time… It wasn't supposed to happen like this. I wasn't supposed to—"

"Tim, I know you've always been a harsh taskmaster with yourself, but even for you this is going too far. Talk to me. Why is this wearing down your spirit so much?"

"Hey. Look, there's a bunch of your colleagues gathered over by the mistletoe, Susie. I think you should probably go over, no?"

"Tim, we're in the middle of talking."

"I'm all right. You can go over. I don't want to hold you here while I stew."

"Why don't you come with me—I've been wanting to introduce you since we got into Montreal. Come, it'll do you good. You'll like them, too. The one on the left there is Solomon Poe, my mentor at my first therapist group, and… To his left is Cindy Chardin, another steadying hand in those shaky early years. And then—well, guess who just crossed under the mistletoe behind them. So Priscilla accepted my invite after all! You remember Priscilla from Minneapolis a couple years ago, don't you?"

"Pr—Priscilla, yeah."

"I see that you do remember."

"No, I mean—I didn't mean to look…"

"Tim, it's OK. Really. I've known Priscilla a long time. I know the effect she has on men—it happens everywhere she goes. Some of my first impromptu psychology experiments were secret observations of everyone from male classmates to married professional therapists, and the various schemes they'd use to sneak a peek at Priscilla as she pranced along by. That's what I find so amusing right now, is that you of all the males in this vast hall are probably the only one not ogling her, at least not quite the same way."

"What do you mean?"

"Well, I don't know, Tim. I was hoping you could tell me."

"It's nothing, except… when Priscilla came in the entrance, I thought that she… I don't know. My peace of mind has been deserting me of late. I'm not sure what kind of clutter is filling my head in its place."

"Come on. No more of that talk. The best antidote to awkward stares is a timely re-introduction. Just follow me and… Tim? What's wrong?"

"Nothing that I know of."

"No, Tim, your right arm it's—what *is* that? It's like your skin is folding in on itself."

"What?"

"Now your left hand's doing it too. Things are coming out of your shoulders and—is that, oh my God, your forehead!"

"My forehead?!"

"Tim, there's an eye, an angry eye opening up right in the middle of your forehead!"

"Susie, please, what the hell is going on?"

"No, Tim, don't come any closer."

"Susie, please, stop. What's happening? Is this a joke?"

"The . . . mirror on the table, next to the cider. Look for yourself."

"The mirror? What? What's happening to me? What's—"

FRIDAY, MAY 23, 2025, 1:49 P.M.
HANCOCK AUDITORIUM
BAUMANN-GRAY MEDICAL SCHOOL

"Aaaaaahhhhhhhrrrgghhh!"

Tim awoke from his pained slumber with a primal, violent holler. He had dozed off on a chair that he had dragged up beside the podium, his head awkwardly slumped against the side of the wooden dais. He was shaking and perspiring feverishly, darting his eyes about the empty auditorium and struggling to catch his breath. As he gradually regained a measure of composure, his dream-fed fright began to transmogrify into an indignant rage. He rose from the chair and hurled it at the first few rows of the audience seats before the stage.

"How dare you!" he exclaimed, choking on each syllable.

He threw some loose items from atop and beside the dais out toward the front rows. Finally tiring, he paused for a moment, wondering if he'd worked off his rage. He hadn't; he'd merely figured out where to direct it. His eyes locked on his briefcase, and, grinding his teeth, he ran at it as if to smash it to pieces.

Instead, he flung it open. He sifted through its contents until he found a familiar manila folder. He nearly ripped it in half opening it, before slamming it down onto the podium beside his sleeping computer.

"How dare you," Tim repeated, directing his rage toward the otherworldly presence in the center of his last dream sketch. Its horrific eye stared back at him in frozen menace.

"How dare you invade my memories of Susan? First you invade Pablo's mind, then you lodge in the precious memories of the others, then you tear into mine. You bastard! They're all I have left of Susan. They're all I have—"

Tim sank his head into his forearms, sobbing silently as he worked through his churning thoughts. To his surprise, however, he soon found himself rising with determination, wiping away his tears as the first wisps of insight seized his mind.

"Children of Mnemosyne," he said, waking up his laptop. He navigated through a series of scattered menus before arriving at a familiar fixture that had been vexing him prior to his fitful nap: the photographed image of the stone tablet. He zoomed in on its bottom right corner.

The strange ceramic object remained an enigma, as did the icon of the preternaturally calm woman to its right. But the three partly-erased Greek letters to their left were no longer a mystery. Tim traced out an erratic series of curves and ovals with his index finger, reasoning through to a conclusion that had been gradually firming in his mind.

"The third letter," he muttered softly, "is an *'eta'* as Mitch confirmed—same as our *e*. The second letter, also lowercase—imaging studies indicate that it's symmetric, possibly sloping, like a lowercase Greek *'nu,'* our *n*. First letter unreadable, but pattern of effacement suggests substantial width and height, symmetry—an uppercase Greek *'mu,'* our *m*."

Tim lifted his head momentarily to substantiate his suspicions, breathlessly resuming his now more loudly vocalized thoughts.

"Put them together, left to right. You spell M-N-E—*Mnemosyne*!"

He returned his gaze to the mysterious woman, nodding in grim recognition.

"You're the embodiment of memory, aren't you? That's what this panel's saying. That the memory of this... being..."

Tim wrinkled his chin and tightened his lips against his teeth, exhaling with a resonant gust of air as he exhausted his deductive powers for the moment.

He then calmly rotated the dream sketch in his manila folder, and, gingerly, lifted it close to his face, staring at the inscrutable entity in the center. And within a few seconds, a stream of insights and forged connections began to trickle into his open consciousness. Tim gasped as the thoughts kept coming. They were soon gushing in all at once in a river of realization, flooding his brain, threatening to overwhelm his capacity to sort it all out before it jumbled together and vanished.

With a hand to his temple, Tim set down his dream sketch and strode to the back of the stage where the unused whiteboard stood like an 8 x 6 canvas. He grabbed a magic marker from the accessory tray and began frenziedly diagramming as he spoke his thoughts to the whiteboard.

"That's the common thread," he said breathlessly. "The premonitions among the Oak Ridge patients, the warnings on that tablet, the heirlooms, my nightmares—"

He scribbled furiously, barely able to make out what his own hand was creating.

"The necklace Susie gave Priscilla, the jade figurine, the... visions of Susan herself... *Memory.* That's the tie that binds them. But not memory confined to an individual mind, and not a mere spotlight on past events. No. Memory as a physical force *binding the world.* Binding all of us. It's why Susie was always citing Proust."

Tim had filled the whiteboard with a vast, heavily marked circle of his thoughts. He now began to connect them with a frenetic series of lines that converged in the center.

Converged on a conclusion.

"Because time itself is framed by memory, and memory is the force that transcends time. That's what Proust understood—as memory evolves, it breaks out of the shell of a single mind. It joins other minds, it joins with the natural world, and then it joins the present to the past. As memory consolidates, as it gains power, the past is no longer a distant island of lost and hazy events, but a rich and abundant land, reborn in all its glory. Because..."

He reached the podium in six long strides, and seized the picture of Susan.

"The past is awakening again. Awakening in the present. It's—"

He shifted his gaze back to the dream sketch, chilling to the bone as he met the furious eye staring out at him.

"The past is devouring the present. Because that's what you are, aren't you? *'Él que recuerda todo'*—the one who remembers all. That's what Pablo called you on that tape. Somehow, you have that power of unbounded memory and yet... you're a memory yourself, aren't you? A malignant memory. Of an ancient horror, a calamity, of... something, and now you, awakening past, you're coming to devour our present. The makers of the stone tablet knew that, and they didn't want to remember you, whatever it is that you represent, that you intend..."

He focused back upon the drawing, this time on the cryptic five-digit number at the top of his drawing, and the blood-drenched memory of where he had first glimpsed it.

"So then why, ultimately, is Pablo remembering you? Why am I remembering you? What exactly is it that we're remembering?"

He dropped the opened folder back onto the podium, glancing about the surrounding dimness of the lecture hall to rest his reddened eyes. He allowed himself one final perusal of the dream sketch before filing it back away. At arm's length, the figure in the center seemed even more insistent, as if delivering a coherent warning to its baffled observer.

"Who are you?" asked Tim. "What do you want from us?"

. . . Wohin gehen, wohin fliehen,

wenn die Finsternis erwacht?

Epilogue: The Dark Devours

THE SAME DAY: FRIDAY, MAY 23, 8:24 P.M.
EAST SHAFT 7A
CARNOCK COAL MINE COMPLEX, LEWISTOWN, KENTUCKY

The lighting near the surface of the shaft was shutting off, creeping downward one level at a time. The miners watched as the phenomenon worked its way inexorably to their level, coming into view three tunnels above them. Kyle eyed Joss with indignation, silently re-affirming his own suspicions. Joss, for his part, turned toward the elderly miner still perched by the broken shaft telephone.

"Earl," said Joss, struggling to mask his own apprehension. "You know what this is? Some sort of—system check, to reactivate the lift?"

"No. Nothing of the sort," the old miner said, also fighting to maintain an appearance of calm. "I've been in plenty of jams like this before, and they never did anything like this. The lighting and the lift are on two separate wiring grids as a precaution; even the backup power feeds are kept apart. But the lamps wouldn't be crackling off one-by-one like that anyway. If there's a blackout, they go off haphazardly, in groups. Someone's doing this deliberately."

"I told you!" Kyle interjected, his face contorted by rage and fear. "We're just fresh meat to them!"

"No," Earl said, firmly shaking his head. "This isn't Pyrrhus. Not their style. They don't care enough one way or another and besides, they couldn't have cancelled all the backups and failsafes."

"That's right!" Joss confirmed. "I remember, Augustus—the old man—modified the vertical shaft lighting to stay on so long as anyone was still down here. It wouldn't cycle off until every miner had punched out."

"And nobody can override that," Earl put in, "not even the owners, except with the prior cooperation of the switch operators in each and every tunnel. Clan Augustus is what it is, but they looked after us down here. The system they rigged up was a good one—a good guard against any errors or mischief in the control tower."

"Then who's doing this?" Kyle said, the last light above them blinking off as he spoke. An odd sonorance, akin to electrical fuzz or crisp static, then percolated through the air about them as the elevator car rumbled irregularly. Again the miners grabbed for the bowed rail along the wall.

They then turned their eyes to Earl. The senior miner merely shook his head and shrugged in resignation.

"All right," said Joss, letting go of the rail and stepping to the center of the elevator car. "Let's not lose our cool here. We still have our personal lamps and flashlights and enough juice for as long as any rescue would take. We're not gonna be in the dark here."

"I wouldn't be so sure of that," Kyle said, his tone of cross disposition now one of helpless apprehension. He darted his eyes toward the members of the group and held up the battery pack attached to his safety lamp. He then flipped its switch, eliciting a collective gasp from the other men. The lamp wasn't working.

"That's impossible," Joss protested as he strained to keep his composure. "Kyle, I saw your lamp on the minute before we arrived at the lift platform. That battery's fine."

"Flashlight's down too," noted another miner standing beside Kyle. The man eyed his coworkers with dread as they too began testing their own devices with similar results.

"Earl," Joss said, now plainly grasping, "has anyone checked the methanometer? Any chance that—firedamp, some contaminant might've snuffed out the batteries?"

"It'd be the first I've heard of it," Earl said as the light vanished at their level, leaving only the scant illumination from below. "I used to work with the old carbide lamps years back, but we switched to battery-powered because they were safer. They were supposed to be impervious to this kind of trouble. I don't know what to tell you."

Joss glanced aside, hoping to conceal whatever fear was not already being masked by the impending darkness. He gathered his resolve amidst the increasingly harried chatter of the men around him.

"OK, everyone," he said, "listen up! I'm not gonna tell you I know what's happening or what's going to happen. But something's coming, and we'd best prepare ourselves for it. It'll be pitch-black in this shaft within about four minutes. In the meantime, everyone, keep your cool. Remember what you learned in training. Don't get lost in your own thoughts, waiting for the folks above to do their job. Just take this one moment at a time, keep talking amongst yourselves, stay warm, and don't lose faith. They will be coming for us! OK? Say it: They will be coming for us."

A mumble rippled through the darkening elevator.

"Say it! Say it now, say it lou—"

"They will be coming for us!" Kyle shouted and Joss fell silent.

The miners hunkered down, Kyle, Joss, and Earl running through safety procedures with the other men until everyone was talking about what they'd been taught in their training. Outside in the shaft the wind was still howling, working its way into the car in quick, chilling drafts.

The last of the lights finally flickered out below them. Still they continued talking safety procedure.

Not but a few minutes had gone by, however, when they began easing off on the training talk. From above them in the shaft came a strange, misty, violet-hued glow that gradually descended the corridor. It hissed with the faint hints of an electrical discharge, cheering the men as they looked up in anticipation of the rescue team sure to follow close behind the peculiar light.

Yet, as the mist-strewn light descended upon them, their relief quickly turned into bafflement, unease, and then terror. The air in their vicinity seemed to be weighted down somehow, with bizarre hints of writhing and curling about itself as the light descended. The miners glanced at each other in further bewilderment at what sounded like distant screaming—like a group of people screaming. Like a small town all gathered together, screaming. The sound would slowly crescendo for a half-second, only to hush itself abruptly then slowly, faintly come back in.

"I don't see any rescuers, Joss!" Kyle exclaimed, covering his nose as the miasma overtook the air inside the elevator. "Is this some—some sort of firedamp?"

"I don't think so," Joss said between coughs that grew ever deeper in intensity, glancing over at Earl as the old man struggled to breathe. "But it could be another toxic gas; everyone, as best you can, hold your breath for this thing to pass!"

The men strained furiously to avoid inhaling the mysterious fumes, but the cloud inexorably overtook them and sent them to the floor of the lift, half-unconscious or fully so. Joss froze his sagging eyelids up in fright as the strange violet beam now scanned his coworkers from head to toe, illuminating their skeletons before fanning out to browse every inch of their heads. His awareness slowly fading, he struggled to memorize every detail of the illumination edging ever closer to him—along with the bizarre, yet undeniable sense of a horrid presence harbored within.

THE END OF BOOK 1

Acknowledgments

Echoes of the Mystic Chords and the Leibniz Demon Trilogy have spanned more than eight years of roller-coaster ups and downs, and quite a few helping hands have gotten me through the ride. The creative spark and nurturing for a novel like this goes well beyond its composition alone.

I began writing *Echoes* while recuperating from a devastating respiratory condition that taxed every resource I had, even as it shaped much of my creative vision. I couldn't have completed that journey without crucial support from many corners. My parents Sam and Anne Ulm and Roselynne and George Cody, my brother Aaron and sister-in-law Lisa, and my wonderful fiancée Gloria were all there to help and inspire me when I needed it most.

My extended family in Georgia, Delaware, and Pennsylvania gave me the kind of support only family can. In particular, Uncle Otis inspired some of the plotlines in *Echoes* with encouraging words and genealogical research.

I have to include Dr. Tan and everyone in the medical team who helped me through my illness. Several people fired up my creative resolve during these trials, offering that spirit-boost to finish the work: Kim Bennett, James Zhou and the volunteer team in China after the Wenchuan earthquake; fellow authors and Jeopardy-ites Bob Harris and Arthur Phillips, Jing Chen, Kazuko Kashiwagi, Aubrey Mabazza, Lisa Houston, Lisa Matsunami; and the many encouraging test-readers and story-testers I met at Volcano Tea (on Sawtelle), Mr. Coffee, and other shops in Koreatown, where I scribed so much of the trilogy after late-night tea boosts.

Wonderful mentors and teachers inspired me with earlier creative projects, giving me confidence and experience to venture out on my own: Pat Herrity, Joel Bonfanti, and Jacqueline Gorski, Rebecca Buckbee, Joel Kaplan, Mary-Jane Addams, Neal Baer, and Gerrie Smith. John Porter gave his ongoing support even after handing over the reins as principal. Lynn Hasher's class at Duke on the mysteries of memory planted many ideas that incubated years hence. Quentin Eichbaum and Isaac Devash help me cut my teeth with *Vision at Harvard*.

Echoes got its start as a philosophical spin-off of intensive investigations within my profession as a clinician and researcher. The encouragement of medical mentors led me down the intellectual path that brought me here: Rick Mitchell and Patty Cunningham, Shahram Yazdani, Richard Palmer, Scott Abrams, Matthew Ellis, Bertram Fraser-Reid, Chris Raetz, Richard Mulligan, and David Frank.

I would like to thank my dedicated book team: Will Chen, my illustrator and long-time collaborator, whose artistic vision has been crucial in forging the haunting imagery of Echoes; Jon Rauch, my content and copy editor, whose nuanced skill and adroitness have helped me turn dozens of drafts into a stirring tale for the mass market; David DePerro, my book designer and typesetter, who brought the novel into a printed form that embodies its sense of mystery; and Karim Lounes, my web designer, who helped me bring the trilogy to multiple media.

And thanks to Madeline Perri and Traci Parks for additional copy editing, Mike O'Connor for multimedia sound design, and Julian Walder for help with public art and social networking. Martin Wallner, Josef Wallner, Felix Lehmann, Ken Reed, and Armi Mack reviewed and edited the German riddle-poems that start each chapter.

Finally, I would like to recognize my Kickstarter donors. First, my sincere thanks to Peter Vanden Bosch and Kimberly Perry. And finally, my special thanks to Steven Mentzel and Ryan Davis for their generous sponsorship and support.

In the end, all of them made this novel possible.

About the Author

J. Wes Ulm is an author, doctor, and medical researcher in Los Angeles. At 22, he achieved five consecutive nights on *Jeopardy!* and made the show's Tournament of Champions. Dedicating his winnings to medical school, he earned an MD/PhD from the joint program of Harvard University and MIT, publishing diversely in gene therapy and pharmacology. His current research pursues the causes and treatments of congenital diseases. He has written for *Democracy Journal*, *Utne Reader,* and the *Vision at Harvard* essay anthology, whose 2003 edition he also edited. He graduated from Duke University in North Carolina and T. C. Williams High School in his hometown of Alexandria, Virginia. If he could tack on a couple extra hours to the day, he'd climb with his guitar to the top of Angel Falls and sing an album of sweet songs to the world below.

Previews: Book 2

SNEAK PREVIEW #1: THE PORTENT

Mitch puzzled over his nephew's remarks before opening another line of inquiry.

"Everything you've been saying about this entity presaged by the stone tablet, Tim – it's reminding me of that day in February of this year, when you said these horrors at Oak Ridge first began to manifest."

"The fifth of the month – El Día del Diablo. It's when the uplink between the Simitalis and the veterans' eye implants went live."

"February 5th," repeated Mitch in a foreboding tone. "I can remember my reaction when you called me on Friday, as if that date was ringing my own bells. Didn't know why at first, but my review of the logs from February confirmed my hunches."

"How so?"

"Whatever happened on that day, the disturbances weren't confined to Oak Ridge."

"You too? You noticed something was off? On the other side of the country?"

"I wasn't in Oregon at the time, Tim; I was down in Concord, North Carolina. Magister Engineering had an old informatics center there, focused on data-mining and recursive selection research. My team was hammering away day and night on a project, and we were there on the

Tuesday of that week, right up to the witching hour. Then things went off the rails, and not for any reason we could pin down. "

"What exactly did you encounter?"

"A spate of brownouts, followed in short order by a weird species of interference with any device tapping into the EM spectrum – anything relaying a signal via radio waves, microwaves, or X-rays. It's like their output got hijacked, amplified and distorted in some way, yet without descending simply into random static. As far as the timing, my logs left no doubt: The dance of these particular gremlins kicked off right after midnight, gradually subsiding over the next hour."

"After midnight? That's right around when Rachel said they flipped the switch at Oak Ridge!" Tim called out in disbelief.

"Yes, and the phenomenon crossed more than one state boundary. I did some sleuthing – and a little hacking – of reports across the area from that time stretch. Social media from night-shift workers, transcribed CB talk from long-haul truckers, images from the yingminghua, that self-tagging database. There were scattered reports of disturbances out to an irregular radius of 300-400 miles from east Tennessee. Clusters in Virginia and West Virginia, Indiana, Illinois, west to Missouri and south to Alabama, with a steady trail-off the farther out you went."

"And only for that single hour from midnight to 1 a.m.?"

"Yeah, in fact there were no accounts of anything along similar lines in the weeks and months that followed. That is, up until only a few days ago, and in a place that may ring some loud bells: Lewistown, Kentucky."

"That coal mine disaster!" Tim exclaimed. "It was all over the news. You're saying there were – there were premonitions of it? Like the anomalies you noted on El Día del Diablo?"

"Forewarnings, yes, but an altogether different flock of strange birds from what I'd logged back in February. This time it was in the air, Tim."

"In the air?"

"Literally. Farmers and gardeners across the region, crews up and out before the crack of dawn – the details vary, but they all saw it: a multi-hued electrical discharge, much like the St. Elmo's Fire that sailors marvel at. And then..."

SNEAK PREVIEW #2: THE RIVER OF BLOOD

Tim stared with an obsessive gaze at the screen as Sanjit Khan, Rachel Bloom's erstwhile colleague at Oak Ridge and self-appointed historian of her team's travails, played back the recording from El Día del Diablo. The original muted video had been overlaid with color-coded visualizations of what could not otherwise be seen: a translucent blue tone for sound and a range of red and pink hues for the radio wave emissions.

"Remember," Sanjit reminded Tim, "the radio receivers in that laser lab could detect frequencies up to 5 gigahertz, right into the microwave range. Anything gushing out of cell phones or other devices would have been picked up. By superimposing those readings onto the acoustic map and the video itself, we should have a pretty good bead on the original signal – and where it came from."

"Then let's dive right back in," Tim said, impatiently resuming the playback. Maybe if he could track the source of that elusive signal, he could pinpoint the origin of the bizarre sound that had so tormented Rachel from that day on – and with it, the madness that would soon overwhelm Pablo and his brothers-in-arms.

"Pause!" Sanjit urged as a dull, pinkish glow emanated from the left side of the screen, like ripples on a pond disturbed by a tossed rock. "There, right on schedule. That's Tara Dreyfus, our systems engineer who flipped the switch to activate your Simitalis. Look, Tim. The moment she does it – boom, a microwave pulse pushes out radially from the device, tuned to the settings on the AP-278 retinal implant. Exactly as we'd expect."

"So it is," Tim replied coolly, impatient for something more. He restarted the playback, looking on as the room's inhabitants kicked off their festivities, the signal from the Simitalis quietly pulsing in the background. Champagne was popping, bleary eyes were widening, faces were smiling. So then what in the world could have happened to –

"Whoa! What the hell?!" Tim startled at a flash of bright blood-red color that filled the screen out of nowhere, followed by a blue tint that creeped in from all directions. The imagery carried a gruesome metaphor, like a gushing stream of blood blotting out the room and everyone within.

"I... I don't know, Tim. It must have been a radio pulse but – far more intense than any I've seen on this sort of overlay. Back up the recording to a few seconds after Tara had flipped the switch, and slow things down to quarter-time. Then dial down the gain, make the signal less pronounced for the radio frequencies."

Tim did so, yet once again the signal swept in like an avalanche.

"Knock the time slices down further," Sanjit suggested, unnerved by what he was witnessing – and the realization he had been there in the midst of it. "Get right to the point before the signal-flood. Move in frames of a tenth-of-a-second each. Now... now try a twentieth. My God, what is this? It's still swallowing up the room! Bring it down to a fiftieth of a second. March it along now, frame-by-frame."

"There, look! A tiny interval before that... river of blood inundates the whole screen, there's another pulse, narrow and sharp – looks like a UHF frequency. And it's pouring straight in from the bottom right corner, from somewhere off-screen. Somehow it – it gave rise to the radio pulse that filled the whole monitor, like it was flipping an invisible switch in the air."

"No, that's impossible. There weren't... That area in the corner was empty."

"Empty?"

"Of transmitters, electronic devices – anything that could have produced a radio signal of any form, let alone of that magnitude peeling through the laser lab. It couldn't have come from there!"

"Sanjit, what was in that corner?"

"The only... We cleared out all the electronics from that side of the room, to make sure the visual guidance signal from the Simitalis would reach him unencumbered."

Tim paused for a nervous moment to ponder a revelation that was soon alarmingly clear.

"Pablo! You're talking about Pablo, aren't you?!"

"I don't know how, Tim, but Lance Corporal Acevedo – he, or something he was linked to, was the source of all you just saw."

"And of all that followed."

SNEAK PREVIEW #3: THE ABDUCTION

Tim wobbled as he came to, struggling to steady his aching head and neck. Something was wrong; he could tell even before his senses had locked in on the world outside. His hands were trapped behind him, and his eyes – they weren't taking anything in, even as his eyelids haltingly parted ways. His ears and cheeks were in contact with a coarse, scratchy material, and the surface on which he was seated was bobbing up and down. What was this? He'd been downtown only a moment ago, he thought, his ear pressed to his phone to update Zach. And then –

"What the hell is this?!" he growled, leaning forward angrily in the car's back seat. "Where are you bastards taking me?"

"So, the good professor's awake," remarked a cynical voice in a forward seat. He redirected his attention to a figure on Tim's right. "Make sure he's secured. No screw-ups with this one."

"You sons-of-bitches." Tim's rage and fear were exacerbated by the muffling from the burlap sack pulled over his head. "I can't see you, but I know who you are."

"Is that so?" taunted the man in front. "Then who are we?"

"They say all the upstart kidnap-and-ransom squads have been doing brisk business here lately, but you chloroformed me in broad daylight, right off a city street. Only the Triantarchy's bagmen would even dare it."

"Why the harsh words?" said the man in mock indignation. "It's just a job for us too, Doc; nothing personal. Gotta make a living any way you can these days, and the Clans have dinero to burn."

"Then why draw this out?" asked Tim, upping his bravado to mask the terror of what awaited him. "If I'm gonna wind up rotting in some hole anyway, might as well pop me right here. Save everyone the trouble."

The three hardened men around Tim laughed coarsely at the outburst.

"Mr. M said he might be a handful," said the one on Tim's right, "but can't say I saw this coming. Gotta hand it to you Doc, you got balls."

"Pete!" rebuked the man in front. "Can you follow instructions for one damn gig? No names, no initials, no hints when it comes to the guy giving the orders."

"Why get so bent out of shape about it?" said Tim, once again willing himself to mock the danger. "If you fine gentlemen would be kind enough to drop me off at the next block – I promise I won't tell anyone."

"You're a piece of work, Professor," chuckled the voice in front. "But don't worry yourself. The Boss only wants a word with you, in fact we're under explicit orders not to harm a hair on your head. He even insisted we keep your gear intact and undisturbed. You'll be getting your cell phone and briefcase back when we reach our destination."

"Which is?"

"C'mon, Doc, you know a detail like that is need-to-know only."

"If your Boss wants nothing more than some face-time with me, there are less dramatic ways to go about it. I have office hours, you know."

"Hey, we're just the muscle. He has his reasons. Look, we got about an hour before we reach our stop. It'll go a lot faster if you keep cool and hang tight."

Tim nodded cautiously beneath the sack about his head, doubting the man's reassurances but seeing little to be gained from further questioning. He settled into an uneasy truce with the anxious meanderings floating through his mind. The sack had been tied loosely beneath his chin, but the wear and tear in its fabric allowed fleeting, fragmentary glances of the drab scenery outside the moving car. He was already in the middle of nowhere; he could scarcely imagine where his captors were taking him.

"Say, Professor." To Tim's surprise, the ensuing silence was broken by the kidnapper in the front passenger seat. "Like I said, it's not like we're the brains of the operation here. But we caught a glimpse of those folders you got stuffed in there. Those numbers, that monster you got staring in closer every time –"

"Staring in closer?" Tim repeated nervously. "The drawings? You've seen those damned drawings?"

"A lot of the folks we 'transport' – you could say they've had better days. Kinda comes with the job. They're down on their luck, neck-deep in debt, then they fry their brains with booze and blow, numb the pain a bit. You on the other hand, seems like you got your head screwed on straight. Yet I never seen nobody give in to them like that."

"Give in to what?" asked Tim, darkly curious at the insights streaming in from a most unexpected source.

"Your demons."

"My – wait, what is it you think you saw on my drawings?"

"I don't know, I figure it's a lot like those things a kid imagines hiding in the night, you fear 'em but never see 'em. But it's like all those things came together in that monster on your pictures. Became real, and nasty, and they're looking right at you, like they know you better every time."

The man paused to murmur instructions to the driver before continuing.

"You're haunted, Doc, and whatever's haunting you, seems like it ain't only in your head either. I don't know why but you can just tell looking at the things you've been drawing out. Hardasses like us, we don't scare easily, but we all got a start looking at whatever it is you dreamt up."

"I couldn't guess what your Boss would want with those pictures, but even if he plans to torture their meaning out of me, he's gonna be disappointed. I don't even know why I draw them let alone what they mean, other than that those scenes anchor themselves in my head sometimes, like someone else's memories forcing themselves on the world all over again. That's all I know."

"We only saw them because they fell out of your briefcase while we were, you know, securing you for transport. The Boss never mentioned the drawings. He has other business with you."

"Look, I don't know what you told him and I realize I'm not in any position to bargain right now. But you said this was nothing personal. So if you guys could do me a solid, keep this all on the down-low –"

"Like I was saying, Professor, it's just a job for us. The Boss didn't ask about it, so as far as we're concerned, we never saw anything out of the ordinary."

SNEAK PREVIEW #4: THE TERROR IN THE TRAIN

Victor hesitated.

"My contact among the Augustans that I mentioned," Victor said, "he's been more agitated than usual in our last couple of exchanges."

Alma sighed.

"Heroism like that requires a measure of paranoia, Victor. I wouldn't read too much into it."

Victor shook his head.

"Maybe. But the last time we spoke, he was going on about... I'm not sure, something about the 'cleansing fires of retribution to which this world would succumb.' He kept repeating that phrase, or some similar apocalypto-babble."

"Might just be he's hit his limit. I can imagine myself cracking under that kind of strain."

Again Victor shook his head.

"His latest ravings have been rooted in a different patch of ground, outside the reinforced compounds of the Triantarchy itself. It didn't strike me as ordinary nerves. He was making all manner of references to a project gone awry. And to some engineering professor out of North Carolina, no idea what his connection is or how –"

The train screeched to a sudden halt, throwing them against the cabin wall. Alma grabbed onto Victor's sleeve to keep from stumbling. Annoyed murmurs rose to anxious chatter that spread down the rows of the cabin as the minutes passed and the train stood motionless.

"All passengers, please stand by," the conductor's voice echoed over the scratchy intercom. "We are experiencing an unexpected delay; we'll be up and running again as soon as possible."

Victor cursed through clenched teeth.

"Must be all the excavations in the old Chinatown. Probably had to close a tunnel on short notice," he said, straining to see out the window into the duskily-lit tunnel.

"At least, that'll be the official excuse," Alma replied bitterly. "And given the track record of our enlightened rulers, I wouldn't expect much more than excuses. We'll be stuck here awhile."

Victor was still trying to see out the dirty window. Alma touched his elbow. He turned back to her.

The two stood impatiently in the cramped train car for several minutes more. Alma fixed her gaze far ahead as if simply bored with the wait; still, Victor saw the pulse in her neck quicken and her eyes widen for a nervous instant.

"Alma," Victor asked, "what is it?"

"I... I can't tell. I could have sworn the lights went out in one of the cars well ahead of us."

Victor turned to the transparent door at the front of the train car, straining along with Alma to gauge the lights in the forward compartments. As they watched, the fourth cabin ahead of them went dark, provoking a contagious panic in the cars immediately behind, where passengers had a better view.

"Ladies and gentlemen, this is your conductor speaking," the train driver's voice rippled over the intercom, this time notably anxious despite his attempt to reassure. "The lights appear to be going down for the cars from the front of the train backward. The PA system is on a separate power feed, so I won't be going anywhere. All passengers, please remain calm and stay seated or standing where you are. We have no indication of a terrorist attack or other danger, so I repeat, please remain calm."

"My God – is this because of us?" Alma said. The other passengers stirred nervously about them. "Have they found us here, Victor?"

"No," he answered firmly, staring dead ahead with ferocious concentration as he weighed the question. "This isn't their M.O."

They and other passengers watched as the third car and then the second car ahead of them went dark. When the blackout struck the car immediately preceding theirs, panic erupted all about them. Passengers scrambled for the emergency door, desperate to exit the train into the tunnel.

Victor clasped Alma's hand as the cabin lights began to buzz.

"Alma, hold on," he said. Their eyes locked as the lights flickered.

"All passengers, please remain inside the train," exhorted the conductor over the intercom. The man had given up his façade of calm. "Do not, I repeat, do not attempt to exit the train. Please remain calm. We have a team of –"

As the lights sputtered and gave out, the conductor's voice faded to silence despite his prior reassurance. The PA system had gone dead. The barest glow came from the two cars behind them, whose lights had not yet extinguished. Alma and Victor held one another tightly. The terror of the other passengers was palpable as they waited in compliance with the conductor's final orders; they sat and stood helplessly as the last remaining light in the tunnel flickered and died in the cars behind them. They were in total darkness.

The Echoes Team

Turn the page to learn about our team members.
Contact them for your creative projects!

Turn to the last page to learn about Book 2 and
how you can help make it a reality!

Ray Sidney-Smith, advisor for release and distribution of Echoes of the Mystic Chords, is author of SoLoMo Success: Social Media, Local and Mobile Web Small Business Marketing Strategy Explained, President of W3 Consulting, providing Web marketing training, strategy planning, and content marketing for Small Business.

Website: w3cinc.com and w3andbeyond.com

Karim Lounes, web designer for www.echomystic.com
Business website: www.askformedia.com
Contact: info@askformedia.com

Mike O'Connor, sound effect designer for www.echomystic.com
Website: www.audioshade.com
Audio Shade specializes in telling stories with sound for film, TV, and web.
Contact: mwosound@gmail.com

Made in the USA
Columbia, SC
13 November 2022

71125005R00236